Author Note

Welcome to *Desired*, book five in the SCANDALOUS WOMEN OF THE TON series! *Desired* is Tess Darent's story. The outrageous Dowager Lady Darent has already been widowed three times and is looking for her fourth husband—but she is determined on a marriage in name only. Step forward Owen Purchase, Viscount Rothbury, who has desired the much-married marchioness for a long time. He is the protector Tess needs, but can he seduce her into realising that a true marriage is what she really wants?

Like the other books in this series, *Desired* is inspired by real-life events. Tess is a philanthropist and a reformer, and in the late eighteenth and early nineteenth centuries the reforming movement was pressing for political change in Britain. The government, however, was afraid of a revolution and sought to repress any opposition by throwing the reform's leaders into prison. Tess, as a secret leader of the reform movement, is in the gravest danger.

I have loved writing all the books in this series! Be sure to visit my website at www.nicolacornick.co.uk and don't miss the final book in the series, *Forbidden*!

Nicola

Nicola Cornick

Nicola Cornick

DESIRED

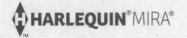

First published in Great Britain 2012.
Harlequin MIRA, an imprint of Harlequin (UK) Limited,
Eton House, 18-24 Paradise Road,
Richmond, Surrey, TW9 1SR

© Nicola Cornick 2011

ISBN 978 1 848 45131 5

54-0912

MIRA's policy is to use papers that are natural, renewable and recyclable products and made from wood grown in sustainable forests. The logging and manufacturing processes conform to the legal environmental regulations of the country of origin.

Printed and bound by
CPI Group (UK) Ltd, Croydon, CR0 4YY

DESIRED

To Kimberley Young with much gratitude
for all the years we worked together.

CHAPTER ONE

London, October 1816

> *Covent Garden: "Artful ways beguile the implicit rake."*
>
> —Taken from
> *Harris's List of Covent Garden Ladies.*

IT WAS THE NIGHT HER LUCK finally ran out.

Tess Darent knew that the net was closing and that someone was coming to hunt her down. Tonight she could feel him very close behind her. Tonight, she knew instinctively, was the night she was going to get caught.

"Hurry!" Mrs. Tong, owner of the Temple of Venus bawdy house held out the borrowed gown to her with shaking hands and Tess grabbed it and slipped it over her head, feeling the sensuous slide of lavender silk against her skin. It was not a bad fit. She was surprised that Mrs. Tong had anything so tasteful in the wardrobe. Fortunate, because she would not be seen dead in any of the harlot's gowns Mrs. Tong's girls habitually wore. Even if she was currently hiding from the law, Tess had standards to maintain.

The bawd's face was pale beneath her paint and powder, her eyes terrified. Out in the corridor the sounds of pursuit were getting louder—voices snapping orders, the tramp of booted feet, the crash as Mrs. Tong's pieces of erotic statuary were knocked to the marble floor.

"Redcoats!" the bawd said. "Searching the house. If they find you here—"

"They won't," Tess snapped. She spun around, lifting the heavy fall of her red-gold hair so that Mrs. Tong could lace the gown. She could feel the bawd's fingers trembling on the fastenings. Mrs. Tong's fear was feeding her own. The panic filled her chest, stealing her breath. Her pursuer was so close now. He was nipping at her heels.

"Even if they do find me here," she added over her shoulder, marvelling at the calm of her own voice, "what of it? My reputation is so bad no one will think it odd to find me in a whorehouse."

"But the papers?" Mrs. Tong's voice quavered.

"Hidden." Tess patted the lavender reticule that matched the gown. "Never fear, Mrs. T. No one will suspect you of being anything worse than an avaricious old madam."

"There's gratitude." Mrs. Tong sounded irritable. "Sometimes I wonder why I help you."

"You do it because you owe me," Tess said. Some months before she had helped Mrs. Tong's son when he had been arrested at a political rally. Now she was calling in the debt.

"I'm no friend to the radical cause," Mrs. Tong grumbled. She pulled the laces of the gown tight in a small gesture of revenge.

"The gown's too big," Tess wheezed, as the breath was pummelled out of her.

"Which is why you need the laces tight." The madam gave them another sharp tug. She threw Tess a matching cloak of lavender-blue edged with peacock feathers and tiptoed across to the door, opening it a crack, finger to her lips.

Tess raised a brow. Mrs. Tong shook her head, closed the door softly and turned the key. "No chance," she said. "They are all over the house like the pox. You'll have to hide."

"They'll find me." Fear clawed at Tess again. For all her defiant words she knew that it would be disastrous if she were to be caught now in possession of the papers. She would be thrown in prison. Everything she had worked for would be lost. The cold sweat trickled down her spine, prickling her skin.

"Buy me some time, Mrs. Tong," she said. "They are a company of soldiers and this is a bawdy house. Distract them."

She grabbed the jacket of the mannish suit she had been wearing on her arrival, extracted the little silver pistol from the pocket, forced it into the reticule along with the papers and pulled the drawstring tight. She tried on the exquisite pair of lavender slippers that matched the gown and winced. They were made for smaller feet than hers. She would have blisters by the time she reached home.

"There's no way of distracting their captain," Mrs. Tong said. "He don't care for women."

"Send him one of your boys then."

"He doesn't like boys either. War wound, they say. No lead in his pencil. Precious little pencil either, if it comes to that."

"Poor man," Tess said. "That's quite a sacrifice to make for your country. Still, if sex fails, money usually talks. Make him an offer he cannot afford to refuse."

She could hear the voices of the soldiers coming ever closer along the landing and the doors slamming back as they searched the rooms with about as much finesse as a herd of cows in a china shop. Mrs. Tong's girls were screaming. Aristocratic male voices were raised in plaintive protest. A lot of people, Tess thought, were going to have their most private vices exposed tonight. The redcoats' raid on Mrs. Tong's brothel would be all over the scandal sheets by the morning. It would be the talk of the ton.

"Time to make a swift exit," she said. She moved across to the window. "How far is the drop to the street, Mrs. T?"

Mrs. Tong stared. "You'll never be able to make this climb."

"Why not?" Tess said. "There is a balcony, is there not? I don't want to risk them searching me." She grabbed the sheets from the bed and started to fashion a makeshift rope.

"That's my best linen!" Mrs. Tong said. "You'll ruin it!"

"Stick it on my bill," Tess said. "Have I forgotten anything?"

Mrs. Tong shook her head. There was a gleam of appreciation in her eyes. "You're a cool one, and no mistake, madam," she said. "How about we go into business together?"

Tess shook her head. Only the direst emergency had driven her to take refuge in a brothel in the first place. "Forget it, Mrs. T. Selling sex is not my thing. I don't even want it when it is offered for free." She waved. "Thank you for your help."

She pulled back the curtains and slipped the catch on the long window. There was a decorative little stone balcony outside with a carved balustrade. Tess knotted the sheet around one of the stone uprights and pulled it hard. The sheet held, though whether it would do so under her not-inconsiderable weight was quite another thing. But she had no option other than to take the risk. Lavender slippers and reticule in one hand, she climbed over the balcony, gripped the sheet in her other hand and slid down the chute to the ground, the wide skirts of the gown filling out like a bell around her.

When she was still some distance from the ground she ran out of her impromptu rope and swung gently backwards and forwards in the autumn breeze. She could see Mrs. Tong peering over the balcony above her, still grumbling about the damage to her sheets. Below, there was a drop of at least four feet to the darkened street. For a moment Tess hung there, trying to decide whether to shin back up the rope or risk the jump to the ground. The sheet creaked and slipped a notch. The laces of the gown groaned as well, cutting into Tess's back as the seams strained.

Then, abruptly, the reticule and slippers were plucked from her hand and a moment later she was seized about the waist and placed gently on her feet.

"Splendid as the view was," a lazy masculine voice murmured in her ear, "I thought you might appreciate some help."

Caught.

Panic fluttered in her throat. So she had been right all along. There was no escape.

Stay calm. Give nothing away.

She tried to steady her breath. Something in the man's touch unsettled her, but deeper than that, deeper and more disturbing still, was the sense of recognition. He had come for her and she could not escape. She knew it and it made her tremble.

She did not even know who he was. She could not see his face.

The gas lamps in the square were out and although the shutters had been pulled back again and faint golden light spilled from the brothel windows it was not sufficient to pierce the autumn darkness. Tess had a confused impression of height and breadth—she was a tall woman but this man was taller, a shade over six feet, perhaps. There was something of resilience and strength about him, of hard chiselled edges and cool calculation. It was in his stillness and the way he was watching her. The impressions confused her; she did not know how she could tell so much whilst knowing so little about him. But her awareness of him was shockingly sharp, intensified in some way by the intimate dark. He still held her, not by the waist but lower, his grip firm and strong on her hips. His touch sent an odd shiver rippling through her. He drew her into the pool of light thrown by the window and released her with meticulous courtesy, standing back, sketching a bow.

The laces of the perfidious gown chose that precise moment to snap. It slid from Tess's shoulders and crumpled artistically about her waist before sighing down to the ground like a swooning maiden. As she was left shivering in her bodice and drawers, her companion laughed.

"What a perfect gown," he said.

"It's a little premature," Tess said coldly. "We have only just met."

She knew him now, recognising him with another ripple of disquiet. It was his voice that gave him away, so low and mellow. It was very different from the clipped British accents she was accustomed to hearing every day. Only one man had that languid drawl, as dark and smooth as treacle. Only one man in the ton

was an American by birth; a man who was as dangerous and exotic and seductive as he sounded.

Rothbury.

Viscount Rothbury was the man sent to capture her.

Tess knew him a little. He was an old friend of Alex,
Lord Grant, her sister Joanna's husband, and of Garrick,
Duke of Farne, her other brother-in-law. Until earlier
in the year, Rothbury had been plain Owen Purchase,
an American sea captain, who had most unexpectedly
come into a title. Now that he was a viscount the ton
fawned upon him but he seemed as indifferent to society's favour as he had been to their previous disregard.
He had visited Alex and Joanna in Bedford Square on
several occasions, but Tess had always kept out of his
way. She met many handsome men on a daily basis.
Almost all of them evoked no emotion in her whatso-
ever. Occasionally she would feel a faint interest in a
man who was witty and intelligent, but the sensation
was gone almost as soon as she had felt it. She had long
ago assumed that any natural desires she might once
have felt had been crushed out of her by the vile experiences of her second marriage. She had assumed she
would never feel a physical attraction towards any man.
She had grown not to expect it and she did not want it.

Rothbury challenged those assumptions and she did
not like it.

It was not merely his physique—tall, broad shouldered, durable, strong. Tess supposed that he was
handsome—no, she was obliged to admit that he *was*

handsome—in a rugged manner that was far too physical for her comfort. She preferred men who were no physical threat, men who had spent their morning in company with their barber and their tailor rather than in riding or in swordplay; men who were brushed, pomaded and as au fait with fashion as she was. Rothbury had fought for the British against the French at Trafalgar and later for the Americans against the British at North Point. He had been a sailor, an explorer and an adventurer. Tess preferred men who had never travelled farther than their country estates.

And then there was his manner, incisiveness cloaked in those deceptively silken tones. She was not fooled for a moment. Rothbury pretended to be indolent when he was in fact one of the most intelligent and perceptive men of her acquaintance.

Her awareness of him was as sharp as a whetted blade. It disturbed her.

He was still watching her. Assessing. Unsmiling. Evidently he had recognised her too, for he gave her another immaculate bow.

"Good evening, Lady Darent," he said. "What an original way to exit a brothel."

"Lord Rothbury," Tess said coolly. "Thank you—I never follow the crowd."

Out of the corner of her eye, she could see Mrs. Tong gesturing wildly at her. The bawd seemed to be trying to indicate that this—*this*—was the man responsible for the raid on the brothel, the man she had been talking about as lacking the wherewithal to sow any oats, wild or otherwise. Rothbury had certainly kept that quiet from his friends, Tess thought, but then no doubt he would. She sensed he was a proud man and it was unlikely he would wish to speak of his incapacity, or for it to become common knowledge. It was not the sort of piece of information one simply dropped into polite conversation.

She tried not to stare at his pantaloons. She had far more pressing matters on her mind other than whether Rothbury was capable of continuing his family line. Such as the fact that she was in a state of *déshabillée* and Rothbury was still holding her shoes in the one hand and her reticule in the other, with the incriminating papers only a rustle away. She was within an inch of being unmasked as well as undressed.

"You might wish to put your gown back on," Rothbury said. "It's optional—" an ironic smile tilted his lips "—but both of us might be more comfortable."

His narrowed gaze had started at her bare toes and was now travelling upwards with unhurried thoroughness, considering the nimbus of red-and-gold hair that fanned about her bare shoulders and finally coming to rest on her face. His green eyes, as cool as a shower of ice, met her blue ones and there was an expression in them that made the breath catch in her chest.

Tess gave a shiver and grabbed the slippery lavender silk and made the best job she could of wriggling back into it. The night air was cold and nipped at her skin and she was grateful when Rothbury wrapped the soft fur-lined cloak about her, its luxurious folds blocking out the autumn chill. But her feet were still bare. She had had no time to put on stockings and now her toes were very cold.

"If I might have my slippers, Lord Rothbury," she said. "I doubt they are your size."

She looked down at his feet, handsome in gleaming Hessians that shone in the faint flicker of light from the only street lamp left burning. She found she was trying to remember the scurrilous gossip she had heard about the correlation between the size of a man's feet and the size of his cock. Was it that men with big feet were well endowed in other regions of their anatomy as well, or that small men had disproportionately large cocks? Lady Farr was having an affair with her jockey, who was extremely short. And Napoleon Bonaparte was also a short man but rumoured to be a prodigious lover.... And why was she thinking about sex when she tried never to think about it at all, and why was she thinking about it *now,* at this most inappropriate moment when she should be concentrating on nothing more than escape? And in conjunction with Rothbury, whose own proportions had, presumably, been utterly ruined by a mortar shell or bullet.

To her surprise Rothbury went down on one knee and presented the shoe to her with a grin that was pure wickedness, his teeth a flash of white in a face tanned by a climate somewhat more tropical than London in winter. He slid one slipper onto her foot, his palm warm for a moment against the arch of her instep, and she felt a strange and disconcerting flicker of response deep within her.

"Thank you," she said, forcing the tiny slippers onto her feet where they pinched like malicious crabs. "Just like Prince Charming."

"I missed the bit of the fairy tale where Cinderella visited the brothel," Rothbury said. He straightened up. "What were you doing there, Lady Darent?" His tone was still as courteous as before but that courtesy cloaked an edge of steel. Tess's instinct for self-preservation snapped another warning. Rothbury was the government's man here, the man sent to hunt her down. She was tiptoeing across a tightrope. One false step and she would fall. The only advantage she had was that he did not know the identity of the person he was hunting.

He was still holding her reticule. Behind him, Tess could see a posse of dragoons rounding up a few ragged protesters. There had been a riot that night and the street was littered with rubble and broken spars of wood. The gas lamps were smashed and someone had overturned a carriage. One of the shutters on the Temple of Venus hung off its hinge. Torn newspapers flapped in the wind. It was quiet now. Once the soldiers arrived the mob had faded away as quickly as they had come, and only the faint smell of burning hung on the cold tide of London air.

Tess shrugged, bringing her gaze back to Rothbury's impassive face.

"Why does anyone visit a brothel, Lord Rothbury?" she said lightly. "If you have an imagination, now would be the time to use it." She arched an ironic brow. "I assume you are questioning me on some authority and not simply because you are impertinently curious about my sex life?"

Rothbury shifted. "I am here on the authority of the Home Secretary, Lord Sidmouth," he said. "There was an illegal political meeting at The Feathers Inn tonight. Do you know anything about it?"

Tess's heart bumped erratically. "Do I look like the sort of woman who would know anything about politics, Lord Rothbury?" she said. "I have absolutely no interest in it at all."

She saw Rothbury's teeth gleam as he smiled. "Indeed," he said. "Then you will have equally little interest in the fact that I am hunting for a number of dangerous criminals including the radical caricaturist known as Jupiter."

Fear breathed gooseflesh along Tess's skin. She was no dangerous criminal. She was a philanthropist and all she wanted was reform. All she had ever worked for was to alleviate the appalling poverty and misery of the poor. But the Home Secretary did not see it that way. He saw the reformers as a threat to public order and a danger that he was set on obliterating forever.

She swallowed the sawdust in her throat. Not by a

flicker of an eyelash could she betray any knowledge of the reformers' cause, still less that she was intimately involved with it. But under the perceptive gaze of this man she felt her defences stripped naked.

Pretend. Playact. You have done it before....

"You are hunting criminals in a brothel?" she said, affecting boredom. "What a singular way to combine business with pleasure, my lord. Have you found any?"

"Not yet," Rothbury said. The tone of his voice sent another warning shiver down her spine. She looked at the reticule with its incriminating papers still sitting snugly in the palm of his hand. If he opened that and saw the cartoons…

"You mentioned Lord Sidmouth," she said. "I do not recall him. Would I have met him at a ball or a party, perhaps?"

"I doubt it," Rothbury said. "Lord Sidmouth is not a man much given to parties."

Tess shrugged, as though the conversation was now thoroughly boring her. She glanced towards the door of the brothel, standing open now with light shimmering across the cobbles of Covent Garden Square. "Well, Lord Rothbury," she said. "Delightful as it is to stand out here in the cold chatting to you, I really am quite exhausted. Worn out, in fact, by my excesses tonight. And I am sure that you have work to do." She smothered a delicate little yawn, improving on the point. "So if you will hand my reticule over and excuse me, I shall take a carriage home."

Rothbury weighed the little bag in one palm and Tess's breath caught in her throat. She knew that at all costs she had to keep her expression blank. If she grabbed the reticule off him or made it clear in any way that she was protective of the contents, Rothbury would look inside and she would be clapped up in the Tower of London as a political prisoner faster than one could say *seditious cartoon.*

"What do you have in here?" Rothbury said.

"The contents of a lady's reticule are private only to her," Tess said. Her mouth dried. "Surely you are gentleman enough to respect a lady's discretion?" she pressed.

"I wouldn't depend on it," Rothbury said. "It feels like a pistol," he added. "You must like playing dangerous games with your lovers." His tone was dry.

"I only shoot the ones who fail to satisfy me," Tess said, smiling sweetly.

She saw Rothbury smile in response, the warmth spilling into those green eyes like sunlight, a long crease denting his cheek. The smile did strange things to Tess's equilibrium. Rothbury placed the reticule gently in her outstretched hand. Tess's fingers closed about the silk and brocade and she felt the relief flood through her, so powerful that her knees almost weakened. Then she realised that there was no rustle of paper, no folded sheets beneath her touch. She gripped

a little tighter, desperately trying to make out the out-
line of the papers. Her stomach hollowed with shock.

They were not there.

CHAPTER TWO

SHE HAD THE PRETTIEST FEET he had ever seen.

It might not have been the first thing about Teresa Darent that most men would have noticed, but Owen Purchase, Viscount Rothbury, was never attracted to the obvious.

He handed Tess up into a hackney carriage and watched as she kicked off the lavender silk slippers and tucked her feet up under the gauzy skirts of the gown. The slippers were far too small for her—Owen had noticed that fact when he had held one of them for her to put on earlier. The gown also could not belong to her. Owen was no expert on feminine attire other than in the removal of it but he had a certain amount of experience of the female form and he knew that a woman with Tess Darent's opulent curves—and Tess Darent's flamboyant reputation—would not wear a gown that was two sizes too large. So the outfit was borrowed, which raised the intriguing question of what Lady Darent had been wearing when first she had arrived at the Temple of Venus and why she had needed to change her clothes.

Tess Darent interested Owen. She had from the first time they had met. It was not merely that she had the face of an angel and the reputation of a sinner. Public opinion held that she was as shallow as a puddle, mercenary, amoral, extravagant. She was an arbiter of fashion who had turned spending money into an art form. She simultaneously outraged and fascinated the ton with her profligate marriages and her decadent behaviour, and she was generally considered an utter featherbrain. There was no reason on earth he would find her interesting. Except that some stubborn instinct told him that she was not at all what she seemed....

"Thank you, Lord Rothbury." Tess smiled at him prettily from the depths of the darkened carriage. The lavender silk gown shone ethereally in the faint light. Taken with the cloud of bright hair tumbling over her shoulders, it made her look impossibly alluring. Owen's body reacted with an unexpected stab of desire. He wanted to peel that gown from her shoulders, to see it tumble to the floor as it had done before, to reveal the impossible curves and luscious, sensual plumpness of the body beneath. He remembered the pure line of her throat and collarbone when the gown had slid off her, so true and pale and tempting. He wanted to press his mouth to the hollow of her throat and taste her skin.

Which was not the matter on which he was supposed to be concentrating his attention.

"We're hunting dangerous criminals here, Rothbury," Lord Sidmouth had warned him when he had offered Owen the role of special investigator for the Home Office. "No bloody respect for law and order."

He had tapped a rather fine caricature that was lying on his desk, a drawing that had evidently been crumpled by Sidmouth's angry and impatient hand. "Treason," the Home Secretary had grumbled. "Sedition. Stirring up trouble, inciting the masses to riot. I'll see them all hang." His brows had snapped down. "You're a British peer now, Rothbury, even if we had to pass an Act of Parliament to make you so." He drummed his fingers on the cartoon. "Need your help against these traitors."

"Yes, my lord," Owen had said, a little grimly. The irony was not lost on him. Once, not so long ago, Sidmouth would have had no hesitation in branding *him* a renegade and a criminal. As an American he had been an enemy of the British state when the two countries were at war. That was before he had inherited a British peerage and turned into a slightly unlikely pillar of the establishment. He owed it to his family to uphold their honour now. Once before he had disgraced the family name under the most appalling circumstances. He would never do it again. Accepting his responsibilities now was his chance to atone.

Tess Darent shifted within the depths of the carriage, drawing his attention back to her as she pulled the peacock feather cloak more closely about her. Owen could smell her perfume, a crisp light scent, tart but sweet, rather like Tess herself. It was perfect for her, pretty and provocative, another element of her charming and flirtatious facade. Owen wondered what it was that she was hiding. Her wide-eyed pretence would fool nine out of ten men into believing her to be every inch as super-ficial as she appeared. It was a pity for her that he was the tenth and did not believe a word.

He had no grounds on which to arrest her, however. Visiting a brothel was not illegal and nor was carrying a pistol, and if she was a secret radical then he was the Queen of Sheba. The idea was absurd.

"Good night, Lady Darent." He kept one hand on the carriage door. "I wish you a safe journey home."

"And I wish you good luck in catching your miscre-ants." Tess's eyes were very wide and innocent. "What did you call them—madrigals?"

"Radicals," Owen said gently.

"Whichever." She made a little fluttering gesture with her hands. Her expression was blank. She even yawned. Owen wondered if she could possibly be as vacant as she seemed. If not, she was certainly an ex-tremely good actress.

"Pray give my best wishes to Lord…Sidmouth, was it?" She paused. "Is he rich? Married?"

"Not at the moment," Owen said.

Tess smiled. "Rich or married?" she queried.

"Yes, Sidmouth is rich and, no, he is not currently married," Owen clarified.

Tess's smile deepened. "Then I should like to make his acquaintance."

"You're looking for another husband for your collec-tion?" Owen said ironically.

"Marriage is my natural state," Tess said. "Is Sidmouth old?"

Owen laughed. "Probably not old enough to be relied on to die anytime soon."

"A pity," Tess said. "I always find that a useful attribute in a husband." Her blue eyes mocked him, sweeping over him from head to foot in knowing appraisal. "What about you, Lord Rothbury?" she asked. "Are you seeking a rich wife to go with your pretty title? I hear that your coffers hold nothing but moths."

"The gossip mongers have been busy," Owen said shortly.

"It is their function," Tess said. "Just as it is the job of every matron with an eligible daughter to parade her under your nose."

"I don't seek a wife at present," Owen said. His feelings felt raw. Odd that Tess Darent's clear blue gaze should, for a moment, strip away his defences. It was common knowledge that he had no fortune to go with his title. Only that morning he had had an awkward interview with his great-aunt by marriage, one of a host of elderly relatives his inheritance had also blessed him with. Lady Martindale was obscenely rich, eccentric and fearsomely opinionated. She had told Owen that if he wed, she would give him sufficient money to put his estates in order and would make him her heir. Owen knew he had reacted to her commands like a small, obstinate child; he had no wish to take a wife simply because Lady Martindale demanded it, and the alternative, to seek a rich heiress, was equally abhorrent to him. He had never yet met an eligible woman who did not bore him.

Except for Tess Darent. She was not precisely eligible but she certainly did not bore him.

The thought caught him by surprise.

Tess was watching him. Owen observed that she had the same lavender-blue eyes as her sister Joanna and the same heart-shaped face. Her hair was a few tones lighter than Joanna's, red-gold instead of golden-brown, but the darkness of the carriage smoothed out all subtleties of shading. Years before, Owen had had something of a passion for Joanna Grant, before she had had the bad taste to prefer his best friend, Alex, to him. Now he felt something move and shift in his chest, a pang of sensation as though his emotions were playing games with him. His rational mind knew that Tess and Joanna were very different women, but gut instinct and desire were not so logical, nor so biddable. He could remember when he had first seen Tess and had been winded by the physical likeness between the two sisters. But Tess Darent was not her sister. He needed to remember that. He could not have the one and he did not want the other, except in the most fundamental physical sense because she was a very desirable woman.

He released the door and gave the driver the word to move off, watching the hackney carriage as it disappeared into the dark. He had the strangest instinct that he had missed something important but he could not put his finger on what it might have been. Shaking off the sensation, Owen strolled back up the white stone steps and into the chequered hallway of the brothel. The last few dragoons were leaving; their captain, a sour-looking man with a permanently pained expression saluted Owen grimly. Owen knew the regular troops disliked having to work with Sidmouth's special investigators.

"Don't mind Captain Smart," his friend Garrick Farne said in his ear. "He took shrapnel in the groin at Salamanca so a raid on a brothel is a particular type of torture for him."

"Poor fellow," Owen said feelingly. "Did you find anything useful?" he added.

"Not much, I'm afraid," Garrick said. "If any of the leaders of the Jupiter Club fled this way they are already gone."

Owen shrugged. "It was always going to be a long shot."

He was accustomed to playing a long game. This sort of work was different from anything he had done before, but it required some of the same qualities of patience and resourcefulness and cool-headedness. It was not the same as exploring or sailing or fighting for his country, or any of the other things that Owen had done since he was old enough to make his way in the world, but it was still a challenge. The only thing Owen knew was that without a challenge, without action, he would fossilise. He might have accepted the responsibilities of his role but he could not see himself becoming the classic English aristocrat, wedded to his club and his country estates, settling into a life of luxurious emptiness. He had too much of his American heritage in his blood, the desire to carve his own future, the need to achieve.

"No sign of Tom either, presumably," he added.

Garrick shook his head. "I'll keep looking."

Garrick had accompanied him that night because there were rumours that his errant half-brother, Tom Bradshaw, had been heard of back in London, and with connections to the radical movement. Tom, Duke's bastard son and master criminal, had wed an heiress the year before and then promptly abandoned her, absconding with her fortune and leaving her ruined. This on top of Tom's attempt to ruin Garrick and murder his wife, Merryn, the year before had been enough to send Lord Sidmouth into near apoplexy. The Home Secretary had decreed that noblemen who had the misfortune to have such disreputable relatives should hunt them down and see them stand trial. Garrick had agreed, although his motives were more straightforward, Owen suspected. Tom had tried to kill the woman Garrick loved and he would move heaven and earth to capture him.

"Was there anything else of interest?" Owen queried.

"This isn't the place for a happily married man," Garrick said, smiling. "I had to avert my gaze on more than one occasion but despite my impaired vision I did find these." He held up a shirt, a jacket and pair of trousers. "No one is claiming them though, particularly as there was this in the jacket pocket." On the palm of his hand he held a wicked-looking knife with a carved ivory grip and a thistle design on the blade.

Owen's brows shot up. "Very nice," he murmured. He picked up the dagger and felt the worn handle slip smoothly into his palm. The knife was light but deadly sharp, with beautiful balance. "We might be able to trace this," he said, "if we ask around."

Garrick nodded. "And even nicer…" He put his hand in his pocket and extracted a set of crumpled papers, unfolding them and passing them to Owen. "I found these in one of the chambers upstairs, hidden beneath a pile of underwear in a dresser. The old bawd swears blind she had no idea they were there and there's no budging her from her story. She says one of her guests must have left them."

Owen looked at the cartoons. They were stunningly executed, conjuring a vivid image in only a few stark lines. One was a particularly cruel but accurate caricature of Lord Sidmouth as a hot-air balloon. The other showed a posse of dragoons trampling men, women and children beneath the hooves of their horses. The banner overhead read Freedom is Not Free. Owen grimaced at the sheer visceral shock and power of the picture. Something in it seemed to grab him by the throat. In the corner of each drawing was the signature of the cartoonist, a loopy black scrawl that simply read Jupiter. He let his breath out on a soundless whistle. "So Jupiter *was* hiding here," he said slowly.

Garrick nodded. "It would seem so. Powerful propaganda, these cartoons," he added. "It is no wonder that Sidmouth hates them."

Owen nodded. "They are dangerous," he said. "An incitement to violence."

He pushed the cartoons into his pocket. The pile of clothes on the floor caught his attention and he stirred it with one booted foot. An evocative scent hung for a moment on the air, crisp and fresh, with a perfume he recognised. He squatted down and picked up the shirt, feeling the fine quality of the linen against his fingers.

So now he knew what Tess had been wearing when she arrived at the brothel. Had she come there incognito because she did not want the ton to hear that she disported herself in a bawdy house? Or was her choice of clothing all part of a sensual game? Did she enjoy having a lover peel off those layers of masculine attire before he made love to her?

Owen thought of Tess Darent's body beneath his hands as he had lifted her down from the rope, the flare of her hips and the delicate curve of her waist. He thought of the heat of her skin through the slippery silk of the lavender gown, then he thought of what she might look like with those curves confined within the stark lines of the jacket and trousers, the thin cotton of the shirt pressing against her breasts. He raised the shirt to his nose, inhaled a long, deep breath and felt his senses fill with Tess, with her scent and her essence. Once again he was impaled by a jolt of lust that was hot and fierce and utterly uncomplicated.

"If you have an imagination, Lord Rothbury, now would be the time to use it...."

Owen, who had had no notion before tonight that he was such an imaginative man, found that imagination positively running riot.

"I met your sister-in-law just now," he said abruptly to Garrick.

Garrick, unsurprisingly, looked completely floored for a moment by the apparent non sequitur. "Joanna— Lady Grant—is here?"

"Is that likely?" Owen said. "No. I was referring to Lady Darent. I found her out in the street, shinning down a makeshift rope from one of the bedrooms upstairs."

Garrick's face spilt into a grin. "Oh, I see. Yes, that sounds exactly the sort of thing Tess would do. She is thoroughly scandalous. She had probably been enjoying an orgy."

Owen grimaced. He had only just managed to force his imagination away from the vision of Tess naked beneath the thin cotton shirt and now he found his mind had filled with an entirely new and darker set of imagery representing the way she might have disported herself here in the brothel tonight. Tess, pale limbs spread in abandoned wantonness, her cloud of red-gold hair fanning over her shoulders, Tess tied naked across a bed… He swallowed hard and fixed his gaze on the middle distance in an attempt to distract his mind. Unfortunately the middle distance consisted of a painting of a nude nymph and a group of lavishly endowed gentlemen indulging in a riotous orgy. Owen raised a hand to ease the constriction of his neckcloth. Evidently the lewd atmosphere of the bawdy house was turning his mind.

He wrenched his thoughts away from wayward visions of Tess and turned to find Garrick watching him closely, his gaze narrowed, perceptive. "Do you have an interest there?" Garrick asked.

Owen ran a distracted hand through his hair. "In Lady Darent? I'd be a fool if I had."

"Which," Garrick said, smiling faintly, "doesn't quite answer the question, does it? Those Fenner girls," he added, shaking his head, "could make a fool of any man."

"I know," Owen said. "Born to drive a man to perdition." He cast a last glance around the hallway. "I have to get out of here," he said. "It's doing strange things to my mind."

"Or you could stay," Garrick said, with an expressive lift of the brows.

Owen gestured towards where Mrs. Tong was leaning over the wrought-iron balcony on the first floor and watching them with a great deal of venom in her dark, disillusioned eyes.

"I think we have already outstayed our welcome,"

he murmured. "That basilisk stare would be sufficient to wither the most ardent man."

"White's, then," Garrick said, "and the brandy bottle?"

"Capital," Owen said. He bent to pick up the pile of clothing from the floor. Tess's scent was growing fainter now. He remembered Garrick saying that the knife had been found in the jacket pocket. So Tess carried both a knife and a pistol. That was interesting. He wondered why she carried them and what she was afraid of. He wondered if she knew how to use them.

Then there were the cartoons, found hidden in a chamber on the second floor, Garrick had said. Tess's resourceful escape down the sheet rope had been from just such a room....

Owen felt the strange prickle of sensation again, an instinct, stronger this time, that he had missed something obvious, something that had been right beneath his nose. A thought slid into his mind, a thought that was so outrageous, so unbelievable, that it stole his breath. It told him that he had been played by a master hand, that he had been misdirected and fooled. He had believed what was before his eyes. He had not questioned it. He had met a notorious widow climbing out of a brothel window and he had believed her when she had pretended to be running away to avoid scandal.

Owen recalled Tess Darent claiming not to know who Lord Sidmouth was and professing pretty ignorance of the radical movement. She had claimed to be in a hurry to get home and sleep off her sexual excesses.

In truth she had been in a hurry to escape.

He let the clothes slip through his fingers and instead took the cartoons from his pocket once more and scanned them. There was nothing, he thought, to say that Jupiter, the witty and dangerous caricaturist, had to be a man. Sidmouth had simply made that assumption, assumed also that the members of the Jupiter Club were exclusively male. But Jupiter could well be a pseudonym for a woman, the type of woman who carried a pistol in her reticule and attended radical meetings dressed in masculine attire. A woman who hid behind her reputation for scandal and pretended to be as light and superficial as a butterfly....

It seemed impossible. And yet…

Owen let out a long breath. No one would believe him, of course. Lord Sidmouth would laugh him out of town if he suggested that Jupiter was the infamous Dowager Marchioness of Darent. The evidence was no more than circumstantial. Even so, Owen was sure that his instinct was right. He had wondered what it was that Teresa Darent was hiding. Now he knew. All he had to do was to prove it.

LADY EMMA BRADSHAW HAD just returned from the meeting of the Jupiter Club and was standing with one hand on the latch of her tiny cottage, listening to the fading sound of her brother's carriage as it rumbled away down the hill towards the city, when a man materialised out of the darkness beside her, flung open the door and bundled her over the threshold. He had one arm locked tight about her waist and his hand over her mouth. It was so sudden and so shocking that Emma had no time to cry out. She struggled and fought, necessarily in silence, kicked him and bit him, and then equally suddenly, she stopped fighting because she had recognised his scent and his touch. Vicious shock flared through her; her knees buckled, she sagged in his arms and he let her go.

"Tom," Emma said. Her voice was hoarse. Tom Bradshaw, her husband, *here,* six months after he had deserted her and left her alone, penniless and with no word....

The shock faded and she waited to feel something else in its place, anger perhaps, or disbelief or even love. *Anything.* Anything but this cold chill that seemed to encase her heart.

The cocky smile that she remembered was gone from Tom's lips. He looked older, not merely because of the pallor of his face and the deep lines that scored it, but because there was something different about him, some knowledge in his eyes that had not been there before, something of pain and suffering. He was emaciated, as though he had been ill. He did not try to touch her again or even to draw any closer to her. He stood just inside the door, watching her with wariness and a longing that did make Emma's heart contract. She had never expected to see Tom look so vulnerable.

She found that she was wondering what on earth to say. Strange, when so many times before she had rehearsed exactly what she would say to the no-good, deceitful, swindling scoundrel should she ever have the misfortune to see him again.

"What happened?" she croaked. "Where have you been?" She immediately hated herself for the banality of the words, as though Tom had merely been gone a few hours enjoying a pint or two at the local tavern.

She saw a faint smile touch his lips as though he too recognised the inadequacy of anything either of them could say. In that moment Emma's feelings came alive, and she hated him with so vivid and bitter a hatred that she could almost taste it. She put her hands behind her back to prevent her from pummelling him with the force of her rage. She could feel the rough plaster of the wall cold against her palms. The rest of her body felt hot, tight and furious.

"I've been on board a ship."

Tom took a couple of steps away from her, down the passage. His steps sounded loud on the flagstone floor. Emma wondered if the maid would wake and think she was entertaining a lover in the depths of the night. She caught Tom's arm and pulled him into the kitchen, closing the door silently behind them.

"On a ship?" She knew she was repeating his words like a parrot. Nothing was making much sense to her.

"Someone didn't like me very much." Tom gave a half shrug. "They paid to have me knocked on the head and thrown into the hold of a ship going to the Indies, no questions asked."

Emma's stomach swooped. She felt a little sick. So this was Tom's excuse for deserting her and running off with her fortune. She did not believe him. She could not. Tom had always been a consummate liar. Of course he would not admit that he had abandoned her of his own free will, not if he wanted her back.

"I'm surprised it took so long," she said sweetly, even though the bitterness was sharp in her throat. "There must be a hundred people willing to pay to get rid of you." She turned away from him, staring fixedly at the little watercolour of a country scene on the wall. The soft pastel colours swam in the candlelight. Tess Darent had painted it as a present for her when first Emma had moved to Hampstead Wells. She had said that it would soften the austereness of the whitewashed walls. Tess had been her staunchest friend when Tom had left her.

"Why did you trouble to come back?" she said. "You are the sort of man who could have made a fortune in the Indies." Despite her attempts to sound indifferent, her voice cracked a little. "I hear that there are opportunities in those places for men of your stamp."

"I came back for you," Tom said. Emma was not looking at him but even so she could feel his gaze on her and knew that its intensity did not waver. "You were all I thought about when I was imprisoned in that hellhole of a ship," Tom said. "It was only the thought of seeing you again that kept me alive—"

He broke off as Emma brought her hand down hard on the kitchen table, sending the bread knife skittering away across the surface.

"Tom, stop!" She took a breath, lowered her tone. "It's too late," she said. A void of hopelessness opened up beneath her heart. "I don't know if I believe anything you say anymore. You always were such a liar."

"I love you," Tom said. "I swear it's true."

Emma shook her head. "Don't, Tom," she said. "I don't want to hear it."

Tom was very pale now. He swayed a little. Emma made an instinctive move towards him but stopped herself and dropped her hand to her side. She could never trust him now. He had abandoned her with no word, leaving her facing a life alone with no money, no home and no reputation left. She had known he was a scoundrel when she wed him. It was that very air of danger about him that she had found so fatally attractive. Now, though, the young girl who had fallen for Tom Bradshaw's charm was like a stranger to her, someone from another life.

"It was your half-brother who helped me," she said, holding his gaze with eyes that burned hot with unshed tears. "You remember your half-brother, Garrick Farne—the man you wanted to ruin, the man whose wife you tried to *kill?*"

Tom was white to the lips. "I admit I have done some

NICOLA CORNICK   43

terrible things," he said, "but that is all at an end. I've changed. I'll prove it to you. I promise you...."

"Oh, Tom," Emma said. "It's too late to do that." She turned away. "If you do love me," she said, with difficulty, "the best thing you can do for me is never to see me again."

"No," Tom said. "Emma—"

"Go," Emma said.

When she turned back Tom had gone and the kitchen was empty and cold. The door swung closed softly with a click of the latch. Moving very slowly, feeling cold all the way through to her bones, Emma locked the door and went back down the passage to the little parlour. The fire had been banked down in the grate; she tried to warm her shaking hands before it. There was a plate of cold ham and bread and cheese for her supper and a glass of wine on the table, but she could not touch it now. Her mouth felt as dry as dust, her throat blocked.

I don't need him, she told herself fiercely, blinking past the tears. *I don't need Tom. He'll only hurt me again.*

The parlour was comfortingly warm but Emma found that the fire could not stave off the cold that was inside her rather than out. With a sigh, she picked up the tray and carried it through to the kitchen, replacing the food untouched in the cold larder and making her way upstairs to bed. It was only once she was beneath the covers, curled around the stone hot-water bottle, seeking a comfort she could not find, that she permitted herself to cry, because she had wanted to believe that there was an ounce of goodness in Tom, that he could reform, but to trust him would have been the most foolish thing she could have done. She had already been hurt far too much.

She wished that Tess Darent were there to advise her. Emma often thought that she would do just about anything for Tess, who had shown her kindness and generosity when everyone else had turned their backs on her. She did not know Tess well and she understood her even less, for there was beneath Tess's outward manner an impenetrable reserve, but she loved Tess all the same with a fierce loyalty she had never felt for anyone else in her life. She had often wondered if Tess, too, had suffered at the hands of men and if that was why she had helped her. Perhaps she would never know of Tess's experiences. But she would always be grateful to her.

CHAPTER THREE

TESS LOOKED FROM THE LETTER in her hand to the flushed, fatuous face of the man standing on her sister's hearthrug, hands clasped behind his back, substantial paunch jutting. He was warming his posterior before the blazing fire. His smug stance said that he held all the cards and Tess, a skilful gambler herself, was rather afraid that he was correct. She was in a bind. There was no doubt.

Play for time.

"Let me understand you properly, Lord Corwen," she said.

You noxious toad...

"You are proposing that I should give permission, as guardian to my twin stepchildren, for you to wed Lady Sybil Darent and if I do not—" her tone dropped by several degrees from cold to frozen "—you will foreclose on a private loan you apparently advanced to my late husband and oblige my stepson, Lord Darent, to sell off all unentailed parts of his estate. To you, of course."

You vile, grasping beast...

Corwen smiled, a lupine smile that left his small eyes cold. "You have it precisely, Lady Darent."

Tess tapped the lawyer's letter against the palm of her hand. News of the loan had come as a shock to her but she could not afford the scandal of challenging Corwen in the law courts and he knew it. She wanted to take him to court because she knew he was a charlatan who had tricked the elderly Marquis of Darent into signing away half his estate in exchange for the loan. Towards the end of his life Darent had been almost insensible from excess laudanum and would have signed almost anything put in front of him. There were plenty of scandalmongers who said that was precisely how Tess had persuaded Darent to marry her in the first place.

"I'll pay the loan off myself." Her heart thumped in her chest and the words stuck in her throat but she forced them out. Forty-eight thousand pounds was no small sum and she hardly wanted to throw it away on Lord Corwen, but three widow's portions, a successful gambling career and some careful investment had made her a rich woman and she could easily afford it. It was also the least painful option for her stepchildren. She would die before she saw either of them fall into the power of this man.

But Corwen was shaking his head, smiling a dissolute smile that made her skin crawl. "I will not accept your money, Lady Darent. The debt is against the Darent estate. And as I say—" he cleared his throat but it did nothing to disguise the thickness of lechery in his voice "—I wish for marriage to Lady Sybil and *then* I will cancel the debt entirely."

"Lady Sybil is *fifteen* years old." Tess could not keep the distaste from her voice. "She is a schoolgirl."

And you are disgusting.

"I am prepared to wait a year provided that we may come to terms now." Lord Corwen rocked back on his heels. "Sixteen would be a charming age for Lady Sybil to wed. I saw her on her most recent visit from Bath. She is a delightful young woman. Fresh, biddable, innocent…" His voice caressed the final word.

Tess set her teeth. Not long ago, a mere ten years, she had been a bride herself when not yet out of her teens. Twice. And Corwen, predatory, hiding his dissolution under that unpleasantly avuncular manner, reminded her all too forcibly of Charles Brokeby, her second husband. A tremor shook her deep inside. Sybil must never, *never,* be subjected to what she had endured.

"And you are…" She looked at Corwen, at his fat jowls and the lines of dissipation scored deep around his eyes. "Forty-five, forty-six?"

Corwen frowned. "I will be seven and forty next year. It is a good age to remarry."

"Not to my stepdaughter," Tess said. "She is far too young. I cannot permit it and, anyway, I share the responsibility for her upbringing with Lady Sybil's aunt and uncle. They would agree with me that such a marriage is out of the question."

Disconcertingly, Corwen did not appear taken aback. Perhaps he thought her protests only token. Since he was threatening to foreclose on a loan of approaching fifty thousand pounds, Tess imagined he thought he could dictate his terms at will.

"Perhaps you are jealous." Corwen's tone dropped to intimacy. Shockingly his hand had come out to brush away the curls that had escaped Tess's blue bandeau. He was running a finger down the curve of her cheek.

"It cannot be pleasant to be eclipsed by a child only fourteen years younger," he murmured. "And my dear Lady Darent—"

Tess knocked his hand away. "I am *not* your Lady Darent, dear or otherwise."

Corwen laughed. "Is that what rankles? A few years younger and I might have suggested you become my mistress in payment instead."

"And," Tess said, "I would have been as little flattered then as I am now." She could feel the panic fluttering in her chest. Corwen was standing far too close to her. He was a big man, fleshy and broad, and his proximity was threatening. She felt the breath flatten in her lungs. For a second she could see Brokeby standing there, reaching for her, smiling that horrible smile. The shudders rippled through her body. Then the vision was gone and she was standing once again in her sister's drawing room with the autumn sunshine warming the bright yellow walls and creating a spurious sense of cheer.

She moved sharply away from Corwen, although the length of the Thames would be insufficient distance from so repellent a man.

Corwen's face suffused with colour. "I offer your stepdaughter *marriage,* madam. You should be grateful for that. And if you think her relatives will object, then I rely on you to persuade them."

"You want to wed a girl who is still in the schoolroom," Tess said coldly. "Do not dress it up as something respectable when it is not." She looked at him. "Let us be quite clear, my lord," she said carefully, her fingers tightening on the lawyer's letter until her grip threatened to crumple it. "I am in receipt of your request for Lady Sybil's hand in marriage. I refuse it. I also refuse to sell any part of the Darent estate on behalf of my stepson, in order to meet this debt. I have offered to pay the full amount myself. You have refused. So you will have to take this matter up with my lawyers. I shall tell them to expect to hear from you."

Corwen did not move. For a moment Tess thought he had not understood her. Then he took a step closer again.

"I believe you have not heard what I am saying, madam," he said. "I *will* wed Lady Sybil." His lips curled. "In a couple of years her aunt will be launching her in society. It would be a great pity for Lady Sybil's debut to be marred by the sort of rumours and scandal that cling to *your* character." He paused. "You had the upbringing of her for five years before her father died. A word here and a whisper there—" he shrugged "—and Lady Sybil is tarred with your brush. Her moral character is questioned, her reputation placed in doubt. Suddenly…" he said, smiling with evident relish, "no respectable man will have her, and Lady Sybil's future is ruined." He inclined his head, eyes bright now. "Do you take my meaning, Lady Darent?"

The blood chilled to ice in Tess's veins. Corwen stood, legs splayed, chest thrust out as though he commanded the room. Commanded her to give him her stepdaughter in marriage or he would besmirch Sybil's reputation out of revenge.

And she had given him the means by which he could do it—she, with her tarnished character and her name for scandal. She should have realised how that might be used against her, but then she had never anticipated the cold calculation of a lecher like Lord Corwen.

Despair slid along Tess's veins. It was her marriage to Brokeby that had done the damage. It had been ten years before but the shadow of it had never lifted. Brokeby had tainted her with his vile reputation for perversion. Then, a year ago, an exhibition of nude paintings of her had dealt her reputation its final blow. Brokeby's wretched paintings… A tremor shook Tess deep inside. She could never reveal the truth about those. Her throat closed with revulsion and she swallowed hard. It was best not to remember that night. It was best to lock those hideous memories away. Except that she had found over the years that she could not forget them. She carried them everywhere with her. They were imprinted on her mind just as she felt they were indelibly written on her body in all their lurid detail. Hateful images she would scrub away if only she could. But they never faded. She was haunted.

The breath hitched in her throat and she blinked to dispel the sting of tears in her eyes. Brokeby was dead and gone to the hell he deserved. She was free. Only, she never quite felt free. Somehow the shame and the horror were etched too deep on her soul to be forgotten.

And now here was Corwen, a man of a similar stamp, waiting for her to succumb to his blackmail. Very slowly Tess raised her gaze to his face. There was a gleam of amusement in his small eyes, the pleasure of a man who enjoyed enforcing his will and making others squirm. So very like Brokeby... But she was not a frightened girl anymore.

"Lord Corwen," Tess said, "if you ever go near Lady Sybil or threaten her reputation, I will person-ally ensure that you are maimed sufficiently never to approach a woman again with your vile proposals." She gave him a smile that dripped ice. "Now—at last—are we clear?"

Corwen made a sudden involuntary movement full of violence, and Tess's mind splintered into terrifying images of Brokeby, brutal, vicious, utterly merciless. She closed her eyes for a second to banish the vile, vivid memories and when she opened them, Corwen was gone, slamming out of the room with a force that shook the mantelpiece and sent the invitation cards fluttering down to the floor.

Tess heaved a sigh and sank down rather heavily onto Joanna's gold brocade sofa. The port decanter beckoned to her but she had had a bad night and her head was already aching, and she knew from bitter experience that trying to lose her memory in drink was a fool's game. She had tried it after Brokeby's death, tried to drown the past. These days she could not look a gin bottle in the eye without feeling sick. She had tried everything, including laudanum, from which she had sometimes thought she would never wake. Nothing helped, not sweetmeats, not even spending excessive amounts of money on clothes, shoes and accessories. In the end she had dragged herself out of the despair through sheer force of will, but by then it had been too late. The ton had seen the drinking and the gambling and the spending to excess, and now there were those hideous paintings. It was no wonder that her reputation was so damaged.

Tess drove her fist so hard into one of Joanna's gold brocade cushions that the seams split. She hastily shoved the stuffing back inside and turned the cushion over so that the rent would not show. Her headache stabbed her temples. She had not been able to sleep after she had got back from the brothel the previous night. Lying in her bed, staring up at the canopy, she had come to the inevitable conclusion that the Jupiter Club was finished. It was too dangerous for them to

meet again when government saboteurs had surely in-
filtrated the membership and were fomenting violence.
Whoever was stirring up the rioters would be acting as
an informer as well. It would only be a matter of time
before the spy would unmask them all, not just her but
her young political protégé Justin Brooke and his sister,
Emma, too.

And now there was this, Corwen's revolting attempt
to blackmail her into serving up her stepdaughter,
Sybil, like some virginal sacrifice to his jaded palate.
The thought made the bile rise in Tess's throat. She
adored Sybil and her twin brother, Julius, and had done
so from the moment she had first met them. It was
intolerable to see both of them at the mercy of Lord
Corwen.

Tess reached absent-mindedly for the chocolate-
flavoured bonbons that Joanna kept in a silver box
on the table nearby. The box was empty. With a sigh
Tess replaced it. She had dismissed Corwen for the
time being but she knew that he would be back, in
one shape or form or another, with his greedy eyes
and his repellent demands. He wanted Sybil and he
would be determined to have her. And Tess understood
all about the driving need a man like Corwen felt to
take something so fresh and sweet as Sybil Darent and
despoil it.

She could keep Sybil physically safe but she could
not protect her reputation. Tess had no doubt that if
Corwen could not have Sybil, then he would ruin her

another way. And the hateful truth was that Corwen was right—a whisper of scandal could kill any debutante's good name and future prospects regardless of whether or not it was based on truth. Sybil's aunt was the most irreproachably respectable chaperone in the whole of London, but Tess was still the girl's stepmother, and her own blemished reputation could do her stepdaughter nothing but damage. She wondered that she had not thought of it before. Corwen would drop a subtle word here and there, poisoning the ton against Sybil for no better reason than that he lusted after her and could not have her.

Tess shivered, her fingers digging into the richly embroidered arm of the sofa. Damn Corwen to hell and back for his callous determination to indulge his most base vices on the body of her stepdaughter. It was unbearable. And damn him to the next level of hell for threatening to foreclose on the loan as well, thereby forcing her to decimate Julius's inheritance in order to pay him off.

She could stall him, but it was only a matter of time.

With a muffled cry of frustration she leapt to her feet and walked over to the window, where a grey cloud stretched from horizon to horizon now, spilling inky darkness over the city. The faint autumn sunlight had been banished and it was a cold, wintry scene.

There was no escape for Julius or Sybil, and yet she had to do something to help them. Their father had entrusted them to her care. She could not fail them.

There was no way out.

Unless…

Unless she married again….

The thought slid into her mind with all the sinuous temptation of the snake in Eden. Tess screwed her eyes up tightly. She had been widowed for two years and she had promised her sister Joanna that she would make no more marriages. Joanna, Tess suspected, was embarrassed to have a much-married marchioness as a sister. But Joanna had also forgotten quite how vulnerable a widow could be.

What she needed was a marriage in name only to a man who had sufficient power and authority to tell Corwen to go hang and to provide the protection of his name for both herself and her stepchildren. Then, once she was irreproachably wed, she would need to transform herself into a reputable matron. No more climbing out of brothel windows. No more gambling. No more Jupiter Club.

No more satirical cartoons.

It would undo all her good work to be clapped in gaol. That was a position from which there really was no return.

Tess pulled a face. The thought of denying her talent for art, of deliberately turning away from the cartoons, the one thing that gave her life such passionate meaning, was almost unbearable. She had been drawing since she was a child, pouring her feelings into her sketches as a means of expression and escape. Sorrow, joy, fear and frustration had all been expressed through her pen.

Yet she could see that now she had no choice. She would have to abandon political satire and choose something blameless like watercolours or sketching, perhaps. Ladies were forever setting up their easels and capturing some idyllic rural scene. She would do the same. Drawing and painting were amongst the few feminine accomplishments she possessed.

A respectable marriage would also offer her the camouflage she needed should Lord Sidmouth's investigators prove efficient enough as to suspect her of sedition. She needed a smoke screen, an elderly, impotent smoke screen. She needed to find a fourth husband and she needed to find him fast.

She crossed the room to the rosewood desk, took out a thick volume, settled herself again on the gold brocade sofa and started to read.

A half hour later she was still engrossed when Joanna came in accompanied by a footman with the tea tray.

"What is that you are reading?" Joanna asked, seating herself beside Tess. *"The Lady's Magazine?"*

"No." Tess felt a little shiver of apprehension. Joanna's disapproval was not something she sought. She tilted the cover of her book towards her sister so that Joanna could see the title. "It is the new edition of *The Gazetteer*."

As Tess had anticipated, vivid disappointment registered on Joanna's face. "Oh, Tess, no!" Joanna exclaimed. "Tell me you are not planning on marrying again! When you came to stay here you promised—" Joanna broke off, biting her lip. Her tone changed. It was cool now, though still indicative of her feelings. "It is your decision, I suppose," she said.

"I have a natural affinity with marriage," Tess said. She could hear the apology in her tone. She did not want to remind Joanna just how insecure her situation was. Her sister knew nothing of her life, least of all her secret political affiliation to the reformers. Nor did she want to tell Joanna of Lord Corwen's threats. Such a discussion would hold too many painful parallels with her marriage to Brokeby. She set her lips stubbornly and tried to ride down Joanna's disapproval.

"On the contrary," her elder sister corrected her sharply, clearly unable to keep quiet for more than a couple of seconds. "There is nothing natural about it. Your marriages have all without exception been most *unnatural*."

Tess could not really dispute that. She knew that Joanna was one of the few people who had realised that she was afraid—*terrified*—of true intimacy, though her sister did not know the reason. Joanna had tried to discuss it with her in the past, but Tess had always refused to talk. Clothes, shoes, hats, gloves, scarves... They could chat about fashion for hours and it gave their relationship a veneer of closeness, but when Joanna tried to get Tess to talk about her marriages, Tess would feel the familiar cold horror spread through her veins like poison and she would turn Joanna's questions away with trivial answers. She knew Joanna was asking not out of prurient curiosity but out of a real concern, and that made her feel even sadder. But there was nothing Joanna could do to help her. The damage wrought by Charles Brokeby had been done years ago and could not be undone now.

"Not everyone has the sort of marriage that you share with Alex," she said. The words came out more harshly than she had intended, perhaps because whilst she was terrified by any thought of intimacy herself, she did at times feel a fierce jealousy of both the physical and emotional bond that Joanna and Alex shared. In public she might scorn such an unfashionable concept as a happy marriage but in reality the warmth and intimacy and shared experience was something she craved.

"Most people," she added, "want no more than a position in society, enough money to sustain it and the promise that they will not need to see their spouse above half a dozen times a year and, if they do, that they need not speak with them above once."

Joanna's pretty face wrinkled into a grimace of distaste. She put down her teacup with a crack that made the delicate china shiver. "Very amusing, Tess. You forget you are talking to your sister and not to one of your casual acquaintances." She flicked *The Gazetteer* with a contemptuous finger. "You hope to find such a husband in here?"

"It is the most marvellous book," Tess said, pressing on although she could feel Joanna's fearsome disapproval. "It gives the rank, fortune and address of every bachelor and widower in the country. It is the perfect husband-hunting guide."

"It does not record whether or not the men are impotent," Joanna said very drily. "That, surely, is your most important criteria."

There was a painful silence. "It gives their ages," Tess said at last, almost managing to conceal the crack in her voice. "That should be a fair guide."

"But not an infallible one." Joanna's voice had softened into pity. She put a hand on Tess's tensely clasped ones and Tess tried not to shudder, not from Joanna's offered comfort but from the cold pain she felt inside.

"Tess," Joanna said. "What happened to you? What is it that you are afraid of?"

"Nothing!" Tess said. The word seemed to come out slightly too loud. The pain twisted within her like the turn of a screw.

"Then why do you only marry sickly boys and old men?" Joanna persisted. "Robert Barstow, James Darent—"

"There was only one of each," Tess protested, "and to be fair I did not know that Robert was going to die so young."

"With Robert you married your best friend," Joanna said. "There was as little passion there as in your last marriage."

Once again the silence was taut and painful. Neither of them had mentioned her marriage to Brokeby but Tess could see the question in Joanna's eyes. Her sister had guessed that Brokeby had hurt her; she wanted Tess to confide. Tess knew Joanna's concern was only to help her but she did not want that help. There was nothing Joanna could do to set right the past or undo the horrific experiences she had suffered at Brokeby's hands. There was nothing that *she* could do except blot out those memories and make sure that such horrors never happened again.

"If you have a fear of physical intimacy," Joanna said suddenly, "I do not understand this obsession you have with marrying."

"You refine too much upon it," Tess snapped, her patience breaking under the strain. "I find myself short of funds, that is all. Marriage is the easiest way to address the deficit." She spread her hands wide in a gesture of exasperation. "For me, marriage is a business option only, preferable to a trip to the moneylenders."

"So you are in debt?" Joanna's exquisitely plucked brows rose disbelievingly. "I don't believe you. You have a fortune to eclipse every other widow in society."

"Clothes," Tess said vaguely. "They are so monstrously expensive."

"That is one matter on which you cannot gammon me," Joanna said robustly. "I know all there is to know about the cost of fashion and not even *you* could spend all your substance on it!"

They stared at one another defiantly. Tess wondered what on earth Joanna would say if she confessed that her money was in fact mainly spent on charitable causes and radical politics. No doubt she would be more shocked than if Tess had confessed to spending it all on sex with handsome young men. There were political hostesses, of course, formidable matrons who supported the Whig or the Tory cause and gave smart dinners to promote their husbands' careers. Reforming politics was a different matter, too extreme, dangerous and inappropriate, with its emphasis on improving the conditions of the working classes. No one in society should concern themselves with such matters. Charity was one thing; political reform quite another.

"My gambling debts are enormous," Tess said, reaching for an excuse that never failed, "and perhaps I may catch myself a rich duke this time. I have no wish to go down the social scale rather than up."

"Then you truly are limiting your options," Joanna said sarcastically. To Tess's relief she seemed to have swallowed this explanation. "Let me see," her sister continued. "We need to find you a duke or a prince, old enough to die within a year or two so that his continued existence does not inconvenience you, sickly enough not to be interested in his marital rights and rich enough to increase your fortune! How very romantic!"

"I do not require romance from marriage," Tess said.

"So I have observed." Her sister sprang to her feet.

"I do not believe that even *The Gazetteer* will be able to furnish you with the direction of such a nobleman."

"I have whittled it down to a list of a few possibilities," Tess said. "There is one duke, Feversham—"

"He died two weeks ago," Joanna said.

"Oh. Well, what about the Marquis of Raymond?"

"Also very nearly dead."

"Then there might still be time to catch him—"

Joanna glared. "Tess, no!"

"Lord Grace?"

"He is in the Fleet." Joanna smiled sweetly. "You could have adjoining cells."

Tess pulled a face. "Lord Pettifer?"

Joanna shook her head. "He is in Bedlam."

Tess deflated. "Then there is no one," she said.

"I told you so," Joanna said, not unkindly.

After Joanna had gone, closing the door with exaggerated quiet behind her, Tess finished her cold tea and picked up *The Gazetteer* once again, flicking listlessly through the pages. Joanna was correct, unfortunately. The list, whilst giving the details of many eligible gentlemen, did not also come with a guarantee that they would see marriage in the same idiosyncratic light that she did. Not many men, when it came down to it, wanted a marriage of no more than convenience. Many wanted an heir, of course. Some wanted to sleep with their wives occasionally if they could not get a better offer. Many thought that a marriage should suit *their* convenience—that that was what the phrase meant. Tess had no intention of being available to service the needs of her husband. That would not suit *her* convenience. And so her choice was limited to the ancient, the infirm, the impotent or those who were attracted to their own sex rather than hers.

With a sigh, she put the book back in the drawer, retrieved one by Voltaire instead and wandered out into the hall.

Tess liked living with Joanna's family in Bedford Square. The house was elegantly appointed and filled with the warmth and laughter of a happy family. It gave Tess a spurious sense of belonging to stay there. She had never had a home of her own, or at least not one she chose to live in. Her various marriage portions had given her a scattering of houses on estates across the country, but any of these would have been under the disapproving eye of her relatives by marriage, not a tempting option. Besides, she hated the country. It was dull and intensified her sense of loneliness. Only in London was there diversion enough to keep solitude at bay.

Tess knew that Joanna would never evict her but she had from time to time thought that she should purchase her own London house. It was embarrassing to be hanging on her family coattails at her age. The idea of living alone did not appeal, however. It made the cold chill in her heart solidify further.

In a sudden fit of irritation, Tess tweaked the bud off the stem of one of the hothouse roses displayed in a wide shallow bowl on the hall table. There. She had completely spoiled Joanna's beautiful arrangement.

The door of the library opened abruptly. Two men came out, deep in conversation: Tess's brother-in-law Alex and Viscount Rothbury. Tess jumped out of sheer surprise. Rothbury was, if not a frequent visitor to Bedford Square, then a regular one. He had even dined here on several occasions. It was no great surprise to see him here. Tess realised that it was simply that he had been in her mind, lurking behind her preoccupation with finding a new husband, the memory of the previous night catching at her heels.

In the daylight Rothbury looked every inch the viscount, elegant in buff pantaloons and a jacket cut with supreme skill, his boots with a mirror polish, his cravat tied in a complicated waterfall of pristine white. Then Tess met his eyes and saw behind the man of fashion the same dangerous challenge she had recognised the night before. This was a wolf in sheep's clothing, an adventurer dressed as a dandy. She had made a good decision in the past to steer clear of him. A pity then that now she had come to his notice, for he showed every sign of paying her a great deal of attention.

Tess realised that she was staring, like a schoolroom miss transfixed by the sight of a handsome gentleman. She saw Rothbury raise his brows in faint quizzical amusement, and she blushed. That was even worse. No man had the power to make her blush. It was not something she did.

Rothbury exchanged a quick word with Alex, who shook him by the hand and went back into the library. The door closed behind him with a soft click. The house was suddenly quiet, the hallway temporarily devoid of servants. Rothbury started walking towards Tess across the broad expanse of chequered tile. She felt a curious urge to turn tail and run away. She shoved the book by Voltaire behind the flower arrangement. It really would not do to be caught reading philosophy, not when she was supposed to be a featherbrain.

"Lady Darent." Rothbury was bowing before her. "Good morning. I trust that you have recovered from your experiences of last night?"

"I trust that you have forgotten them," Tess said. "A gentleman would surely make no reference to our last meeting."

A wicked smile lit Rothbury's face. It deepened the crease he had down one tanned cheek. "Ah, but there you have the problem," he drawled. "Surely you have heard that I am no gentleman, merely a Yankee sea captain?"

"I've heard you called many things," Tess agreed smoothly.

He laughed. "And none of them flattering, I'll wager." He kept his eyes on her face. The intentness of his expression flustered her. "I am glad I saw you this morning," he continued. He put a hand into the pocket of the elegant coat. "I have something here I think must be yours."

Tess's heart did a sickening little skip. She had wondered about the loss of the cartoons. She had wondered about them all the way home and for the best part of the night. She had not thought Rothbury had them, for surely he would have asked her about them if he had found them in her purse. Now, though, it seemed she might be proven wrong. For a moment her mind spun dizzily, then with a fierce sense of relief she saw that it was not the drawings he held in his hand but the thistle knife.

"My dagger," she said. "How kind of you to reunite me with it."

She saw a flash of surprise in Rothbury's eyes. Perhaps he had expected her to deny it belonged to her. But the thistle knife had been Robert's and was of great sentimental value to her if of no real worth. Tess was not going to sacrifice it.

"Did you find anything else of mine?" she asked, very politely.

Rothbury's keen green gaze met hers. "Did you lose anything else?" he asked.

Their eyes locked with the sudden intensity of a sword thrust.

He knew about the cartoons. She was sure of it.

Tess suppressed a shiver, schooling herself to calm. Rothbury might have the satirical sketches, but he could prove nothing. And she must give nothing away. She knew she should be afraid, yet the beat in her blood was of excitement, not fear. It felt like drinking too much champagne, or dancing barefoot in the grass in a summer dawn. She had almost forgotten what it felt like for her senses to be so sharply alive.

"Only my clothes," she said lightly.

Rothbury smiled. "Is that a habit of yours?" he enquired. "Losing your clothes?"

"Not particularly," Tess said, "though gossip would tell you different." She smiled back at him. "Pray do not trouble to return them. Men's clothing never suited me anyway."

Rothbury's gaze slid over her in thorough, masculine appraisal. "You do indeed look charming in your proper person," he murmured, in that voice that always seemed to brush her nerve endings with fire.

He gestured to a drawing of Shuna, Tess's niece, which was framed on the wall above the vase of roses. "Your work?" he enquired softly.

It sounded like a complete change of subject, but Tess knew it was not. He knew she was an artist. It was only one small step from there to her being a cartoonist. She looked at the pencil portrait of her niece. Unfortunately she had signed it. Her heart missed a beat as she noticed that the signature bore more than a passing resemblance to Jupiter's arrogant black scrawl. How careless of her....

"You seem unsure if this is your work or not." Rothbury's voice was faintly mocking now.

"No, yes!" Tess tried to pull herself together. "Yes,

that is one of my drawings. Art is one of the few things at which I excel."

Once again she felt Rothbury's gaze on her face as searching as a physical touch. "I am sure you sell yourself short," he said. "You must have many accomplishments."

"I don't sell myself at all," Tess said. She gave him a cool little smile. "Pray do not let me keep you, my lord," she added pointedly.

So clear a dismissal was difficult to ignore and she saw Rothbury's smile widen in appreciation. "Oh, I am in no hurry," he said easily. "I enjoy talking to you. But if you wish to escape me, then pray do run away." There was more than a hint of challenge in his voice—and in his eyes. He retrieved the Voltaire from behind the rose bowl and held it out to her. "Don't forget your book."

"Gracious, that isn't mine," Tess said. "French philosophy? It must be one of Merryn's vast collection."

"My dear Lady Darent," Rothbury drawled, "it has your signature on the bookplate."

Damnation.

Tess snatched the book from his hand and flicked it open. The title page held no bookplate at all. She looked up to see Rothbury watching her closely. His lips twisted into amusement.

"So it is yours."

"Very clever," Tess snapped.

"I think you must be," Rothbury said thoughtfully. "So why pretend to be a featherbrain, Lady Darent?"

Checkmate. If she was clever then Rothbury was at least one step ahead of her.

Tess shrugged. "A woman is no more than a fool if she lets a man see she is a bluestocking," she said. "Or so my mama told me."

"I don't think you believe that."

Tess's heart skipped a beat at his directness. There was something predatory in his eyes now, the intensity of the hunter. Her mouth dried with awareness.

"Why pretend?" he repeated softly. "There is no need to dissemble with me, I assure you. Confident men are not afraid of bluestockings."

Tess laughed. She could not help herself. "You may have a remarkably good opinion of yourself, my lord," she said, "but there are a lot of very insecure men in the ton."

"I don't doubt it," Rothbury said. "Is that why you feign ignorance, Lady Darent—so that you do not out-shine any of your male acquaintances?"

Tess smiled. "It is easier," she said. "Some men do have a very large—"

Rothbury raised a brow.

"—sense of their own importance," Tess finished.

"How fascinating," Rothbury said. "I suspected that you were a consummate actress." He glanced at the book in her hand. "And I see that it is in the original French too…." His gaze came up, keen on her face. "So you read French Republican philosophy, Lady Darent.

You sketch beautifully, you carry a knife and a pistol when you go out at night—"

Tess could see where this was heading. "Excuse me," she said. "I have detained you quite long enough, my lord. I could not possibly keep you any longer."

Rothbury's laughter followed her across the hall. As she hurried back into the drawing room, Tess was all too aware that he had stepped closer to Shuna's portrait and appeared to be examining the signature very carefully. She could feel the trap closing.

She shut the door behind her and leaned back against it for a moment, shutting her eyes. How could she throw Rothbury off the scent? He was too quick, too clever, right on her heels now. The only way she could keep him quiet, assuming he had told no one else of his suspicions, was to kill him, which seemed a little extreme, or…

Or she could marry him.

The room tilted a little, dipped and spun. Suddenly Tess's heart was racing with a mixture of fear and reckless determination. A husband could not give evidence against his wife in court, for under the law they were considered indivisible, one and the same person. If she were to marry Rothbury she would be safe.

She groped her way to a chair and collapsed into it.

This was madness, utter folly.

It was the perfect solution.

Leaping agitatedly to her feet again, Tess ran to the rosewood desk, pulled open the drawer and grabbed

The Gazetteer, flicking through the alphabetical list to the appropriate page:

Owen Purchase, Viscount Rothbury, on inheritance of the title as the grandson of the cousin of the 13th viscount...

Gracious, the connection had been as distant as all the gossips were saying.

Principal Seat: Rothbury Chase, Somerset. Also Rothbury House in Clarges Street, Rothbury Castle, Cheshire, and five other estates in England...

In that respect at least, Tess thought, Owen Purchase's endowments were not to be underestimated. He also had an income from those estates that was reckoned to be in excess of thirty thousand pounds per annum, which was not outrageously rich but not to be sneezed at either. There was more invested in the stock market. He was, of course, a mere viscount and so she already outranked him, but...

Tess put a stop on her galloping thoughts, placed *The Gazetteer* gently on the fat gold cushions of the sofa and stared fixedly at the rioting rose pattern on the Aubusson carpet. Her chest felt tight, her breath shallow. She was not sure that she was really considering what she *thought* she was considering. Viscount Rothbury as her next husband...

Normally she would not countenance such a marriage because Rothbury was not the sort of man she felt comfortable dealing with. He was too young, too handsome, too authoritative, too *everything.* But she was, if not a beggar, then certainly not in a position to choose. And Rothbury possessed several advantages. Marriage to him would remove the threat that Sidmouth posed, since not only would Rothbury be unable to testify against her, no one would suspect his wife of sedition in the first place. He was also powerful enough to protect her and the Darent twins from Lord Corwen. Plus of course his most priceless attribute was that he would not expect her to occupy the marriage bed.

There was only one flaw in her plan. She was sure that Rothbury already suspected her to be Jupiter, so if she were to approach him proposing marriage he would surely be very suspicious indeed. On the other hand, he had no proof or he would have arrested her already. If she were clever and careful she might be able to persuade him of her innocence. Plus Rothbury had little money and a keen need for some to repair his estates, and she was very, very rich. He might well be tempted enough by her fortune to marry her anyway.

Tess realised she was clenching her hands together so tightly that her nails were biting into her palms. There were, in truth, precious few other options open to her in the husband stakes.

With a quick, decisive gesture she picked up *The Gazetteer* and tucked it under her arm. If Rothbury had returned directly to Clarges Street, then he would be home by now. There was no time like the present. She had a call to make before her courage deserted her.

CHAPTER FOUR

It was in fact three hours before Tess was ready to go out, since to her time was a relative concept normally measured by how long it took her to dress. Usually she did not have a great deal of difficulty in selecting an outfit for any occasion. Today was different, however. It was seven years since she had made her last marriage proposal, to the Marquis of Darent. On that occasion she had worn holly-green and had been well pleased with her appearance. She was not sure Darent had noticed it, though. She suspected he might have dozed off during her proposal, overcome by a laudanum-induced stupor.

The thorny question of what to wear to make Lord Rothbury an offer he could not refuse was not so easy, however. After trying on a few outfits, she finally settled on a jonquil-yellow gown and matching bonnet. She was disturbed to see that when she checked her appearance in the pier glass she looked young and apprehensive, her blue eyes wide and dark and the faintest hint of nervousness in the tense line of her cheek and jaw. She stood straighter and tried to smile. It came out more as a grimace. Anxious was how she felt, unusual for her, but not how she wanted to look. With a sharp sigh of irritation she picked up her matching cloak and reticule and hurried out to the carriage.

Rothbury House was in Clarges Street, not far from Joanna's home in Bedford Street and a most quiet and respectable address. The house itself looked dusty and shuttered although Rothbury had been living there for at least a year. It was interesting, Tess thought, that the viscount had not sought to make an impact on society when he came into his inheritance. It was the ton that had courted him rather than he seeking recognition from the ton.

The carriage halted. Tess clenched her fingers briefly inside her fur-lined gloves. There was a curious pattering of nervousness in her stomach. This, she reassured herself, was not in the least surprising. She had proposed to a man only three times before and none of those men had been anything like Lord Rothbury.

For a moment she sat frozen still on the carriage seat, wondering if she had made a terrible mistake in choosing the viscount. It was not too late. Except it *was* too late, for the carriage door had opened, allowing a swirl of cold autumnal air inside. It was no servant standing there, waiting to help her alight, but Rothbury himself. Evidently he had called elsewhere on his way back from Bedford Street for he was still in outdoor dress and looking impossibly broad shouldered and tall in the beautifully cut coat. He had taken off his hat and there were snowflakes settling in his tawny-brown hair.

"Lady Darent," he said. "I had not expected to see you again so soon. What may I do for you?" His voice was smooth as honey, that deep drawl rubbing against her senses like silk. It would be very easy to be lulled into a false sense of security by such mellow tones. And that, Tess thought, would be another big mistake. She did not want to be lulled into anything by Lord Rothbury. She needed her wits about her.

He extended a hand to help her out of the coach and after a moment Tess reluctantly took it. She did not want to touch him. She rarely touched anyone. Brokeby's cruelty had bred in her revulsion for physical contact. No matter how impersonal the touch was she shrank from it.

Rothbury's touch was not impersonal. His fingers closed about hers and Tess could not quite repress the tremor of awareness and apprehension that quivered through her. He felt it too; his eyes narrowed momentarily on her face, a perceptive flash of green. Tess felt the heat burn into her cheeks. She was blushing again, so rare an occurrence that she had almost forgotten how it felt. Except that around Rothbury it was not rare at all. She concentrated on descending the carriage steps neatly. Falling into his arms at this or indeed any other moment was not part of her plan.

Once her feet were firmly on the pavement, Rothbury released her and stood back, but his gaze was still fixed intently on her face. He was, Tess realised, still waiting for her reply to his question.

"There is a business proposition I would like to discuss with you, Lord Rothbury," she said, "but not out here in the street." Her voice was not quite as steady as she might have wished. It lacked authority and she hated that.

Rothbury bowed ironically. He looked completely unsurprised, as though his female acquaintances frequently appeared unannounced on his doorstep to discuss some sort of mysterious business. Perhaps they did, Tess thought. She had heard enough about his past as an adventurer to know that her unexpected arrival was probably the least exciting or unforeseen thing that had happened to him all year.

"Then please step inside." He stood back to allow her to precede him up the steps and into the hall. Tess's immediate impression was of darkness. The hall was so full of statuary and enormous china vases that she was afraid she might blunder into one of them in the gloom. The previous Lord Rothbury, she recalled, had been a scholar of ancient civilisations. The collection must represent some of his research. She repressed a shudder. The house felt as dry and lifeless as a museum display.

"A mausoleum, I know." Rothbury's voice cut through her thoughts, reading them with uncanny accuracy. "I have yet to decide what to do with it." He glanced at her. "Did you ever meet my cousin, the previous viscount, Lady Darent?"

"Not that I recall," Tess said. "I heard he was a prodigious academic, always travelling and adding to his collections."

Rothbury nodded. "We shared a love of travel, he and I. It makes for a bond between us even though we never met." He smiled. "I assume that you know the rest of my inherited family though—my great-aunts Ladies Martindale, Borough and Hurst?"

Tess looked up sharply. This was even better than she had imagined. Ladies Martindale, Borough and Hurst were a trio of the most fearsomely upright dowagers in society.

"Lady Martindale is a very high stickler—completely terrifying," Tess said.

"Even to you?" Rothbury murmured. "I thought you impervious to the disapproval of society."

He loosed his coat and handed it with a word of thanks to a butler who looked as though he was part of the statuary.

"Would you like Houghton to take your cloak, Lady Darent, or will your stay be of short duration?" There was gentle mockery in his voice.

Tess hesitated. The house was not cold but she felt as though she required the extra layers of protection her cloak gave her, rather like a suit of armour. The conviction beat in her mind that she was about to make a very serious mistake. Despite all of Rothbury's advantages—impotence, respectable relatives—she could not quite get past her discomfort.

But whilst she had been thinking, he had taken her

arm and steered her into the library. The double oak doors shut behind her with a stealthy snap and it felt like another trap closing.

"I apologise if you think me high-handed." His smile stole her breath, something that happened so rarely to her that for a moment Tess wondered if the tightness in her chest meant that she was ailing. The charm of handsome men generally left her utterly cold.

Rothbury leaned back against the library doors, arms crossed, broad shoulders resting against the panels, another barrier to her escape.

"I am at your service," he murmured, "whenever you are ready to acquaint me with this business proposition you have."

Tess's throat dried. "I wanted…" She groped for the words that had scattered like petals in the breeze. "That is, I thought…"

One dark brow rose quizzically as Rothbury surveyed her confusion.

"I came here—" Gracious, she had lost all her town bronze. This would never do.

"I came here to ask you to marry me," she finished, with all the finesse of a tongue-tied schoolgirl. "In name only, that is. I wish for a marriage of convenience."

Mortified, she stood pinned to the spot whilst a burning blush seemed to creep up from her toes to engulf her entire body. It was difficult to see how matters could have gone more painfully awry. She had wanted to be so cool, so composed. She had wanted to be *herself,* Teresa, Dowager Marchioness of Darent, poised and self-assured. Instead, this man had taken all her confidence and turned it inside out. She should have known not to engage in this dangerous game of using Rothbury for his name and his protection, because any moment now he would call her bluff, accuse her of sedition and very likely have her thrown in the Tower of London.

Rothbury was silent for a very long moment. Finally, when Tess was about to stammer an apology and climb out of the window in her desperation to escape, his shoulders came away from the door and he started to move towards her. Panic gripped her by the throat as he drew closer to her. There was something about his physical presence that was so powerful, so authoritative, that it made her supremely uncomfortable. She did not feel threatened by him in the same way as she had by Brokeby, with that terrible fear that had made her skin crawl. Rothbury, she knew instinctively, was not a man who would ever hurt a woman. Even so his physical proximity filled her with unease.

Rothbury took her chin in his hand and turned her face to the faint light that penetrated the room from the long windows. Tess tried to remain still beneath his touch although the impulse to break away from him was strong. No one touched her. Ever.

"An extraordinary suggestion," he murmured. "A marriage in name only. Why would you wish for that?"

He allowed his hand to fall and Tess felt the relief swamp her, heady as wine, enough to turn her dizzy for a brief moment. Rothbury took a step away from her and then turned sharply back on his heel.

"It was not a rhetorical question," he said.

Tess jumped. "Oh!" Her mind was a blank. Why had she not anticipated that Rothbury might ask that question—and a great many more difficult questions besides? She had hurried off to proposition him without laying the groundwork first. She should have realised that he was not the kind of man, like Darent before him, to accept such an arrangement without debate.

Rothbury was still watching her with one eyebrow raised in an odiously quizzical manner. And her mind was still blanker than a blank canvas.

"No doubt you will share your reasons with me before too long," he said, still in the same gentle drawl. "Meanwhile, I have another question. This may seem impertinent, Lady Darent—vulgar, even—but I have to ask it." He smiled. "What exactly is in this for me?"

OWEN HAD HAD A VERY entertaining ten minutes, possibly one of the most unexpected and interesting ten minutes that he had experienced in his entire life. He had received a number of marriage proposals over the course of his thirty-two years. Some had been from enterprising courtesans on the make, others from respectable young ladies seeking to escape the tedium of life in the schoolroom. One had been from a fabulously wealthy princess wanting to run away from an arranged marriage to a fellow royal. None had been as brazen as this proposal of a marriage of convenience from so notorious a widow who collected husbands with a similar reckless abandon to which King Henry VIII had gathered and shed his wives.

Owen had never imagined himself as anyone's fourth husband. Until ten minutes before, the idea of marriage had been the last thing on his mind. And marriage to Teresa Darent, of all people... It was an absurd notion.

It was a fascinating notion.

What interested him in this moment was why Tess was asking. He had a very strong suspicion that she was playing a game of bluff and double bluff with him; she knew he suspected her of being Jupiter so she had come to defuse the threat he presented to her. Marriage was a hell of a way to do it. He admired her tactics. It was a daring move, risky but brilliant, demonstrating a breathtaking audacity. The decision he had to make was whether he was prepared to play her game, and all Owen's gambling instincts told him to engage. He had been an adventurer all his life even if he now had the respectable cloak of a viscount's title and fortune.

Owen had not expressed his doubts about Lady Darent and her role as Jupiter when he had met Lord Sidmouth that morning to discuss the events of the political meeting and riot. He was not sure what had held him silent; lack of evidence perhaps, the fact that he still only half believed it himself, or even a powerful feeling of protectiveness that made him want to defend

Teresa Darent rather than condemn her. This last was as
inexplicable as it was disturbing. He had no sympathy
with the radical cause and he thought Jupiter no more
than a dangerous criminal intent on destroying law and
order. Yet still he had kept silent; something had held
him back.

He was not the only man investigating the Jupiter Club, however. Sidmouth had plenty of men at his
disposal—infiltrators, informers and spies as well as
his formal investigators. Owen knew it could be only
a matter of time before Jupiter was unmasked and the
club destroyed. Tess would guess that too. So here she
was, seeking protection.

"Most men would see marriage to me as a prize in
itself and not ask for more." Tess's answer to his question was full of disdain. Her chin had come up. Owen
repressed a smile. Ten generations of Fenner family
pride was in those words. She made him feel as though
he had committed a faux pas in even questioning her.
Perhaps her previous three husbands had snapped her
up before she had finished making the offer. Owen had
heard that she had proposed to each and every one of
them, that approaching her chosen prey was Tess Darent's style, whether she had selected a man to be her
husband or her lover. She did not wait to be asked. She
was the one who did the hunting.

That was the gossip. The truth, Owen thought, was
probably a deal more complicated. He was already

coming to the conclusion that Teresa Darent was in almost all particulars the opposite of how she appeared.

At the moment, for example, he could tell that she was ill at ease. He sensed the nervousness that beat inside her, a fear that she was making strenuous efforts to hide behind a flawless facade. She had chosen to stand a good distance away from him, by the long windows that looked out across the terrace to the neat garden with its clipped box hedges and yew. The autumn day had taken a long time to brighten that morning and now the grey light was behind Tess, concealing as much as it revealed. Owen could not see her expression at all. She stood straight and still, like a pale flame in a dress of yellow silk that made her the only bright thing in a dull room. The gown should have clashed with the russet of her hair, so cunningly arranged beneath the matching bonnet, and yet it did not. Instead it was a breathtaking contrast, framing her face like a halo of fire. Each item of clothing she had chosen had been for obvious effect, and it worked. Owen knew nothing about fashion and cared less. He had an innate taste and wore his clothes with the sort of careless elegance that his valet deplored. Tess Darent, he thought, deployed her wardrobe like a weapon. She knew the value of appearance and the way it could give you protection as well as confidence.

He walked towards her very slowly, very purposefully, his footsteps ringing on the bare wooden boards of the library floor. There were no deep rugs or carpets here to soften the austerity of the room. Rothbury House had been woefully neglected under his cousin Peregrine, who had been widowed for years and had seldom been in England. All the Rothbury estates were in disrepair and would take thousands to renovate. Marriage to an heiress was an obvious solution, as his aunt Martindale had pointed out. If he wed and produced an heir, she had said, she would settle the Rothbury debts and pay for the estates to be restored.

Lady Martindale would not approve of Tess Darent as a bride. The idea of marrying a woman who would incur his great-aunt's deepest disapproval pleased Owen, a small act of rebellion when he was hamstrung by so much of his new inheritance. It was not a good reason for marriage. He knew it. Yet it appealed to him.

He stopped when he was no more than a couple of feet away from Tess. Her violet-blue eyes met his very directly. There was now no nervousness in them. Owen wondered if he had imagined the tension he thought he had sensed in her. But no. He felt it again, and saw the way in which she stepped back, almost imperceptibly, to put more distance between them. She was withdrawing from him. Evidently she was not comfortable with physical proximity. Which was very odd indeed if the rumours about her were true.

"I doubt most men would see marriage to you as a prize if they are not permitted to sleep with you," Owen said drily. "Forgive my plain speaking," he added, seeing the flash of anger in her eyes. "I always find it best to be quite frank in discussions of an intimate nature."

"I have never thought of marriage as an intimate matter," Tess snapped. The pink colour had come into her face now. "I fear you have a sadly *colonial* view of the institution, Lord Rothbury. Marriage in the ton is for profit alone. You profit from my beauty and connections and I gain the protection of your name."

"Forgive me again," Owen said, "but is that an equal bargain?"

"No," Tess said, "the bargain favours you by far. I would be the one compromising by marrying a mere viscount."

"One does not need to possess a thoroughbred horse to admire its beauty," Owen said.

Tess raised a haughty brow. "I beg your pardon? Is one of us an *animal* in your analogy?"

"And as for connections in the ton," Owen continued, "I do not value them."

"That is short-sighted of you," Tess said. "So short-sighted I doubt you have the vision to appreciate your thoroughbred."

Owen smiled. Oh, he appreciated her. She was beautiful enough to turn any man's head. And at the very least, he thought, if he married her he would never be bored. Conversation with Tess Darent had the astringency of a dose of salts. Though no doubt she would say that a fashionable husband and wife spoke to one another as little as possible and preferably only via the servants.

"And your reputation?" he said. "Many men might balk at taking a wife with the sort of reputation for sin one would normally hope for in a mistress."

Once again he had been brutally frank and he awaited her response with interest. Her defences were so perfectly in place, however, that he could discern not one flicker of emotion in her: no shock, no anger, nothing. She looked him over with that detached blue gaze he was starting to know.

"You," she said, after a moment, "have a reputation as a pirate and a mercenary soldier. Most women would prefer such a man as a lover rather than a husband."

Touché.

Owen inclined his head. "I was not a pirate, though I suppose you could say I was a mercenary soldier," he admitted.

"Whereas I have never been a whore," Tess said. The coolness of her response made him smile. She certainly had nerve. "And were we to wed," she continued, "I would behave with the utmost propriety. I am marrying to try to rescue my reputation, so there would be no point in my sinking it further."

"I feel I must point out," Owen said, "that I found you climbing out of a brothel window last night."

Her pansy eyes lit with mockery. "We were not betrothed last night, Lord Rothbury."

He had to give her credit. She played the coolest

hand of anyone he knew. Which was perfectly in keep-ing with a woman who might lead a secret life as a radi-cal sympathiser, who carried a pistol in her reticule and who might well have been in Mrs. Tong's brothel for purposes other than a night of debauchery.

He was intrigued. Owen admitted it to himself. He had a low threshold of boredom, the product of a life-time of constantly moving onward and seeking new challenges. He had gone to sea when he was in his teens and had spent his life exploring, fighting and carving out a future. He liked unpredictability and risk. It was what made him feel alive.

Tess Darent was enough of a challenge for one man for an entire lifetime.

"Of course," Tess said, very casually, "there is also my fortune. I am accounted very rich indeed."

That got his attention. Owen realised that he had been vaguely aware that she was a wealthy widow but had no idea whether that meant she was merely plump in the pocket or wildly affluent.

"How rich?" he said.

Once again her blue gaze mocked his directness. "Over one hundred and fifty thousand pounds rich," Tess said, frank as he. "Is that sufficient to tempt you, my lord, where my other advantages do not?"

Truth was he had already been deeply tempted. Now her words stole his breath.

"Extraordinary how very attractive a lady may sud-denly become when she is adorned in gold," Tess said, seeing his expression. "Now I am become a gift horse, in your analogy, or possibly a goose laying golden eggs." But for all the dryness of her words there was a flicker of something else in her eyes that looked like disappointment. Owen wondered if she had wanted him to accept her for herself alone. It seemed unlikely that she would care.

"I cannot deny that a fortune of one hundred and fifty thousand pounds is a strong inducement," he said.

"Well, at least you would never lie to me and pretend you cared more for my charming person than you did for my money," Tess said, still dry. "You may be famously blunt, Lord Rothbury, but actually I prefer it. It saves trouble in the end."

"Then perhaps we will deal well together," Owen said. Their eyes met and he felt a flare of awareness, an attraction that was most certainly for her rather than for her fortune.

"You mentioned that you wished to marry to save your reputation," he said. He gestured to a chair. "Why don't you tell me more?"

She hesitated. There was real vulnerability in her face now and it was so unexpected that it touched Owen more than he wanted, more than he had expected. He had wondered if she had been using her desire to repair her reputation as a convenient excuse for marriage but now he saw that she was sincere. The problems she faced, whatever they were, were huge and they distressed her deeply.

"Please," he said, still waiting for her to take a seat. "You can trust me." He had moderated his tone before he realised it, gentleness sweeping away his previously rather abrasive frankness. He smiled ruefully to himself. Tess Darent's skill at disarming a man was formidable. If he were not careful he would soon forget she was a dangerous political renegade and be taken completely off his guard.

This time she sat, perching upright on the edge of one of the hard library seats as though she half expected it to explode beneath her. Given the state of the springs this seemed a distinct possibility. Owen found himself studying the delicate line of her throat and jaw, a delicacy that seemed at odds with the stubbornness of her chin and the determination in her eyes. Tess Darent, it seemed, was all contradiction.

"My late husband, Lord Darent, took out a loan," she began. A shade of exasperation touched her voice now. "His creditor is demanding payment."

"Marriage is a rather extreme way to settle a debt," Owen said, taking the seat across the table from her. "You could try the moneylenders first. And anyway, you have just told me that you are obscenely rich. Surely you can pay?"

"There is nothing obscene about my fortune." Her tone was hard. "But you misunderstand me, my lord. It is not money Lord Corwen demands."

"What then?" Owen said. He watched her face and felt a jolt of shock at what he saw there. "You?" he said.

The possessive anger caught him unawares as it leapt and burned within him. He leaned forwards. "He wants *you* in settlement of the debt?"

She was already shaking her head. Her face beneath the brim of the bonnet was shadowed, her expression hidden. "No." She took a deep breath as though she had to steel herself to force out the words. "He demands payment in the form of marriage to my stepdaughter." Her face crumpled into disgust and a sort of despair. "Sybil is currently at school in Bath. She is a mere fifteen years old. Corwen wishes to wed her next year on her sixteenth birthday." She raised her eyes to his. "You should understand that his lordship is seven and forty and that he requires a wife who is biddable and—" a shudder shook her "—innocent. He will take her in return for cancelling the debt."

Owen felt a rush of revulsion. He stared at her, brows lowered. "But that is grotesque, monstrous. Surely—" He had been going to say that surely it could not be true, but he recognized the words were hollow.

Tess met his eyes. He could see something there that was deeper than abhorrence at Corwen's behaviour, something of pain and grief that was sharp as an imprint on her soul. He glimpsed it in a second's brief flash and then the expression was gone and he wondered if he had imagined it.

"Surely you have refused him," he said.

"Of course." Suddenly she looked tired. "I have offered to pay the debt in full but he has declined. Instead he threatens to ruin Sybil's future. A word here and there that, like her stepmother, she is not virtuous...." She shrugged eloquently. "You know how fragile a young lady's reputation can be, my lord. A debutante's reputation is not like a lost reticule—it cannot be replaced. Once gone it is lost forever."

"Corwen can have no grounds to slander her," Owen said.

Tess shook her head. "Of course not," she said, very quietly. "But it is *my* poor reputation that will taint Sybil's life unless I can prevent it. Corwen will point to me as the worst of bad influences. He will say that I had the upbringing of Sybil for five years, that I am corrupt and that my immoral ways must surely have contaminated her. And he will be believed because people prefer to think the worst." Suddenly her tone was fierce, ringing with sincerity. "I will *never* let that happen to Sybil. She deserves better than that. Her father left both his children in my care and I will not fail them."

Owen got to his feet. He understood now Tess's earlier pledge to behave with absolute propriety should they wed. She had made her choice: marry, gain a modicum of respectability and protect her stepchildren. To do so she would need to abandon any wild behaviour and become a pattern card of propriety. Owen wondered if she would be able to keep the bargain.

His lips twisted. "You wish me to be your fig leaf,

Lady Darent," he said, "to make you appear respect-able."

Tess laughed, a real laugh full of genuine amuse-ment. Those pansy-blue eyes warmed, full of mischief. It startled Owen to see her in so unguarded a moment. Startled him, but pleased him as well. He found that he wanted to know more of this real Tess Darent away from the bright, brittle pretence. He wanted it a great deal. The intensity of his hunger for it was another shock.

"My fig leaf," Tess said. "How very picturesque a description, my lord."

"And how appropriate, since it seems that your clothes are always coming off," Owen said. "At the brothel, in those paintings by Melton that everyone is talking about…"

The light died from her eyes. "I concede that that is certainly how it appears," she said. She sounded cold now, lifeless. She shifted on the chair. "The paintings are from a collection belonging to my second husband," she said. "They were never intended to be on show to the public, but—" she shrugged "—Mr. Melton must make his fortune as he sees fit."

That shrug, Owen thought, covered more than a little distaste and a healthy dose of anger. Teresa Darent might pretend aristocratic indifference towards Melton and his impudence in making his fortune from her body, but Owen could sense that she had been deeply hurt and offended by it. Once again his protective instincts stirred. He reined them in sharply.

"If we are speaking of gossip and scandal," Owen said, "there is also a rumour that you have a young lover in Justin Brooke."

"Society has been quick to acquaint you with my poor reputation," Tess said drily. "Which rather proves my point."

"Is it true?" Owen persisted. "Call me old-fashioned but I would prefer that my future wife is not embroiled in an affair before we wed and preferably not afterwards either."

"Mr. Brooke is not my lover." Tess's gaze was very direct. It challenged him to disbelieve her. "I do not have a lover nor do I intend to take one. I've never—" She stopped and bit off what she was about to say. She looked away, colour stinging her cheeks.

"You've never had a lover?" Owen queried softly. He was surprised, but then she was a creature of surprises.

"No. Never." She sounded annoyed to be caught out in the admission, as though she was revealing too much. Her gaze fell from his, her lashes veiling her expression. "I've had three husbands," she said, after a moment. "Surely that is enough."

"Evidently not, since you are seeking a fourth," Owen said.

She smiled a little, spreading her hands in another pretty gesture that Owen suspected was completely false. "What can I say? It's a compulsion."

Owen doubted that. Tess Darent seemed far too carefully controlled to fall prey to any kind of compulsion.

"Is there anything else I should know before I give you an answer?" he asked. It was her opportunity to be honest with him about her political allegiance, her chance to confess to her involvement in the Jupiter Club. He waited, and realised that he was holding his breath.

He saw the flash of calculation in her eyes and could almost feel her weighing the merits of confession. She caught her lush lower lip between her teeth. She seemed to tremble on the edge of revelation. But then he saw her withdraw behind that cool facade again. Those formidable defences came down. She was shaking her head.

"There is nothing else, my lord." She arched a brow. "Is that not enough?"

It was plenty but it was not the whole truth.

Owen felt the disappointment like a dull weight. He had wanted Tess to trust him, which was foolish of him, since she had every reason not to do so. He was Sidmouth's man, bound to hunt down and arrest the wanted criminal Jupiter. Tess would hardly walk straight into his house and confess she was the woman he sought. No, instead she would do precisely what she had done. She would tell him half-truths and compromises, tempt him into marriage with her money and try to use him, to hide from Sidmouth in plain sight.

He should refuse her proposal, of course. He should,

in fact, have her arrested and investigated. But he would not. Tess Darent's devious and daring game appealed to all his gambling instincts. She had thrown down a challenge. Very well, he would take her on. He would play and he would win.

He remembered the political cartoons, their visceral power. They were full of anger and passion, the perfect counterpoint to this cool, poised woman sitting before him. He wanted to discover the real Tess Darent, to tear away those layers of cold composure with which she disguised herself, and expose the woman beneath. He wondered if she really would take this challenge as far as the altar—and beyond that into the marriage bed.

There was only one way to find out.

He stood up. "Lady Darent." He gave her an immaculate bow. "I am sensible of the honour that you do me…" Was that not the terminology one used on receiving an offer? Owen grinned. He had no idea.

"But you are going to refuse me," Tess said, before he could finish. She jumped to her feet. "Of course. Which is a blessing, I think." She was smoothing her gloves on and was so transparently anxious to be away that Owen was fascinated. "Because I have changed my mind too. You would not have done for a fashionable husband *at all*. You are far too…" She broke off.

Owen was about to correct her misapprehension but he was too amused and curious to do so straight away. So cool, collected Lady Darent had lost her nerve at the last moment. Clearly she was not quite as brazen as she seemed.

And he was not going to let her off the hook so easily.

"I am far too what?" he prompted.

"Too forthright, too forceful, and you ask far too many questions," Tess said. "It will not do."

Owen moved to block her way as she headed for the door.

"Before you leave," he said, with deceptive quietness, "please do give me some pointers for the next time I receive a proposal from a lady. How should one respond in a suitably *fashionable* manner?"

"With gratitude," Tess said tartly, "if the lady in question is someone like me."

"There is no one like you," Owen said. "And I accept your proposal, Lady Darent. With gratitude."

Her blue gaze was stunned. Her mouth formed a round, silent, astonished O.

"Unless," Owen added gently, "you have withdrawn your offer already. In which case I am most disappointed."

He watched with interest to see whether, now it came to the point, she had the bravado to go through with it.

She recovered very quickly.

"In that case," she said crisply, "it is agreed."

"Don't tell me," Owen said drily, "I have made you the happiest of women. Is that not the accustomed response, albeit generally from the man since our roles are reversed?"

"I would not go so far," Tess said. "I am grateful to you, Lord Rothbury."

"So flattering."

"This is business. I do not flatter my business associates." She pinned him with a look that said she was back in control. Owen found it amusing. He had to smother a smile. In a moment he would take that control and give her a foretaste of what marriage to him might entail.

"You will send a notification of our engagement to the papers, if you please," Tess said.

Owen bowed. "As you wish," he said. "And I will get a special licence."

He was interested to see the panic flowering in her eyes. Evidently she still had reservations about what she was doing.

"There is no need for haste," she said.

"On the contrary," Owen said, enjoying her discomfiture, "there is every need. Whilst our betrothal will give you a measure of the respectability you seek, it cannot be as effective as our marriage will be."

He saw her bite down hard on her lower lip. "Well, I..."

"And I will call on you tomorrow," Owen finished, with a great deal of satisfaction.

A tiny frown wrinkled her brow. "Call on me?"

"Unless," Owen said, powerless to prevent the

heavy irony that now coloured his voice, "you prefer me simply to send you a note with the wedding date so that you can meet me in church?"

"Oh…" She smiled deliciously, an echo of the superficially charming Tess Darent who was all pretence. "Yes, that would be extremely helpful of you. As this is a marriage of convenience I don't think we need see each other a great deal before the ceremony."

She started to walk towards the door. Owen took two strides backwards and reached for the handle just before she did. Her body collided with his. She felt warm, soft and yielding; Owen's senses clouded with the scent of her and the heat of her skin. Desire flowered through him again as fiercely as it had done the previous night. He caught her wrist.

"I will not be a conformable husband, Lady Darent," he warned. "You do not issue me with my tasks and expect me to obey without question. I am not reversing the wedding vows along with everything else."

Beneath his fingers he could feel her pulse racing. Her glove was no protection against the insistence of his touch.

They were so close now that she had to tilt her face up in order to meet his gaze. He could read an element of anger in her eyes now, though her tone was still level. "Just as long as you do not expect me to obey you either," she said.

"You will be promising to do so in the marriage service," Owen said. "Or do you pick and choose those vows you honour?"

He felt her pulse kick up another notch. Something flickered in those blue eyes, something that looked like fear.

"You seem uncertain," Owen said silkily. "Would you like to reconsider—cry off before it is too late?"

There was a moment when he saw a welter of emotion cloud her face before she wiped her expression clear.

"No, thank you." She sounded as cool as though she were placing an order for tea with the footman. "I cannot afford to be too particular. Would you like to withdraw *your* agreement, my lord?"

Owen had absolutely no intention of withdrawing.

"No," he said. "I will marry you."

"So gracious," she said, in mocking echo of his words earlier.

Owen tugged on her wrist. One step brought her into his arms. He was astonished to realise that he wanted to kiss her very much. The challenge she presented, the game between them, lit his blood.

He brought his lips down on hers.

For a brief second it felt bewitching. She was all heat and light, all sweet fierceness in his arms. Desire exploded within him, sensual darkness enveloped him. He reached out to draw her closer.

He felt the shock rip through her like lightning. This did not feel like the startled reaction of someone merely taken by surprise by a kiss, but a far more profound response built on something that felt disturbingly like fear. But before Owen could analyse it fully Tess froze, stiller than a hunted mouse, utterly unresponsive, her lips cold and unmoving beneath his, her body as stiff as a corpse in his arms.

Owen's ardour died as swiftly as it had been born. He drew back. Tess's eyes were closed, her lashes a sharp black fan against her cheeks, her lips parted, curls of red-gold hair framing her face. She looked enchanting but lifeless, like the princess in "Sleeping Beauty," dead to the world and certainly dead to his touch. Owen released her. It was a while since he had kissed anyone and perhaps his technique needed practice but he had never experienced a response, or lack of response, such as this.

Tess opened her eyes. Their expression was as lifeless as her reaction to him. Owen felt his stomach hollow with something close to despair. If this were a foretaste of his married life, it would be barren indeed. Perhaps he should have taken the opportunity to withdraw his suit a moment ago when he had the chance. Perhaps he should hope that they never got as far as the altar.

"Good day, Lord Rothbury." Tess was smoothing her gloves and adjusting the jonquil-coloured cloak, tying the ribbon with fingers that were quite steady. She appeared unmoved. And it seemed she was not going to refer in any way to their kiss. Perhaps that was what passed for an embrace in a fashionable betrothal, Owen thought—a cold acknowledgement of the unemotional tie that now bound them. If that was Tess's expectation of their engagement and potential marriage, she was going to be extremely shocked.

He held the door for Tess and she walked out, negotiating the maze of statuary in the hall with elegance and aplomb. She was once again in control, every inch the modish society beauty.

It was only as the ring of the carriage wheels faded away down the street that Owen realised Tess had never answered his question as to why she had wanted a marriage in name only.

CHAPTER FIVE

TESS WAS CAUGHT BETWEEN the devil and the deep blue sea, as her old governess, Miss Finch, had been inclined to say. She could not withdraw her offer for her charges' sake but she was not at all sure she could go through with her plan to marry Rothbury. He was too forceful, too difficult to control.

For the second night in a row, she could not sleep. She opened the drawer beside her bed and took out her sketching book and charcoal. As always, the act of drawing soothed her with its clean lines and the soft scratch of the pencil against the paper. She drew a cartoon of the tree of liberty with Lord Sidmouth dressed as a forester, hacking at the trunk. Then she caricatured the scene in the brothel with various peers falling out of their breeches and Mrs. Tong shrieking like a witch and her girls diving for cover as the dragoons trampled all the whips, crops and erotic paraphernalia underfoot. Each smooth sweep of her crayon brought the scene to life, sharp, vivid and full of character.

With a sigh, she laid the sketches aside, pushing the pad away across the counterpane. She was itching to publish another cartoon. Tomorrow she would slip away to the printers. She knew she had promised herself that the Jupiter Club was finished, but a few more cartoons could not hurt, and she would burst if she were unable to express the feelings she had inside. And after she had been to the printers she supposed she would have to go back to the brothel and confront Mrs. Tong over the missing sketches. She was sure that the bawd, opportunistic as ever, must have taken them, seeing them as a way to extort money from her perhaps. Mrs. Tong had helped her because her son was a firebrand radical, preaching reform. That did not mean, however, that the mercenary bawd owed her any loyalty. That would be foreign to her nature.

Tess's shoulders slumped. There were so many complications now. She had become a philanthropist because of her first husband, Robert Barstow, who had inspired her. When he had died she had taken his cause and his money to fight for reform to alleviate poverty and disease, violence and misery. Now she was embroiled in a mire of intrigue.

She tapped the crayon against the palm of her hand. Common sense suggested that Rothbury knew nothing of the cartoons. Five minutes in his presence this morning had shown her how blunt was his approach. She had never met a more direct man in her life. If Rothbury had found evidence to incriminate her he would surely have confronted her. Yet, though she tried to reassure herself, she could not be certain. She was playing a very dangerous game with him.

She pulled the sketching pad towards her again. In a few strokes Rothbury's face came to life on the page, the determined line of his jaw, the slash of his cheekbones, the fall of his hair across his forehead and the cool, direct gaze. Tess gave another little shiver. Rothbury was so very different from Robert Barstow, and from James Darent for that matter.

She opened the drawer of the nightstand again and her searching fingers closed around the miniature portrait of Robert that she kept by her bed. She could feel the chased silver of the locket, worn almost smooth now after ten years. She always felt an ache of unhappiness when she thought of Robert, even now, so long after his death. Her first husband had never had the chance to be more than an idealistic boy, but he would have grown to be a good man had he lived, the sort of man who had integrity and courage and belief, a man of honour.

Her gaze fell on the drawing pad again. She wished Rothbury had not kissed her earlier. She pressed her fingers to her lips. For a brief second when he had touched her she had felt a jolt of something fierce and bright, but then she had remembered the past, and the fear and revulsion had swept any sweeter feelings away. It had been that way with every man. Brokeby's cruelty had damaged her past mending. For a moment though, with Rothbury, she had thought… She gave her head a sharp shake before the thought formed properly. Rothbury was no different. He could not help her, and she was a fool even to wish it.

She was not sure why he would want to kiss her anyway, except perhaps as a formal way of sealing their betrothal. There could be nothing else for either of them, no love and certainly no physical desire. A cold kernel of misery hardened inside her. She had never known true physical love. Robert had been her best friend but no lover. And after Charles Brokeby, every thought she had had about erotic love had been shadowed by the carnage he had wrought on her.

She picked up the drawing book and closed it, blotting out Rothbury's face. Men of honour, in her experience, were few and far between. A pity she had met this particular one when it was far too late for both of them.

"WHY DIDN'T SHE TELL ME?" Joanna Grant burst into the library and brandished *The Morning Post* beneath her husband's nose. "Am I supposed to learn of Tess's latest betrothal from the newspapers now? She's marrying Owen! Owen, of all people!" She threw the paper down on the shiny rosewood desk on top of Alex's estate papers, scattering them to the floor.

Alex laid down his pen. His grey eyes were very steady. "I am not entirely sure why you are so upset, Joanna."

Upset. Yes, she was upset. Joanna was shocked to realise quite how upset she was. Her heart was thumping and she wanted to hit something. Or someone. For a second she felt a violent antipathy towards her sister. Then she wanted to cry. She sat down so heavily on one of the rosewood chairs that it creaked.

"Well, I..." Alex's steady gaze and his cool tone were unnerving her. This was not how she had expected him to react. She had wanted him to understand her indignation.

"She didn't tell me," she said, a little forlornly. She felt hurt that Tess had not confided in her. She had tried endlessly to help her sister. She had reached out to her time and again, encouraging her to open her heart. And Tess had always denied her. They were so close in age, they had shared so much, and yet Joanna felt despairing that they would ever be friends. Tess simply did not allow anyone close enough to be her friend. So yes, she felt hurt. But she also felt betrayed.

Alex raised one shoulder in a half shrug. "I agree it would have been nicer to hear the news from Tess herself," he said, "but perhaps she realised that you would react like this."

"Like what?" Joanna demanded. The anger was fizzing in her blood.

"As though it was all about you, not about your sister," Alex said calmly. "Tess is getting married to an old friend. We should be happy for them both."

"I *am* happy!" Joanna protested, whilst a fat tear rolled down her cheek and splashed onto the carpet. "But it isn't fair! Owen was supposed to be—"

She stopped but it was already too late. The expression in Alex's eyes, already cool, was now icy.

"Owen was supposed to be—what?" he said. The edge to his voice made her shiver. "In love with you? Do you want to tell Tess that he wanted to marry you first? That she is second best? Perhaps," Alex said as he shifted on the chair, toying with the quill, turning it over and over between his fingers, "you want to tell Tess she cannot marry Owen because he is your property?"

Joanna blinked back the tears that stung her throat and blocked her nose. Indignation and a sense of betrayal had been replaced by a chill fear wreathing her heart. Had she meant that? She could not quite see how matters had slid so far, so fast. She had been upset and had not thought to censor what she had said.

"That's not what I meant at all," she protested, and her voice rang lame in her own ears. "Whom Owen marries is nothing to me."

So why did it hurt so much? Joanna examined her feelings and realised with a rush of fear that she did not want to know.

"As long as he does not marry your sister," Alex said, and the sarcasm in his tone set her teeth on edge. He shook his head. "I'm afraid I do not believe you, my love. You sounded jealous. Can it be that you care for Owen more than you pretend?"

Joanna felt as though the ground was slipping and sliding away beneath her feet. She glanced across at the newspaper with the little box of print written in such harsh black lines:

The betrothal is announced between Teresa, Dowager Marchioness of Darent, and Owen Purchase, 14th Viscount Rothbury... Her heart squeezed again, the breath blocking her throat.

"No!" she said. Her voice was high with desperation. She tried to moderate her tone. "It isn't like that, Alex," she said. "I don't love Owen. I never did. I chose you!"

"But Owen was your white knight, wasn't he?" Alex said, a wealth of bitterness colouring his voice now. "He rescued you from your first husband when David threatened you. He kept you safe. He loved you for years."

Joanna put her hands over her ears. They had talked about this before, long ago, when first they had wed. She had thought it was all settled between them. Heaven help her, she had thought that Alex had not minded.

"Don't," she said. "Alex, please. I don't love Owen. I love you."

Alex stood up. He came towards her, pulling her to her feet, taking her by the wrists and drawing her hands down to her sides. She felt open and vulnerable, as though all the complicated emotions within her were exposed. She knew in that moment that she could not pretend. They knew each other too well and pretence would be an unbearable deceit.

"Very well," she said. She raised her chin in a brave little gesture of defiance. "Owen is a good man. I admire him. He did me a tremendous service in protect-

ing me from David and for that I will always love him."
She met Alex's eyes. His expression was dark and cold,
giving nothing away. She could feel the tension in him,
spun taut as she told him of her love for another man.

"But I am not *in* love with Owen," she said softly, her
eyes pleading with Alex to understand. "Perhaps there
was a time when I almost fell in love with him. Perhaps
there was a time when I might have run off with him.
But by the time he asked me it was too late because I
had already met you and we were wed and for better or
worse you were the one in my heart. I had my chance to
elope with Owen and I refused him because you were
the only one I wanted."

There was a moment of absolute stillness and then
Alex pulled her into his arms so tightly that all the
breath was knocked out of her body. His mouth was
pressed against her hair and his arms were tight about
her.

"I'm sorry," Alex said, muffled. His voice was
hoarse. "I suppose I have always been afraid…
He loved you first, and I thought there might be a
chance—"

"Never," Joanna said firmly, all the lovely confidence flowing back into her veins to hear the emotion
in his words. "Only you, Alex. Always."

She freed herself a little, doubt clouding her eyes.
"I worry though," she said, "that Owen wants Tess because he cannot have me and that Tess is simply not
good enough for him."

"Both of those comments are most presumptuous, my love," Alex drawled. His voice was his own again, cool and incisive, but the love and amusement still blazed in his eyes. "In the first place, you have no notion whether Owen still cherishes a hopeless *tendre* for you, and in the second, you do your sister an injustice."

"Do I?" Joanna asked, genuinely taken aback.

"Tess has a great deal more to her than you think," Alex said.

"How do you know?" Joanna said.

"Because I have caught her in the library reading Rousseau," Alex said.

"Who?" Joanna asked, mystified.

"Merryn," Alex said, not without satisfaction, "is not the only bluestocking in this family." He hesitated. "And I suspect Tess is a philanthropist too."

"Tess!" Joanna's face wrinkled up into genuine confusion. "Surely you jest? Tess cares for nothing but the cut of her gown! Or the identity of her next husband," she added sharply. "Must she have four, Alex? It's so greedy!"

"Enough!" Alex said, drawing her into his arms again. He pressed his lips to the hollow beneath her ear, a hollow that was wonderfully sensitive and sent ripples of sensation skittering along Joanna's skin. "I find I am bored already with your sister's nuptials," he whispered, his tongue tickling her. "I want to discover my own wife all over again. Come to bed."

A delicious little shiver whipped through Joanna's body. "Now?" She glanced at the clock. "In the afternoon? But people will be calling—"

"We shall tell them we are busy," Alex said, his fingers already delving beneath the fine lace that edged her bodice.

"Alex!" Joanna squeaked.

"Of course," Alex murmured, his lips exploring the tender line of her collarbone now, "if you would rather do something else—"

"No!" Joanna squeaked again, her stomach hollowing with lust as she realised quite how much she wanted him. "I cannot think of any pressing engagements."

Later, much later, as the grey shadows of autumn dusk were gathering outside, Joanna rolled over in luxurious abandon in the middle of her tumbled bed and propped herself on one elbow.

"Alex," she said.

Her husband made a sleepy sound indicative of nothing other than that he was too exhausted to talk.

"There is just one small matter to do with Tess's wedding that I feel we should discuss," Joanna persisted.

Alex groaned. He half opened his eyes. "Must we?" he grumbled.

"Tess only marries impotent men," Joanna said baldly. "Therefore she must imagine Owen to be impotent."

Alex shot up in bed. *"What?"* he said. "How on earth
do you work that out?"

"Ha! Now I have your attention," Joanna said. She
pressed a kiss to his shoulder blade, licking experimen-
tally, tasting the salt on his skin. "After Brokeby she
never wanted an intimate relationship again," she said.

Alex rolled over, trapping her beneath him. "Did
Tess tell you this?" he demanded.

Joanna shook her head. "Not in so many words. Tess
tells me nothing. But I know it's true. He hurt her in
some way." She ran a finger down Alex's arm, feeling the muscle beneath the skin and the fine scattering
of hair beneath her touch. His body was hard against
hers and already she was starting to feel weighted with
desire again. It pulled deep inside her, making her feel
soft and heavy with languor, sharp with need. How
could anyone, she wondered, not want this delicious
fulfilment? A wave of acute pity for her sister assailed
her.

"The question," she whispered, "is whether we tell
Tess the truth or not."

"How do you know Owen isn't impotent?" Alex
asked mildly.

Joanna blushed. "I don't," she admitted, "but it
seems unlikely."

"Very unlikely," Alex agreed with a reminiscent
smile.

Joanna poked him sharply in the ribs. "I don't want
to hear about your joint exploits in the brothels of the

world," she said crossly. "I just want to know what to say to Tess."

"There were no brothels in the parts of the world Owen and I were exploring," Alex said. He bent his head and kissed her softly. "As for Owen and Tess, it is nobody's business but their own, Joanna. Leave them to sort it out themselves."

"But—" Joanna started.

Alex kissed her again with more deliberation this time, and her thoughts scattered, her body rising to the demand in his touch. By the time he lowered his head to her breast she had forgotten Tess's marriage completely in the pleasure of rediscovering her own.

OWEN FLATTERED HIMSELF THAT his great-aunt Lady Martindale already had a soft spot for him even though they had known one another for no more than a year. Lady Martindale had been the previous Lord Rothbury's eldest sister. She was a childless widow who was habitually squired about town by some distant family connection called Rupert Montmorency, whom she treated rather as she would a pet dog. Rupert, Owen had quickly discovered, was not the sharpest wit in the family tree, a rather vacuous dandy who nevertheless seemed a good sort. Lady Martindale's tolerance of him, Owen suspected, said a great deal about the kind nature beneath her rather formidable manner.

When he had first met his great-aunt, Lady Martindale had walked around him, examining him through her quizzing glass as though he were an exhibit in a freak show, then she had announced that she had heard he was a scoundrel and that she liked that, and had told him bluntly that he would see not a penny of her fortune unless he married to oblige her.

Over the past few months he and Lady Martindale had started to build a wary regard for one another. Owen admired Lady Martindale's wisdom and her tenacity. With her, he felt a sense of family and a fierce residual loyalty to his British connections.

This morning, however, he could see that her good opinion of him had come crashing down. Perched on the overstuffed sofa in the lemon drawing room, tall and thin, clutching her reticule in one sharp claw of a hand, her dark eyes snapping with fury, she looked like an angry bird of prey. Beside her, Rupert, resplendent in a brightly embroidered waistcoat that made Owen's head ache just to look at it, fidgeted as though he were seated on hot bricks.

"No refreshment for me, thank you," Lady Martindale had snapped when Owen had offered, "and nothing for Rupert either."

"Brandy?" Rupert had said plaintively.

Lady Martindale ignored him. "I hear you have offered marriage to Lady Darent," she said. She enunciated each word as though it had a full stop after it. She spoke in the sort of tone that suggested that Owen had committed some unforgivable social blunder. "Why would you do such a thing?"

"Splendid little filly," Rupert put in helpfully. "I like

Lady Darent. Frightfully tempting. Brandy?" he added with a hopeful lift of the brows.

"Be quiet, Rupert," Lady Martindale said. "You do not understand. Gentlemen do not *marry* women like Lady Darent."

"I would," Rupert said longingly.

"Three gentlemen already have done," Owen pointed out.

"Two gentlemen and a rogue," Lady Martindale corrected. "Brokeby was no gentleman. Well?" she added impatiently. "You have not answered my question. Whatever possessed you?"

"He wants to marry Lady Darent so that he can s——" Rupert broke off as Owen shook his head sharply, and subsided back against the sofa cushions like a deflating balloon.

"It is a business arrangement," Owen said smoothly. "Lady Darent requires the protection of my name for herself and her stepchildren. She is in some financial and personal difficulty and I have offered to help her."

"Capital," Rupert said, brightening again. "Nice work, Rothbury, generous to a fault. Plus you will get to s——"

"To strengthen an alliance with the Grants and the Farne Dukedom," Owen said quickly. "I know how much you value good family connections, cousin Agatha."

"True." Lady Martindale's icy expression had thawed

a little. "Teresa Darent is an earl's daughter and is very well connected. If only her reputation were not so s—"

"Brandy, Rupert?" Owen said desperately.

"I was going to say scandalous," Lady Martindale said coldly. "Really, Rothbury, must you persist in interrupting? It is very frustrating."

"Just like your situation, Rothbury," Rupert said, a twinkle in his eye. "Most frustrating, I imagine, since Lady Darent is nowhere near as scandalous as she appears. Frightfully chaste, in fact. I should know—I've tried to seduce her often enough."

"Have you indeed?" Owen said smoothly. He turned swiftly back to Lady Martindale. "You have been encouraging me to wed since I came into the title, Aunt Agatha," he said. "I am doing this to oblige you."

He heard Rupert make a choking sound.

"Well, I find it very disobliging for your fancy to alight on so unsuitable a person," Lady Martindale said. "Why could you not make an offer to a debutante?"

"Boredom," Owen said briefly. "May I offer you hartshorn, Aunt Agatha?" he added. "You look as though you need it."

"Don't be absurd," Lady Martindale said. "I'll have a brandy."

Owen poured for her, a double measure, and another for Rupert who grasped at it like a drowning man. Lady Martindale imperiously patted the sofa with her beringed hand. Rupert shuffled up. Owen sat.

"I suppose," Lady Martindale said, her sharp black

gaze skewering him, "that the saving grace is that Lady Darent is most gratifyingly rich."

"Indeed," Owen said. "Very, very rich."

The tightly drawn line of Lady Martindale's mouth relaxed a little. "It is almost worth it," she allowed. "If only she were not so *soiled*. Have you seen the frightfully common portrait exhibition mounted by Mr. Melton? No? Then in that case you can be the only man in London who has not seen your future wife in the nude."

"I will try to possess my soul in patience until I can see the real thing," Owen murmured. He was getting heartily sick of hearing about Melton's exhibition. And he did not care to hear his great-aunt refer to his future wife in such disparaging terms either.

"The exhibition is dazzling," Rupert confirmed eagerly. "Absolutely spectacular. I've been three times—"

"Rupert!" Lady Martindale said. She drained half of her glass in one swallow. "The only protection you will be giving Lady Darent, Rothbury," she said, "is as a cloak to her scandalous affair with Justin Brooke."

"He is not her lover," Owen said. "She told me so."

Lady Martindale looked down her nose. It was a nose designed, Owen thought, for precisely that manoeuvre. "And you believed her?" she said, in tones of outright disapproval.

"Yes," Owen said shortly. "I did."

He *had* believed Tess and he had no idea why. He had taken the word of a woman he suspected to be hiding far greater secrets than a mere *affaire*. Perhaps Lady Martindale was correct and his wits had gone begging, all his good judgement swamped by the need to possess Tess Darent and make his sensuous fantasy a reality.

"Of course, Lady Darent has not had any children with any of her previous three husbands," Lady Martindale said. "One would hope…" She let the sentence hang.

"One would indeed hope," Owen said.

"I wouldn't leave it all to hope," Rupert said. "I'd have a damned good go at trying."

Lady Martindale withered him with a look. "Thank you, Rupert." She sighed. "You know, Rothbury, I cannot tell whether you are the most honourable man I know or just a damned fool," she complained.

"No doubt time will tell," Owen said. "And if Lady Darent does indeed make a fool of me," he added, "at least I will still have her money."

Lady Martindale gave her sharp bark of laughter. "I'll say this for you, Rothbury—you do not cave in under duress."

Owen grinned. "With respect, Aunt Agatha, I have experienced a great deal more duress than this, although your persuasion does rate second only to the combined forces of Villeneuve and Gravina at Trafalgar."

Now the gleam of amusement in Lady Martindale's eyes was even more pronounced. "You know that you will forever be defined as Lady Darent's fourth husband," she said. "You will not be a man in your own right, Rothbury. Such is the way when you marry a notorious woman."

"We'll see about that too," Owen said.

"Well," Lady Martindale said. "I wish you joy in your betrothal." She got to her feet. "I will put Rothbury House in order for you as a wedding present," she added casually. "I hear Lady Darent's sister is a talented designer. Perhaps she could draw up some plans." She fixed Owen with a sharp gaze. "And when Lady Rothbury delivers your first child I will remake my will in your favour provided that the baby is recognisably yours, of course. Come along, Rupert."

And she went out, leaving Owen choking on his brandy.

LADY FARRINGTON'S ROUT THAT evening was one of the highlights of the Little Season, and despite the press of guests in the ballroom, Owen had no trouble in picking Tess Darent out of the crowd as soon as he arrived.

He had called on Tess in Bedford Street earlier that afternoon, only to discover that she had gone out. He thought it highly unlikely that she had forgotten that he had promised to call, so he could only assume that she had not seen the necessity of being at home to him when he did so. Her independent spirit amused him; he had seen how badly she had reacted when he had assumed control of their engagement. But she was mistaken if she thought that she could dictate to him and he was here tonight to prove it to her. The Marquis of Darent and all his predecessors might have let this wayward widow go her own way; Owen had no such intention. Besides, Tess had claimed that she wished for respectability, so tonight was the first step she would take to repair her damaged reputation.

Owen stood unobtrusively in the shadow of a huge potted palm and watched Tess. Tonight she was gowned all in black, which should have been in outrageously bad taste and yet on her seemed merely elegant. She should have looked dreary but instead she looked stunningly dramatic. There were diamonds in her hair and diamonds on her black velvet fan and diamonds sewn onto her bodice that trembled with every breath she took. Her slippers were shimmering silver and she sparkled as radiantly as the moon, cool and ethereal, evoking the hint of a promise and not fulfilment. That promise was enough to draw a coterie of men to her side, vying for her attention, pressing her for a dance. Tess flirted and sparkled; it was easy to see how she had gained her reputation and what fed it, for the women were left hating her as their men spun in her orbit. Most women, Owen thought, cultivated other women's friendships and so were accepted even if they were beautiful. Tess simply seemed not to care whether other women liked her or not.

Yet the more he watched her the more he could see how false her claim to notoriety was, flimsy and insubstantial, a magic trick done with smoke and mirrors. Her gown, though it dazzled, was high-necked and long-sleeved, as befit a dowager. She showed as little bare flesh as a modest debutante. She danced rarely and then only with men she knew, such as Alex Grant or Garrick Farne. She never waltzed. And though Justin Brooke hung on her sleeve like a jealous lover, she treated him indulgently, more as a younger brother than an admirer. Owen wondered that no one else could see it. Perhaps it was simply the case that they did not want to. They had tarred Tess Darent as a wanton widow and had no desire to change their minds.

He watched Tess glitter in the diamond dress, saw the expressive gestures of her hands as she spoke, observed the smile that tilted those lusciously rounded lips and came to the conclusion that it was the very containment in her, the distance and the restraint that made men want to claim and conquer her. He felt it himself, a fierce impulse to possess her, to take that fantasy and explore it in all its sinful, sensuous depth. He wanted Tess's eager nakedness beneath him, her mouth open to his. He wanted to drive them both to the excess of pleasure and to see the expression in her eyes when she was sated. He wanted...

Someone near at hand cleared their throat very loudly and Owen recalled himself to his surroundings and concealed himself even more thoroughly behind the enormous palm until his erection had subsided.

A helpful debutante had left her dance card on a nearby rout chair. Owen perused it briefly and saw the waltz was next. It was perfect for his purpose. He walked across to Tess, knowing she would have no other partner for this dance. A rustle went through the crowd as people recognised him. The group of men about Tess fell back rather gratifyingly as though they expected him to run them through on the spot. Sometimes, Owen thought, it was useful to have a dangerous reputation.

"Lady Darent." He bowed to Tess with impeccable elegance.

"Good evening, Lord Rothbury." He was sure she was taken aback to see him but not by a flicker of an eyelash did she betray it. "How delightful," she added lightly. "I had no notion that I would see you again so soon."

"You would have seen me this afternoon," Owen said, "had you not been from home." He took her hand and pressed a kiss on the back of it. He felt her fingers tremble in his grasp before she withdrew them from his grip.

"My appalling memory…" She sounded genuinely regretful. Her smile was charming, her gaze limpid blue. "I do apologise."

"I'm sure your memory will improve in future," Owen said.

He saw her gaze flick to his face as she took in the meaning behind his words. "As no doubt will your manners," she said sweetly.

Owen smiled. "I am sure," he said, "we shall both find the influence of the other most…stimulating."

The orchestra started to tune up, the opening bars of a waltz mingling with the chatter of the guests.

"I came to claim the waltz with you," he added.

He saw Tess's eyes widen. Those cherry-red lips curved upwards in a provocative smile that made him want to kiss her. "You should know that I never waltz, my lord."

"But if you cannot show preference to your betrothed," Owen drawled, "who can you show it to?" He looked pointedly at Justin Brooke, who took a step back, then another, almost falling over his own feet in his haste to get away.

"It would be irredeemably unfashionable to dance with my future husband." Tess stifled a little yawn behind her diamond-encrusted fan.

"Try it." Owen had his hand under her elbow and was already drawing her to her feet. "You might even like it."

The candlelight shimmered on the expression in her eyes. She was annoyed and he could not really blame her for it. His actions had been high-handed, his claiming of her very public and very possessive. She did not, however, refuse him.

He led her out onto the floor and heard the speculation swell around them as they took their place amongst the dancers.

"Was it your intention to be the *on dit,* my lord?"

Tess sounded no more than slightly curious. "If so, you have succeeded admirably."

"It was my intention to show I would not be an indulgent fiancé," Owen said. "I did warn you."

"So you did." A faint smile touched her lips. "Yes, I see. You refuse to be designated Lady Darent's latest husband." She said the words as though quoting. "I do not think anyone would believe you anything other than your own man, my lord. And if they did they would never dare say it to your face," she added drily.

The music swelled, the irresistible lilt of the notes sweeping around them. "I trust that you can actually waltz?" Owen said. "I know you usually choose not to but I assume you know the steps?"

"I had lessons," Tess said ironically. "What about you?"

"I waltz indifferently to badly," Owen said.

"What a treat for me," Tess said. She rested her hand on his upper arm with all the delicacy of someone touching live ordnance.

"I won't break," Owen said, "or explode." He placed his hand on the small of her back and drew her firmly towards him.

"Do we need to be quite so painfully close?" Tess enquired. "I barely know you."

Owen could feel the resistance in her. He could tell that she did not like being in such physical proximity to him and was doing all she could to hold back. Her reluctance dragged in her steps, setting them a little behind the beat of the music. Owen pressed his hand more firmly to her waist and felt a tiny shiver rack her as his thigh brushed the silk of her skirts. What that meant, he was not sure. It did not feel like desire but there was certainly awareness burning between them as hot and sharp as a flame.

"I lead," he said. He slanted a look down at her. "That is not negotiable on the dance floor."

"Nor at all, it seems," Tess said.

"I will not be defined by my wife," Owen agreed. He paused and let the silence gather for a second. "I apologise for forcing your hand just now—"

A scornful flash of her eyes silenced him. "I do not believe you regret it for a second, my lord," she said crisply.

"Touché." Owen laughed. "I do not." He leaned closer. "I am claiming something that no one else has." His lips brushed her ear in a brief caress. His voice fell to a whisper. "The right to take what I want from you."

He had the satisfaction of feeling her entire body jolt in his arms. Her gaze shot up to meet his, startled and smoky blue.

"A dance," he said smoothly, "a waltz that you will grant to no one else."

"Oh…" Her body softened against his as the relief washed through her. Her steps came more easily. The music flowed around them now, carrying them with it. A thousand dazzling lights spun off the diamonds of her gown.

"You are staking more than your claim to a simple dance," she said, after a moment.

Owen's lips twitched. "Am I?"

"You know you are." Her look was as sharp as the diamonds. "You are making a very public statement of possession." She shook her head slightly. The stones in her ears shimmered. "There is no need for theatricals, my lord. I told you I would behave like a model wife and give you no cause to doubt my fidelity. For my stepchildren's sake, if nothing else, I must repair my reputation as best I can."

"I understand that," Owen said. "And I believe that you will honour your word. I am merely at pains to make sure that everyone else respects it too. You must give up your harem, I fear."

"My harem!" He felt laughter shake her. "What a quaint concept, my lord."

"But an appropriate one." Owen glanced across the room towards the spot where Justin Brooke and Tess's other admirers lingered, looking slightly disconsolate now that they had lost the bright star at the centre of their universe. "How will they cope without you, I wonder?" he added derisively.

Tess raised one shoulder in a careless little shrug. "By finding some other object to admire, I imagine." She sounded supremely unconcerned. "It should not take them long to find one."

"And how will you survive without their admiration?" Owen enquired softly.

She smiled. He saw a rich depth of mockery in her eyes. "What a shallow creature you must think me if you imagine I would care, my lord."

"And we both know you are not that," Owen said. He watched her face. "You are a talented artist, you read French philosophers in the original and you embrace reformist ideas...." He felt the tension whip through her body, saw her eyes narrow to a calculating flash of blue. "Don't you?" he finished softly.

"Do I?" She was not giving an inch. Her feet were moving instinctively now to the steps of the dance, for all her concentration was on his words.

"Of course you do," Owen said. "Was it not Mary Wollstonecraft who said that a woman should not be subject to a man's rule but should be his equal? Surely you agree with her?"

Tess laughed. "Most women I know would agree with that, my lord, whilst reserving the right to believe that in many ways they are infinitely superior to the male sex, never mind its equal."

Owen smiled lazily. "Then perhaps we may discuss philosophy together on the long, dark winter evenings," he said.

"How the time will fly by." She sounded amused.

"I am sure you will find it more congenial than having to play the dutiful wife in public," Owen said. "Unfortunately the price the ton will demand for the restoration of your good reputation is that you are seen to be both biddable and submissive to me."

He saw the expression of disgust in her eyes and tried not to laugh. "I know it will be difficult," he added, gently mocking, "but I will try to make it as pleasant as possible for you to obey me."

"How gracious of you," Tess said. Her narrowed gaze scanned his face. "You are enjoying this," she accused.

"I am," Owen admitted readily. He was indeed enjoying the look of plain fury on Tess's face, enjoying the stiff outrage in her body, so at odds with the sinuous shift and swell of the waltz. It was this passion that she kept so well hidden, this passion he wanted to explore in her. She had been spoilt, he thought, having so much money and being the sole mistress of it. Now she was in a situation she could not control. She was at his mercy. His blood quickened at the thought.

"No gambling," he said, "no extravagance, no drinking, no lovers, a diet of improving books and worthy causes… You may even develop a taste for it."

"It is more likely to kill me first," Tess said bitterly.

Owen smiled. "All in a good cause," he said.

He saw the anger fade from her face to be replaced by resignation as she realised he was right; she really did not have a choice, not if she wished to wash her own reputation clean to save that of her stepdaughter.

"Damn it," she said after a moment. "And damn you, Rothbury, for taking pleasure in my predicament. It was not supposed to be like this." Her tone had changed on the last words, from frustration to utter desolation.

"You do not like ceding control," Owen said, watching her.

"Of course I do not." Her eyes were fierce. "It's…" She paused. "It's dangerous."

Dangerous. It was an interesting choice of word.

"Why?" Owen asked.

"Why is it dangerous to be at the mercy of others?" Tess's gaze was dark, inward looking. Owen wondered what she was thinking. "I would have thought that was obvious," she said. "It makes one vulnerable."

"Do you think I'm dangerous?" Owen said.

Her gaze swept his face. She laughed. "Think it?" she said. "I know it."

The dance was drawing to an end, the last few bars of the music hanging on the air with rousing sweetness. Owen let Tess go as the applause rippled out and the musicians took a bow. She dropped him a deep curtsy, there in the middle of the dance floor before everyone, a perfect parody of abasement, skirts spread about her, head bowed. It looked subservient but Owen knew it was all pretence. He gave her his hand and raised her to her feet and she smiled into his eyes with such docile charm that he almost laughed aloud.

"Is that submissive enough for you?" she whispered. "Will this convince the crowds?"

In truth, her sham obedience only sharpened the lust Owen felt for her. Such neat defiance provoked everything in him that enjoyed a challenge. He pressed a kiss on her hand and could have sworn that she blushed for the onlookers.

"You are perfect," he said mockingly.

"Oh, good." Her smile had widened but her eyes were cold. "I would not wish to disappoint our audience. You must forgive me, my lord." She raised her voice so those close by could overhear. "I am tired and would like to return home. Do I have your permission to retire?"

"Doing it too brown now," Owen said drily.

Her gaze teased him, her look for him alone. "You wanted a biddable wife," she murmured. "Now deal with her." And with another curtsy she swept out of the ballroom without a backward glance, every diamond on her gown sparkling defiance, leaving Owen short of breath from an emotion he had no trouble in identifying as acute lust. Already she had him tied in knots.

CHAPTER SIX

"MY LADY!" THE URGENT TONES of her maid dragged Tess up from the deepest sleep. She came awake with a start, her heart pounding. For a second her mind felt hazy and confused, sluggish with dreams. She could see that there was light creeping around the edge of the bedchamber curtains but it was a very pale grey early-morning light.

"What is it, Margery?" she said, propping herself up on one elbow, forcing her eyes to open. "Is the house on fire?"

"No, ma'am," the maid said. "Lord Rothbury is here to see you, ma'am."

"Rothbury?" Tess squinted at the clock but could not see it in the deep shadows of the room. "But it can only be eight o'clock."

"It is nine-fifteen, ma'am," the maid said, in the tone of one who had been up and at work for at least four hours.

Tess gave a muffled groan and flopped back on the pillow. "Nine-fifteen? But no one makes morning calls in the morning," she said. "It is far too early."

"Lord Rothbury is doing so, ma'am," Margery

pointed out, with the brand of logic that was peculiarly her own.

Tess was extremely tempted to burrow back into the cocoon of the bedclothes and leave Rothbury to enjoy the pleasures of the early morning alone. The room felt cold and there was little incentive to set her bare toes on the chilly floor. This could only be the latest of Rothbury's high-handed attempts to show her that she was at his beck and call. She should tell him she was never at home until after one o'clock, roll over and go back to sleep until an acceptable hour, when Margery could awaken her with a cup of hot chocolate, as was her custom.

Except… She hesitated. She had enjoyed crossing swords with Rothbury the previous night. Most balls were as dull as ditchwater, tedious, predictable affairs, lacking any kind of novelty. Last night, in contrast, had been unexpected, and it was Rothbury's presence that had given it the edge. She could not remember the last time she had enjoyed herself so much, especially not in the company of a man and certainly not in the company of any of her previous husbands. Rothbury had been challenging, provocative and *dangerous*….

She gave a little shiver.

Well, she was awake now and it would be impossible to get back to sleep. She might as well resign herself to that fact and go and tell Rothbury that he needed to learn the etiquette of ton society.

The clock was striking a half hour past ten as she

came down the stairs. The morning sun cut through the high window on the landing, casting pools of light on the stairs and polishing the deep walnut of the banisters to a rich lustre. The brightness made Tess narrow her eyes. She had not even realised that the hall and landing caught the sun at this time of day. The house smelled of coffee and beeswax polish. It was rather pleasant. From behind the closed door of the breakfast room she could hear the sound of voices. She had not imagined that Joanna would be out of bed at this time either but perhaps her sister rose early to spend time with her daughter, Shuna, in the nursery. The thought made Tess pause on the last step. She lived in this house and yet she had a very separate existence from the rest of her family. She had always kept her distance. Suddenly she felt hollow with loneliness.

Perhaps it was this uncharacteristic melancholy that threw her slightly off balance as she entered the drawing room to see Rothbury comfortably seated before the fire reading *The Times*. Certainly she felt rather odd as he cast the paper aside and stood up, odd and a little gauche, just as she had done the morning she had gone to propose to him. She remembered that she had thought to lecture him on the standards of etiquette expected by the ton when it came to morning calls. At the least she had to admit that he was dressed perfectly for it. He looked immaculate. He gave her a formal bow but then he smiled as well, and Tess felt an unexpected curl of pleasure ripple down to her toes.

Her gaze fell on *The Gazetteer,* which was resting on the rosewood table at Rothbury's elbow. She could see her embroidered bookmark sticking out of the top and felt a quick rush of mortification. Rothbury had had over an hour on his own waiting for her. Had he taken a peek inside the book and realised that she had chosen him from a cast of hundreds?

"Good morning, Lord Rothbury," she said. "It makes a change for a gentleman to be encouraging me *out* of my bed rather than trying to get me into it."

Rothbury smiled. "I apologise," he said. "I rise so early myself. Navy training."

"I hope that Lord and Lady Grant offered you breakfast whilst you waited?" Tess said.

"Oh, I had breakfast at seven," Rothbury said easily, as Tess repressed a shudder. "Though I did join Alex and Joanna in a cup of coffee."

"I am glad that someone was up in order to greet you," Tess murmured. She waited for him to acquaint her with the purpose of his visit. He did not. Instead his gaze travelled over her with the same slow, considered appraisal as it had done on the first night they had met.

"I am not at my best in the morning," Tess said, as the silence stretched. "In fact I try very hard to ignore the fact that the morning even exists."

"On the contrary," Rothbury murmured. "You look lovely."

You look lovely....

It was a very simple compliment to give Tess such

pleasure. She imagined that Rothbury was not a man given to flattery and somehow that made her value his words all the more highly. But those same words made her nervous. She did not want his compliments. They felt too intimate. She did not seek such a relationship with him.

"I don't think you should say things like that to me," she squeaked, her sense of discomfort deepening. She felt taken unawares, as though she had not had time to wake up properly and had been caught out without the facade she wore for the world, vulnerable and unprotected.

Rothbury smiled at her. Her pulse fluttered. She grabbed the corner of the sofa and sat down. She was starting to feel hot, dizzy and confused. The last time she had experienced such perplexing emotions had been at the age of fourteen when she had developed a *tendre* for her piano teacher, a crush that had rendered her completely tongue-tied. She remembered that both the piano playing and the *tendre* had been a disaster. This had better not go the same way.

Rothbury's smile had deepened as he watched her. "Why should I not compliment you?" he enquired.

Tess hesitated. "It's not…"

"Fashionable to admire one's fiancée?" Rothbury shrugged his broad shoulders. "I beg your pardon. If I make any further faux pas I am sure you will be trading me in for another gentleman in your husband hunter's charter." He gestured to *The Gazetteer* on the table.

"The only mystery is that, with such a broad spectrum of manhood to choose from, your decision alighted on me."

Tess blushed. So he *had* looked through the book and found her bookmark on the page for his entry. Under the circumstances she could hardly pretend it was a co-incidence or that the book belonged to someone else.

"It is unaccountable, is it not?" she said. "I am questioning that very decision myself."

Rothbury's lips twitched. "Well, before you do change your mind," he said, "I called to see if you would care to go driving with me."

Tess gaped. "Driving in the morning? Why on earth would anyone do that? No one will be about."

"You've answered your own question," Rothbury said. "I'd far rather drive in the park when I don't have to fight my way through the crowds."

"But the purpose of driving in the park is to be seen," Tess said. "No one will see us."

"We are at cross purposes, Lady Darent," Rothbury said. He arched a sardonic brow. "My intention is to enjoy a beautiful autumn morning rather than to see and be seen."

"My concept of a beautiful autumn morning involves curling up at the fireside with a copy of *The Lady's Magazine,* Lord Rothbury," Tess said. "To go outside would be most singular."

Amusement and surely an element of disappointment registered in Rothbury's face. "You do not wish to come with me," he said. "Very well." He sketched a bow. "Good day, Lady Darent."

"No, wait." Tess put out an impulsive hand. She spoke before she thought, because for some odd reason the sincere disappointment she had read in his eyes had given her a pang of regret. "I'll come with you," she conceded. "If you give me a half hour to dress appropriately."

Rothbury shook his head. "I'll give you five minutes," he said, "or I come and fetch you. If I have to wait as long as I did earlier we'll arrive at the same time as all the crowds I'm trying to avoid."

Fifteen minutes later, he was tucking her into a chocolate-coloured curricle with the Rothbury crest on the side. It was an extremely elegant equipage, its huge black wheels mirrored in the polished coachwork. The interior was lavishly padded with buff-coloured squashy leather seats that Tess sank into with a little gasp of pleasure.

"Good gracious," she said. "We became betrothed under false pretences, Lord Rothbury. I was sure you were poor and yet this is the height of opulence."

Rothbury grinned, his teeth a flash of white in his tanned face. "All thanks to you, Lady Darent," he said. "All on tick against my expectations."

"What happens if I jilt you?" Tess asked innocently, and his grin broadened.

"Then I end up in the Fleet for debt," he said.

"So perhaps," Tess pursued, "I am not quite as much at your mercy as I had thought."

"Touché." Rothbury gave her a look that made the colour burn hot in her cheeks. "It seems we are already mutually entwined."

Tess had taken the precaution of wearing a fur-lined pelisse with matching hat, fur tippet and gloves as well as a muff. There was a hot brick for her feet and several layers of thick blankets to protect her against the cold. For it was exceptionally cold. The thick grey fog of the previous days had lifted, the sky was clear and the sun rising, but the frost still lay on the shadowed grass and the wind cut like a knife. For a moment Tess could barely breathe and certainly not speak as the icy draught filled her lungs.

"You are trying to give me consumption," she gasped. Her breath crystallised into a cloud in front of her.

Rothbury laughed and the curricle dipped and swayed as he swung up beside her and took the reins. "You will soon warm up," he said.

"I doubt it," Tess said, teeth chattering.

Whilst Rothbury was fully occupied with his team, Tess peered about her at the bustling street. Some people, it appeared, *did* get up in the mornings, quite a lot of them in fact.

"I had no notion it would be so busy," she said without thinking, then realised that Rothbury had given her another laughing glance. Suddenly she felt naive and spoiled. "I do know that people have to work," she said sharply.

"Of course," Rothbury said. "But I imagine that for you, marriage has been a full-time occupation."

Tess shot him a sharp look. The smile still lingered on his lips but his green gaze was cool now. She had the oddest feeling that he did not approve of her leisured life and she supposed that it was in stark contrast to his own career as sailor, explorer and adventurer. He, it seemed, had never stayed still, never ceased working. She wondered how he felt now that he had been obliged to give up a career at sea to take up his title.

"I certainly worked hard at my marriages," she said, with feeling. "So pray do not disparage my efforts. You have no notion how tiring it was accumulating three husbands."

"I imagine you are held up as an example of what can be accomplished by such a career," Rothbury said in his laconic drawl.

"On the contrary," Tess said. "If I am held up as anything, it is as a terrible warning. You said so yourself last night."

"Disapproved of by those who are convinced you had more fun than they did," Rothbury said, with a grin.

"They should try it," Tess said bitterly, before she could help herself.

He shot her a sideways look. "It was not fun?"

"Being wed to a lecher and a gambler and a man insensible with laudanum?" Tess questioned. "No, it was not."

"Which was which?" Rothbury enquired.

"Darent was laudanum and drink, and Brokeby—" Tess managed to keep her voice steady "—was lechery and drink. And gambling. And laudanum. And every other vice." For a second she closed her eyes to blot out the memory of it. She wished she had not mentioned Brokeby's name. The cold shadows wreathed about her heart. Somewhere in her mind a door closed, trapping her in the dark. She could hear the hurried catch of her breath and feel the terrified patter of her heart. Hands reached for her, Brokeby's face set in a mask of lust and cruelty, the laughter, the clothing stripped from her body...

"And your first husband?" Rothbury was saying. His attention was on the horses and he had not noticed her discomfort. Thank God. Her racing heart steadied.

Tess smiled, allowing herself to relax into warmer memories. "Oh, Robert was a wonderful friend," she said.

"An interesting choice of words," Rothbury said. Tess could see that he was leaning forwards now to try to see her expression beneath the brim of her bonnet. "Was it a love match?"

"I did love him," Tess agreed. *But I was not in love with him....*

She turned her face away, feeling too vulnerable. Rothbury had a knack of asking very blunt questions that seemed to prompt her to divulge far too much personal information. With Rothbury, she found herself tempted into indiscretion before she had even thought about it. His presence acted on her like some sort of drug that loosened her tongue—and that was frightfully dangerous. She did not know how or why it happened, only that he was able to circumvent her defences with the greatest of ease.

"You should tell me something of your own romantic history, my lord," she said, "to make this a fair discussion. Have you never met a woman you wished to marry?"

She wondered if it was her imagination or if Rothbury really had hesitated for a second before replying. There was an opaque look in his eyes. She could not read his expression at all. She wondered too if she had been insensitive in putting the question when he could not offer a woman a full marriage in every sense.

"I've met women I have admired," Rothbury said, easily enough, after a moment. His gaze was steady on some point in the distance. "But marriage is a serious business." He turned to look down at her and smiled. "I do not wish to make a mull of it."

"Don't worry," Tess said. "I have sufficient experience of the institution to count for both of us."

The smile Rothbury gave her made her feel quite dizzy. "An institution," he mused. "That sounds not only frightfully dull but something one is locked into without escape." His voice fell, the tone deep and thoughtful. "I hope our marriage may be much more than that."

The sincerity in his voice made Tess's breath catch in her throat. In a society that thrived on artifice, Rothbury was a man of a very different stamp and his honesty challenged her to be equally sincere, challenged too the barriers she had erected about her guarded heart. For a moment her emotions felt terrifyingly naked.

She fell silent as they turned into the gates of the park and the gravel of Rotten Row crunched under the carriage wheels. She was suddenly assailed by all the images of autumn. The trees were every shade of brown, the falling leaves swirling down to lie on the frozen grass in a bright carpet of orange and gold. Vivid pictures came into her mind of the watercolours she'd drawn as a child when, bored with her other lessons, she had wandered outside with her paint box and brushes. The hot summers had been full of long hazy days when she had lain in the grass, her tongue poking out with concentration as she had tried to capture in pictures the enquiring dark eye and feathered breast of a blackbird, or the flimsy beauty of a rose petal. She felt a sudden sharp pain in her chest. She had not thought of those days for a very long time and never with the warmth of memory, always with the need to escape. Yet now, as she looked at the branches of the beech and oak against the cold blue sky, she felt a pang of nostalgia.

She realised that she had lost herself in memory.

Rothbury was watching the play of emotions across her face and his gaze was disconcertingly intent.

"You look sad," he said. "I'm sorry. That was not my intention in bringing you here."

Something twisted in Tess's heart. "I was thinking about my childhood," she admitted, wondering as she did so how he seemed to be able to draw secrets from her that she would confess to no one else.

"And that made you unhappy?" His voice was very quiet.

Tess nodded. "Because it all ended so abruptly when my brother died, I suppose." She had not spoken of Stephen's death for years, yet now it seemed easy, natural, to do so. "You know that Garrick Farne shot him, that Stephen had been having an affair with Garrick's wife?" Rothbury nodded. "I knew about it at the time although I never said a word to anyone. I felt terribly guilty afterwards." Something of that guilt eased at last, now that she was finally telling someone of it. "But it made me realise how dangerous passion was, I suppose. Stephen died because of his affair with Kitty Farne." Tess shivered. "All our lives were ruined by it. I swore I would never do anything so foolish as love blindly like that."

She looked up, blinking back the tears and with them the memories of the old scandals and hurts. Rothbury's gaze was very steady on her face and she realised that his gloved hand was covering hers where it lay on the rug. Although there were two layers between them she felt a tingle of warmth and a very great deal of comfort. She did not want to move from beneath his touch.

"I am not sure that it was like that," he said, very gently. "Garrick told me that Stephen never loved Kitty at all."

"I know that now." Tess sniffed. "Merryn told me everything after she and Garrick wed. But at the time…" She stopped.

"At the time, you ran off and married your best friend so that you would always be safe from love, because it was too powerful an emotion," Rothbury said.

Tess's heart dropped with shock. Her eyes opened very wide. "I cannot see how you could possibly know that," she said. How could Rothbury see so much, see straight into her heart, when she had not even realised the truth herself until a second before?

Rothbury smiled at her. "I know because you told me yourself, just now," he said easily. "You said that Robert had been a wonderful friend. You omitted to say that you were in love with him."

"I *loved* him." Tess knew she sounded defensive. She also knew her protestations had come too late. She had already given away far too much.

"You did not love him with a passion." There was something in Rothbury's voice that made Tess burn. She turned her face away. This felt too intimate, as though she was giving away far more of herself than she had intended. She did not want to speak to Rothbury of love and passion. It felt far too dangerous and she did not understand why. She had believed that the threat he posed related purely to his ability to unmask her as Jupiter. She had not even considered that there might be other perils here, yet the powerful affinity between them made her feel extraordinarily vulnerable.

"It's beautiful here," she said quickly.

For a moment she thought Rothbury was not going to allow the subject to drop but then his face broke into a smile and her heart did a little errant skip. "I'm glad you think so," he said, and Tess felt it again, that little shiver of pleasure that she took in his company. She seemed powerless to help it.

"It is almost like being in the country," Rothbury said, beside her. He had allowed the carriage to slow almost to a stop and his gloved hands held the reins idle in his lap.

"Do you not care for London?" Tess asked.

His shoulders moved beneath his coat as though he were trying to shrug off a weight. "London hems me in," he said. He smiled down at her. "I'd rather be at sea."

"Do you still sail?" Tess enquired.

"Only a rowing boat." He sounded rueful. "I still have *Sea Witch*," he added. "She is in dock at Greenwich. No money to pay for a crew though, and where would I go?" His shoulders lifted in a helpless little shrug. "I have responsibilities ashore now."

"*Sea Witch*," Tess said. It was an evocative name. "Why did you call her that?"

Rothbury laughed. "I used to claim it was because she handles like a woman in a temper," he said, "but in truth it is because I am more than a little bewitched by her." His voice fell. "I had thought to sell her though. She is the only asset I still possess."

"You can't do that!" Tess said quickly, instinctively.

He raised a quizzical brow. "Why not?"

"Because we were speaking of passions just now," Tess said. It was odd to feel envious of a ship and yet for a second envy was precisely the emotion she felt, a resentment that so much of Rothbury's life had been wrapped up in sailing the world aboard *Sea Witch,* in adventures she could never know or even dream. "*Sea Witch* is your passion," she said. "I can hear it in your voice."

"Can you indeed?" Rothbury sounded startled, then his tone warmed into amusement. "What a perceptive woman you are, Teresa Darent."

It was the first time that he had used her name. No one had called her Teresa since her childhood. The way Rothbury said it ruffled the edge of her nerves. Tess found that she liked it. She liked it a lot. Too much, probably, for it felt as though he was effortlessly stripping away more of the formality between them. Again it felt too intimate, threatening her defences.

"Why do you call me Teresa?" she asked.

There was a smile at the back of his eyes. "Because everyone else calls you Tess," he said.

"But not you."

"I'm different."

Tess's stomach gave a little flip. She turned her face away. He *was* different. She was only now beginning to realise quite how much, and quite how dangerous it was to her.

"At any rate," she said lightly, "you have the promise of my money now. There is no need to sell your ship."

"Despite what I said earlier," Rothbury said, "I do not like living off the expectation of my future wife's fortune." There was an edge to his voice.

"You have too much pride," Tess said.

"How much pride is too much?" Rothbury said softly. He laughed suddenly. "If your money enables me to renovate Rothbury Chase, then I shall indeed overcome my pride and be grateful. It is a beautiful house, criminally neglected."

"Have you visited all your estates?" Tess asked.

He nodded. "I'm told that legally I cannot sell any of them."

"Of course not!" Tess was appalled. "They are in trust for future generations—" She broke off abruptly, feeling grossly insensitive as she realised that for Rothbury there would be no begetting of another generation. The Rothbury title and the lands would have to move sideways to a cousin yet again. She wondered whom he had as his heir.

Rothbury appeared not to have noticed her insensitivity. Tess was vastly relieved.

"Do *you* enjoy the country?" he was asking.

"I try never to go there," Tess said. "I grew up in the country. That was enough for a lifetime."

Rothbury laughed with genuine amusement. "Is that true?" he enquired. "Or just another of your fashionable statements?"

"It's true enough," Tess said. "The country bores me. All the hunting and shooting."

"But surely," Rothbury said, "that is the height of fashion? And as a leader of society it is your duty to set an example by killing as many foxes as you can."

"You are teasing me," Tess said. "Fox hunting is no pursuit for a lady unless she is some dyed-in-the-wool country squire's wife. Which is fortunate, since I do not share society's passion for maiming and killing furry and feathered creatures."

"Well, as to that I cannot see it is sport," Rothbury agreed. His tone hardened. "There is sufficient killing without adding to it for fun."

Tess stole a glance at him. This was a man, she reminded herself, who had been a professional soldier and sailor, who had seen action in a number of campaigns and had been a prisoner of war. She wondered what marks his experiences had left on his mind as well as his body. No wonder he sounded bitter when speaking of the violence and cruelty of killing.

"So you never visit Darent Park?" Rothbury asked.

Tess shook her head. "The house is closed. Mr. Churchward administers the estate until Julius reaches his majority."

"But you see your stepchildren?" Rothbury persisted. "You visit them?"

A very hard knot formed in Tess's chest, stealing her breath. "No," she said. It sounded stark, a mirror of the pain inside her. She tried to find the words, words that would explain her situation without giving away too much emotion.

"Julius is at Eton," she said carefully. "And Sybil is at school in Bath."

"But during their holidays—" Rothbury said.

"They stay with their aunt," Tess said in a rush, "my late husband's eldest sister."

She could feel Rothbury looking at her but she did not turn her head to meet his gaze. The brightness of the day stung her eyes. There was a hot burn in her throat.

"So you never see them?" Rothbury repeated. There was a very odd tone in his voice.

"I told you yesterday," Tess said, "that you ask too many questions."

"Forgive me—" he sounded impatient "—but I want an answer to this one. Your late husband entrusted the administration of his children's affairs to you and to his lawyer and yet you never see them?"

Tess thought about the harsh words that had been exchanged when Lady Nevern had discovered that her brother had not only cut her out of his will but had also left the sole running of the Darent estates to his widow and his lawyer. Legally, Lord and Lady Nevern had had

no claim on the Darent twins, but Celia Nevern had
known Tess's weakness. She had asked in the sweetest
possible tones whether Tess thought that her less-than-
savoury reputation could possibly be an asset to the
Darent twins in their future. Would it not be far more
politic for her to leave the upbringing of her stepchildren to their blood relatives?

"We agreed that it was for the best," Tess said. She
knew she sounded wooden. She felt as though she was
shrinking inside, curling up in an effort to hide and
protect herself from the pain she always felt when she
thought of the loss of her stepchildren. It was like missing a step in the dark, a jolt, and her heart would stutter
before she found her way forward again.

"Best for whom?" Rothbury's words cut like a knife,
straight through her pitiful defences. Then, as she did
not reply: "Best for whom? Look at me, Teresa."

It seemed inordinately difficult to do so because in
looking Rothbury in the eye and telling him about her
stepchildren, Tess found that she was accepting the
truth for the first time. She had always skirted around it
before with evasion and falsehood, claiming that Julius
and Sybil were better off living with their aunt, uncle
and cousins, pretending that she did not care. People assumed that she had packed the twins off to school and
never saw them because it interfered with her social
commitments. The reality was a great deal more painful.

She felt Rothbury's gloved hand smooth against her

cheek, raising her chin so that she was forced to meet his eyes. His own cool green gaze was unflinching, demanding the truth.

"Well?" he said softly, with an expressive lift of his brows.

"Lord and Lady Nevern, Darent's sister and brother-in-law, thought it best that they should have responsibility for the twins when they were not at school," Tess said. "I agreed."

In the end she had been browbeaten into it by Nevern's threats to bankrupt the estate by contesting the will in court. And there had been only one of her against a barrage of Darent's siblings, all of them siding with Lord and Lady Nevern. Tess had often thought it a shame the marquis's parents had been so fecund. It meant that there were so many more relatives who disapproved of her.

Even so, her capitulation shamed her. She wished she had stuck out longer for the right to see Julius and Sybil sometimes. She had been so very fond of them and they of her. She missed them terribly.

"Your stepchildren had grown accustomed to seeing you as a mother," Rothbury said, and there was a barely concealed edge of anger beneath the silk of his tones now, "and your late husband trusted you to run the estate and care for them, yet his sister thought she knew better?"

"We both knew that my poor reputation would reflect badly on my stepchildren," Tess said, erasing all bitterness from her voice, "and so it has proved."

Rothbury's fingers brushed the line of her jaw in something perilously close to a caress. Little shivers of sensation cascaded over Tess's skin. He was still watching her and she saw anger in his eyes but knew it was not for her. She saw understanding there too and once again felt the tug of a dangerous affinity that threatened to undermine her completely.

Rothbury's hand fell. "So even then you were sacrificing yourself for the children's sake," he said, "and tacitly agreeing with their relatives' judgement that you were a bad influence." He tightened the reins. The horses checked.

"Sometimes," Tess said, "one needs to recognise the odds one is fighting against." Her voice strengthened. "Besides, Lady Nevern is a most respectable matron with a spotless reputation. In a few years she will bring Sybil out, and since I shall be married and behaving like a pattern card of propriety there will be nothing to dim the future prospects of my stepdaughter."

There was a taut silence between them.

"You are very generous," Rothbury said gruffly. "More generous than your late husband's odious relatives deserve." His voice warmed a little. "A respectable matron with a spotless reputation, eh? She sounds like a ghastly judgemental harridan to me. One can only hope she will do something shocking before she chokes on her own virtue."

Tess gave a spontaneous burst of laughter. "Now, that I would like to see."

"I am always suspicious of those who profess the greatest morality," Rothbury said. "Usually they are shockingly perverted."

"What a ridiculous generalisation!" Tess said, still laughing.

"Isn't it?" Rothbury agreed cordially. He set the carriage in motion again and as they moved off a barouche swished past in the opposite direction, the ladies inside raising their lorgnettes to peer at them.

"Lady O'Hara," Tess said, shuddering. "She is a frightful old gossip. I did not expect to see her out so early but maybe she cannot endure to lie late abed in case she misses the latest *on dit*."

She remembered that once, when Lady O'Hara had cut her dead at a musicale, she had drawn a couple of extremely cruel but accurate caricatures of her and had affixed the pictures to the supper room doors. The expression of utter horror on Lady O'Hara's face when the entire assembly had gathered around the anonymous portraits had been a sight to gladden Tess's heart.

But there would be no more of that sort of thing. No more little revenges for the slights she had suffered. She glanced sideways at Rothbury. There would be no more reforming politics either and no more Jupiter cartoons. If she was good, if she was lucky, she might just get away without being unmasked. But her life would be eminently the poorer for it. She would have no purpose.

She would be a wife locked into another fashionable marriage of convenience. It was what she had thought she wanted and yet for a second Tess felt frighteningly empty and unsure what she was going to do with her future.

The park was filling up. A gentleman cantered past on a roan gelding, then a pair of dashing young bucks who raised their hats to Tess as they passed and were almost unseated by their mounts as the horses started to prance and pirouette. The bucks disappeared in a welter of curses and flying hooves.

"Restless stallions," Tess said. "So difficult to control."

"I imagine you must have some trouble with them," Rothbury agreed. There was a small frown between his eyes as he watched the two gentlemen out of sight.

"Indeed," Tess said. "Men are always trying to get into my…"

Rothbury raised his brows.

"Bank deposit box," she finished. She smiled demurely. "And my bed as well."

"A stern husband should be a fine deterrent," Rothbury said, with a twitch of the lips.

"Very true," Tess said. "I doubt any amorous libertine would risk getting on the wrong side of you, my lord, by making advances to your wife. Is it correct that you once snuffed the candles on an entire chandelier with a brace of pistols?"

"No," Rothbury said. "That would be a pointless waste of bullets."

"How prosaic you are," Tess said. "And the story that you sailed into Cadiz under the cover of darkness and captured three Spanish ships?"

Rothbury sighed. "Wasn't that Sir Francis Drake?" he said. "You are several centuries out."

"Are none of the stories about you true?" Tess said plaintively.

"Perhaps," Rothbury said noncommittally.

"But you do not have anything to prove," Tess said. One would not catch Rothbury boasting in his cups of his adventures as a privateer, she thought. There was something so self-contained about him and yet so formidably confident.

"The story about me winning fifty-thousand pounds and a maharajah's mistress in a game of chance was true," Rothbury said, a smile tilting his lips.

"What happened to the money?" Tess asked.

"Spent."

"And the mistress?"

His smile deepened. "She preferred someone else." *More fool her.*

The thought ambushed Tess, surprised her. Hot on its heels came a second thought: what must it have been like for a man like Rothbury, a virile man, a man who had no doubt known plenty of women in his time, to lose the ability to take sexual pleasure? She felt a sharp pang of regret for him, followed by a very pleasant feeling of relaxation. It was delightful that this was one man she need not worry would try to bed her. She snuggled further down beneath the blankets, matching her emotional comfort to the physical warmth of the fur-lined rugs.

"I'm hungry," she said, surprised.

Rothbury laughed. "You had no breakfast."

Tess realised she had not and that her stomach was rumbling. They turned out of the gates and Rothbury pulled the curricle over, jumping down to purchase muffins and buttery crumpets from the baker whose barrow was on the corner. Tess stripped off her gloves. The butter ran between her fingers and she laughingly licked it off, looking up to surprise an expression in Rothbury's eyes that she could have sworn was desire. For a second she felt afraid as her heat bumped against her ribs and panic dried her throat, but then he smiled.

"Is that enough," he said, "or would you care for some milk and cake?"

"You sound like my nurse," Tess said, and the patter of fear in her stomach faded away and the day was bright again and the crumpet was warm and the butter salty and it tasted better than anything she had ever eaten before, because of course Rothbury did not desire her. The idea was absurd, and there was absolutely nothing she needed to fear.

WHITE'S CLUB WAS QUIET, opulent and shockingly rev- erential. At first the club servant had seemed disin- clined to allow Owen entrance because he was not a member, but Owen had explained very courteously that he was there to see Lord Corwen on behalf of the Home Secretary. The servant had considered Owen's height, breadth and general air of polite danger and had stood aside. He had recognised him as Viscount Rothbury and had known that whilst he was not a member in his own right, preferring Brooks's Club instead, he was a friend of several most influential members of the nobility. Decidedly it would not be a good idea to throw him out.

Owen followed the man up the wide wrought-iron stairs to the landing above, along several thickly carpeted corridors and through a heavy wooden door into a room where five men sat at play. The servant approached one and bowed deferentially, bending to murmur a few words in the peer's ear. Owen waited. He could feel his muscles tense beneath the skin.

This was for Tess. From the moment she had told him of Corwen's squalid blackmail he had been determined to make the corrupt peer see the error of his ways. When Tess had told him that morning that she was estranged from her stepchildren, Owen had become doubly determined she should suffer no more shame from Corwen's malicious tittle-tattle. He had felt Tess's grief when she had related that she no longer saw Sybil and Julius Darent. It was a small private tragedy but it had hit him in the stomach like a blow. Tess had given up her stepchildren because she was perceived as a bad influence. She did not wish to damage their future. It was a most selfless act from a woman branded as selfish and manipulative.

Corwen threw down his cards with a bad-tempered slap and rose to his feet. His gaze, more than a little inebriated, rolled over Owen.

"Who the devil are you?" he demanded, despite the fact that Owen knew the servant had given his name a second earlier. "And what the hell do you mean by interrupting my game?"

"Careful, Corwen." One of the other players looked up. He looked like a country squire with a nose as red as the port in his glass and a certain arrogance in his bearing. "Don't forget he outranks you," the man said.

Corwen gave a dismissive snort. "I won't be outranked by a damned Yankee pirate."

"It is not something you have any control over, my lord," Owen said very politely. "I am and you are."

The other man laughed. "Join us in a game, Rothbury?" he asked, gesturing to the table. "I hear you play a fine hand, with all that experience gained in gaming hells around the world."

"You flatter me, sir," Owen said. "Thank you for the invitation but I am merely here to speak to Lord Corwen about his marriage plans."

An odd ripple went around the table like the movement of wind through corn. Two of the other players—the third was insensible with drink and nodding over his cards—looked up and then quickly down at the cards in their hands. The squire, inured to the atmosphere either through insensitivity or port, laughed. "Told you that you should have been more discreet, Corwen."

Corwen's eyes darted from his companions back to Owen's face. "What's it to you anyway, Rothbury?" he demanded. "Do you have a fancy for Lady Sybil Darent yourself?"

Owen felt a flash of violence ripple through him. He itched to take the peer by the throat and throttle him with his own cravat. He kept his hands clenched tightly at his side. He could not allow himself to be provoked. Deep within him, buried but not forgotten, was a thread of violence that had haunted his past.

"My sexual preferences are not for children," he said coldly. "I am betrothed to Lady Darent and as such I have to tell you that any threats you make against her or her stepchildren are my business and I shall deal with them." He paused. "Do you understand me, Corwen?"

"I understand that you are nothing but a fool to betroth yourself to Darent's widow," Corwen sneered. "Could you not find yourself anything less shop-soiled, Rothbury? The virtuous ladies all spurn a foreigner?"

Owen smiled. "Don't give me further cause to hit you, Corwen," he said silkily. "I want to do it very much."

"You wouldn't do it here," Corwen said contemptuously.

"You mistake," Owen said. "I'd do it anywhere." He shifted. "Another word against Lady Darent, Corwen, or against Lady Sybil, and the whole array of your sexual misdemeanours will be paraded before the ton. Lord Sidmouth has quite a file on you, I assure you."

Corwen paused, the blood leaching from his face, his eyes narrowed. "All lies," he hissed.

Owen shrugged. "Maybe so, maybe not. But who would care when the gossip would be so much more piquant than the truth anyway? Was that not what you said to Lady Darent, Corwen?" He took a step back and saw Corwen's shoulders slumped with pitiful relief.

"My lawyers will contact you about the payment of Darent's debts," Owen said. "In the meantime remember what I said about Lady Darent and Lady Sybil." He smiled. "I think that you will find that your estates require your attention, Corwen. For a good, long time." He nodded to the others. "Gentlemen…"

The slumbering card player awoke just as Owen was strolling out of the door.

"Who the devil was that chap?" he heard the man say. "Damned cool hand."

Once out in the night air, Owen stopped and took a deep breath, feeling the icy cold sweep away the heated anger from his body. The violence in his blood died away. He had restrained that aggression for his entire life. Violence had dogged his steps since his youth but he had learned the hard way to keep a grip on his temper; only once had he lost that icy control. Once, fatally, in an incident never to be forgotten, a shame buried deep in his past. He had dishonoured his profession and shamed his family and as a result he would never again fail them.

He straightened and squared his shoulders. Sometimes it felt as though he spent his whole life atoning for that failure. He had fought for the causes he had held to be just and he had tried to help those who needed saving. He had almost taken a life and he had given his in return, over and over. For a second his thoughts veered back to Joanna Grant, the only woman he had ever loved. He had saved Joanna from her first husband's cruelty. He had wanted Joanna herself to be his prize. But fate was tricky like that; it did not always give one what one wished for. Owen smiled ruefully in the darkness. Instead of Joanna, fate had sent him Tess, Tess who was in her own way as fascinating as her sister, Tess who also required protection, Tess who for all her courage and her independence was vulnerable and needed him.

He had started out seeing Teresa Darent as a deceitful jade without an honest bone in her body, a woman who was both sensuously desirable and dangerously cunning. Yet after only two days he was realising that she was so much more than that: complex, passionate for the causes she believed in, loving. He could not deny that he was enjoying the game of bluff and double bluff between them but he was also starting to want much more. He wanted Teresa Darent. He wanted all of her. He needed to strip away the pretence and uncover the woman beneath, to take her, and keep her and know all her secrets. He, the hunter, was falling prey to the very woman he was intent on capturing. And he did not know how the game would end.

CHAPTER SEVEN

TOM BRADSHAW STOOD ON LONDON Bridge and watched the waters of the Thames slide below, black and smooth, shifting light and dark. It was a bad night to be out, a cold night with a haze of snow on the wind. The sky was impenetrably dark.

There was a cold feeling in Tom's heart too and the knowledge that matters were not falling out according to his plans. Twice now he had tried to persuade Emma to take him back and twice she had refused him. He knew she was not going to change her mind. The Lady Emma Brooke he had known a bare year before, the girl he had courted, seduced and married was gone. That Emma had been sheltered and spoiled, a product of her class and her upbringing. Lady Emma Bradshaw was a different matter, her character honed by loss and despair; she was stronger, wiser and all the more desirable for it.

All his life Tom had had success with women and he had never believed for a moment that he could not persuade Emma to come back to him. They had been two of a kind. They had had an attraction, an affinity that bound them together. Emma was the only woman that Tom had genuinely loved—although he had said the words to plenty of other women, he had never meant them. It was for Emma alone that he had returned to England, wanting to take her with him to start a new life.

It was not to be. Tom leaned his elbows on the stone parapet of the bridge and watched the water tumbling beneath the arches. The cold cut through his thin jacket like a knife. His fortunes had turned. He had always been lucky in the past but not anymore.

He had suspected at first that it was his half-brother, Garrick, who had been behind the abduction that had seen him on the ship to the Indies. Now he knew better. Garrick Farne was an honest man who might have Tom arrested for attempted murder but would never act against him in an underhand manner. No, Tom's enemy was more deceitful than that, slippery and dangerous, a threat to all around him. Justin Brooke. Justin had pledged Emma his love and support whilst ruthlessly, secretly, attempting to rid her of her husband.

Tom's fist smashed down onto the parapet. He knew that the Brookes had disapproved of him, of course. Oh, they had made the best of their daughter's marriage in public in order to avoid a scandal but he suspected that from the first they had been plotting to be rid of him. That was understandable, almost forgivable. What he could not forgive was that in the process they had made Emma suffer too, his beautiful Emma, disgraced and cast out, sacrificed to their pride. And now Justin had the hypocrisy to pretend that he loved his sister and wanted to protect her....

Emma was not the only one Justin threatened. Teresa Darent, the only person who had helped Emma and shown her kindness when her family had abandoned her, was in jeopardy too. Tom knew that Justin Brooke would sell out his political principles—and his allies— for the sake of gaining power. Brooke had already gone to Lord Sidmouth and promised names in return for a deal.

Tom shifted. He was assailed by two very unfamiliar emotions. The first was selflessness and it was the impulse that prompted him to keep Emma safe. No matter that she wanted nothing more to do with him, no matter that she could never be his again, Emma's future was now more important to Tom than his own.

The second emotion was guilt.

Tom had never in his life been troubled by guilt. He had done many bad things but had never regretted them. Now, though, Teresa Darent haunted him. He was obsessed by the terrible thing that he had done to her ten years before. He had been much younger, of course, and he had not realised at the time how serious the repercussions of his actions had been, not until he had heard about Melton's art exhibition. Tom could of course blame Brokeby—Brokeby had been the ringleader, the libertine, a man steeped in dissipation. But where Brokeby had led, Tom had followed. He had not known who Tess was at the time, had not even recognised her when he had met her again eight years later. It was not until he had heard some throwaway remark in a coffee shop about Lady Darent and her previous marriages that he had made the connection. The horror of it had filled his thoughts ever since.

He owed Tess Darent a double debt. And the one thing he would do, besides protecting Emma, was to ensure that those who wanted to bring Lady Darent down, to frame her for their own crimes, would never succeed. The powers ranged against Tom were substantial but he thought he might have one ally. Lord Rothbury was the Home Secretary's man but he was also Lady Darent's betrothed. And he was an honest man. Tom was sure of it. Rothbury was not deep in the conspiracy and double-dealing that reached as high as the Home Secretary himself.

Tom drove his cold hands into the pockets of his jacket and started to walk back towards the docks, the place he had come from as a child, the warren of back-streets and rookeries that was his home. He had work to do. He would write to Rothbury—anonymously, of course—and warn him to keep Lady Darent safe. It would go a small way to repaying his debt to her and easing the guilt.

"My lady!"

"Don't tell me." Tess rolled over and buried her face in the pillow. "Lord Rothbury is here to disturb my sleep again." She yawned, forcing her eyes open a crack. "Pray tell him to leave me in peace."

isiting the Tower of London, they went to
ion at the Dulwich Picture Gallery.

you like paintings," Rothbury said
n Tess asked him why. "Often when you
ery visual imagery and when we are out
king at things with an artist's eye." He
have a lot of talent."

ittle talent," Tess admitted warily. She
e political cartoons she'd recently com-
a pang of guilt. The previous afternoon
three of them to the printers in Cheapside
ing they were on sale on the streets for a
he one depicting the government seated
binet table like a line of fat suet puddings
ple outside the window starved was prov-
ly popular.

s smile broadened at her qualified ad-
are too modest," he said. He helped her
e carriage and guided her into the gallery
l on the small of her back. Even through
of her pelisse Tess could feel his thumb
y along her spine. It was distracting, as
of him. As he moved she caught a hint of
air and clean linen. She was accustomed
ere polished and pomaded to within an
ves. They smelled so strongly of cologne
into the room before they did. Rothbury,
nelled of masculinity and the outdoors,
would have expected him to do. At the

"His lordship requests the pleasure of your company
on a trip to see the Tower menagerie, my lady," Margery said. "I have lovely hot water here for you," she
added coaxingly. "And the fire is already lit and the
room is warm."

"The Tower menagerie?" Tess grumbled, sliding further beneath the covers. "I do not like animals."

"Yes, you do, my lady," Margery, literal as ever, corrected her. She was already warming Tess's petticoats
before the fire. "Do you remember the time you bought
that kitten in the market from the man who had it in a
cage, and the bird that flew into the window and you
fed it milk?"

Tess gave a sharp sigh. There was no chance of sleep
now, not with Margery's chatter dragging her awake.
"I dislike seeing animals in captivity," she corrected.
"That sad leopard at the Tower... One cannot blame it
for moulting, trapped in this climate." She slid out of
bed, wincing at the cold that wrapped about her and set
her shivering.

"I really do not know why I am doing this," she muttered.

"It's because you like Lord Rothbury, my lady." Margery was unanswerable in this mood. "Admit it. You
know you do."

"It is a marriage of convenience," Tess said shortly,
"though what is convenient about being dragged from
one's bed under cover of darkness is anyone's guess."

Nevertheless she was shocked by the pleasure she

felt when she descended to the drawing room—they were so early that no one else but the servants were awake this time—and found Rothbury waiting for her. He was standing by the window looking out on the snow that was tumbling from a sky as lumpy and grey as an old mattress. The room looked dull and dark but when he turned and smiled at her, Tess felt a happiness so acute that for a moment it robbed her of speech. She could feel a smile starting and turned it into a severe look.

"My lord—here again? And so early?"

Rothbury's answering smile rocked her heart. "I wanted to see you again," he said easily.

"Why?" Tess asked bluntly. Such frankness was not her usual style. She wondered if his candour was contagious.

"Why not?" He looked puzzled. "I enjoy your company too much to waste the day spending it without you."

I enjoy your company...

Tess could feel a tide of colour flooding her face. It was such a simple statement to make her feel so flustered. She had thought her town bronze burnished to the highest polish. It was extremely disconcerting that Rothbury could agitate her like this. And when he did she was in danger of forgetting everything; forgetting that he was the man who could ruin her, forgetting that she had set out to use him, forgetting everything in the sweet pleasure of knowing him better each day.

"I really do not like nagerie," she said quic sion. "It feels unnatura as downright cruel to our British winters."

"What a soft heart rior." Rothbury had co now. He was rubbing of it, which did nothi "Who would have tho proving," he added, earlier today expecti three-quarters of an with an appraising breathless, "that you

"You flatter me," had not had time to into one braid and p ardly that strands w

"I never flatter," His were such a clea so compelling. "Yo me," he said. "I ne and cannot see a u

The hot, giddy, intensified. "I do depart this mornin so that she did not

Instea see the e "Beca smoothly talk you I see you smiled. "
"I hav thought o pleted and she had ta and this m penny eac around the whilst the ing particu
Rothbu mission. "y down from with one ha the thickne moving ger was the sce it, of cold fr to men who inch of their that it walke in contrast, exactly as sl

same time there was something knee-weakeningly familiar about his scent. Her body seemed to respond to it and the knowledge made Tess feel hot and aware.

Fortunately, once they were inside Rothbury released her and so she was able to concentrate on the collection rather than on his proximity. The elegant rooms of the Picture Gallery housed some marvellous Dutch landscapes and English portraits, and Tess was soon engrossed, wandering from room to room, discussing light and style with the curator, who was only too happy to have a knowledgeable visitor. Even so, she was very conscious of Rothbury watching her as she viewed the paintings.

"I'm sorry," she said at one point. "I am taking so long and I am sure that you must be bored." But Rothbury only smiled.

"It is reward enough for me to see your pleasure," he said, and Tess blushed as she felt the happiness slide through her in response to his words.

Eventually she was obliged to admit that her feet were too sore and that she was too tired and hungry to stay a moment longer. It was only when Rothbury commented that the gallery was closing in ten minutes that she realised how late it was.

"I liked all the collections except the still-life paintings," she said, as Rothbury handed her up into the carriage.

"Too many dead pheasant and rabbits?" he said quizzically. He was still holding her hand, looking up at her, the wind disordering his hair and the pale late-afternoon sun striking across his eyes. "I said you had a soft heart," he said, "though you pretend otherwise."

Tess blushed again. It was becoming a bad habit. She felt quite ridiculously gauche.

"I like being able to put you to the blush," Rothbury said, swinging up into the carriage beside her. His eyes were warm as they dwelled on her face. "You give the impression of being such a sophisticate, Teresa. It is good to know that there is some vulnerability in you."

As far as Tess was concerned she was a mass of vulnerabilities, never more so than now when her hand was resting in his and his touch was insistent and called to something in her that Tess neither recognised nor understood. She withdrew her hand from his with rather more haste than finesse and saw him smile as he recognised her susceptibility. He looked damned pleased with himself, she thought, yet she was powerless to cut that satisfaction down to size.

Rothbury took her to the Fountain Tavern on the Strand for dinner and they ate mutton pie and drank warm beer.

"Goodness," Tess said as she took a seat in a booth tucked at the back of the inn, the table bare wood, the floor stone strewn with sawdust, "you do know how to show a lady a good time, Lord Rothbury."

Rothbury grinned. "I think that as we are betrothed, you should start to call me Owen," he said. "I am not a great one for formality and have no desire for my wife to sound like my butler."

"Our mother always called our father Lord Fenner," Tess said, giggling. "We did not realise he had another name until we were well into our teens."

She looked around at the clientele. "I do believe this is a Whig tavern." She cocked her head. "An interesting choice for one of Lord Sidmouth's men."

"I like to live dangerously," Owen said. His eyes, brilliant with challenge, mocked her and Tess felt her heart flip.

"Don't you?" he added softly.

Tess almost choked on her beer. She met the dazzling demand in his gaze and felt a strange, heated sliding sensation in her stomach. She did not understand how Owen could tempt her so close to confession. Each day they spent together built the intimacy between them and with it her instinctive desire to trust him. But it was all an illusion. Just as she was using him, so he was trying to entrap her into indiscretion. She knew it. That was the game between them.

She gave him a cool little smile. "I think," she said deliberately, "that the real reason you chose to dine here is because you cannot afford better." She raised the beer glass in ironic toast. "I have not forgotten that your pockets are to let."

Owen gave a crack of laughter. Tess could see admiration in his eyes for the way she had so skillfully evaded his trap. She smiled demurely.

"Have you ever been rich?" she asked.

His eyes were still bright with amusement. "A few times," he admitted.

"What happened to the money?"

"Gambled away or spent."

He was certainly spare with the words, Tess thought. But always direct. She found it so attractive. She had to remember it was all part of the armoury he was deploying to make her fall.

"How odd," she said, cutting into the pie crust and inhaling the fragrant steam. "You do not strike me as a reckless spendthrift."

"When I was younger I did all manner of reckless things," Owen said. "Violent, even." There was a shade of something in his voice that Tess could not place. It sounded like regret, or bitterness. She was not sure. Owen was always so considered, so controlled. It made him very hard to read. He paused and for a moment Tess had the conviction that he was about to confide something in her. Then he shrugged. The moment passed. His throat moved as he took a long draught of the beer. "I was careless then," he said, "and I never thought of the future. I lived for no more than the moment and the next adventure."

The idea of a heedless young adventurer appealed to Tess. "Tell me about that," she said.

To her surprise, he did tell her, in more detail than his usual terse style. He told her all about his youth in Georgia and his family of two brothers and three sisters, and his father's business and the way that they had all gone without so that there would be enough money to buy him a commission in the American Navy.

By the time he was twenty-five he had sold out, bought his own ship and was his own master, and so it had stayed until he had received the letter that changed his life.

"The whole concept of inheriting wealth and title is foreign to me," he confessed. "I never sought to be Viscount Rothbury, never even imagined it."

"Yet you did not refuse the title," Tess said.

He looked at her, putting down his tankard with slow deliberation. "Can a peer do that? Damnation, I had no idea."

Tess burst out laughing. "You would not have done!"

"And disappoint my mother?" Owen shook his head. "No, you are right, I would not have done."

"Not just for your mother's sake," Tess said. "You are not a man to abandon your responsibilities or shirk the demands made on him."

Owen looked at her for such a long time that she started to feel uncomfortable. Once again she had the strangest feeling that he was about to say something important, something that was not a part of this game of bluff and double bluff between them but was a real insight into his soul. Then he smiled, that long slow smile, and Tess felt hot and giddy, as though she had drunk too much ale. His hand covered hers.

"Thank you, ma'am," he drawled, and Tess thought

she would melt into a puddle right there on the stone floor. She snatched her hand away.

"Don't practise that Southern charm on me," she said. "I'm too old a hand to be seduced like that."

Another smile. "Are you sure?" Owen said. There was a light as bright as a flame in his eyes and Tess felt as though she was dissolving in the heat of it. In that moment she was not sure of anything other than the fact that he was at least ten times more dangerous to her than she had imagined.

She cast around hastily for something else to say to cover her embarrassment. "You cannot be a Yankee if you come from Georgia," she said.

His mouth twisted. "The British tend to call all Americans Yankees," he said. "They are not particular, especially if they mean to be insulting."

His tone was mild but Tess sensed something deeper beneath the words, an edge of anger that he had found hard to forget. "I imagine you suffered a great deal of that when you were a prisoner of war," she said.

He nodded. His face was shadowed now. "It was no more than I expected."

Tess reached out impulsively across the table to touch the back of his hand. "Was it very bad?"

He stilled for a moment. His gaze was on her slender fingers as they rested against the tanned skin of his wrist. Tess realised with a little shock what she had done; normally she never touched anyone spontaneously. Then Owen looked up and, as their eyes met, she felt dizzy, as though she was falling. She wrenched her gaze away from Owen's and snatched back her hand.

It seemed a long time before he spoke.

"Physically I was well treated," he said, as though nothing had interrupted their conversation. "But I hated that I was not free. I cannot bear to be confined for long."

"Yes," Tess said. For a man accustomed to the high seas and wild empty spaces, to be penned in a parole town or locked in a gaol would have been near intolerable, his every move watched, all his activities circumscribed.

"I don't know how you could bear it," she said with a little shudder.

His eyes gleamed with amusement. "I'm a very patient man," he said. He shifted one booted leg across his knee. "I am always prepared to wait for the things I want."

For some reason his words sent another ripple of emotion—anticipation, nervousness—skittering down Tess's spine. She took a hasty gulp of her beer.

"I spoke to Corwen last night," Rothbury continued. "He should not trouble you again. I hear he left early this morning for an extended stay on his Herefordshire estates."

Tess looked him in the eye. "What did you do to him?"

Rothbury shrugged. There was a shadow of a smile about his mouth. "I spoke to him," he repeated.

"Is that all?" Tess said. "You spoke to him and he decided to leave London for his estates?"

The smile deepened. "What else?" Rothbury said. He lounged back in his chair, his body relaxed but his gaze cool and watchful.

"I don't know," Tess said. She felt confused. She had asked for Owen's help and he had given it freely. She had drawn on his strength and he had not failed her. Suddenly she was deeply ashamed of her deception. More than ever she wanted to trust him, to beg for openness between them. But it was too late. She was too frightened, in too deep. She hated the thought that Owen's help might have been calculated, nothing more than another step on the path to lead her to trust him. The web of deceit was getting so tangled and she could not bear it.

She felt the prickle of unexpected tears in her throat.

"Thank you," she said. Her face puckered. "I...I am truly grateful."

Owen took her hand and kissed the palm. "My pleasure," he said. His lips were warm against her skin, sending all kinds of ripples of sensation to the core of her. He sounded so sincere.

"I have the special licence," he added. "We may marry whenever you choose."

Tess jumped, snatching her hand from his. A tremor of disquiet shook her. "Marry?"

"It tends to follow a betrothal," Owen pointed out.

He was watching her, his green gaze lazy but still very acute.

"I need time to buy my trousseau," Tess said quickly. She knew she was prevaricating. The idea of actually marrying Owen still disturbed her and she was not sure why.

"A week?" Owen suggested.

"A week to do my clothes shopping?" Tess was horrified. "Certainly not! I need a month at least."

"Too long," Owen said. "Ten days."

"Two weeks," Tess said.

"Ten days," Owen repeated.

This time, Tess did not argue.

She slept surprisingly well that night and woke the following morning just as Margery was drawing back the curtains. She joined Owen downstairs thirty minutes later. They went to the Monument to the Great Fire of London and climbed up to the top to see all of London spread out below them, the smoke from a thousand chimneys lying across the cold city like a veil.

"You are such a tourist," Tess complained, as she tried to catch her breath from the three hundred and eleven steps. She had been appalled to discover that Owen actually expected her to join him on his ascent. "No one who lives in London bothers to climb up here."

"Then they are missing a wonderful view," Owen said, taking her hand and drawing her over to the rail. "Only see how beautiful London looks from here."

Tess leaned one hand on the rail, trying not to pant

with the exertion. Owen, she noticed, was not even breathing hard, as though the exercise had been no more than a walk in the park to him. The wind was cutting and cold but she had to admit that the view was stunning. The breeze threatened to pull her bonnet right off, teased her hair into knots and stung her cheeks bright pink. She could feel them radiating like beacons.

"You look lovely," Owen said, as she put up a hand to catch the wayward bonnet. "Tousled and ruffled and nothing like a lady of fashion." The expression in his eyes was warm and, despite the coldness of the day, Tess felt as though she were standing near a furnace. This tendency she had to feel heated was starting to worry her. She had wondered the previous day if she had been developing an ague from going out so much in the cold weather.

"You can descend first," she said, "so that if I trip you will break my fall."

"It would be my pleasure to have you land on top of me," Owen said very gravely.

The following day he took her to the British Museum. "All shrunken skulls in boxes," Tess said, though she found it fascinating. In the evening they joined Alex and Joanna, Garrick and Merryn at Vauxhall Gardens for a winter concert. It felt odd to be part of a couple. Owen paid her the ultimate compliment of focussing his entire attention on her; he did not doze over his wine as Darent would have done, or watch other women like many of the rakes and bucks who ogled her from the boxes opposite whilst their wives sat ignored. It felt as Tess imagined a proper courtship might feel, though of course she had no real idea, never having had one.

That night Tess sat in front of her mirror and wondered what it might be like to kiss Owen, to kiss him properly without the shadow of fear that hung over all her thoughts of intimacy. She pressed her fingers to her lips and felt a little sensual quiver run through her and a heat in the pit of her stomach. She was so enrapt that she did not hear Margery come into the room to help her undress and jumped almost out of her skin when the maid spoke to her.

That night she could not sleep for hours, and when she did, her dreaming was feverish and full of strange images. She was dancing with Owen, waltzing with him, but the music was muted and all she could feel was the heat of his hands on her through the thin silk of her gown and the brush of his thigh against hers as their bodies moved against one another, and all she could hear was the thundering of her heart. Owen's touch and the slip and slide of the silk on her skin made her feel heavy and lush with a curious sensation of excitement. Then she was running with him out of the ballroom and out into the night, where they tumbled over into a yielding pile of snow as soft as a feather mattress. Then it *was* a mattress and she sank deeply into it, Owen beside her, and he kissed her and she felt blinding pleasure, a pleasure that dissolved all fear. She had a sense of knowing him down to his soul and a wrenching desire to know him more deeply still.

In her dream he stripped the clothes from her with sure hands and she felt the tug of his mouth at her breast and her whole body rose to meet his, and she woke up abruptly, hot and panting, to find the sheet wrapped tightly about her. She felt ripe and full with wanting and for a moment she lay unmoving in the darkness, her senses dazzled by such strange and unfamiliar sensations. It was extraordinary to her that in her dreams, in her *fantasies* of Owen, she could step beyond the painful memories that were an absolute barrier to physical intimacy in real life. She had felt no fear or revulsion. There had been nothing but pleasure and deep, sensual fulfilment, and now she wanted to cry because she reached after that satisfaction only to feel it leach away as the familiar terror took its place, filling all the dark corners of her mind.

When she woke in the morning the dream was no more than a faded ghost, but even so she wondered if she would blush when she saw Owen and remembered the dreams of what he had done to her. In any event she need not have worried; she waited and waited but Margery did not come to wake her. Owen, it seemed, had not come that morning.

"You have a face as miserable as a wet Wednesday," Joanna commented when Tess came down for breakfast at nine, "and since when did you get up at this hour?"

There was a note from Owen waiting for her in the

hall. Tess knew immediately he had written it himself from the brief, blunt style of the wording. He apologised for not calling on her, explaining that he had arranged to see Mr. Churchward about the marriage settlements that afternoon. Tess moped about the house for a few hours, picking up magazines and casting them aside, then decided to go shopping and spent a thoroughly miserable time in Bond Street before going home and drawing some vicious cartoons. She had not meant to do it again but it was the only way to give vent to her feelings.

When she had agreed to be the pattern card of propriety that society demanded in order to save her reputation, she had intended it all to be for show. But she knew that what she was starting to feel for Owen was not pretence and it scared her. It scared her very much. She had let him get too close to her. She had started to need him. And that could never be allowed to happen.

CHAPTER EIGHT

OWEN HAD ARRIVED VERY promptly at the offices of Churchward and Churchward, lawyers to the noble and discerning, and was shown into the inner sanctum with commendable speed. The room was beautifully proportioned with a very pleasant aspect over a courtyard at the back, though today it looked out on a leaden sky and a tree with only a few sad leaves left to shiver in the late-November breeze.

Mr. Churchward stood up to shake Owen's hand and show him to a chair, subjecting him to a very shrewd look as he did so. Owen had the impression that Mr. Churchward was sizing him up, and reserving judgement for the time being.

"I am very pleased to make your acquaintance, Lord Rothbury," Churchward said, "and even more pleased to have your business." He waved a hand over the pile of papers stacked neatly on the desk. "Lady Darent has entrusted me to act for her in the matter of the marriage settlements." Rueful amusement touched his voice. "I fear that financial matters bore Lady Darent."

"And yet Lady Darent is nowhere near as feather-brained as she pretends," Owen said gently.

A gleam of humour lit Mr. Churchward's eyes. "If you have ascertained that already, my lord, then it seems you are a most perceptive man."

"I hope so," Owen murmured. "Of course, I am not the only one to admire Lady Darent's sharp mind. I understand that her late husband made her a joint trustee—with yourself—of his children's estate?"

"Ah," Churchward said. He paused. "Yes. I was going to broach that matter with you later, my lord, but as you raise it…" He leaned his elbows on the vast expanse of mahogany desk and steepled his fingers. "Lady Darent requests that, as her husband, you be appointed as a third trustee to the Darent estates, and I am happy to agree. That is, if you are prepared to take the responsibility, of course."

Owen felt surprise, then a rush of warmth and pleasure that shocked him. He had not expected this. It floored him. He knew Tess might be hiding other secrets from him but when it came to Julius and Sybil she was loving and protective. She would never use them, so the fact that she wanted him to share the trusteeship of her stepchildren meant that she must have confidence in him. She was starting to trust him. Owen knew at once that he had to have the matter of the Jupiter Club resolved between them. He must confront Tess and force her to be completely honest with him.

To take their relationship any further when it was based on deceit would be a travesty.

Mr. Churchward was saying, with careful lack of emphasis, "Of course, if you do not care for the idea, my lord—"

"No." Owen pulled himself together. "Of course. I should be honoured to accept."

Churchward allowed himself a prim smile. "Thank you, my lord."

For the next half hour they discussed the details of the marriage settlement. Tess, Owen was shocked to discover, was worth almost two hundred thousand pounds rather than the conservative estimate of one hundred and fifty thousand she had told him. He felt a little winded to think of it. He was also interested to realise that Mr. Churchward, who had a mind like a steel trap and judgement to match, clearly approved of Lady Darent. That made him very curious, for Churchward was no fool, nor a man to be influenced by charm and a pretty face.

"You mentioned that you administer all of Lady Darent's financial affairs," Owen said slowly, "and clearly you have done an excellent job, Churchward—sound investments, judicious expenditure..." He waited. Churchward inclined his head to accept the compliment but did not say anything.

"I wonder," Owen said. "Do you also pay Lady Darent's gambling debts?"

Mr. Churchward permitted himself a rueful smile. "Lady Darent never loses," he said. "Or very rarely."

Owen narrowed his gaze. "Then these sums here—" He tapped the deficit column on the accounts where small, regular sums were annotated in Churchward's neat hand. "These payments must be for something other than debts?"

Just for a second he surprised on the lawyer's face an expression that could almost be described as shifty. Certainly it was the expression of a man who had nearly allowed himself to be trapped into indiscretion and was thinking very quickly about how he might get himself out of the fix he was in.

"Mr. Churchward?" Owen prompted smoothly.

Churchward took off his glasses and polished them a little feverishly on the tails of his coat.

"I had no notion you would wish to look at the accounts in such detail, my lord," he said. He sounded slightly reproachful.

"No doubt it is *bourgeois* of me," Owen agreed pleasantly. "My father was a shopkeeper and—" He shrugged. "Old habits…"

"Quite," Churchward said, not budging an inch.

Owen smiled. "So," he prompted again. "These sums of money…"

Churchward huffed. "You would have to ask Lady Darent about that, my lord," he said.

"There are regular payments to a variety of different concerns," Owen pursued. The payments were all numbered but anonymous. He raised his eyes from the columns of figures to see Churchward watching him very closely.

Owen thought about Tess Darent, of what he had learned of her in the past ten days. He took a guess.

"These must be charitable donations," he said. "Gifts to philanthropic causes."

Mr. Churchward's gaze flickered. "My lord," he said repressively. "I cannot help you. You *must* speak to Lady Darent."

"Or perhaps they are political affiliations," Owen said ruthlessly, and saw the lawyer's shoulders tense. "Money given to radical charities and political groups."

"My lord." There was steel in Churchward's tone now.

"When Lady Darent and I wed," Owen said, throwing the papers carelessly down on the desk, "I will be in control of this enormous fortune. Does that affect your discretion in any way, Churchward?"

Now there was no doubting the lawyer's ire. "Certainly not, my lord," he snapped.

"I thought not," Owen said. He smiled. "My apologies, Churchward. I was but testing your loyalty. Forgive me. You are the soul of discretion and I would be honoured if you took on my business in future."

He watched the tension slide from Churchward's shoulders. The lawyer, he thought, not only admired Tess Darent but also exhibited a fatherly care for her. It was telling that she could inspire such liking and such loyalty in a man of Churchward's integrity.

"Thank you, my lord," Churchward said. "I am very glad. If I may make so bold, my lord," he added, as he escorted Owen to the door, "there is something I think you should know."

Owen waited.

"Mr. Barstow, Lady Darent's first husband," Churchward said, choosing his words very carefully, "was the godson of the noted political reformer Sir Francis Burdett." His voice was dry. "Just in case you wondered at the origins of her ladyship's loyalty to the reformers' cause."

"I see," Owen said slowly. He remembered Tess telling him of Robert Barstow, the childhood friend who had given her security through marriage after the death of her father and brother. For the first time he felt a glimmer of understanding for her political allegiance. Tess was fiercely loyal. He already understood that. Barstow's cause had become her cause, he thought, and a way of giving her future some meaning when she had lost everything. He was racked with pity for the girl she must have been, widowed at nineteen, losing her father, her brother and her husband within so short a time.

OWEN WALKED BACK THROUGH the sleet and found a letter waiting for him on his return to Clarges Street. It was anonymous, short and very much to the point:

Ask Lord Sidmouth who is responsible for violence

in the reformist movement. And keep Lady Darent safe.
Someone close to her is set to betray her.

Owen almost threw the letter in the fire. He detested
anonymous letters and had no time for their insinua-
tions. As far as he was concerned, Sidmouth worked
to protect the rule of law, and in taking the Home Secretary's commission he had pledged himself to do the
same. Yet even as he discarded the letter, it troubled
him. The reference to Tess was too specific to ignore.
Only a week before he had sworn to entrap her, to play
her at her own devious game. Now his ambitions had
changed.

He went out again, this time to the Home Secretary's
office, where Lord Sidmouth kept him waiting a full
hour.

Sidmouth was in a bad temper. There was a crumpled cartoon on his desk, a caricature of the government sitting around a long table like a row of fat suet
puddings. Looking from the picture to Sidmouth's fat
jowls, so cruelly and accurately parodied, Owen found
himself almost betrayed into a wry smile.

"Of course I incite the radicals to violence," Sidmouth said contemptuously, in answer to Owen's question. "Good God, man, don't be so naive! I need an
excuse to arrest them! The political reformers had been
peaceful for years before I planted agents provocateur
amongst them." He brought his fist down on the desk
with a crash that made the papers jump and scatter.
"We don't need reform here! Perish the thought!" He

glowered at Owen from beneath drawn brows. "Do you want a revolution here like the damned French? Do you want to lose that pretty title of yours already and your head with it?"

Owen felt as though he had been kicked in the stomach. "Forgive me, my lord," he said tightly, "but the only danger here seems to come from the violence that you are deliberately stirring up, if I understand you correctly."

Sidmouth made a very rude noise. "You are too scrupulous, Rothbury," he sneered. "A man in my position has to make accommodations and compromises to succeed."

Owen felt his temper soaring dangerously at the sheer cynicism of it. "You do it to keep yourself in power," he said softly. "No better reason."

He was furious with Sidmouth for his duplicity and with himself for accepting the Home Secretary's commission at face value. He should have known better, he thought bitterly. When he had believed he was working for a just cause he had been no more than Sidmouth's dupe.

"I do it to keep the peace," Sidmouth roared. "Damn it, man, we need these repressive measures or we'll all be murdered in our beds!"

"By the men you have paid," Owen said coldly. He picked up the cartoons. "So if you captured Jupiter, you would hang him," he said slowly.

"Hang him? I'll make a bloody exhibition of him,"

Sidmouth said viciously. "And once I have bought Justin Brooke's loyalty, I'll know exactly who Jupiter is."

A cold trickle of apprehension slid down Owen's spine. Justin Brooke, the man the ton said was Tess's lover. He remembered the wording of the anonymous letter. *Someone close to Lady Darent is set to betray her....*

"Brooke?" he said. "He's a radical?"

"He's one of the leaders of the Jupiter Club," Sidmouth said with satisfaction. "I can buy him off though. He'd sell his own grandmother for political power and he'll sell the names of his conspirators for a lot less."

Hell. Owen could feel the net closing inexorably on Tess.

"Your methods make my hands feel dirty, my lord," he said very politely. "I am afraid I have no choice but to resign your service."

"Go, then." Sidmouth waved a dismissive hand. "Knew you'd turn native. Damned revolutionary! That's the trouble with you Yankees—don't know when you should be grateful."

"On the contrary, my lord," Owen said. "I never felt more grateful to be an American than I do now."

He went out into the cold afternoon and drew several appreciative breaths of cold winter air. Sidmouth's cynical manoeuvring left him feeling sick, but Justin Brooke's potential to betray his colleagues troubled him more. Now more than ever he needed the truth between himself and Tess. There was no one else who could protect her.

He went directly to Bedford Street, but Tess was not there. Once again she had left him no note and no direction. This time Owen was not remotely amused. Urgency and fear drove his steps; he returned home to throw on his evening clothes and took the carriage to Lady Marriott's ball.

Tess was not there. Fortunately Merryn and Garrick Farne were, and it was Merryn who remembered that Lady Dalton was also holding a rout that evening.

"You may find Tess there," she said dubiously, "but I cannot be certain. She is something of a law unto herself."

"She is indeed," Owen said, with a touch of grimness. He gritted his teeth as the carriage rattled and pushed its way at a snail's pace through the busy streets.

He felt the atmosphere as soon as he walked into Lady Dalton's ballroom, the flutter of comment as people noticed him, the flash of a fan hiding a smile. The reason for their interest was not far to seek, for across the vast acreage of polished floor Owen could see Tess and, beside her, Justin Brooke. Tess was wearing scarlet tonight; a scarlet gown, scarlet slippers and a scarlet ribbon threaded through her curls. Beside her Brooke looked tall, handsome and arrogant, presumptuous in a manner that Owen found deeply offensive in a youth whose entire life was a testament to privilege.

Justin Brooke, Owen thought, had had everything he wanted served up to him on a silver platter.

Everything, it seemed, including Teresa Darent.

For as Owen watched, Brooke bent his head and whispered intimately in Tess's ear and a moment later Tess left his side and slipped out of a door on the opposite wall. Brooke waited only a second before following her.

It was blatantly, breathtakingly indiscreet. Owen could barely believe it.

Slowly, carefully, he stalked around the edge of the ballroom, acknowledging the greetings of his acquaintances, pausing to exchange a word here, a smile there, wondering all the time just what these people could read on his face, knowing they thought him a cuckold before the marriage lines were even written. He could feel the fury seething inside but he kept a cool head. There might, of course, be some rational explanation as to why Tess had chosen to behave with such indiscretion when she had promised him only ten days before that she wished to reform her reputation. On the other hand, he could not imagine what it might be.

He reached the door that Tess had gone through and slipped out of it to find himself in a smaller hallway; from there a passage ran down to a garden door at the end, and halfway down, almost obscured by an arrangement of ferns and foliage, stood Tess and Justin Brooke.

Tess's auburn curls were brushing Brooke's shoulder. His dark head was close to hers as he spoke to her.

Owen could not hear the words but sensed the urgency and the intimacy. Brooke had a hand on Tess's arm and as Owen watched he slid that hand down to take hers and press it between both of his in a heartfelt gesture. Tess smiled up at him. Brooke drew her closer and kissed her cheek, his lips lingering as though he wanted to do a great deal more.

Shock and anger punched Owen in the gut. Tess showed none of the physical reticence with Brooke that she had done with him, no reluctance for his touch. What a fool he had been to believe her when she had told him that she and Brooke were not lovers. He had imagined them no more than political allies. He had been more than a fool, in fact, since he had been utterly duped into providing not only security for Tess against Sidmouth's investigation but also cover for her *affaire*. He had sought her out tonight, anxious to have the truth out between them, prepared to offer her his protection because he despised what Sidmouth was doing to entrap her and he admired her for her loyalty to her cause and he had thought her sincere. Yet instead of binding her closer to him he had found her with her lover. And of course Brooke would never betray her to Sidmouth. She was his mistress and whatever political advancement he received, he would take Tess with him.

Owen saw Brooke gesture slightly with his head towards the garden door. He went out. A few seconds later Tess came back down the corridor and passed Owen so closely that he could smell her jasmine scent.

Her scarlet skirts brushed the statue of Apollo he was hiding behind. She went through into the hallway and headed for the ladies' withdrawing room. A second later she emerged, cloaked and hooded, and slipped away out of the front door and into the street. There was a clatter of hooves on the cobbles as a hackney carriage pulled away. Brooke evidently had had one waiting.

"Rothbury! Capital stuff!" Rupert Montmorency accosted Owen as he was hurrying towards the door. "Already paid my compliments to the lovely Lady Darent." Rupert winked. "She seemed to be leaving in a hurry—"

"Not now, Rupert," Owen said. "I have to go—"

"Frightfully bad *ton* to interrupt your future wife with her lover," Rupert said. "Give them an hour. Or perhaps two to be on the safe side," he added thoughtfully.

"Thank you, Rupert," Owen said tightly. He was aware that a number of people had emerged from the ballroom and were watching him, eyes avid and scandal tripping from their tongues. Tess's departure had not gone unnoticed, then. The gossip was already starting to filter through the ball, rippling around the edges of the room and sweeping inwards like the tide.

There was a light touch on his arm. "I imagine you are thanking God now that you are such a cool hand at cards," Alex Grant said, in his ear. "I assure you, no one looking at you would realise you wish to break Brooke's neck and I only realise it because I know you so well."

"I'm not sure that his is the neck I wish to break," Owen said grimly. He was remembering again Tess's claim: *Justin Brooke is not my lover....*

What sort of fool had he been to believe her?

"Are you going to let her get away with it?" Alex asked, with an expressive lift of his brows.

"What do you think?" Owen beckoned to the footman. "The carriage for Lady Darent," he said. "Where did it take her?"

The man's face was completely blank. "I'm sorry, my lord—"

Owen swallowed a curse. "Lady Darent and Mr. Brooke," he clarified. "Where did they go?"

The man's face cleared. He looked inordinately relieved to be able to help. Owen realised that such was his anger the man probably thought he would strangle him if he could not answer the question. He strove to bank down that anger and moderate his tone.

"It was an address in Hampstead Wells, my lord. Belsize Terrace," the footman stuttered.

"Thank you," Owen said, and the man shot away as though his life depended on it.

"That'll take you the best part of an hour," Alex said.

"I don't have anything better to do," Owen said drily. "Hampstead Wells," he added. "Where is that?"

"North of town, very genteel, very respectable," Alex said, a little grimly. "Good luck, old fellow."

Luck, Owen reflected, was not precisely what he needed. Better judgement when it came to women might serve him well in future. Nevertheless he would see Tess Darent and have the truth out with her before he broke their engagement and abandoned her to her sensual excesses with her young lover.

The journey out of town did indeed seem interminable, endless ill-lit streets giving way to darkened roads along which the carriage jerked and jolted. Finally Owen alighted in front of a small row of cottages. The footman had only heard a partial address. Impossible to tell which of these houses held his errant fiancée, but perhaps he could start with the one that still had candlelight showing behind the shutters.

His knock brought a housemaid scurrying. She looked terrified. No wonder. Owen was not at all sure what was showing on his face now that he did not have to conceal his feelings and since he had had the best part of an hour to dwell on them. He had never been a possessive man, or so he had thought, but now he felt every drop of the white-hot fury a man would feel when he caught his woman with a lover. He felt as though he cared. It angered him that he had been deceived; it angered him that his name had been dishonoured and, more than anything, it angered him that it mattered.

"Is Lady Darent here?" he demanded, when the door opened to his peremptory knock.

The housemaid, mute, eyes wide as dinner plates, nodded.

"I'll announce myself," Owen said, pushing the door wide and striding into the hall. The house was tiny, the

corridor so narrow he felt as though the walls were closing in on him. His fury needed more space than this.
He felt hemmed in and could feel the anger boiling up
in him. He exerted absolute control to keep it down. No
point in frightening the maid. She was already trembling and her face was pale as milk.

He strode down the passageway. The house was
very simple; plainly decorated, a couple of good quality
paintings on the wall and a thin strip of carpet woven
in bright colours. He would have expected that Tess
would wish for a great deal more luxury from her love
nest than this. Surely she would want a deep feather bed
and plump pillows, and smooth satin against her naked
skin?

The image was unexpectedly erotic and did nothing
to sooth his temper. Devil take it, Tess Darent was *his*
betrothed, not Brooke's, and he had treated her with
absolute respect. He had not even kissed her yet. More
than once in the past week he had wondered why not.
His desire for her had not diminished. If anything it
had become keener because he had started to know her
and to like her very much. He had no longer lusted after
Tess simply because she was beautiful, a physical em-
bodiment of some sinful fantasy. The real Tess Darent
had seemed quite different from the dream, sharp and
sweet, strong yet vulnerable, a woman of decided opin-
ions and determined will. He had admired her very
much. He had wanted her very much.

Owen was not a man accustomed to delayed gratification where women were concerned. Generally he took his pleasure as he saw it. His liaisons had been enjoyable but in the past they had lacked the depth to hold him. With Tess it had been different—or so he had thought.

He could hear voices from a room to the left. At least if they were talking he would not catch them in the act of making love, though it was not going to be pretty. He could imagine it all: Tess in a state of undress perhaps, her bodice undone to give a glimpse of the curve of her breasts beneath, her hair unbound in all that glorious red-gold profusion. Brooke would be lying back against the pillows with that curst youthful arrogance of his and beckoning her to come to his bed....

Owen opened the door.

And realised that he had made a monumental mistake.

The first thing that he noticed was that there were three people in the tiny parlour and they were all fully clothed. Furthermore they were drinking tea from bone china and could not have looked more respectable had they been at a vicarage garden party.

Tess was seated in an elegant old wing chair before the fire. There was a sketching pad with pencil drawings open on the table beside her. Opposite her was a young lady of strikingly pretty appearance who overset her cup when Owen burst in and sent tea cascading onto the worn rug in front of her. A fair proportion of it showered Justin Brooke, who had been kneeling in front of the fire toasting crumpets.

Toasting crumpets... Owen had rushed in expecting to find his fiancée *in flagrante* and instead found her alleged lover toasting crumpets. A faint sense of the ridiculous possessed him. He could not help himself.

Tess got to her feet with exquisite, unruffled calm. Or perhaps she was not so calm, Owen thought. Certainly she was very careful to surreptitiously cover the sheets of sketches as she moved forwards to greet him.

"Good evening, my lord," she said, as though Owen's precipitate appearance was both expected and extremely welcome. "I am so happy that you could join us." Owen doubted that, but Tess was already turning to the young lady. "May I introduce Lady Emma Bradshaw?" she said. "I believe you are already acquainted with her brother, Mr. Brooke."

Brooke gave Owen the very slightest and most awkward of bows. "Rothbury," he said.

"Brooke," Owen said coldly. Whatever the situation here—and clearly he had misjudged it somewhat—this was a man for whom he had absolutely no respect and he did not trouble to pretend otherwise.

Brooke's face took on a deep flush. Sensing Owen's blatant hostility, Tess once again threw herself into the breach.

"Lady Emma," she said, drawing the girl forwards. "This is my fiancé, Viscount Rothbury."

Owen found himself the subject of a very frank gaze

from Lady Emma's enormous blue eyes. It was evident from a single glance, he thought, who had inherited the strength of character in the Brooke family.

"I hope," Emma said, "that you are good enough for Lady Darent, my lord."

It was not a concept that Owen had ever considered before. He cast a glance at Tess and saw her lips twitch as she tried to hide a smile.

"I am not certain that that is the thought uppermost in Lord Rothbury's mind at present, Emma," she murmured.

"Well, it should be!" Lady Emma took Owen's hands in a firm clasp and drew him down to sit beside her on the settle. "You should know, my lord," she confided, "that when my husband deserted me last year and my family disowned me, it was Lady Darent who took me in and persuaded the Duke of Farne to provide for me—" Her gesture encompassed the little parlour and all that was in it. "She has been the best and most generous of friends to me."

Out of the corner of his eye, Owen saw Tess shift uncomfortably in her chair. He could see that Lady Emma's words, however well intentioned, disturbed her.

"Not only that, but Lady Darent has enabled Justin to visit me, my lord," Emma was saying. "When my family cast me off, my parents forbade him to see me ever again. They threatened to cut him off without a penny but he was determined not to abandon me."

It was Brooke who shifted this time and Owen hoped it was with guilt to be given so much credit for so little. The pieces of the picture were beginning to move into place in his mind. He could see precisely how Tess had enabled Justin Brooke to continue to visit his sister. Their supposed affair was the most perfect cover for his clandestine visits, not to a mistress but to a sister he could no longer publicly acknowledge. Owen deplored the craven way in which Justin had used Tess and he could not understand why she had permitted it. He had been right before when he had sensed that there was not one iota of sexual attraction between them. The idea was absurd. He felt an enormous relief, but it was still edged with anger for Tess's indiscretion in publicly dishonouring his name and the protection he offered her, as well as ruining her own reputation so carelessly.

"There must have been a very important reason that led you to ask Lady Darent to come here tonight, Lady Emma," he said softly. "What was it?"

He felt Tess stir. She took a step towards him.

"My lord—" she began.

Owen turned his head and looked at her. "Do you wish to tell me," he said coolly, "or permit Lady Emma to do so?"

Tess looked across at Justin Brooke, and Owen felt his temper soar dangerously again. No, Tess and Brooke were not lovers, but there was something very strong that drew them together. He could sense it. They were political allies but it was more than that. He remembered the payments on Churchward's balance sheet. If Tess had been funding Brooke, perhaps in the manner Sir Francis Burdett had funded her first husband's political ambitions, it might explain why she had taken both of the Brooke siblings under her wing in different ways. She was Justin Brooke's benefactor. Owen felt an even greater contempt for the man then, thinking of his clandestine meetings with Sidmouth and his pledges to change allegiance and give up the names of his radical allies.

Brooke made an instinctive move towards Tess, quickly checked when Owen turned sharply on him. Brooke was running a finger around the collar of his shirt as though it were so tight it was cutting off his breath. Which would be no bad thing, Owen thought. He wondered when—or if—Justin Brooke would develop a spine and not only stand up for himself but also openly defend those he claimed to love. The man was weak through and through.

"Do you have anything to say, Mr Brooke?" he asked with immaculate courtesy.

"No, my lord," Brooke mumbled. He did not meet Owen's eyes. "This is my sister's business, not mine."

"Tom has come back," Emma said in a rush. "Tom Bradshaw. My husband." Her fair, open face was flushed and troubled, her blue eyes pleading. "I didn't know what to do." She wrung her hands in a gesture of unconscious distress. "I was fearful, upset, so I sent to Justin to ask Lady Darent to help me." She stopped.

"I didn't know what to do," she repeated, more softly. "I love Tom and I don't want to see him arrested, but I cannot trust him and I know he has done some terrible things." She stopped. The misery was palpable in her voice. "I thought that Lady Darent would know what to do," she said, turning towards Tess. "She always helps me."

Tess took both of Emma's hands in hers and drew her close, as gently and unselfconsciously as a mother might do. Owen saw Justin Brooke watching them.

"You should turn him in," Brooke said viciously. "We could set a trap for him—"

"No!" Emma's cry was wrenching. "You always hated him—"

"Of course I did," Justin said. "Look what he did to you, Em. He's ruined you!" But Lady Emma had cast herself into Tess's arms now and was sobbing as though her heart would break. Owen watched Tess stroke the girl's bright hair and murmur soothing words to her, and he thought of the Darent twins and all the love Tess Darent had within her to give. He felt torn between tenderness for her and the deep anger that still burned in him.

He caught sight of Justin Brooke. Brooke was also looking at Tess and what Owen saw in his eyes gave him pause, for Brooke's expression was yearning, almost hungry. It might be the case that Tess had no romantic interest in Brooke, but Brooke most certainly wanted her, and that, Owen thought, made him more dangerous still.

CHAPTER NINE

THE SILENCE IN THE HACKNEY carriage was intense. Tess had never thought silence could be so loud. The atmosphere between them had changed as soon as they had stepped out of the house. She had not been naive enough to imagine that Owen would not be angry with her for what she had done that night, but she had hoped that by now the anger might be muted, knowing that she had come here only with Emma's best interests at heart. She glanced sideways at Owen's tense profile. There was a frown between his brows and his jaw was set hard. His disapproval, his censure, was so intimidating that she quaked. And it mattered to her. She felt as though her stomach had dropped away as she realised how much it mattered to have Owen's good opinion.

"You are angry with me," she said unsteadily.

The glance he gave her shredded her with its contempt. "How very perceptive of you, madam."

"It is instructive," Tess said. "I have never seen you angry before. I was beginning to think it was an emotion foreign to your nature."

His eyes were dark, inward looking. "You have no idea, I assure you."

Tess shrivelled a little. His words only served to emphasise how little she understood him. She had wondered what might move Owen to anger or passion. Now she knew. She had done it through her reckless lack of regard for his feelings and his honour.

"I'm sorry," she said. She had to start somewhere and abasing herself was probably the best place.

"Are you?" His tone was still clipped. He slanted a look at her. Tess could read nothing from it other than that it was not particularly friendly.

"It seems that you cannot help but be careless of your reputation," Owen said, and his tone stung her. "That is your choice. But you should not be so careless of my good name."

"No." Tess knitted her fingers together. She was all too aware that when Owen had agreed to wed her she had sworn to behave in future with the utmost propriety. He had taken her word. Then she had created a scandal before they were even married by leaving a ball with the man everyone assumed to be her lover. Owen's fury was entirely justified. Her behaviour had shown nothing but disdain for his name and his honour. It pained her to see his disappointment, more so because he had trusted her and she had let him down. She had not expected to feel his hurt. Yet within a few days, Owen's strength and generosity had already made her care and she could not escape that emotion.

"No," she said again. There was a hollow of misery under her heart. "I know. I am truly sorry."

She felt him shift his shoulders against the back of the seat and sensed the very slightest easing in his anger.

"Brooke is weak through and through," Owen said, "to hide behind your skirts." His tone held biting scorn.

Tess flinched. "You are harsh," she said, "but I suppose there is some truth in what you say. Justin—" She felt Owen shift at the familiarity and quickly corrected herself. "Mr. Brooke was not prepared to defy his parents openly and risk being cut off without a penny, but he still loves his sister and wishes to see her."

"Of course I am harsh," Owen said. "This is a man who has not only failed to stand up for what he believes in but also allows an older woman to take a very public responsibility for his actions." He turned directly towards her. "Was there no other way?" he said. Tess could feel the anger and frustration swirling in him. "No other way than to allow people to think he was your lover?"

Tess sighed. "People will think what they will," she said. "They always have done that. I realised long ago that I could not stop them and I ceased trying to change their minds."

"You should have tried harder," Owen snapped, turning away. "Behaviour such as this only encourages the rumours that Lord Corwen, for one, sought to exploit."

"I realise that," Tess said tiredly.

"Then why go tonight, in full view of everyone?"

Owen said. "Tell me, Teresa." He sounded exasperated. "I want to understand."

Tess was silent for a moment. She could feel his impatience as he waited, wound tighter than a loaded spring.

"I'm sorry," she said for a third time. "It was an error of judgement. Emma needed me and so I went to her." She rubbed her forehead. "It was a stupid thing to do. I see that. I should have sent word to Garrick and asked him to go to help Emma instead, but I knew he would wish to capture Tom and have him arrested. Emma did not want that, so…" She shrugged hopelessly.

"So you kept Emma's situation a secret and went yourself," Owen said grimly. "With Brooke. The least sensible option in front of an entire ballroom of people."

"I know." Tess felt miserable to her soul. She had thought about it so long and hard. When Justin had first approached her with Emma's news her heart had sunk to her slippers because she knew Emma had nowhere else to turn. She had hoped that as Owen was absent he might not hear of her apparent indiscretion or that at the least she would be able to smooth him over and make light of the matter. She glanced again at his profile, the harsh lines of his face in the skipping shadows of the carriage. She had underestimated him.

Owen was silent for a moment. "You have been a good friend to Lady Emma," he said. "It is not the first time you have helped a young woman in trouble, is it?

I heard that when Tom Bradshaw ruined Lady Harriet Knight a few years back you also gave her your aid."

"Oh, yes." Tess had forgotten about Harriet, who had married a very rich elderly squire and was no doubt creating havoc in the shires.

"One might almost say," Owen said, "that you have a compulsion to help people who are in trouble." His tone had eased but Tess was not fooled. Owen was going somewhere with this, somewhere dangerous. A quiver of apprehension ran along her skin. This was a side of Owen she had seen that first night at the brothel, cold and relentless in pursuit of the truth. She had forgotten quite how intimidating was the ruthlessness beneath his equable exterior.

"Two acts of charity do not make a compulsion," she said.

"Once again you are too modest," Owen said. "I understand that you are most generous in your charitable giving. You donate to the Foundling Hospital and the Blackfriars School—"

"You forgot the Magdalen Hospital," Tess snapped. "For penitent prostitutes. Appropriate, is it not?"

Owen laughed. "I hardly think so." He paused. "You do admit to being a philanthropist?" Then, when she did not reply, he said, "You are unconscionably bad at answering my questions. Teresa." Again there was exasperation in his voice. "I am not asking you to confess a thousand-guinea-a-week gambling debt. Why is it so difficult to admit to charitable giving?"

The answer was that her philanthropy was intimately linked to her political causes and in admitting one Tess knew she would inevitably betray the other. But she could feel Owen's gaze on her through the dark and she knew he knew the truth already. There was no point in dissembling.

Her heart took a dive down into her slippers. She felt wretchedly sick. Owen was going to confront her about the Jupiter Club. Here. Now. She sensed it. Swept up in the pleasure of the time they had spent together, she had almost forgotten that it was all based on dishonesty. She felt empty and lost.

"You know, don't you?" she said, and she was not referring to her philanthropy.

She felt him shift as he turned slightly towards her. "Know that you are Jupiter?" he said. "Yes, I do." He took something from his pocket and laid it on the rug between them. In the faint light of the carriage lanterns Tess could see it was the cartoon of Lord Sidmouth as a balloon. Owen smoothed his palm over it.

"It's an excellent likeness," he said. "Lord Sidmouth was not amused. He wants your head on a platter." He looked at her. There was a long silence. Tess knew what was coming and her stomach tumbled. The feeling of sickness at her betrayal thickened in her throat.

"Tell me," Owen said. His tone had hardened. "When you first came to me proposing marriage, was that a deliberate ploy because you knew that as your husband I would be unable to give evidence against you?"

Tess closed her eyes. Regret twisted inside her at the deception she had practised on him.

I did not know you then....

She wanted to cry out those words, but it was pointless to say them or to try to persuade Owen that she had come to like and respect him. He would never believe her. And what she felt for him was stronger than mere liking now. All of a sudden the tears stung her eyes.

"I...I thought... It's true that I..." She stopped again. She could feel Owen's gaze on her through the dark and it seemed to strip her defences to the bone.

"You thought that you would deceive me and use me as the perfect disguise to hide you from Sidmouth?" Owen said. His voice was very steady and very cold now.

"When I came to you my most pressing concern was for Corwen's threats and Sybil's and Julius's futures," Tess said. Her voice faltered. She could hear the plea in it.

"But any number of people could have helped you with that," Owen said. "Your brothers-in-law, for example. Both Alex Grant and Garrick Farne are influential enough to force Corwen to hold his tongue."

"I needed to do more than that," Tess argued. "I needed to repair my own reputation, for Sybil's sake. Only marriage could do that."

"But you chose me specifically," Owen said. "I wondered about that from the start. It was because of my connection to Sidmouth." Suddenly his hands bit into her shoulders. "Tell me the truth, Teresa," he said. "No more lies."

"I didn't lie!" Tess said. Desperation coloured her tone. She gulped in a breath. "Very well, I did seek to deceive you," she said. "But you knew it, Owen. You suspected me from the first! I know you did. You only let me play out my game because you were waiting to trap me."

There was a loaded silence. Tess realised how much she wanted him to deny it. She knew he would not. They had both played the game. And now it seemed they had both lost; lost the burgeoning trust and the closeness and the promise that had been between them.

"Touché," Owen said, after a moment. "I did indeed." His hands slid down her arms and Tess shivered. As his touch left her she felt very alone and utterly bereft. For a moment she thought she saw something in his face of regret, or disappointment, but as the shadows moved she saw only the coldness in his eyes and the harsh line of his jaw.

"The Jupiter Club is disbanded," she said. "We meet no more." Her heart felt sore and bruised now that the truth was exposed between them. It made their relationship feel so hollow and empty when it could have been so much more. "If you could be generous enough not to pursue the other members," she said stiffly, "I give my word that after our betrothal is broken I will not engage in further reformist activity—" She stopped as Owen put his hand on her wrist. His touch seared her like a flame, silencing her completely.

"My dear Lady Darent," he said, and all the smoothness was back in his voice, "I do not think you quite understand. Our engagement is not at an end. You are still going to marry me. You have even less choice than you had before."

OWEN WATCHED WITH AMUSEMENT as Tess struggled to assimilate his words. In the skipping darkness he could see the play of various emotions across her face: shock, puzzlement and a certain icy hauteur that suggested she disliked very much being dictated to. That, Owen thought, was too bad. He had had a difficult evening and he was in no mood to be chivalrous anymore. Tess was completely in his power now and that was where she would stay. He shifted, turning so that one shoulder was against the side of the carriage and he could see her face more easily.

"There are things you do not know," he said. "Specifically, Mr. Brooke, your political protégé." He allowed his contempt of Brooke to colour his tone. "He is in discussion with Lord Sidmouth to join the government. He blows with the wind. He will never be the leader that you wish, the leader the radical cause needs."

He saw Tess's face blanch in the lamplight, leaving it pale and drawn. "You must be mistaken," she whispered. Her shock was too vivid to be feigned. Owen felt a faint easing of the tension within him. It seemed she had never known of Brooke's betrayal; her allegiance to the reformers had at least always been true even if he still had to live with the bitterness of knowing that she had chosen him only to use him.

"I'm afraid I am not mistaken," Owen said. "I had it from Sidmouth himself. Brooke is ambitious. He will sacrifice anything for political power. Including you."

He saw Tess's eyes narrow. "I do not understand," she said. A little shudder racked her.

"I think you do," Owen said grimly. "Sidmouth wants to arrest Jupiter. Brooke knows who you are—"

He heard her give a gasp of shock. "Justin would never betray me," she said, but there was an undertone of uncertainty in her voice as though she was already afraid of the possibility.

"I hope you are right," Owen said, "but I would not lay any money on it." He shifted. "So you see how vulnerable you are. If you do not wed me you will be utterly unprotected."

Tess was silent for a very long time. "You are very generous not to withdraw your offer of marriage to me," she said, at length. Her tone was as cool and unemotional as his now.

"I have my reasons," Owen said. His reasons were simple. He still wanted Teresa Darent. He was angry with her and he felt betrayed by her, but he still wanted her in his bed.

Her gaze on him was unreadable. "I shall have a

great deal more money now that it will not be going to support the radical cause," she said ironically.

"And I shall have a great deal less," Owen said, "since I no longer work for Lord Sidmouth."

Her eyes opened wide. "You resigned? But why—"

"Give me credit for some principles," Owen said shortly. "I cannot knowingly wed a woman I know is a criminal whilst working for the man who seeks to arrest her."

He heard her breath catch to hear herself described in such brutal terms. "I suppose not," she said. "Well, then…" Her tone was dry. "You may take my money as recompense."

He would take her as recompense, Owen thought. For a second he was wrenched with sorrow that their marriage would be so shallow, the very fashionable affair that she had claimed she wanted. He had sought more than that in his wife, had wanted more, more of trust, more of belief, more of respect. But with their mutual deceit uncovered now it felt impossible.

"There is another price for my protection," he said.

He saw her look sharply at him. "A price," she said dully. "Yes, of course there would be. There always is a price." She sounded very tired all of a sudden, disillusioned.

"You have to give me your word of honour that you will never draw political cartoons again," Owen said, "or take an active role in the reformist movement."

He waited. She did not respond. She was fidgeting

with the braiding on her cloak. Suddenly he was shot through with regret and bitterness. He had not wanted it to be like this.

"Teresa," he said, a little roughly, after a moment. "It's too dangerous. Sidmouth will hunt all reformers down. Give me your promise."

Her head came up. He saw a tiny spark of warmth come back into her eyes to hear the ring of genuine emotion in his voice. It was such a small thing when the truth had torn apart the relationship they had only just started to build, but Owen knew in that instant that it had not all been pretence for either of them.

"Very well," she said, very quietly. "I give you my promise."

Owen felt his tense muscles relax. "Thank you," he said.

She turned her face away but not before he had seen the glint of tears in her eyes. Pity wedged in his throat; she was not the sort of woman to let him see her tears. She was not the sort of woman who willingly took help or comfort from anyone.

"Why do you cry?" he asked, and was almost amused when the look she shot him in return was pure anger rather than sorrow.

"Because of what I am losing." Her tone was crisp. "My drawing…" She rummaged in her reticule and withdrew a ridiculous scrap of lace, which she scrubbed fiercely at her eyes. "It matters to me. You wouldn't understand."

He did, actually, or he suspected he did. When he had taken his title he had given up his previous way of life, given up the sea and the exploring and the life that had made him the man he was. Like him, Tess was losing her passion and she would have to find a different way of living. He felt an impulse to tell her, to reach out and comfort her, but her shoulder was turned against him and she was staring fixedly out into the blind dark.

Owen sighed. "Are there any other secrets I should know before we wed?" he asked, and he did not miss the very slightest hesitation in her before she shook her head.

"No," she said, her tone quiet and unemotional again. "Of course not."

Almost he pressed her on it but in the end he let it go. Her shoulders were slumped now and for a moment she looked so small and poignantly alone that he had already put out a hand towards her before letting it fall again.

He wondered what it was that Tess was not telling him. It was nothing to do with the Jupiter Club or her radical politics. He was certain of that. She had been very candid about her identity as Jupiter and he had appreciated that honesty even whilst he had been angry with her for her earlier deceit. There was still much to admire in Teresa Darent, he thought. She had a loyalty to those she cared for, whether it was Julius and Sybil, or the foundling children of Blackfriars, or the members of the Jupiter Club.

He thought this final secret must be something to do with her choice of philanthropic causes amongst the poor and the dispossessed. They all involved women and children, those who had fallen from grace or been born out of wedlock. Had she perhaps had an illegitimate child during those wild early days after Charles Brokeby had died? There were those shocking nude paintings of her which, coupled with the stories of Brokeby's famous debauchery and Tess's uninhibited drinking and gambling after his death, all pointed to a phase of her life that had been recklessly out of control. Owen had been no saint himself and had a past as chequered as a draughts board, so he could not lay blame, but he did wish Tess would confide in him. Some people preferred not to expose the truth of the past, but in his experience it almost always came out anyway, and usually in the most painful way possible. But he had known Tess so short a time, and if he truly wanted to unravel all her secrets he would have to wait now. They would have to start to build again, slowly and carefully, on the foundations they had laid before. And this time there must be no deceit or betrayal.

He looked at Tess, at her profile turned away from him, so pure and clear. Every line of her body was taut and defensive, keeping him at bay, forbidding his touch.

He wanted her more than ever.

CHAPTER TEN

THEY MARRIED TWO DAYS LATER at Southwark Cathedral.

Lady Martindale's brother was Bishop of Southwark, a fact that Tess considered both convenient and marvellously respectable. It also solved the difficult issue of venue. Tess had been uncertain which London church to choose for her fourth trip up the aisle. She had certainly not wanted St. George's in Hanover Square, fashionable as it was, since she had married Brokeby there.

Her second wedding had been a huge affair even though she had been a widow and good taste might have suggested that she settle for something smaller. Brokeby, of course, had been a stranger to good taste. He had wanted to show off his beautiful young bride to the entire ton. It had been a bright May morning with resplendent sunshine and the cherry trees in blossom in the square. Within an hour, however, the brightness had turned hazy and the spring rain had started to fall heavily, washing away the blossom. Tess thought she really should have recognised the omen for what it was.

On this particular day the sky was a pearly grey with snow clouds blowing in over London like smoke. It felt chilly and raw. Tess tried to ignore the cold, tried too to banish the chill from her heart, which felt frozen with a chip of ice. The confrontation with Owen, revealing their mutual deception, had left her feeling like she had lost a true friend. Somehow, despite her intentions of making no more than a marriage of convenience, she had come to value Owen a great deal. And then she had lost him. The hollow sensation in her heart made her want to cry and she did not understand why.

It was fortunate that Southwark Cathedral possessed a very small chapel since the wedding party was sparse. Joanna was there, dazzling in cherry-red silk with a saucy hat. Merryn was in sapphire-blue. Both Tess's sisters sported the definitive accessory of a handsome and adoring husband. Joanna even had the ultimate trophy of a beautiful little daughter. Tess tried hard not to feel jealous and failed comprehensively. Rampant adoration of her sisters was all very well, she supposed, but not at *her* wedding when she was making a marriage of convenience. The contrast seemed too bleak.

It was not that Owen did not look handsome. In fact, when she had first seen him waiting for her at the altar, Tess had experienced a very peculiar fluttering sensation in her midriff. Owen had paid her the compliment of being immaculately turned out, unlike Darent, who had arrived late for his own wedding with his shirt hanging out. And Owen was not drunk, unlike Brokeby, for whom it had almost been a permanent state. In fact Owen did not take his eyes off her all the way up the aisle—she was alone because she was damned if

anyone was going to give her away other than herself—
and there was something in his gaze that made her feel
very hot even though it was snowing outside.

"You look beautiful," he whispered to her when she
reached his side, and for a second she had felt as though
it was summer and the sun was out.

But her feeling of pleasure was fleeting and shallow.
One glance at her sisters shot her through with another
pang of envy so sharp and painful she almost caught
her breath aloud. The longing tightened in her gut like
a knot, and she did not even know what it was she cov-
eted. She glanced at Owen again but he was concentrating on the bishop's words.

There were no smiles on Owen's side of the church
where the Ladies Martindale, Borough and Hurst sat
like a vast wave of disapproval with Rupert Montmorency sandwiched between them, his shirt points so
high he could barely turn his head without impaling
himself. Tess was surprised that the ladies had not worn
mourning dress.

The bishop spoke the words of the marriage service
but Tess did not really hear them. She made her vows.

"To have and to hold…" Her voice faltered a little
over the words and she felt Owen's fingers tighten on
hers. She looked up and met his eyes. There was something very steady and reassuring in them.

Owen made his vows too, his voice a great deal
firmer than hers.

"With my body I thee worship…"

A fierce shudder went through Tess as she remembered Charles Brokeby slurring the same words, remembered his hands hot on her body, grasping, brutal hands reaching for her, his lust plunging her into the depths of horror.

"Teresa?" Owen's voice was soft. Tess blinked, forcing the images back in the dark recesses of her mind. She trembled.

Owen slid the ring onto her finger. It felt too big; her hands were very cold and she was still shaking. She did not really understand why she should be nervous, not when she had done this three times before and could recite the words of the wedding service in her sleep.

The service over, they all went out of the church and into the snow. Tess was feeling colder and colder, shivering beneath the beautiful golden cloak that covered her matching gown of gold tissue. She had thought when she set out that she looked very fine, her hair dressed with pearls, her cloak trimmed with white fur. Now, though, the clothes could provide physical warmth but not the usual confidence that fashion gave her. She could feel her assurance leaching away and was baffled and angry with herself. She should be happy. She had achieved her marriage of convenience; Julius and Sybil were safe, and Owen had promised that he would protect her from Sidmouth's investigations. But then she watched Joanna slide her hand through Alex's arm and press her cheek to his shoulder in a little caress. She saw Merryn slip her hand into Garrick's. And she felt a sting of tears.

Something of how she was feeling must have communicated itself to Owen, for he covered her hand briefly with his gloved one.

"All right?" he murmured. His head was bent close to hers and his touch was reassuring. Tess wanted to cling to him. She nodded, even though she was lying. Owen smiled at her, the warmth lingering in his eyes. His lips brushed her cold cheek and she jumped.

"Rothbury!" Lady Martindale claimed Owen's attention abruptly and Tess felt lost again, adrift from the others, lonely and frighteningly alone.

Back in the gloomy house in Clarges Street a wedding breakfast had been set up in the dining room. Houghton and the rest of the servants were lined up in descending order of precedence, like the other statues in the hall, to welcome their new mistress.

"I look forward to your improvements to this museum piece, Lady Grant," Lady Martindale boomed as she sailed through the statuary of the hall like a galleon negotiating a reef. "When will you start work?"

Tess swung around on Joanna, who was looking slightly embarrassed.

"You are going to be decorating the house?" she said.

"Lady Martindale suggested it," Joanna murmured, "but of course I was going to speak with you first, Tess." There was a note of pleading in her voice, an apology Tess did not want to hear. All she could think was that Lady Martindale had not chosen to speak to *her* of the plans—had not, in fact, acknowledged her in any way since the engagement had been announced—but that she had been quick enough to approach Joanna on a project.

Perfect Joanna who had everything Tess wanted....

Another sliver of ice pierced her heart. The thought, so instant, so instinctive, frightened her. She did not want a marriage like Joanna's and she especially did not want a child of her own, not with the process one had to go through to get one. She had what she wanted. Yet even as she framed the thought she knew she lied. She wanted what Joanna had, yet she was so fearful of it too. She wanted to be cherished, she ached to be loved in every sense, but the chasm of fear that was Brokeby's legacy to her seemed to yawn at her feet, taunting her that she would never be whole again.

Her gaze sought out Owen, who was across the other side of the hall chatting to Garrick and Alex. Tess wanted to draw reassurance from the sight of him, but she was starting to feel so odd and disconnected from reality that it felt as though he was already slipping away from her. She put a hand out to steady herself against one of the pieces of statuary, which promptly swayed and almost toppled over.

"Probably drunk," Lady Borough said loudly. She was deaf and seemed to assume everyone else was too, judging by the way she shouted. "Or pregnant with Justin Brooke's child. Did you hear the latest *on dit?*

Mr. Melton celebrates Rothbury's wedding by exhibiting some more nude portraits of the bride. To think the Rothburys have come to this—"

Lady Martindale, clearly neither as deaf nor as vulgar as her sister, hushed Lady Borough, but the damage was done. There was an odd, heavy quiet in the hall as everyone fell silent. The servants stared at the floor, frozen into immobility.

Tess felt a huge burning wave of shame start at her toes and work its way up her entire body. She knew that everyone was looking at her. Merryn looked stricken. Joanna put out a hand to her but Tess could see the pity in her eyes. It made her want to scream. She looked at Owen again but he seemed so far away from her, across a vast expanse of marble littered with those hideous busts of dead Roman emperors. She knew that she had to get away. She headed for the door, past Lady Borough, ghastly old gossip, past Lady Martindale, past Lady Hurst, who was saying plaintively, "What did you say, Amelia? I can't *hear* you!"

Owen was calling her name but she ignored him too.

Then she was out in the snow and running down the street because she realised that if she needed somewhere to hide, to be alone, there was nowhere for her to go now. Her bags had been brought over from Bedford Street that very morning; she was Lady Rothbury now. She had no other home but this, and the house in Clarges Street was no refuge, full as it was of people who either scorned or pitied her.

But really there was only one place to go, a place she should have gone a long time ago. She had tried to ignore Melton's paintings, tried to pretend that they did not exist because they had belonged to that dark and shameful and utterly repugnant place that she only ever visited in her deepest nightmares. But now she knew she would finally have to see them. She would have to confront them and the damage they had done to her life. There was no other way she could go on, not if she was to have a future that was different from the past.

Suddenly she saw very bright, very clear, exactly what she had to do.

She jumped into a hackney carriage and set off for the Strand, still in her golden wedding dress and with the snow settling amongst the pearls in her hair.

THE SNOW LYING IN THE backstreets off the Strand was not white and pretty. It was a dirty grey, melting, mingled with the rubbish and slops. It fell from a dark grey sky. Night was already closing in.

In the chaos that had followed Tess's abrupt departure from her own wedding celebrations, Owen had not known where to look for her. He had had visions of accosting every passerby and hackney-carriage driver and asking them if they had seen a woman in a bridal gown running full tilt down the street. Then Joanna had taken him aside.

"I think you will find her at Melton's studio," she had said. She was distressed, visibly shaking. "Poor Tess, she has never said a word about the exhibition—" she paused and shot Lady Borough a furious glare "—but I know it hurt her deeply."

So here Owen was in this shadowy, insalubrious corner of the Strand, where London suddenly seemed a great deal more shabby and shop-soiled than it did in the glittering ballrooms of the ton.

The door to Melton's art studio stood ajar. As Owen paused on the step, someone opened a window above and the contents of a chamber pot rained down onto the snow beside him.

"He's not open yet!" a female voice called. "Come back later!" A woman was leaning over the sill above, chamber pot dangling from her hand and the neck of her dirty white nightgown drooping open. Her hair was a wild tangle and she looked as though she had only that moment arisen from her bed.

"Here for the exhibition, are you?" she said, looking Owen up and down. "You and all the other bucks in town."

A sudden loud crash from inside the building distracted her attention and she withdrew her head hastily. Owen heard her swear. Ignoring the instruction to come back later he pushed the door wide and stepped into the hall. He was instantly assailed by two unpleasant smells, cabbage and paint fumes, both of which stuck in his throat. The hallway was dark; he could dimly see a bare staircase rising to the first floor.

He had not expected Melton's premises to be quite so ramshackle. A fresh wave of anger assailed him that the artist should not only debauch Tess's reputation by exhibiting such lurid paintings of her but that he should do so in such unsavoury a setting. He knew this was ridiculous. Clearly it would be no better for nude paintings of his wife to be exhibited in Buckingham Palace. Yet it seemed just another sign of disrespect for Melton to hang them here in the backstreets and invite every lecher in the ton to come and view them.

From above came the sounds of raised voices, Tess's words sharp and clear.

"You have one chance, Mr. Melton. I ask you to act as a gentleman and remove these offensive pictures from exhibition. If you do not do so I shall do it for you."

And the artist's tones, oleaginous, gloating. "My dear Lady Darent, you should be proud to display such luminous beauty—"

"Lady Rothbury," Tess corrected. "It is my wedding day, Mr. Melton, as no doubt you are aware."

Owen paused as he heard Tess claim his name as her own. An unfamiliar emotion made his heart clench. He set his foot to the bottom stair just as there was another crash from the room above. He heard Melton's voice. "Lady Rothbury—" And this time the gloat had gone and there was an edge of fear in it. Owen raced up the stairs and flung open the door of the exhibition room.

He had not been sure what to expect. He had thought to visit the exhibition himself before to see what all the fuss was about, but it had made him feel too voyeuristic and too much like all the other rakes of the ton who lusted after Tess. He had wanted the real Teresa Darent, the one he had started to know, not the fantasy version with the painted smile and the tempting body. Now, though, as the naked images of Tess surrounded him on every side Owen was struck momentarily dumb, utterly overwhelmed by the collision between fantasy and reality. There was Tess reclining on a red velvet couch, creamy skin illuminated in the pale lamplight, a little sensual smile playing about her lips and gleaming in her half-closed eyes. There was a painting of Tess from behind, leaning over the back of the same couch, all voluptuous curves and tumbling hair. And— dear God—there was Tess lying on an enormous bed, arms stretched wide, thighs parted, her lower legs entangled in the sheet, the lazy look in her eyes indicative of the fact that she had been pleasured to within an inch of her life. Owen felt his body harden in sheer visceral response to the image and hated himself for it. In a flash he imagined all the other men who had stood there feeling as he did now and he felt sordid and furiously angry.

A palette of paint whizzed past his ear to splatter with an almighty crash against the enormous painting to his left. In it Tess was lit from behind in ethereal white light. She was actually wearing some clothes in this one—a long transparent white robe that only served to emphasise the lushness of the body beneath with its beautiful curves and angles. The picture showed her nipples rosy-pink through the fine lawn and the shadowy triangle of hair at the juncture of her thighs.

Red hair. Owen was really struggling now.

Another palette thudded into the wall, liberally splashing both Owen and the painting. The transparent white robe was now a gown of many colours, the picture despoiled beyond repair.

The artist was wailing. "Lady Rothbury! I beg you! No…"

Owen regained the power of movement just in time to avoid the final pots of blue and green paint that hit the portraits to his left, one after the other, with the precision of bullets. Colour splashed like blood, coating the pictures, the walls and the floor, running in rivulets down the paintings until they were nothing but an unrecognisable blur.

Owen doubted that Tess had even registered the fact that he was there. Her glorious golden wedding gown was smeared with paint, as were her hands. She had taken her cloak off so that she could throw more accurately, and the violence of her actions had loosened her hair from the pearl pins so that it fell about her flushed face in soft waves. But it was the look in her eyes that made Owen catch his breath. He could understand why Melton was afraid. Not even in battle had he seen such utter concentrated fury in anyone.

Tess dropped the last of the empty pots and turned back to the artist's easel. There were two paintings left undamaged. She picked up a knife. Owen started forwards. Paint was one thing, a knife quite another.

"Teresa," he said.

Tess ignored him. She spun around on Melton and Owen heard the artist give a little whimper. But she ignored Melton too. Slash went the blade across one canvas, so violently that the frame splintered and the portrait came away from the wood. Owen felt his heart lurch. He heard Tess make a little sound, half satisfaction, half sob. She raised the knife again and cut the last remaining picture from top left to bottom right. Owen could see her hand shaking now. There was a cut across her palm, the blood red amidst the green and blues of the paint. He put his own hand on her wrist and she dropped the knife with a clatter on the bare boards of the floor.

"That's enough now," he said very gently.

The dark inward gaze of her eyes faltered then. She looked about the room, from canvas to canvas, paint-spattered and slashed. Her breast heaved suddenly with a huge sob, and then she was crying as though her heart would break. Owen grabbed the cloak and wrapped her in it, swinging her up into his arms. On the floor Melton was almost crying too, cowering and scrabbling amidst the overturned pots and fallen frames.

"You were lucky it wasn't you," Owen said grimly.

"Yes, my lord." The artist's eyes were wide and terrified.

"Leave town," Owen said. "And don't ever come

back. And if I hear that you have ever displayed a single portrait of my wife again—"

"Yes, my lord," Melton said, before Owen had even finished the sentence.

Owen nodded. He turned his back on the ruined studio and went out, carrying Tess as carefully as though she was brittle china. He could feel her shaking with grief and reaction. Her face was buried against his neck. Her hair tickled his throat. He carried her to the waiting carriage and placed her gently on the seat, climbing in after her. He took her hand and examined the cut to her palm. It was not deep but it was bleeding slowly and he ripped a strip of material from his sleeve and bound it about her hand.

She did not speak one word. After a while her trembling started to abate a little, and a while after that Owen felt her body soften and relax in his arms. She opened her eyes, blinked and sat up.

"Owen." She sounded exhausted. "You came to find me."

Owen smiled at her. "Remind me never to get in your line of fire," he said.

Her face lightened into a smile but it faded almost immediately. A little frown dented her forehead between her brows. "Yes… Did I…did I really do that? Destroy Mr. Melton's exhibition?"

"Yes," Owen said. "You obliterated it. Do you feel better for it?"

Tess sat up straighter. "I should have done it years ago," she said.

"Why did you not?" Owen asked.

The light died from her eyes. "Because I wanted to pretend it did not exist," she said. "I tried to disregard it. But today—" A little shudder ran through her. Her voice shredded, turned thin. "Today when I heard Lady Borough…"

Owen was shot through with a bolt of protectiveness so powerful that he felt physically shaken. "She should be ashamed of herself for speaking like that," he said gruffly.

"No," Tess said. "I am the one who is ashamed."

"Don't be," Owen said. He saw the single tear that escaped from the corner of her eye to slide slowly over the curve of her cheek. She was trying so hard to hold the tears in check.

"You don't know," she whispered. "You don't understand."

"You can tell me if you like," Owen said. "But not now. Don't think about it now."

She nodded. Her shoulders had slumped again and she looked so frighteningly pale Owen thought she might faint. He remembered that she had not eaten all day, that she had run out before the wedding breakfast. He drew her gently to him and after a moment she relaxed against his shoulder, her eyes closing. She stayed like that, tucked into his side, until they reached Clarges Street.

"We're home," he said softly as the carriage drew to a halt.

Tess was so stiff as he helped her down from the carriage that she almost stumbled and fell. Owen put his arms about her to steady her. She looked like a fairy princess in the golden cloak and gown with the snow settling on her hood and swirling around her. A very woebegone princess, he thought, paint-spattered and dishevelled. A wave of emotion swept through him, tender and protective. On impulse he leaned forwards and kissed her gently. Her lips were cold.

"Come inside," he said softly. "Come to bed. Let me hold you. I'll make everything better, I swear."

He kissed her again, still careful to be gentle.

A shiver impaled her. For a moment he thought her trembling was from desire and that the high emotions of the day had made her turn to him for love and comfort, and he felt inordinately glad. His body surged in reaction to the quickening response he felt in hers, his erection hardening.

Tess made a sound of distress and wrenched herself away from him. She cast him one horrified look, then turned, tumbled up the steps of the house in a welter of golden gauze and disappeared inside. The door slammed behind her with so much force that the house shook. Owen stood still, the shock driving every last vestige of lust from his mind.

That went well.

Tess had not been nervous. She had been frightened.

She had been scared and repulsed and horrified. No woman, Owen thought ruefully, had ever responded to his kiss with quite such repugnance. It was far, far worse than the first time. No woman had ever run from him in terror before.

The footman was still standing on the pavement, his face studiously blank. The horses shifted, snorting and stamping in the snow.

"Thank you, Cavanagh," Owen said to the coachman. "Pray get the horses into the warm." He ruefully reflected that he was turning into the perfect aristocrat, able to ignore the most outrageous things going on under his nose and carry on as though nothing were amiss. The footman held the front door for him and he followed his wife into the house. He was relieved to see that the wedding guests, with great tact, had taken themselves off. The house was empty and quiet.

A couple of overturned statues in the hallway showed Tess's path to the library. Apollo, Owen saw, now had a chipped nose. Aphrodite's arm had come off. No doubt Owen's predecessor was spinning in his grave.

Owen hammered on the library door. "Teresa, open the door!"

The sound reverberated through the silent house, bouncing off all the statuary with their knowing eyes and shuttered faces. Owen did not really want to have to break down the door. In the first instance, it was made of old oak and was very fine. In the second, it was strong. He could not simply put his shoulder to it. His mind boggled at calling Houghton and asking for an axe in order to hack a path through to his wife.

"May I be of assistance, my lord?" Houghton had materialised silently beside him.

"I doubt it," Owen said grimly. A thought occurred to him. "Actually, yes, Houghton, you can help. Pray go to the kitchens and fetch a tray of cold food for myself and Lady Rothbury."

He went back to the library door, which remained stubbornly shut. He knocked again.

"Teresa," he said, "open the door." He paused. "I have food," he added cunningly.

He heard the key turn. The door opened a crack.

"Where is it?" Tess said.

Owen grinned. "Houghton is fetching it."

"Oh." She started to close the door again.

Owen inserted his foot into the gap. "Let me in," he said. "We need to talk."

There was a moment when he thought Tess might just slam the door on his foot but she did not. She let go of the door and stood just inside it, staring at him. There was a fire lit in the grate and the room was hot. She had removed the cloak and was standing there in her paint-spattered golden dress. Her blue eyes were drenched in tears, rimmed in red. Owen was astounded to see that she could actually look ugly. Not that it would help matters to say so at this point.

"Right," he said. It came out more roughly than he

had intended but he was tired and it was the end of a very long day. "What the hell was all that about? Why did you run away?"

She was upset. He could see that. But she was angry as well. And somehow, even though he had been married for only a day, Owen knew it was going to be his fault. She stared at him, accusation in her eyes. Then she stared down at his pantaloons as though trying to work out exactly what was concealed in them.

"You were supposed to be impotent," she said.

CHAPTER ELEVEN

IT WAS TURNING INTO ONE HELL of a wedding night.

Owen rocked back on his heels. His first thought was that he had misheard.

"I beg your pardon?" he said.

"I expected you to be impotent," Tess repeated. "I *wanted* you to be impotent. And then, when you kissed me, I felt—" She broke off, glaring at his pantaloons again.

Owen gestured her to sit down and took the place beside her on the sofa. Tess immediately moved farther away from him and curled up in a corner, her feet tucked under her, arms wrapped about herself.

"I am sorry that I cannot oblige you," Owen said. "But what on earth gave you the idea that I was impotent?"

Tess looked confused. "It was understood."

"By whom?" Now he was the one who was confused. Had the entire ton been discussing his supposed incapability?

"You had been injured fighting the French," Tess said. "It was common knowledge that you…" She paused. "That you had sustained a debilitating wound."

Her eyes touched his face then she looked away. "Mrs. Tong told me so that night at the brothel. She said that you…that the Captain of the Dragoons had no lead in his pencil." She looked up and there was indignation in her eyes. "You were in charge of the troops that night!"

"No, I was not," Owen said. "I was merely there in my capacity as one of Sidmouth's special investigators."

Tess stared at him for a moment and then her face crumpled as she realised the extent of her misunderstanding.

"But Alex and Joanna…" Her breath caught on a gasp. "They said it was true!"

"Grant told you I was impotent?" *Hell.* Owen thought he probably owed Alex something for trying to elope with his wife all those years before, but he thought they had got past that. This was a devil of a way for his friend to take revenge. "What did they say?" he asked.

Tess ran a hand through her disordered curls. She looked ruffled and cross and bewildered. Owen found he wanted to touch her, pull her into his arms and comfort her. He wanted to offer her comfort because he was not impotent and she had wanted him to be. Dear God, what a coil they were in.

"Well…" Her voice had softened into hesitation. "When I say that they told me, that is not quite true. But when I announced that I was to marry you, neither of them warned me."

"Warned you that I might want to sleep with you?"

Owen raised his brows. "It is the done thing in many marriages."

"Not in my marriages." Tess looked harried. "You never tried to kiss me," she said. "You never tried to take advantage."

So this was what he got for behaving like a gentleman, Owen thought. There really was no justice. "I'm old-fashioned," he said.

"Everyone tries to seduce me." Tess looked confused again. "Are you sure you really are—"

"Yes," Owen said. "I am sure. Why did you not ask me directly?" He added, "If you needed to be certain?"

Now Tess looked even more cross. "I would not be so indelicate," she snapped. Colour the shade of deep rose stung her cheeks.

She was shy.

It was another shock. Owen knew that Tess was nowhere near as brazen as she pretended, but the extent of her naivety and her reticence surprised him. No one would believe it and yet the defiance in her eyes and the blush that was spreading down her neck told the truth of it. She had been too shy to tackle such a personal subject directly with him and so she had relied upon gossip and hearsay. And as a result... As a result she was married to a man who was not only very far from incapable of consummating their marriage but had a positive desire to do so.

Which brought him neatly to the most important question of all.

"Why did you want an impotent husband?" he asked.

Instantly her shoulders tensed and her body became even more hunched and rigid. Her lavender-blue gaze slid away from his and fixed on the velvet cushions.

"I told you that when I proposed," she said. "All I required from you was the protection of your name. A marriage in name only," she repeated dully. "That was what I wanted."

Owen spared a moment to reflect on the irony of it all. When Tess had first come to him she had said she needed protection for herself and her stepchildren. He had suspected her of deceiving him by seeking protection from Lord Sidmouth's investigations too. In the process of untangling both of those issues he had completely forgotten her original demand for a marriage of convenience. Now he could see it was the most important element of the entire arrangement and it was far, far too late to put it right.

"That is not an answer," Owen said. "The question was why—why you want a husband who does not desire you."

She was not looking at him, but even so he saw something flicker in her eyes before her expression shut down altogether.

"That is none of your concern." She sounded cool and haughty, the Teresa Darent the world saw, the woman who gave nothing away and whose composure was as impermeable as steel. Except that she was fidgeting with the threads of the cushion until they were twisted and ragged between her fingers.

Owen shook his head. "You mistake," he said. "I am your husband and what I expect from our marriage is that you share my bed and provide me with an heir. Those are my requirements and as they in no way match yours I think that is a matter of considerable concern."

He had to credit her with perfecting the art of silence. She did not say a word. He knew no women and very few men who had the nerve to let the silence run and refuse to break it. He had thought that over the past ten days he had learned all her secrets. But then he remembered the moment in the carriage on the way back from Hampstead Wells. He had asked her if there was anything else he should know and she had denied it. But here it was, something so vivid and painful and deep that he sensed she was fighting it with all her strength. But he had to know.

"Well?" he said.

There was a knock at the door. "The food, my lord," Houghton said, peering into the library as though he half expected to be stepping into a pitched battle. He came forwards reluctantly and placed the tray on the table between them. "There is pigeon pie and beetroot salad and ham and cheese."

Owen looked at him and he fell silent. "Thank you, Houghton," Owen said. He had lost his appetite and it seemed Tess had too. She was looking at the beetroot with barely concealed loathing.

"Well," he said softly, shifting his attention back to Tess as Houghton exited the library with indecent haste.

"Perhaps we should have spoken of this before." Her steely composure was still in place. "Now it is too late. Unless…" She paused. "Can I persuade you to see my point of view? A marriage in name only has certain benefits." She moistened her lips with the tip of her tongue. "You could keep a mistress with my blessing."

Owen drew a short breath. *Well, hell.* It was his wedding night and his wife was suggesting he take a mistress. Some men would be gratified to have married such an understanding woman. He was not one of them.

"Such a tempting offer," he said, his voice loaded with sarcasm. He saw Tess wince. "You are all generosity, madam. But," he said, and shrugged, "I am afraid I wish to sleep with my wife, not with a mistress. Unfashionable of me, I know, but there we are. Besides, a mistress cannot give me an heir to Rothbury, can she?"

Tess rubbed her forehead. "There I cannot help you, my lord. I fear you will have to divorce me and remarry in order to gain the heir you clearly desire. Or—" her gaze slid over him and lingered on his pantaloons "—perhaps an annulment would be more appropriate, given the circumstances."

"I am sure that would enhance my fictitious reputation greatly," Owen said. "No, thank you. I am not encouraging further debate about my supposed impotence." He shook his head. "You move very fast, madam. From marriage to divorce without stopping for a wedding night in between."

Tess shrugged. Every muscle was tight with tension now. It seeped from her skin; for all her assumed nonchalance she could not disguise it. Owen knew she wanted him to stop questioning her. She wanted him to leave her alone. But he was not giving up until he learned the truth.

He could feel his temper rising. Could she not *see* that they had had an opportunity to build something that could become tender and precious if only she gave it a chance? Was she truly as shallow as she had always pretended? The Teresa Darent he had started to know was a very different woman, generous and loyal with the capacity to love deeply. The thought of her denying that, denying him, made his heart ache. Yet she sat there with so unyielding an expression on her face he did not know how to penetrate that facade and he was not sure he even wanted to try anymore.

"There will be no divorce," he repeated. He stood up to leave.

She put out a hand to stop him, caught his sleeve in urgent fingers. "But we will be married in name only," she said. "You would not force me to consummate—" She came to an abrupt stop.

Owen's temper shattered. "Dear God," he said cuttingly, "what sort of a man do you think I am?"

He felt Tess shudder. Her face went completely blank

as though in that moment she had utterly absented herself, not only from him but also from the power of her own thoughts. There was the oddest silence Owen had ever experienced, then something snapped in his mind, and the words, the memories, the images reformed, and he felt the shock hit him for a third time that evening, with jarring force. He looked again at Tess's pale, frozen expression. Whatever it was she was blotting out of her mind had nothing to do with him. It was some other man she was thinking of, some other situation that was intolerable to her.

"You're afraid," he said very slowly, and saw the confirmation of his suspicions in the terror that leapt in her eyes.

"No!" Her denial was instantaneous, forbidding him to trespass. She curled up even more closely like a tightly closed flower.

"Yes, you are," Owen said. "You are terrified of intimacy." At the back of his mind he could hear the echo of her words, like a ghost:

Darent was laudanum and drink, and Brokeby was lechery and drink. And gambling. And laudanum...

She had given him all the clues, Owen thought, whether she realised it or not. She had wanted a marriage in name only; she had turned to ice in his arms when he had first kissed her and she had been too shy to broach directly with him the issue of his supposed impotence. She had said that Robert Barstow had been her best friend and that Darent had entrusted her with his children's futures.

She had never spoken about Brokeby.

Others had. Even his aunt Martindale had said Brokeby was no gentleman, but Owen, like everyone else, had read the situation the wrong way round and imagined that Tess had been a willing participant in Brokeby's wild and licentious ways. There were the paintings to prove it. Those pictures that Tess had destroyed that very afternoon.

"I tried to pretend it had never happened...."

He remembered the stories he had heard of Tess's gambling and drinking and wild ways in the wake of Brokeby's death. Not indulgence, but a desperate attempt to forget....

A feeling of sick horror slid between Owen's ribs like the blade of a knife.

"Brokeby," he said slowly. His voice was heavy and harsh. "What did he do to you?"

Tess made a broken little sound of distress. Owen took her hands in his. They were frozen, trembling. He thought that she might resist and draw away from him but she did not.

"He can't hurt you anymore," Owen said. "You're safe now."

Tess shook her head. "It's too late," she said. "It's too late. It's inside my head." Her face crumpled and Owen thought she was going to cry again, but she took a deep breath and steadied herself, and then she began to talk quickly, urgently, the words tumbling out in an unstoppable tide that once started could not be quelled.

"I didn't know about the paintings," she said painfully. "There was a house party. Brokeby and I were newly wed and he had taken me to the country along with a group of his cronies and some of their mistresses. It was all very disreputable and I thought it strange when we were on our wedding trip, but I was young and naive and a little lonely, and so I said nothing...." A frown puckered her forehead. "Anyway, Brokeby must have given me something, in my food, my wine, I am not certain. But I remember feeling very unwell and then everything became very confused."

Owen felt a shiver ripple through her. "I knew I was not asleep," she said, "and yet I dreamed—" She stopped. Her voice was thin. "Horrible nightmares, waking nightmares. I could not tell the dream from the reality. I remember I was dressed only in my shift and sometimes...sometimes I was wearing nothing at all. I remember the cold on my body, and sometimes the heat of a fire, and there were shadows about me, hands on me, people touching me, *displaying* me." The despair shuddered in her voice. "It was grotesque, almost impersonal, as though I were some sort of exhibit. I realise now that Melton was sketching me in different poses, but at the time I did not understand...." Her voice caught. Owen saw her swallow very hard. "I wanted to break away, to escape. I tried, tried to run, but I could barely stumble as far as the door. I saw a crack of light and reached for it, but someone laughed and closed the door in my face…." She turned away from him. "After that I had no strength to fight. It was too difficult, so in the end I gave in to it. I let it claim me, let them do what they willed. I never wanted to wake again."

Owen tightened his grip on her hands. He focussed solely on her. The emotions inside him, the dark, turbulent anger, the violent rush of protectiveness, the primitive need for revenge, those feelings could wait. Tess was all that mattered now.

"Eventually I did wake, even though I did not wish it." She was speaking very quietly now, her gaze on their clasped hands. "I found I was alone, in my bed." Her gaze was blind, inward looking. "Brokeby came to me then," she said. "He had not bedded me before." She stopped. "I was a virgin when I wed him and I think that in some twisted way he saw me as his trophy. He was excited and he had come to claim me. At the least," she said drily, "it was over quickly and after that I was not so innocent and I learned to deal with it."

"What of the others?" Owen said. His voice was so rough he barely recognised it. He did not want to know the answer to his question but he knew he would have to bear it. If he was to help Tess he needed to know the whole truth, no matter how painful. But she was shaking her head. She did not pretend to misunderstand him.

"Brokeby was a jealous man," she said, "so although he wanted his cronies to see what he possessed and to envy him for it, he was not prepared to share me. Not then. Maybe when he had tired of me." She smiled but there was no amusement in her eyes. "Lucky for me he died before that happened."

"How long?" Owen said. He was so angry he was not sure he could even get the words out. "How long before he died?"

"Two months," Tess said, "but mercifully he was up in town for one of those."

Dear God. She had spent a whole month with a whore-mongering, libidinous bastard like Brokeby. Owen felt his throat close with despair for her.

"I ran away whilst Brokeby was in London," Tess said. "I went back to my uncle and aunt's house, but my uncle was a most God-fearing vicar and he said I was breaking my wedding vows. He took me back to Brokeby in person to make sure I could not run again. I should have gone to Joanna," she said bitterly, "but she had difficulties of her own. She and I had a talent for choosing the wrong husbands."

"You have both made up for it now, though," Owen said, and just for a moment he saw a smile filter like sunlight into her eyes and he felt a fierce desire to bring that laughter back into her life and banish the shadows for good.

"Maybe we have," she said slowly. The smile vanished from her eyes. "After Brokeby died I found some of the portraits in his effects and destroyed them. It never occurred to me that there would be more. Foolish of me, but I was not thinking clearly and—" She gave a shrug. "I tried very hard to not think about it at all. I tried to wipe Brokeby from my mind, obliterate him." Her eyes clouded with pain. "You will have heard that I was very wild. I tried everything in order to forget—gambling, drinking… But no lovers." Her gaze snapped up to meet his again. "I could not bear anyone to touch me." The words, so desolate, dropped into the silence of the room. "Darent found me in the gutter one night after I had drunk too much at a ball. He was a kind man." She smiled faintly. "We came to an understanding. His health was ruined through the laudanum." She made a slight gesture. "I was…safe… with him."

"He did not want to bed you," Owen said.

"No." Tess shifted, sighed. "After Darent died I made my home with Joanna and Alex, but the damage was done in terms of my reputation. And then Melton mounted his exhibition—" again Owen saw her hands clench "—and ruined me all over again. I tried to pretend it was not happening. I never went to see it. But the knowledge of it burned at the back of my mind all the time. I could not escape it." She made a slight gesture that had a wealth of hopelessness in it. "So you see, my lord, why I wished for another impotent husband. I can never be a true wife to you." Her eyes begged for his understanding. "It truly is for the best that we should part."

No.

Owen's reaction was an instinctive refusal. He did not speak the word aloud but he was never going to accept it. What damage had been done, and it was terrible damage, hideous violation, could surely be undone with enough time, patience and care. He had to believe that because he wanted it to be true.

"We'll discuss this in the morning," he said gently.

It was late—almost dawn—and she looked exhausted, every nerve stretched tight. She was translucently pale. He could not leave her here in the library, for the fire had gone out and she would be chilled to the bone within minutes. She was already shivering, though Owen doubted that was entirely with cold. Tiny shudders racked her.

Upstairs there was a room that had been prepared for her to occupy. All her portmanteaux had been sent round from Bedford Street. He had seen them earlier, standing in serried rows, waiting to be unpacked. He wondered whether it would comfort Tess to have her belongings around her or whether it might simply send her running back to the place she probably thought of as home, a place where perhaps she felt safe. He could imagine her climbing out of the window and running off into the night, driven by desperation and despair.

Perhaps his room might be better. There were no bulging suitcases there to remind her just what a lonely stranger she was in this house.

Well, she could not stay here, whatever the outcome. He scooped her up in his arms to take her upstairs.

As soon as he touched her, her body went rigid as a board and he heard her breathing escalate to a pant of terror.

"Calm yourself." He spoke very soothingly, as he would to a frightened horse, and held her with impersonal gentleness. "I won't hurt you. I'm just taking you upstairs so that you can get some rest."

He could hear the frightened flutter of her breath and feel the erratic rise and fall of her chest against his. Her entire body was stiff with dread. If she could not bear him even to touch her, Owen thought grimly, they were in deeper trouble than he had ever imagined. But after a moment her breathing slowed a little and some softness came back into her limbs. She relaxed against him, her head brushing his shoulder, her hair tickling his cheek. She made no further protest as he carried her up the stairs and into the warmth and light of his room. Her head lifted from his shoulder; she looked at the bed and he felt her give a slight shudder.

Hell. He sat her down on the side of the bed and drew off her evening slippers.

"I'll call your maid," he said. "You need to undress. Your gown is covered in paint."

Tess nodded slightly. She already looked more than half asleep.

The maid came so quickly Owen wondered if all the servants had been listening at the door. Very probably they had. The events of his wedding day would have circulated halfway around London by now, he was sure.

The maid was a thin, plain girl, but she looked practical and there was a fierce light of affection in her eyes when she looked at Tess.

"I'll look after her, my lord," the girl said. "You can trust me."

Owen nodded. "Thank you," he said. "What's your name?"

"Mallon," the girl said. "Margery Mallon."

"Thank you, Margery," Owen said. Regardless of convention, he hated calling servants by their surnames and would even have called Houghton by the name of Harold had he not thought that the butler would have expired with disapproval to be so addressed.

"Come and find me when Lady Rothbury is asleep," he said. "I want to stay with her to ensure she is safe."

"Yes, my lord." Margery's gaze was quick and approving. She went over to Tess and talked to her gently, easing her from the paint-spattered gown. Owen watched Tess lean back against the pillows and heard her give a tiny sigh, as though she felt safe at last. He looked at her. Tess, his beautiful, damaged bride. It all made perfect sense to him now; the way that she had helped Harriet Knight and Emma Bradshaw and all those other women who had been lost, broken and betrayed, how she had given away money to the charities that saved women and children ruined on the whim of men, her utter determination that Sybil Darent would never be sold into marriage with a middle-aged lecher…. Tess had known the desolation of such a life and had resolved to do everything she could to prevent that misery ruining the lives of others.

The fury that had possessed Owen earlier flared back into vivid and vicious life. It was fortunate for Brokeby that he was already dead. But the others, the men who had been there at that fateful house party... He wanted to hunt them down and kill them one by one with all the anger and violence that was in his soul, especially the man—whoever he was—who had so cruelly, so carelessly, closed the door and trapped Tess in a world of misery and fear. Owen felt something very close to despair twist his gut. Only once before, on the night he had almost killed a man, had he felt such fury fill his entire being. Now he was not sure that he could control that anger. White-hot and vicious, it seeped into every corner of his being. He would find them, every last man of them. And he would make them pay.

TESS SLEPT FOR A WHILE OUT OF sheer exhaustion but woke on the edge of a nightmare, uncertain where she was. For a second she felt the darkness and the nameless fear bear down on her and a gasp rose to her lips, but then the room swam into view, the candle burning low, the fire a glow of comfort in the grate. In the faint light she could see the outlines of the room. It was bare and plain, the sort of chamber that belonged to a man who took only what he needed and was accustomed to travelling lightly and moving on. She was in Owen's chamber. She could smell his scent on the sheets and it pierced her with desolation. Earlier, all she had wanted was to be free of Owen, to run away from him and from her fears, to be alone again because that was the only way she knew. Now she realised that she needed him. She needed his strength and his comfort and his reassurance, but she had no right to claim them because she could offer him nothing in return.

The ragged edges of the nightmare taunted her again. Despite herself, a little sob broke from her lips. She tried to stifle it but the fear pressed closer, smothering the air in her lungs.

And then someone was beside her, his hand smoothing the hair away from her hot forehead, his arms about her, holding her with gentleness she craved but had never found.

"Sweetheart." His lips were against her hair. "Hush. You're safe now."

Owen.

He was there for her when she needed him. She had thought to push him away, uncomfortable with his physical proximity, but found herself clinging to him instead, burying her face in his shirt and holding him as though her very life depended upon it. She inhaled his scent and it felt so familiar and reassuring that her body softened into acceptance. There was no danger here. Owen would never hurt her. She knew it in her soul.

After a moment he drew her back beneath the sheets—it was cold in the room, even with the flicker of the fire. Her head was on his shoulder, and his arms about her were as strong as steel bands.

"Safe…" She murmured the word and felt his lips brush her brow. She was so tired; habit and an instinctive wariness told her that she should stay awake, that she should be vigilant. A deeper instinct told her that she could trust him and sleep. The warmth crept from his body to hers, wrapping her about with comfort, a drug on her senses. She could not resist any longer. Sleep ambushed her and with slight surprise she succumbed.

When she woke the next time, the entire length of Owen's body was pressed against her and she felt hot, as though she had a fever. His lips were about an inch from hers. She could feel his breath on her skin. Through the tangle of her nightgown she felt his erection—no, he most certainly was not impotent—and her gasp of shock brought him awake so fast she barely had time to register it. One moment his face had been vulnerable in repose. The next he was staring into her eyes, and his own were dark with desire, sleep fading fast. Tess froze, the terror pouncing on her, turning her body to ice. But then an extraordinary thing happened. Owen's lips curved into a smile. He kissed her with the briefest and most fleeting of caresses, and rolled away from her onto his back, one arm behind his head.

"I apologise," he said, "if I shocked you."

"I…" Tess grabbed her scattered thoughts. Her heartbeat was slowing, the patter of fear easing from her body leaving her weak with relief. "I thought you would—" She stopped.

"You thought I would make love to you?" Owen said. His face was tilted towards her. She could barely see his expression in the shadows. "I don't force my attentions on an unwilling woman."

He had told her that earlier but it was still a revelation to meet a man with restraint, even though she had known they must exist.

She frowned. "But you were aroused…" The heat flooded her body, embarrassment mingled with something else. She had never left so many sentences unfinished in her life.

"I find you very attractive." He sounded matter-of-fact. "I won't lie. Nor apologise." A thread of amusement came into his voice. "However, I don't actually have to do anything about it."

"Oh." She felt naive. In fact she felt a whole welter of emotions, but for the first time fear was not the strongest. She snuggled closer to his side, seeking his warmth again, and immediately felt him stiffen. She drew back. She had done something wrong. She knew it from his reaction.

"I'm sorry." She was mortified.

"No." He pulled her very firmly into his arms. "I was surprised, that's all." His breath stirred her hair and sent delicious shivers skittering over the skin of her neck. "I'm glad you trust me."

Tess relaxed. Her head was resting on his shoulder

again, her lips only a couple of inches from his throat. The scent of him was like rainwater but with something in it that was uniquely his. Once again the relaxation seeped into her limbs but it had a different quality to it now. It felt peaceful, undemanding.

She lay like that for a long time, watching Owen, listening to his breathing as he fell asleep. She felt different and strange, humble, filled with awe and happy. The happiness rippled through her like sunlight and she revelled in it, revelled in Owen's closeness and the uncomplicated pleasure she could take from it. It was like a revelation to her. But slowly her awareness of him changed. Contrarily it was spiked with attraction now. She felt very awake. *Excited.*

This time her gasp of shock was from a different cause. Impossible. It was impossible that she should want him.... And yet she did.

She shifted imperceptibly closer to Owen. He was lying very still with his eyes closed, deeply asleep. Tess pressed her lips softly to the skin of his throat. It was warm, skin soft, stubble rough. The contrasting sensations jostled within her. So did the curiosity and the apprehension. Greatly daring, she parted her lips and tasted him with the tip of her tongue. Again that uniqueness; she tasted salt, fresh air, clean linen, Owen... Her head spun. She touched her fingers to his hair, feeling the smoothness of it like the flick of feathers.

She wanted to kiss him. She wondered if she dared.

In truth she wanted to touch all of him, the hard, corded muscles of his arms, the breadth of his shoulders, his chest... She gulped. It was too much, too soon. The idea simultaneously intrigued and frightened her. The desire in her shimmered, but it was still locked away behind that closed door. She had to breach those barriers in her mind first before her body could follow and find satisfaction.

No, together *they* had to breach those barriers. She knew that Owen would help her if only she could trust him. She leaned over and kissed Owen very softly, and he murmured something and drew her down into his arms again and finally she slept without nightmares.

CHAPTER TWELVE

"THE DUKE OF FARNE AND LORD Grant are here to see you, my lord." Houghton, very stiff, bowed Garrick and Alex into the breakfast parlour. Owen wondered what he had done this time to incur the butler's disapproval. Perhaps there was some sort of social procedure that a newly married viscount should perform. Very probably retiring to the library at six in the morning and drinking half a bottle of brandy was not on the list of approved activities of the morning after the wedding, though knowing the ton, perhaps it was positively encouraged. Who knew? Owen certainly did not. All he knew was that he had left Tess sleeping under Margery's watchful eye because he had had enough torture for one night. Lying with Tess curled safely in his arms had been both agony and delight. He had been astonished and humbled that she had trusted him but there was only so much that a man could stand, and when she had started her innocent exploration of him he had thought he might come apart beneath her questing fingers. He had lain awake, feeling her curiosity, feeling her hesitation, until finally she had slept. Then he had lain awake some more wanting to slake his hunger for her and knowing full well he could not in all honour. Finally he had got up and hit the brandy. Now it was ten o'clock and he felt vile. Not even the strongest coffee could soothe the monster of all headaches.

"We thought we would see how you were this morning after the drama of the wedding breakfast," Alex was saying. He grabbed a chair and poured himself a cup of coffee. "You look appalling," he added.

"No sleep," Owen said succinctly.

"Congratulations," Garrick said.

Owen shot him a look. "Not like that." He swung around on Alex. "What the hell do you mean by telling my wife that I was impotent, Grant?"

Alex almost choked on the coffee.

"Bloody hell," Garrick said. He backed towards the door. "I'll leave you to deal with this one on your own, Grant."

"I didn't have you down as a coward, Farne," Alex said sardonically.

"Stay," Owen said, hooking out another dining chair with his foot. "I might need you as my second, Farne."

Alex peered at him. "Hangover?" he asked. "Is that the cause of this vile temper?" He reached for the bell. "Surely Houghton has something for that."

"Not sure the butler can cure thwarted desire though," Garrick said. "Looks like a bad case."

Owen shot him a filthy look. "Shut up, Farne," he said.

"So Tess thought you were impotent and you didn't

discover this...problem...until after the wedding, then," Garrick observed.

Owen rolled his eyes. "Well, obviously not." He looked from Garrick, who was trying not to laugh, to Alex, and spread his hands. "Devil take it, what can I say? I'm a gentleman. I'm old-fashioned. Lady Darent and I had only been engaged a fortnight. Naturally I had not tried to seduce her—"

"It's all right, Rothbury." Alex patted him on the shoulder. "You don't need to explain yourself to us."

"This is all your fault, Grant," Owen said.

"What was I supposed to do?" Alex protested. "Mention that just in case Lady Darent was not aware of it, you were in no way impotent?" He shook his head. "I don't go around talking about my friends' sexual exploits, Rothbury."

There was a brief hiatus in the conversation as Houghton came in bearing a tray. "I have brought you a remedy against the drink, my lord," the butler said, with deep disapproval. "Your predecessor, the late Lord Rothbury, swore by its reviving qualities."

"Had no idea my predecessor hit the bottle," Owen said. "Not quite the dull stick he appeared, then."

He tossed the liquid back. It tasted utterly vile. His admiration for the previous Lord Rothbury went up another notch.

"I'm sure you can overcome the problem, Rothbury," Garrick said as the door closed behind Houghton.

"I'm not so sure," Owen said. Before the previous

night, he would have said there was no hope. Now he had to believe there was a chance. He looked from one to the other. "The problem," he said slowly, "is Brokeby."

Alex and Garrick exchanged a look.

"Brokeby," Alex said. His voice flattened. "Joanna wondered…" He stopped. "Hell," he said.

"Literally," Owen said drily.

"I'd forgotten Lady Darent had been married to Brokeby," Garrick said. "It was over so quickly."

"Not quickly enough," Owen said grimly.

"What happened?" Alex said.

"The exhibition," Owen said. He was not going to tell them everything but he wanted their help. "Teresa didn't know," he said. "Brokeby drugged her and Melton painted her."

Shock flared in Alex's eyes. "Christ, Rothbury," he said faintly.

"I want to find Brokeby's cronies," Owen said. The anger surged in him again, bitter, violent, no less sharp with the passage of time. "They were there. I'm going to find them and I'm going to kill them."

Alex shook his head. There was sympathy in his eyes. "Don't do it, Rothbury," he said. "I understand your feelings, but—"

"If you tell me it's not worth it," Owen said through his teeth, "I'll probably punch you."

"It's worth it a thousand times over for Tess," Alex said with a faint smile, "but it will never change the past." He shifted. "Violence did not serve you so well before, did it, Rothbury? You lost your commission and you damn near lost your everything else."

Owen came to his feet. "Why, you—"

"Don't call me out," Alex said calmly. "You've spent fourteen years putting that behind you. Don't let it master you now." His gaze was steady and watchful on Owen's face. Very slowly, Owen sank back into his chair.

"Curse you, Grant," he said morosely. "Why are you always right?"

"Because I've been in the same place," Alex said. "When you told me what David Ware had done to Joanna I wanted to kill him. If he had not already been dead…" Owen saw him shrug, a little uncomfortably, as though the memory still had the power to hurt him. "But I realised that the only thing that mattered was how Joanna felt, not how I felt. You are the only one who can help Tess and you won't do that by getting arrested for murder, no matter how tempting it is."

Owen let out his breath on a long sigh. "You're damned persuasive."

"Most of Brokeby's set are dead anyway," Garrick put in. "Carver broke his neck on the road to Brighton a few years back. Helmsley was shot by his gamekeeper, and Towton was trampled at the Newmarket races."

"Couldn't have happened to a more deserving bunch," Owen said.

The door opened and Tess came in. She was dressed

in a rose-pink morning gown and looked pretty and fresh and very young. Owen felt a rush of pleasure on seeing her and a greater rush of relief that the first thing she had done was to seek him out, not to run away from him. He saw Garrick shoot Alex a look and they both rose from the table with almost indecent haste.

"Did I chase them away?" Tess asked, looking slightly baffled as her brothers-in-law made their bows of greeting and departure at one and the same time. "I did not intend—"

Owen took both her hands in his and she fell silent.

"I think," he said, smiling, "that that was their attempt to be subtle and leave us alone together."

"Oh." Tess's smile was mischievous. "Subtle." She nodded. "I see."

"You are well this morning?" Owen asked softly.

Her eyes searched his face for a moment, wide, wary and very blue. She looked uncertain and very shy. Owen felt the look like a physical punch in the gut. It stole his breath.

"I am very well, thank you, my lord." She sounded very slightly breathless.

Owen kissed her hand and felt her tremble slightly but not, he thought, from fear. Last night, deep in the horror of all she had to tell him, she had recoiled from his touch, but later she had turned to him with complete trust. He had to try to build on that. He smiled at her and saw an answering smile leap into her eyes and

268

DESIRED

he felt a ridiculous surge of pleasure, as though she had given him a present.

"What do we do now, my lord?" she said.

Owen liked that she was prepared to tackle the matter so bluntly. It was brave of her.

"We are married," he said, "and we will stay that way."

A shadow brushed her face. She looked down at their joined hands. "I told you yesterday that if you wish for an heir you would do a great deal better to divorce me," she said. "I still feel it might be better. For you, I mean."

"Teresa," Owen said, "that is a terrible plan. It's the worst plan since your last bad plan."

"The one to propose to you because I thought you were impotent?" Unbelievably, there was a little smile playing about her lips now. "Yes, that was a very poor idea."

"And yet in other ways it was not," Owen said. He drew her a little closer. "I like being married to you. So we will stay married." He paused. "And I will demonstrate to you the many benefits of not having an impotent husband."

He saw the flicker of nervousness in her eyes but behind it, surely, a shade of something else, something that looked like a shy curiosity. His heart leapt.

"You are very sure of yourself," Tess said slowly, "if you think that you can persuade me."

"Yes," Owen said. "I am."

The smile was back in her eyes now, delicious, irresistible. "You are confident," she murmured. Her lips curved. "I find I like that though. One of us has to be."

Her smile was doing all sorts of dangerous things to his self-control. Owen wanted to kiss her. He ruthlessly subdued the impulse.

"Give me leave to persuade you," he said. He eliminated all urgency from his voice so that she would not know how much he already wanted her and run from that knowledge. "It doesn't have to be like it was before for you. It would not be like that with me. I swear it."

Again she smiled a little. "I know."

"Then take the risk. Give me that chance."

She still looked uncertain. Owen reined in his galloping lusts and drew her slowly towards him until their bodies were just touching. There was a different sort of awareness in her eyes now but still she did not break away from him. The soft pink muslin of the gown brushed his thigh. Her hand rested against his shirt front, over his heart.

"Teresa," he said. "Before we wed, when we were starting to get to know one another, you liked me then, didn't you? Admit it."

Her gaze flickered warily. Still she did not answer. He could feel the caution in her, as though she was on the edge of fleeing from him.

"All right," Owen said. He could see he was going to have to be very honest. "I liked *you*," he said. "I liked you very much. Why do you think I came to see you every day? It wasn't only because I wanted to trap you into admitting you were Jupiter. It wasn't even because I wanted your money. It was because I—" He stopped. *Liking* seemed so pale a word for the heady mix of emotions he felt for her. "I loved spending time with you," he said.

"You wanted my money as well," she corrected him, a hint of laughter in her voice.

"Very well." Owen bit back an answering smile. "I did. I do. But—"

She pressed her fingers to his lips and he stopped abruptly.

"I liked you very much too," she whispered, and Owen felt as though the sun had come out.

"And you trusted me," he said.

Her hand fell. She gave a little nod and Owen felt his whole body jolt with the release of tension.

"Last night," he went on, "even though you were exhausted and afraid, you turned to me. I would never betray your trust. I promise."

She nodded again. A shade of colour came into her cheeks. "Last night," she said. "When I…" She bit her lip. "When I kissed you… You were asleep?"

"No," Owen said. He did not pretend to misunderstand her. "Not for a moment." He felt her jump. Shock flared in her eyes. Her colour deepened. "You wanted to explore," he said. "It's all right. I thought I would let you do what you wished."

He watched the emotions chase across her face. "You understand," she whispered.

"Yes," Owen said. "You are curious but you are frightened as well. It's natural." He gave her fingers a comforting squeeze. "I promise not to do anything you do not want," he said. "One word from you and I will stop."

Now her eyes were huge as she contemplated all the things he *might* do to her. Owen watched with interest. Yes, there was apprehension there, but again there was more than a glimmer of interest as well. She moistened her lips and he felt a kick of lust so violent that for a second it stole his breath. Then she looked up and met his eyes.

"Very well," she said. "When do we start?"

"Right now," Owen said.

TESS WONDERED IF SHE had been quite mad to go with him. When Owen had thrown down the gauntlet and announced that not only were they to remain married but he would seduce her into liking it, she had not anticipated that the first thing that they would do together was visit *Sea Witch*. Yet here she stood on the cobbled quay at Greenwich, the pale sun rippling on the water and the river air keen on her face. Her shoes were dirty, there was the scent of fish and rotting seaweed in her nostrils, and she had no notion how she was going to get aboard the ship that lay so gently at anchor before her.

Sea Witch, Owen's great love. This was her rival for his attention. Tess smiled. She might have known that

Owen's ideas of a romantic courtship would not be the same as anyone else's.

Courtship. She shivered a little at the word. It sounded extremely gentle, harmless, even. What could be sweeter or more chaste than a courtship? Yet she knew that what Owen wanted from her was not chaste at all. That frightened her, but she had to be honest and admit that it intrigued her too.

In the relative anonymity of the dark the previous night, believing Owen to be sleeping, she had felt safe to explore her desires a little. Now, though, it was bright daylight, and Owen was wide awake and back in control, and she felt more than a little fearful of what lay ahead of her. She did not know if she could be the wife Owen wanted, be his wife in the fullest sense of the word. She knew that not all men were like Brokeby. But she had never wanted an intimate relationship with any man before. It was quite a shock to her to acknowledge she might want one now. She trusted Owen and she knew she could either try to be his wife or she could run away, and perhaps it was time to stop running.

Sea Witch was a trim little craft. Even Tess, who knew nothing about ships and cared less, could see that.

"How do we get aboard?" she asked.

"Like this." Owen picked her up in his arms and strode up the gangplank, which was at a vertiginous angle. He placed her, breathless and shocked, on the deck.

"My apologies," he said, smiling into her eyes. He

was still holding her lightly by the elbows. Her whole body tingled from the suddenness of the experience and the contact with the hard lines and muscles of his. He stood back, allowing her to find her feet. "It's easier that way," he said. "Avoids discussion."

Feeling mildly disturbed, Tess followed him through a small doorway and into a narrow passageway. Instantly the wooden walls of the ship closed about them and her consciousness of Owen's physical presence became very strong. A stifling feeling of awareness rose in her throat.

"Down here." Owen had disappeared down a set of steps that seemed to descend into darkness. Tess looked down the hatch and saw him grinning up at her.

"How on earth am I supposed to get down there?" she asked.

"Turn around and come down backwards," Owen instructed.

When she was halfway down the steps she was mightily relieved to feel his hands close about her waist and swing her to the floor. She had been concentrating so hard on her footing that it was only several minutes later that she realised that he would have been able to see up her skirts as she descended, just as he had when she had climbed out of the window at the brothel. She glared at his back. His shoulders looked very knowing. He was enjoying this, damn him.

But so was she. There was a little flutter in her stom-

ach when she thought about what might happen between them, the uncertainty and the possibilities.

"Nothing will happen that you do not want," Owen
had said, and she shivered to think of all the things she
might want. There would be nothing to frighten or hurt
her. He had promised. So it might be quite safe to kiss
him....

"The captain's cabin," Owen said, throwing open a
door, breaking into her thoughts.

"It's tiny!" Tess said. "How did you find room—"
She stopped, realising the way her thoughts were tend-
ing. Suddenly, from never thinking about sex it seemed
to be the only thing she was thinking about. "To move,"
she finished quickly.

He gave her a wicked smile. "One becomes accustomed to making the best use of the space." He was already moving away down the corridor. His steps were
quick and light. Tess sensed the pleasure it gave him
to be back on his ship, even here, at anchor. She felt a
sudden fierce desire to see him sailing *Sea Witch* out
on the open ocean. She tried to imagine all the expedi-
tions he had been on and felt hopelessly parochial. Her
travels had all been within England. Even Scotland had
seemed impossibly distant and too barbaric to visit. But
Owen was an explorer and explorers changed the world.
She felt humbled. She also had a glimmer of the sense
of entrapment he must feel to be tied now to a landed
estate, a responsibility he would not shirk, because he
was not a man to evade his duty.

"The mess room." Owen threw wide another door.

The room smelled of dust and tar. It was very sparsely furnished, containing only a round wooden table in the center and a few chairs. There were some battered books on a shelf cut into the panelling and a chess set carved from what looked like ivory.

"Whalebone," Owen said briefly. He was rummaging in some cupboards. "Your sister was remarkably good at chess. She beat Alex every time."

"Our uncle taught us to play chess," Tess said. She ran her fingers over the pieces, feeling the worn smoothness of the bone. "My game was always vingt-et-un, though."

"We must play sometime," Owen said, and something in his eyes made her catch her breath.

"I hear you never lose."

"I hear the same thing of you," Owen said. "They say that you must cheat because no one could be so lucky."

Tess replaced the Queen gently on the dusty chessboard. "I don't cheat," she said. "It's simply that I can picture all the cards and so…" She shrugged. "I count them."

Owen looked taken aback. Then he laughed. "So that's how you do it," he said. "Counting cards. Some do call that cheating."

"I have a good memory," Tess objected.

"And a huge fortune as a result." Owen straightened up, two glasses in one hand and a bottle in the other.

"I'm glad this is still here," he said. "It should have matured nicely by now."

"That," Tess said, eyeing the bottle mistrustfully, "looks disgusting, whatever it is."

"It's called bumbo," Owen said. He polished the glasses on his jacket and filled them. "Rum, water, lime, sugar and nutmeg. A favourite tipple of pirates." He raised his glass and saluted her.

"To you, madam gamester."

Tess took a mouthful of the bumbo and almost choked. It tasted as vile as it looked, sweet and yet unpleasantly sharp in flavour and wickedly strong. She groped for one of the wooden chairs and sank into it, her legs already feeling a little weak from the spirit.

"So you *were* a pirate," she said slowly.

Owen shook his head. She saw the flicker of something in his eyes. "I was never a pirate," he said. There was a harsh edge to his voice. "I always sailed under the rule of law. Where there is no law there can only be chaos."

"You do look more like a Navy captain than a privateer," Tess said. "You're not flashy like Devlin, all pearl earrings and gold-embroidered waistcoats. He looks like one expects a pirate to look." She took another absentminded mouthful of the bumbo. It tasted less unpleasant this time, the spice stronger, the rum less of a fierce burn in her throat. She thought about Owen making his fortune, buying his own ship, an adventurer, an explorer, a man who took what he wanted with such quiet ruthlessness that one would only notice once it was taken.

"But that's what is dangerous about you," she said slowly.

"What is?" Owen said. He was sitting very still and his lazy gaze on her made her feel hot all over.

"That you are so controlled," Tess said. "You are relentless and determined and—" She swallowed. "You have the patience to wait for what you want."

Owen smiled. The expression in his eyes was vivid and watchful. "How well you know me already," he said.

Tess drained her glass. She was starting to feel very odd. The winter sun was low over the water, dazzlingly bright. The ship rocked gently on the current. She felt a little dizzy, her senses adrift.

"Why did you marry me?" she said suddenly. She knew it was the drink talking but she could not seem to help it. "Was it only for the money?"

Owen did not answer immediately but he did not take his eyes from her face either.

"I married you because I wanted you," he said.

His words hit her straight in the solar plexus and she almost gasped aloud. Well, she had wanted to know— and now she did. He was making no pretence of his desire for her. It was something she had to face. She reached for the bumbo and splashed a little more into her glass, drinking it down almost recklessly.

"You should not," she said, not looking at him.

"Want you?" His words were very quiet. Tess looked up and was almost scorched by the look in his eyes.

"I can't promise..." Her mouth dried. All the excitement, all the anticipation she had felt earlier drained away in an instant when confronted by the stark reality. Owen wanted her but she was so damaged she did not know if she would be able to bear his touch or if she would run away in despair.

"I can wait." He sounded philosophical even though his expression belied the words.

"You should not wait for me." She wanted him to understand. "I may never be able to be the wife you need." She swallowed what felt like a sharp wedge trapped in her throat. "Sometimes I think that Brokeby damaged me beyond mending."

Owen stood up very slowly. He took her hands and drew her to stand also. "The question," he said softly, "is do you want to try to mend?"

In that moment all Tess knew was that he felt very strong and sure, holding her, and that her head was spinning from the bumbo and that she thought her knees might give way at any moment.

"I think I do," she murmured, and he smiled, the dazzling smile that always made her feel warm through and through.

"This morning you trusted me," he said. "I am glad that you have not changed your mind."

"I'm scared," Tess said. Her tongue really was running away with her now. "I want to try but it terrifies me."

He shook his head slightly and she fell silent.

"You don't need to be afraid of me," he said. "I'd never hurt you." His expression changed. "I'd like to kiss you," he said. "One kiss. That's all. May I?"

Excitement laced with fear coursed through Tess again, as sharp and fierce as the kick of the drink.

"Always so polite," she managed to say. "You do not simply take what you want."

Owen's eyes went so dark with lust that she knew exactly what he wanted. Knew, too, that she should not play dangerous games with him when she could not follow through.

"No." He sounded constrained. "I ask first."

Tess felt another shiver of anticipation. Could it really be so easy to forget the past? A ripple of apprehension shook her, chasing away the excitement. No, of course it was not. She could play these games because she felt safe with Owen, but once it became serious, once it became real, the fear would return and swamp her and drive away all pleasure.

"Trust me." His fingers swept across her cheek, a feather-light touch. There was a smile in his voice. "Close your eyes."

She obeyed. Her heart was beating light and fast now, with nervousness, not anticipation. She waited for the touch of his lips on hers. He would be gentle. She was sure of it. She was also sure she would feel nothing at best and would run screaming from him at worst.

The pad of his thumb brushed the fullness of her bottom lip and she gave a little gasp of surprise, then his lips were covering hers.

Tess waited, stiff in his arms, her back rigid, feeling nothing at all. Despair welled in her.

Owen was kissing her softly, persuasively, with such tenderness that it made her want to weep. That was not, she was sure, the reaction he would want, nor the one he was accustomed to from the woman in his arms.

Nothing. She felt Owen pause, and knew he was about to withdraw. She felt hollow and cold, distressed to have lost all the lovely warm promise. Owen's lips moved on hers again and then—she did not know how it happened—she felt something shift deep within her, something instinctive that she barely understood. She felt herself tremble and heard a tiny sound that she realised was hers. Her lips softened and parted, she found she was pressing closer to Owen rather than drawing away, and then he was kissing her again and this time it was not gentle at all but hot and fierce. He tasted of rum and spice and something else delicious, and Tess's head swam and the floor most definitely shifted beneath her feet in a way that had nothing to do with the tide.

In a second it was all over. Owen released her so fast that she had to grab the edge of the table to steady herself.

"I'm sorry." He was breathing as though he had been

in combat. He rubbed his forehead, looking dazed. "I was expecting a rejection."

"And you could not deal with a response instead?" Tess arched her brows. There was a new emotion stealing through her, wicked and powerful. It shocked her to recognise it as triumph. Extraordinary. But she could not deny that the confusion in Owen's face made her feel very good indeed.

His gaze came back and focussed on her intently. Desire flared in his eyes. He took a step towards her.

It was then Tess felt the fear. It was swift, visceral and it ambushed her with ruthless intensity. She caught her breath on a gasp and took a hasty step back, bumping into the wood-panelled cupboard, setting the glasses clinking. Owen caught her arm to steady her but then released her immediately.

He leaned the palms of both hands on the table. His mouth twisted into a rueful smile. "I'm sorry," he said. "Don't look like that. I have no intention of pouncing on you like an untried youth."

Tess put a tentative hand on his arm. "I didn't intend to tease," she said uncertainly.

Owen's expression lightened. He covered her hand with his, brief and reassuring. "I know, sweetheart."

The endearment filled her with sweetness. "It's new to me," she said. "And…" She hesitated, wanting to be honest, not provocative. "I did like it very much when you kissed me."

She saw the light leap in Owen's eyes "We could try it again," he said, a little huskily, "if you would like."

"May we?" Tess said.

This next kiss was better, almost startlingly so, so good it shocked her. It was as though she had learned so much already and had a hunger for more. Her body responded instantly this time, with no hesitation or fear. Owen kept the kiss frustratingly light, his lips a mere whisper against hers, but even so when he released her the cold day felt hot and Tess shivered a little with emotion.

Owen took her hand in his. "Come along," he said. "I am minded to show you the Blackheath Caverns before we have dinner and return home." He looked around the dusty mess room. "I would not consummate our marriage here anyway. There are almost certainly ship's lice. And weevils."

"I thought that weevils lived in biscuits," Tess said.

"You are remarkably well-informed on the habits of maritime parasites," Owen said. "I knew you were a bluestocking all along."

"So are you going to keep her?" Tess asked, as Owen helped her down onto the quay. "She could do with a lick of paint, poor creature, but she's a beautiful ship and she deserves all the love you can give her."

Owen looked at her quizzically. "Do you think so?"

"Oh, yes," Tess said. She ran her hand along the shabby peeling paint of *Sea Witch'*s side and tried to imagine her crashing through the Atlantic breakers, the wind whipping through her sails and the sun beating down, or nosing her way through the Arctic ice under a frozen blue sky. The thought excited her. She was not sure why. She had never been interested in travel before but now she was hungry for it. She wanted to sail beside Owen and see what the world had to offer.

"She'll take every penny of your fortune," Owen warned her. "And then more. It's a monstrous extravagance owning one's own ship for pleasure rather than industry."

"I don't care," Tess said. She pressed her palm to *Sea Witch's* side. "I think I may have fallen in love with her. And besides," she added, "you will need to escape sometimes, Owen. I feel it in you. You cannot be tied to the land for too long or you will start to feel trapped."

She saw some expression shimmer in Owen's eyes and then his hand came up to touch her cheek and he twined his fingers in her windblown hair.

"What a wonderful woman you are, Teresa Rothbury," he said, and there was a tone in his voice that Tess did not understand. "I'll see the broker next week," he said. "Make all the arrangements. If you are sure," he added, with another keen look at her.

Tess nodded. She was sure. But she wished that Owen had said he wanted her to journey beside him.

The drive through Greenwich to Blackheath was fascinating, through the narrow cobbled streets with ancient taverns on the corners and the shops with their signs swaying in the breeze. After a few minutes the older, more cramped backstreets gave way to wider tree-lined avenues and grand mansions.

"It's like a miniature version of Bath," Tess said, craning her neck to study the crescent of elegant houses that formed Gloucester Circus. "Except that it has a whiff of gunpowder and salt and leather about it."

"So you do travel outside London occasionally then," Owen said.

"All the world goes to Bath," Tess said. "It's fashionable."

"I'd like to be a country gentleman," Owen said, as they passed a row of neat villas with well-kept gardens. "It would have suited me much better than a viscounty."

"You can be a country gentleman at Rothbury Chase," Tess said.

Owen laughed. "I didn't want twenty-thousand acres," he said. "That seems greedy. I don't need so much."

There was such a warmth in his eyes when he looked at her that Tess's heart tripped a beat.

"I like these outings with you," she said. "When we did this before we wed it felt as though we were becoming friends. Naively I thought how good it was to have a male friend. But now..." She stopped, trying to untangle her feelings. "I feel as though I have lost you in some way," she said slowly.

Owen shifted along the carriage seat and took her hand. "Why can there not be friendship between us?" he asked.

"Because men and women generally cannot be friends," Tess said.

"As I recollect," Owen said, "you were the best of friends with your first husband."

"That was different," Tess argued. "Robert and I had known each other from childhood. In most cases, however, other things get in the way."

"Other things?" His brows rose.

"You know what I mean!" Tess said. "Sex always gets in the way."

She saw that Owen was trying not to laugh. The amusement danced in his eyes and lifted the corner of his mouth. "You mean you do not think we will remain friends if we sleep with one another?"

Tess was starting to feel very hot and bothered. She wished she had not introduced this topic of conversation at all. Talking about sex was one of the things that she never did, second only to not doing it. Sitting in the enclosed space of the carriage, holding Owen's hand beneath the pile of rugs, felt cozy and intimate but there was an edge of something else to it now as well, something sensual and hot.

"You are twisting my words," she said.

"I beg your pardon." He sounded extremely courteous. "Correct me."

Tess made a little huffy sound. "Now you are making fun of me."

"On my honour I am not."

Tess dared a quick look at him and saw he could not

quite banish the glimmer of amusement from his eyes. She felt a strange, giddy, sliding sensation inside her as his fingers interlaced with hers.

"I swear it," he said. "I am…fascinated…to hear your thoughts on the relationship between us and how it might change if we…ah…make love with one another."

Oh. Tess's breath caught. She wished Owen had not used those words. Her mind translated them instantly into pictures of erotic excess. She felt very heated. The giddy sensation had transmuted into a tight coil of excitement in the pit of her stomach. Her lips parted. She felt no fear now, only an intriguing sense of what might happen.

Owen was watching her, his eyes so intent on her face it was almost like a physical touch. His thumb was brushing the palm of her hand and it was creating the most delightful sensations in her.

"Teresa," he said. "You won't lose me, if that is what you fear. We will still be the best of friends. Our marriage will simply be—" He paused. "Different." His voice dropped. "Better, possibly, if you find you like it." There was a thread of amusement in his tone. He brushed the hair away from the hollow of her collarbone. "My worship of your body," he said softly, his eyes intent on the slow, sensual stroke of his fingers against her skin, "as well as my sincere admiration for your mind."

Her mind, Tess thought dazedly, was in danger of splintering into tiny pieces if he carried on like this.

My worship of your body...

She gave a tiny sensual shiver, remembering the way she had felt when he had kissed her on the ship, remembering that shift of sensation deep inside. Her body twitched again in recognition. It shocked her. Somewhere she possessed a knowledge she had not even guessed at.

"I would like to worship every curve and every hollow you possess," Owen whispered, "with the touch of my hands and my lips…" This time his mouth brushed her throat and Tess felt the echo of that touch in the pit of her stomach. The images rampaging through her mind now were setting her on fire. She did not understand what Owen was doing or how he could make her feel like this. His fingers were against her cheek and his touch felt good, as gentle as his next words. "There will be no more fear or revulsion," he said. "I promise you, Teresa. There will be nothing but pleasure."

The tight knot of heat in Tess's belly intensified. Instinctively she leaned into the caress of his fingers as they fell to the hollow at the base of her throat.

"You like me touching you," Owen said. "That's good." There was an edge of roughness to his words that unsettled her nerves. And she did like it. She was shocked at the knowledge, shocked by her reaction. She was so accustomed to thinking herself cold, but this heat in her blood was like a fever. Yet from the first, she had liked Owen touching her; his palm against the arch of her foot when he had helped her with her slippers outside the brothel; his hand on the small of her back when they had visited the Picture Gallery. Her heart contracted as she realised the truth.

She not only liked him touching her, she ached for him to touch her. She wanted him.

She closed her eyes and allowed the fear to empty from her mind so there was no thought, nothing but sensation, and when Owen's mouth claimed hers a second later she felt pleasure so hot and sweet she almost groaned aloud. She recognised the taste and touch of him now and she craved it. When she felt the tip of his tongue coaxing her to open for him she parted her lips and allowed him in, and was at once lost in the mysterious feelings created by each delicious sweep of his tongue against hers.

Nothing but pleasure…

She felt starved for him, pressing closer into his embrace, hearing Owen groan against her lips with a ragged need that was an echo of the emotion that drove her.

The carriage jerked to a halt, almost depositing her in Owen's lap. Not that she would have minded.

"We are here," he said. His voice was a little hoarse. "I'm tempted to drive around in circles for a while but we had better not. I have no intention of consummating our marriage here any more than I had on the ship, and if I do not exercise a bit of control that is exactly what will happen."

"You are very particular," Tess said. She sat for a moment trying to work out how she felt. The overriding sensation was one of strangeness. Her body felt thwarted with wanting. It was the most unfamiliar and curious feeling. Just as the kisses on the ship had ended too soon, so she had started to want to explore the feelings this kiss had aroused. Owen had definitely stopped before she was ready. She wanted him to kiss her again, for longer, thoroughly, properly or perhaps more improperly. A wedge of frustration lodged inside her.

"Are you going to join me?" Owen was waiting to hand her down from the carriage.

"I suppose so," Tess said, sighing. "Though why you imagine I should wish to explore some sort of cave is quite beyond me."

"For the same reason you wished to ascend the Monument or visit Greenwich," Owen said. "You like being with me. You said so yourself."

"Such arrogance," Tess said, biting her lip to repress a smile.

Owen swung her down to the ground and kept his arms about her for a second. "You know you like me, darling," he murmured, his lips nuzzling her ear. "You have just shown me how much."

"I do," Tess said. "I confess it." She put a hand on the nape of his neck and brought his mouth down to hers. "I think," she whispered against his lips, "that I am discovering something I enjoy almost as much as sightseeing."

Kissing Owen in the open air made her feel as wicked and carefree as a young girl, she discovered. It was a very long time since she had felt so light and alive. Her lips parted to allow his to fit them and delicious sensations swept through her again. Oh, she had such a curiosity about this now. It all but consumed her. Cold snowflakes drifted down to melt against her face as the hot, languorous desire took her.

"Teresa," Owen said, pulling back, "we will become a tourist attraction in our own right if we carry on like this. Besides—" Tess heard his voice change as he felt her shiver in the bitter winter breeze "—on a practical note, it will be warmer underground."

"I had heard that Greenwich was an indecorous place," Tess said, allowing him to take her hand and lead her towards the entrance to the caverns. "Now I know it's true."

The attendant took Owen's money and handed him a candle. Tess followed him down the deep steps cut into the rock. As they descended under the white archway of chalk the air grew warmer and the shadows deeper.

"How frightfully gothic," Tess said, shuddering as the caverns below glowed ghostly white in the candlelight. "When were they discovered?"

"They were rediscovered a few years ago," Owen said, "though no one knows when they originated. Perhaps they were quarried by the Romans." He held the candle high as they reached the bottom and the natural light receded to a speck above their heads. "They hold dances down here. See the chandelier?"

As Tess looked up, a stray draught of wind blew down the steps and set the chandelier tinkling like ghostly music. It doused the candle flame with a soft puff. Far above them the door slammed shut. Immediately the darkness closed around them and with it came a damp chill that seemed to seep from the walls and sink into her bone-deep. Tess shivered. Suddenly she felt much colder in the unrevealing gloom. Her memory was full of darkness, of a door closing and the light being extinguished. She fought the fear but it pressed in on her. She gave a little gasp of panic.

Owen groped for her hand. "Are you all right?" he said urgently.

"Yes." Tess's teeth were chattering. "I'm sorry. I am scared of the dark."

Owen gave a soft curse. "I was a fool for bringing you down here."

"No!" Tess squeezed his hand. "You said it yourself, Owen. I cannot spend my life in fear."

Owen drew her close. His arms were strong and comforting around her chilled body. Tess's world steadied.

"They will be down with a candle to light us out very soon," he said.

Tess turned her face up to his. "Why did it happen?"

"A draught from above, or a lack of oxygen, perhaps," Owen said. "Such things are enough to douse the lights completely." His cheek brushed hers in the darkness, cool and a little rough. She felt his breath ruffle her hair. Instantly her senses filled with the scent of him, of cologne, ship's tar, fresh air. She felt dizzy. She remembered their kisses, the feel of his lips against hers, the blaze of desire and the driving need to be closer still.

But this felt different. Tess hesitated for a moment and then took a step closer and rested her hands against Owen's chest. She pressed against him, instinctively seeking reassurance and comfort. She felt safe and loved and at the same time her heart pitched over and she felt as though she had stepped right off the cliff and into thin air.

She felt his chest move against her cheek, felt his lips brush her brow, and her need transformed from the search for comfort to something sharper and hotter. Desire. She had so seldom felt it before. Now it burned her at every turn.

She could feel Owen's heartbeat beneath her fingers, felt it accelerate as she stood on tiptoe and pressed her lips inexpertly to the corner of his mouth. The darkness was intimate, tempting. It made her feel brave. He had kissed her before, taken control. Now she wanted to try.

Tess heard him draw a sharp breath and in the same moment realised that she had never kissed a man and did not know how to do it, particularly when she could not even see what she was doing. She stood still, frozen into mortification, her lips an inch from his. Trapped between desire and embarrassment, feeling her body heat with what was surely the latter, not the former, she was about to withdraw when Owen bent his head.

"You think too much," he whispered against her lips. "Just do it."

That this was not bad advice was her last coherent thought before his mouth claimed hers unerringly in the darkness. Tess felt relief but it was banished as soon as it came, swamped by a wave of excitement and lust so fierce that she gasped against his lips. She had not expected it to be so ferocious; it swept her away. Owen's tongue was in her mouth, twining with hers in a kiss so intimate and intense she thought she might melt. His hands were on her shoulders and the cloak fell. She felt one of his palms warm against the small of her back, holding her still against him as the kiss deepened with escalating hunger.

Tess clutched at Owen's forearms to steady herself and felt him shift, felt her back come up against the cold wall of the cave. Hot and cold, her body shivered as though with a fever. Owen was pressing kisses against her throat now and she tilted her head back against the wall to make it easier for him. His lips brushed the hollow at the base of her throat, then the edging of the neckline of her gown, and she arched against him in sheer instinctive need. She drove her hands beneath the superfine of his coat, feeling the smooth linen of his shirt beneath and the warm muscles of his back beneath that. Owen groaned and Tess felt a flash of power so victorious that she smiled with the pleasure of it.

His fingers slid over the curve of her breast beneath the bodice and her nipple rose instantly against the touch. She felt a tug, and the sting of the cold air was against her bared skin. Her mind spun; it was astonishing, delicious. She had had no idea. And then his mouth was on her *there*.... Her thoughts splintered in shocked delight. Her knees buckled and she thought she was going to faint. Owen caught her before she slid to the ground.

"Too fast." He was breathing so hard she could barely discern the words. He held her tightly, his cheek pressed close against hers. "Teresa. We must slow down."

She did not want to. This was all she wanted now, his mouth on hers, his hands on her body. But already the pleasure was slipping away from her, as elusive as water clasped in the hands. Her heartbeat slowed and her breath steadied. She was no longer afraid of Owen but she was uncertain, inexperienced and utterly taken aback by her own responses and emotions.

"Don't tell me," she said, striving for control. "You have no intention of consummating our marriage in a cavern two hundred and eighty feet underground."

She heard him laugh, still shaken, still close to the edge. "No indeed."

Candlelight flared; the voice of the attendant called, "Where are you, sir?"

They fell apart, torn from the intimate cocoon that had held them. Tess hauled up her bodice and bent to grab her cloak, wrapping it tightly about her with hands that shook. She felt adrift and disoriented. Her body was still singing from Owen's touch, craving more. In the growing light she could see that his face was taut, his breathing still hard. He tucked his shirt back into his pantaloons and smoothed his jacket, and Tess realised with a pang of shock that she had been the one who had undone those buttons in her desperate quest to be as close to him as she could.

It was fortunate, she thought, that in the face of the anxious attendant she was able to ascribe her flushed cheeks and shaking hands to the effects of being trapped in the dark rather than to the fact that she had been so close to begging for ravishment.

The man was frightfully apologetic, anxious perhaps for his tip. "I don't know how it happened, my lord. The wind got up and the door slammed…."

Tess listened absentmindedly to Owen assuring the man it was in no way his fault and hurried up the steps towards the square of light at the top. Although it was snowing heavily by now she drew in deep breaths of the clear fresh air.

"Are you all right?" Owen said as he handed her up

into the carriage and she sat down rather shakily on the velvet seat. His touch was warm and reassuring now. Her hectic pulse settled, and the turbulent emotions inside her simmered down. She felt safe again.

"What happened?" Tess said. "What happened between us?"

Owen looked moody, almost as though he were angry. "Lust," he said shortly. "And lack of self-control on my part."

Tess thought about it. "I've never felt lust before," she said. "How singular." She thought about it some more. "I rather liked it," she admitted.

Owen's expression had lightened a little. "Any time you would like to experience it again…"

Tess laughed. "Thank you, but I think I was getting a little out of my depth by the end."

"You were not the only one," Owen muttered.

Tess sat staring out of the carriage window as the snow thickened, turning the heath to a white haze beneath a pewter-grey sky. She knew she had a decision to make. She could retreat into caution or she could take the risk. The two emotions tugged on her, pulling in opposite directions, the deep, habitual fearfulness versus an utterly unfamiliar frisson of desire, wicked, wanton, thrilling.

She had not wanted to learn about physical intimacy. Now she did. She wanted to overcome her fears and she wanted to entrust herself to him.

Poor Owen. What a heavy responsibility to place

on a man. A rueful smile curved her lips. "I'm sorry," she said, as the carriage lurched over the snow-covered track. "This whole matter must be a great strain for you."

The spectacular smile that lit his eyes made her heart give one of its giddy leaps. He drew her closer so that her body was just touching his. "I do believe that you are worth it," he said. He gave her a brief, hard kiss. It left her breathless. "But yes," he added wryly, "it is rather like trying to sail *Sea Witch* through the passage of The Needles. One false move and we are wrecked."

Tess gave a spontaneous giggle. "You are comparing me to a shipwreck?" She touched her hand to his cheek. "I was thinking more in terms of the strain on your self-control."

"That," Owen said, "is very thoughtful of you." He turned his head and kissed her fingers. "That too. It is completely wrecked. I have decidedly less self-control than I thought I had." He kissed her again, more slowly this time, lingering, sensual, until Tess felt as though she was melting with the bliss of it. She drew back. Owen's eyes were dark with the intensity of his desire. Her heart thudded. To entrust herself to him… She did not know if she had the courage.

"You think too much," Owen had said. *"Just do it."*

It had been good advice. Her heart took a huge leap. The nervousness closed her throat. But her decision was made. It was time that she opened the door and banished those dark memories for good. It was time she stepped into the light.

She was going to seduce her husband. And she was going to do it tonight.

OWEN SAT IN THE CORNER OF THE carriage and watched Tess as they wended their way back to the Old George Inn in Greenwich for dinner. She was leaning forwards and gazing out of the window, her face averted from him. Given that it was almost full dark outside and that the snow was falling like a shroud now, he doubted that she could see much of the heath.

He wondered if her avoidance tactics were because she was shy, shocked by what had happened between them in the caverns. It did not seem likely given her incendiary response to him and he hoped it was not the case. He had seen the bemusement on her face when the candlelight had first fallen on it and there had been astonishment in her eyes but no dread and no fear. Tess was discovering something she had never known, something that she was amazed to find she enjoyed very much, and, truth to tell, he had been equally astonished by her eagerness and her unrestrained response. Owen bit off a smile. He had never seen himself as a tutor. The women he had known had been as experienced as he. But this was exciting stuff. Introducing Tess to physical pleasure, watching her delight in the discovery, was going straight to his head as well as to other fundamental parts of his body. And they had barely started. Soon, if he were not careful, he would believe himself God's gift to women.

Soon she would be driving him to the edge of madness.

He had promised himself and promised her that he would take matters slowly, but twice now Tess's passionate reaction to him had almost made him lose that control. He had been taken by surprise. He had underestimated her. She might be damaged by what had happened in her past but she was brave enough to try again.

Tess caught the edge of his glance and their eyes met. She gave him a smile he had never seen on her lips before, a smile full of promise, wickedly teasing. Owen realised with a shock that she had not been avoiding his gaze because she was shy, quite the contrary. She had been exploring all manner of decadent thoughts. She was intrigued by what had happened between them, not repulsed.

The air between them instantaneously seemed to heat and burn. Owen felt his body start to harden into arousal. He wanted to grab her, tumble her onto the carriage seat beneath him and make frantic love to her. The need he had for her seized him by the throat so hard and fast his mind reeled.

Hell. How could Tess do this to him with only a few kisses?

This was going to be excruciatingly difficult. He had had no idea. And now he was committed. He was honour-bound to take this very slowly indeed.

"Will we be there soon?" Tess said innocently, her blue eyes wide. "I am very hungry."

Hell and the devil. So was he. Owen turned his mind away from the many and varied ways he wished to slake that hunger.

CHAPTER THIRTEEN

IT WAS DANGEROUS FOR Tom Bradshaw to venture into Mayfair where so many people might recognise him and where so many wanted him arrested, tried and hanged. But it was more dangerous to stay away, because Tom knew that fate was closing in. It was the end game.

He had been following Justin Brooke all day, noting the places he went and whom he met. Now his quest had brought him to this shabby house in Dover Street, tucked almost unnoticed between Green's Hotel and the Dragon Club. He slid around the back of the house, scaled the wall with considerable ease and dropped down onto a snow-covered terrace that looked directly through the dusty windows of a library.

There were three men in the room, hunched around a table before the fire. Tom had already known that Brooke would be there. A second man he accurately and contemptuously identified as Catesby, one of Lord Sidmouth's most treacherous agents. Sidmouth would not attend such a meeting in person, of course. He would want total deniability that he had ever been involved in a plot such as this. But Tom knew the Home

Secretary was implicated. He was in it up to his neck, in fact.

The third man was unknown to Tom and he viewed him with some interest. He was not young but neither was he old. He had an equine face framed by excessively large shirt points, a ridiculously dandified waistcoat and a rangy body slumped in one of the battered wing chairs. He was a gentleman by birth perhaps but no gentleman to be part of such an unholy trinity as this.

Tom watched as Brooke took from his pocket some drawings and laid them on the table. Sidmouth's spy stooped over them like a hawk. The dandy picked one up, perused it lazily and dropped it with a laugh. Tom pressed closer to the window. Even from here he could see the cartoons with their strong black lines and the arrogant signature by Jupiter. For a moment Tom was shocked that Rothbury must have ignored his warning and not told Tess of the danger in which she stood if she continued to act as the radicals' cartoonist. Then his stomach dropped as the truth hit him. These were not Tess's drawings. They were Emma's work. Justin Brooke must have persuaded his sister to take up the mantle of Jupiter as caricaturist for the radical faction, and Emma, always so ardent in support of those causes she believed in, had agreed. Tom beat his fist against the rough stone of the wall. Emma had been in enough danger before when she had merely attended the radical meetings. By becoming Jupiter, the figurehead of the radicals, she was stepping directly into the line of fire.

Sidmouth's spy was addressing Justin, firing off questions at him. From what Tom could gather they were going to use the caricatures to incite violent trouble at the next big radical meeting the following week. But that was not all. Sidmouth wanted to capture Jupiter, the figurehead, the talisman, and Brooke was nodding. The dandified wretch in his gold brocade waistcoat was suddenly alive as though someone had jerked his strings and was sitting forwards, and it was Tess Rothbury's name that had caught his interest. Catesby was talking now about how they could use the cartoons to trap and arrest Tess, and Brooke looked as though he wanted to protest, but in the end he slumped in his seat, his face grey, and said nothing at all. Tom could see that Brooke had betrayed Tess, just as he had suspected he would. And now Sidmouth's spy also knew that Emma had been complicit in the drawing of the cartoons and that made Tom's heart contract with terror because Sidmouth was ruthless and Emma was in terrible danger and her own brother had put her there.

Tom felt a wave of despair sweep through him. He did not know how to warn Emma. She would never believe a word against her brother, least of all if the warning came from him. Emma had steadfastly refused to see him and Tom knew that Brooke, who had orchestrated his removal from Emma's life in the first place, had completely poisoned her mind against him. Yet still he had to try to persuade her of her brother's perfidy before it was too late. And he had no notion how he was going to do it.

TESS WAS NOT HUNGRY. IT WAS A shocking waste of good food, she thought, but there was no getting away from it. Ever since she had decided that she was going to seduce Owen she had been simultaneously exhilarated and terrified, completely unable to eat a crumb. Nature was conspiring with her too; by the time they had reached Greenwich the snow was too thick for them to return to town and they were marooned at the Old George Inn for the night.

The inn parlour was deliciously warm, with an open fire that had soon thawed the cold from the caverns and soothed Tess after the long, slow drive through the snow. The beef pie steamed deliciously and there was hot soup to tempt her if the pie did not. The landlord had already been in twice, his brow increasingly furrowed when he saw she had not touched the food and drunk only a drop or two of her coffee.

"You'll make the poor man most unhappy if he thinks his food not good enough for the Viscountess Rothbury." Owen had discarded his jacket and was sitting opposite her, elbows on the table, shirtsleeves rolled up and showing his muscular forearms dusted with golden hairs. His voice was cheerful but in his eyes was the same concentrated intensity with which he had been watching her since they had arrived. Something clenched inside Tess, released and clenched again, and she found the latest mouthful of pie had turned to sawdust in her mouth and the breath was trapped in her throat.

"It's your fault." She wanted to sound cross but the words came out too faint to contain any authority. She drew a jerky breath. "All you do is look at me. Like that."

A smile she could only describe as smug curved Owen's lips. "And so you lose your appetite?" he said.

"Yes, damn you." She pushed the plate away. The soup slopped. "I'm hungry. Starving. But when you look at me like that you make me nervous."

The smile in Owen's eyes made her heart ache fiercely. "I'm sorry," he said. "You have nothing to fear." He stretched. Tess watched the ripple of muscle beneath the linen of his shirt. "I have booked two separate rooms."

"I don't want my own room," Tess said. "I want to stay with you." She felt hot, mortified, and yet there was a razor-sharp edge of excitement in her stomach. She swallowed convulsively. Well, the words were out now. Let him make of them what he would.

Owen stilled. He put down the beaker of ale he was holding. "If you are concerned that you will not be safe on your own I can assure you that this is a very respectable inn."

"Please don't be obtuse," Tess whispered. "I do not want my own chamber as I wish to be with you. I want to make love with you."

She pressed her palms together. They felt slightly damp. Her whole body felt strange, aware of each shift and slide of her gown like a caress against her skin. She was burning up inside, part anxiety, part wicked delight. She was not sure if she was mad to take this risk and entrust herself to Owen when she was so uncertain of everything. She only knew that her instinct prompted her to give herself to him. She had been alone for ten long, barren years and now that could change only if she took a leap of faith.

Owen looked completely winded. In the light from the fire Tess watched his expression. There was shock there, she thought, but also temptation. She felt a flare of hope.

"Teresa," he said. "It's too soon."

"Ten years is not too soon," Tess said.

Owen rubbed his forehead. "This morning you wanted a divorce."

"I didn't really," Tess said. "But fear has become a habit for me. I was accustomed to running away, but you made me stand and face it." She spread her hands in a gesture of appeal. "Owen, if we wait I shall only become more anxious, not less so. I shall be forever worrying about what will happen when finally you… we…" She stopped, groped for words. "The longer it goes on, the worse it will be."

"So you want to get it over with." Owen's face was impassive. "Not precisely the approach I would wish."

"It's like riding a horse…." Tess stopped again and

blushed. "Well, perhaps that is an infelicitous analogy, but what I mean is that I should have tried again long ago, instead of becoming imprisoned in my own fears." Her voice dropped. "But until now I had not met anyone I would have trusted sufficiently to make love to me." She raised her eyes to his. "Please don't refuse me."

She could sense the conflict in him. "Teresa," he said. "Damn it, I'm trying to do the right thing here."

"This is right," Tess said. She came across to him and laid her mouth on his. "It could not be more right," she whispered against his lips.

For a moment Owen did not respond, but then his hand came up to cup the back of her head and his lips parted hers and he kissed her back, fierce and sweet.

Then he put her away from him. "Teresa," he said.

Tess was not going to give him the chance to refuse her again. She slid onto his lap and kissed him again, her hand delving beneath the linen of his shirt to find the warmth of the skin beneath, splaying her fingers over his heart.

"You know you want me," she said. "Owen, please…"

Owen gave a small groan. The heat and light in his eyes was so bright it scorched her, arousing in her an excitement that eclipsed the fear as the sun eclipsed the moonlight.

"Please," she whispered again.

Owen made an inarticulate sound that Tess interpreted as encouragement to kiss him again. She snuggled closer and felt the resistance in him falter. He pulled her to him with sudden need and then he was kissing her deeply, desperately, and the light burst in Tess's mind like a scattering of stars and she was not afraid at all, but fiercely glad.

"Oh, thank goodness," she said, as his lips left hers briefly and she was able to draw breath. "At last—"

He kissed her again. It was blissful, wicked and delicious. She opened her mouth to the demand of his and every desire flared into life.

Owen drew back a little. He rested his forehead against hers. He was breathing hard. "You can change your mind at any point, you know," he said. There was amusement, desire and deep understanding in his eyes and it made Tess's heart turn over.

"Yes," she said. "No. I won't want to."

She wanted to run from the heat she saw in his eyes. But she wanted to be caught as well.

"You think too much," she said, smiling. She drew his head back down to hers for another kiss.

"Not here." A long, breathless, heated time later he released her. "Upstairs."

It was fortunate that the night was so inclement and the visitors to the inn so few so no one could see them as they stumbled up the twisting stairs and into one of the rooms that the landlord had set aside. Tess barely noticed it, registering only that it had a huge, deep bed. The curtains were closed against the snowy night and the room was warm and intimately dark with only one candle and the light from the fire.

Owen closed the door and stood resting his palms against it, looking at her. He looked wonderfully dishevelled, she thought, his shirt hanging open, the hair falling across his brow. Her pulse was hammering, nervousness and anticipation inextricably bound together in a taut knot inside her.

"Are you scared too?" she asked.

Owen laughed. "It would be an unusual man who would admit to such a thing."

"You are an unusual man," Tess said. "So?"

"A little." He lightly touched a curl of auburn hair that nestled in the hollow of her throat. "It's a responsibility as well as a privilege."

It was not, she soon realised, a responsibility that he was going to hurry. He drew her down beside him on the bed and kissed her until she felt dizzy and wanting, and her body felt heavy with desire and her clothes felt as though they were an intolerable imposition.

"I need…" She struggled for a moment to be free and Owen released her instantly. He was pale and breathing hard.

"To get rid of my clothes," Tess finished, and his expression relaxed.

"I can help," he said, with a wicked smile, "but you will find me a poor lady's maid."

"No matter." Tess started to unfasten the buttons on her bodice. Her hands shook and slipped a little with impatience, matching the quiver of eager need that was inside her. Owen was watching the movement of her fingers, his head bent and his expression intent. Tess looked up.

"I thought you said you would help."

His methods, she found, were as direct as the man himself. Direct and intensely exciting. He tumbled her back down onto the bed, pushed aside the bodice of her gown and tugged the ribbon on her chemise. His hands were warm on her bare shoulders as he slid the material down over the curves of her breasts. Tess lay still, pleasurably, sublimely shocked, absorbing the kiss of the air against her naked skin, absorbing too the heat and desire in Owen's gaze as he looked on her.

"You're so beautiful…."

He sounded almost reverent. His hands swept over her, every curve and every hollow, worshipping her just as he had promised. He feathered kisses along her neck and down to the tender line of her collarbone. His tongue flicked the hot skin there and moved on to taste the base of her throat. Tess found she wanted to arch upwards to the mastery of his touch.

He bent his head to her breasts then paused, his lips an inch away from her nipple. In a second she was back in the Blackheath Cavern, remembering the tug and pull of his mouth on her. The memory conjured a hot, sliding excitement inside her. She could not help herself then; she arched to meet his lips and gave a broken cry as he took her in his mouth.

She wanted more of this. More of the sensuous flick of his tongue over her, more of the teasing nip of his teeth, more of this extraordinary pleasure. She had never known this, never imagined it.

"You taste delicious." Owen raised his head a little. "I want to eat you."

He did. Tiny biting kisses that raised the goose bumps all over her breasts as his teeth grazed her and his tongue salved away the hurt, and Tess groaned at the ecstasy of it and writhed against the covers, feeling the provocative chafing of the brocade bedspread against her naked back.

"I should have shaved," Owen said, looking up, seeing the stung pink skin of her breasts.

"No," Tess said, with feeling. "You should not."

He laughed and came down beside her. "My darling." He kissed her, deep and hot, his hand replacing his lips at her breast, fingers teasing the hard nipple until she squirmed.

She wanted to ask him to hurry. She wanted to beg him to make love to her. There was such a hot, demanding ache inside her. Her legs were all tangled in the weight of her skirts and the linen of her petticoats. The folds of material felt unbearably heavy, holding her down.

"Please..." The word slipped from her lips before she could prevent it and she saw his lips curve into a smile of delight.

"You like it." He sounded relieved. He licked the underside of her breast and she gave a laugh that broke on a moan. *Liking* was far too small a word for what she was feeling. She reached out and unfastened his pantaloons, fumbling a little with the button. She heard his breath hiss through his teeth in shock.

"Teresa—" There was a harsh edge to his tone, a warning that if she really was not certain she should stop now. But she was not afraid. She tested her feelings and felt the triumph. The fear had been crowded out, banished by wicked, wanton desire. She wanted to touch him. She needed to touch him.

She raised herself on one elbow and turned towards him. She tugged stealthily on his drawers, pulling them down. His cock sprang free, smooth, hard and hot in the palm of her hand. No indeed, he was not impotent and she could not remember why on earth she had wanted him to be.

"Ah..." His gasp told her how close he was to the edge of control.

"Keep still." She pressed her lips to his ear. She could feel every muscle tense in his body. "You have to be patient with me, Owen. Remember? You said I could explore." She ran a hand along his length to emphasise her words and felt the shudder rack him. Such power she had. She loved it. She tried another caress, from base to tip. She squeezed.

His hand closed about her wrist like iron.

"Not this time, unless you want to kill me." He did genuinely sound as though he was in extremity. His eyes were tightly shut. He looked as though he were making some complex mathematical calculations in his head. His fingers gentled on her wrist. "You probably don't understand," he said, "but I will not last two seconds if you touch me again."

Tess might never have experienced it before but she understood his predicament perfectly well. She put out a hand and cupped his balls, just to test the truth of his words.

"Liar." She breathed the word against the hot skin of his neck.

"Ah…" The groan was wrenched from him. He rolled her over so that his weight held her down, drove his hands into her hair and kissed her hard.

For a second Tess felt a flicker of fear at the sheer physical power he was exercising over her. She felt her mind stray towards those dark places and the force and the compulsion that had been imposed on her before. But she was starting to realise that such domination, such taking without consent, had nothing to do with love. With Owen it was different; his kiss held a demand she wanted to meet. He was easing back now, cupping her face, kissing her gently, softly, with such persuasive seduction that she felt her tense body softening into acquiescence again, and from there sliding into eager, sensuous wanting.

He kissed her throat, the tender hollow beneath her ear, the sides of her breasts and then the valley between them. Tess wriggled. The knot of her skirts binding her lower body was becoming intolerable. She was too hot, too constrained.

Owen's hand slid down over the bare curve of her stomach until it reached the edge of her gown, bunched about her hips. The muscles jumped deep in Tess's belly. *Now.* She had to be rid of these horribly constricting layers of material.

"Take it off. *Please.*"

She heard him laugh at the abject entreaty in her voice. She could hear it herself, so uneven, so eager. She would have been ashamed to give away the depths of her desperation had she not been so utterly desperate that actually she did not care.

He laughed. "Oh, all right then. As you ask so nicely."

She felt anything but nice. She felt wanton and wild and full of shock and delight to be that way. Her feelings should have scared her. Instead she was stunned to realise that she felt hopelessly aroused. Her entire upper body was naked, exposed to the cool air, the candlelight and to Owen's gaze. Below she was weighted down with silks and linens, unable to move except to shift restlessly against what felt like unbearable pressure.

Then, at last, she felt the ties of her skirt loosen. Something shifted, the tightness easing, and then she felt cool air against her legs.

"I'm afraid your gown is crushed." Owen sounded polite but not particularly repentant.

"I don't care."

It had been a pretty dress but it was in the way.

Tess felt Owen's hand warm against her ankle and then on the curve of her calf. She was still wearing her stockings; she felt his fingers reach the edge of her garter and pause. She wriggled. She could not help herself. Time spun out whilst she hung suspended in an agony of waiting, then Owen's hand resumed its stealthy slide, inching up the soft skin of her inner thigh. He reached her drawers and paused again.

It was intolerable.

Owen kissed her, his tongue stroking hers, plunging deep, and Tess's mind spun away, fracturing with delight. It took her a moment to realise that the drawers were gone now too. She had not noticed.

"Oh," she said, as she realised, "you are very good at this."

His lips twitched into a smile but his eyes were dark, his jaw tense, and she realised with a pang of shock just how much control he was exercising over himself. There was no haste, no hurry. He was waiting for her every step of the way. His fingers moved gently, persuasively, touching the very core of her. Tess arched again, cried out in shock and astonishment, cascades of sensation shivering through her body. He touched her again and again, such subtle strokes, and Tess thought she would come apart. She ached in the most delicious and wicked ways imaginable. Except that she wanted Owen, not just this blinding delight. It was her last thought before the light exploded in her mind and her body was seized by wave after wave of raking pleasure.

When she came back to herself she was in Owen's arms, skin against skin, lying along the whole length of his body, his lips against her hair. He gathered her close and held her slick body against his, kissing her with persuasive tenderness.

"Did you like that too?" Tess could feel his arousal hard against her thigh and she lay quite still, absorbing the thought that she was naked with a man for the first time in ten long years. She allowed herself to think about the last time, to think about it properly, when before she had always pushed the memories away before they were no more than half-formed. Tears stung her eyes, not for what had happened to her then but for the difference now, for the tenderness and the wonder. Owen brushed the tangled curls away from her cheek, his fingertips gentle against her face.

"All right?" he said, and Tess nodded. Now that the moment had come she realised that she had been wrong to think this might be easy just because she wanted him. But equally she had been wrong to think it would be bad.

He kissed the corner of her mouth. "It won't be perfect."

She smiled. "You do yourself an injustice." It already was perfect no matter how it ended.

His lips moved to claim hers fully this time. "We'll see."

Owen kissed her until she was hot and shaking again, reawakened to the need between them, and then he kissed her some more until she could not think straight anymore and did not want to. They were intimately entangled now, their skin damp and heated everywhere it touched. It felt so luxuriously decadent to be lying here naked with him that Tess wanted to sink into the feeling and let it devour her.

Owen's hand came up to her breast, and her body, already stirring to his touch, restless for more, arched as another wave of need broke over her. She parted her legs and Owen rolled over between them. She tensed, waiting for him to move inside her but instead he slid down the bed until his head was between her thighs, the fall of his hair tickling her sensitised skin.

"Ah…" His voice was a whisper. "So beautiful. So silken."

He spread his hand on her belly, pressing down gently with the heel of his palm to open her even more, then swept his tongue over the sweet centre of her. Tess's body jumped and her mind splintered in disbelief and sheer sensation. Again he tasted her and she lost the last vestiges of all rational thought. She could only feel; feel the pleasure build over and over as his tongue plunged deeper and deeper. She groaned aloud, shifting beneath the renewed caress of his hands. It was impossible, she thought faintly, to bear more. And yet her body was rising to Owen's touch; it seemed to have a will and a knowledge all its own, something she had not known, yet now understood with an awareness as deep as time.

Owen moved over her and then he was there, resting against her. He raised his hips and stroked her core with the tip of his cock. Once, twice, a third time whilst she writhed under him. She grabbed him and tried to hold him still, and he, damn him, just laughed. Then she tried to pull him into her but he held back, bending to kiss her with such tenderness she thought she would melt.

"Patience," he whispered, and there was mischief in his eyes.

Tess dug her nails into the smooth muscles of his shoulders and heard him groan before he slid into her, slow and deep.

It was not as she remembered. It was nothing like anything she had ever experienced. This was smooth and tight and hot and delicious. It was so gloriously intimate and so honest that she felt her heart contract with astonishment.

Owen paused to allow her body to adjust to his presence before resuming a long, slow stroke that seemed to draw the soul from her body. Tess watched his face as he moved, the strength and the concentration, desire distilled, and she wondered to be able to do such a thing to such a man. It filled her with awe to be able to give him so much pleasure.

Yet she knew that for her it was not going to work.

It felt marvellous but somehow it was not enough for

her to completely abandon herself now. She had come such a long way but not quite far enough. The deep, delicious pleasure started to drain away from her. Then she felt the first cold flicker of despair.

Owen sensed it at once. He swooped down to kiss her. "You have to trust me, Teresa." His voice was a harsh whisper. "Don't fight me. We're on the same side."

Tess wondered if she could surrender herself. It felt as though she was relinquishing everything, giving herself up to him utterly. She wanted to do it, she ached for it, but fulfilment shimmered so frustratingly just beyond her grasp.

She was within an inch of giving up. Then Owen bent his head and licked her nipple and the fire shot through her from her breast to deep in her belly and she forgot for a split second to think about anything. He did it again, his hair brushing the sensitive skin of her breast, his mouth hot and relentless on her and she moaned. His hand was there, where their bodies joined, trailing pleasure, igniting fire. And suddenly Tess did not want to fight him, did not want to deny either of them. She wanted to eclipse the past in the intensity of the present. She surrendered completely and in the next instant felt herself fall hard and fast into astonishing bliss. Her body clasped his and she heard Owen call her name and felt him spill his seed inside her, and they broke together, falling over and over into the joy of blistering-bright consummation.

Some time—some unmeasured time—later Tess woke. She stirred and Owen shifted, drawing her closer into his arms. She realised that he had been awake, watching her. His fingers stirred in her hair, caressing.

"I trust you have worked up an appetite now," he murmured.

Tess smiled. "I do seem to be hungry," she murmured. "How helpful you have been."

"My pleasure." Owen's lips tickled the lobe of her ear. His teeth closed about it. He sucked on it. Tess felt the goose pimples cascade over her skin as she shivered with voluptuous sensation.

"We'll send for some food," Owen whispered. His hand was resting low on her stomach, warm and intimate. Tess could feel little ripples of sublime pleasure tightening her belly.

"In a little while," Owen finished. "But first I understand your need to make up for lost time."

This time he made love to her with such slow extravagance that the food, and indeed everything else, was completely forgotten.

CHAPTER FOURTEEN

"MARRIAGE SUITS YOU THIS TIME around." Joanna poured tea into Tess's dainty china cup and offered her an equally dainty cake of sponge and cream. They were in Joanna's drawing room, which glowed warm on this dull November day, bright with hothouse flowers and jewel-coloured porcelain. Joanna, Tess thought with more than a hint of envy, certainly had exquisite taste. Perhaps she might be the best person to transform the old Rothbury mausoleum in Clarges Street after all.

"You look radiant," Joanna continued. A mischievous smile played about her lips. "Am I to assume that you have discovered certain benefits to being married that you had not been aware of before?"

"It has only been ten days but I like marriage very well," Tess admitted, biting into her cake and feeling the cream and jam splurge. She licked her fingers. "Yes, I would say that being wed does indeed have something to recommend it."

"I am glad," Joanna said. She eyed her sister shrewdly. "That, I suppose, is the difference between a marriage of convenience and a love match."

Tess almost choked on her tea. "I'm not in love

with Owen!" she said automatically. The idea seemed absurd, yet as soon as the words were out she felt strange, disloyal, as though she had committed a betrayal.

Love. Now that the word was out it was like the genie from the bottle; she could not force it back in again. She went hot all over with panic. Her cup rattled in the saucer as she put it down. She could not be in love. It was impossible. She had never been in love in her entire life. She did not know how to do it.

"Yes, you are," Joanna said calmly. "You are in love with him."

"No, I'm not," Tess contradicted. The exchange showed signs of degenerating into a schoolroom squabble of the type that had been all too familiar since their childhood.

"You are always running away from things," Joanna complained.

"And you always have to be right."

They glared at each other.

"Well, you *should* be in love with him!" Joanna was looking as angry as Joanna could look, which was to say she looked pretty and disordered and really quite cross. "Why are you not? Because you think it is not fashionable?"

A cold void had opened beneath Tess's heart with each denial. She felt very, very afraid. She knew Joanna was right. Now that the truth was staring her in the face she did not know how she had missed it for so long.

Somehow, when she had not been paying attention, she had lost her heart to Owen. She was no longer in control of her own emotions. She had thought that all she had surrendered was her body and she had liked that. She had enjoyed the discovery of physical pleasure. But all the time Owen's seduction had not been merely to do with physical love. It had involved trust and reassurance, protection and comfort as well as desire. She had fallen hard. Owen had seduced her into loving him with all her heart and all her soul, and now she was terribly vulnerable. She had no defences at all and she was undone.

She picked up her cup again and took a delicate sip of the cold tea. "I've barely come to terms with the concept of lust," she said lightly. She could hear the note of panic in her voice. "I confess I like it extremely. I'm in love with lust."

"You're in love with Owen," Joanna corrected bluntly. "Admit it, Tess."

"Nonsense," Tess said. The sliding panicked feeling inside her intensified. "I *like* him. I like him very much. I feel about him much the same way that I felt for Mr. Chasuble, the dancing master, when I finally learned the steps of the quadrille. A sort of *tendre,* I suppose."

Joanna made a very rude noise. "The two cases are very different and you know it. You light up like the Vauxhall Garden fireworks whenever Owen is near you."

Tess stared blindly into the dregs of her teacup. "Are

you sure?" she said. "I mean, how would you know?" She had never known love. She had closed her life and her mind to it. She had never realised how terrifying— how exhilarating—love might be, how it meant giving everything that she had to give. But now she could not deny it. She felt torn between fear and excitement, lost and found at the same time.

"Believe me," Joanna said. "I know."

Tess felt a tiny shred of hope and warmth. It was a shock to discover that her emotions were engaged but that was only because she was so naive in the ways of love. She had trusted Owen with her body. She could surely trust him now with her heart. But only if he loved her in return, or the balance between them would be too unequal. She frowned. She did not know how Owen felt about her. He had been endlessly tender but that did not mean that he loved her. She was painfully unsure.

"I am glad for Owen," Joanna said. "He deserves someone of his own—" She stopped abruptly.

There was a very curious, very long silence, as though time hung suspended on the thinnest of threads. Tess felt a little dizzy. Joanna was evading her gaze now, fidgeting with the teapot, filling up her cup although it was already almost brimming over. The pale November sunlight shone on the arrangement of hot-house roses in the bowl on the table. They were scentless. Tess could hear the clink of Joanna's cup and the sound of carriage wheels from the street outside, and somewhere in the depths of the house a door closed.

This was the moment when she knew she could simply draw back and make some remark about the weather or the winter fashions or Lady Meriton's ball that night. She could ignore Joanna's remark and pretend that it had not occurred. They would never refer to it again. And yet she could not do it because it was already too late.

"Owen deserves someone of his own," she said softly, "as opposed to loving someone who is in love with someone else?"

A wave of guilty colour washed up from Joanna's neck, staining her cheeks bright pink. Even in guilt, Tess thought sourly, her sister looked very pretty indeed. She wondered how she could have been so slow to understand. She had been aware that Joanna and Owen had known one another for years, since the days of Joanna's first marriage, long before Joanna had married Alex. Owen had taken them to Spitsbergen aboard *Sea Witch*. Tess thought of the cramped accommodation on the ship and the enforced proximity and the adventures they must have shared....

Joanna and Owen. Owen and Joanna...

A wave of violent jealousy crashed over her. She was utterly unprepared for it and it left her feeling physically sick.

"It was you, wasn't it?" she said slowly. "Owen was in love with you." She remembered the day in the park when she had asked Owen if he had ever wanted to wed and he had hesitated for one betraying moment before replying. She knew now; the answer had been, yes, he had been in love. Yes, he had wanted to marry.

He had wanted to marry her sister.

She waited for Joanna to contradict her. She waited with a slowly sinking heart where hope dwindled from a tiny spark to nothing at all. She wanted Joanna to deny it more than anything in the world because the lovely warm confidence she had started to feel in her relationship with Owen was so precious but so fragile. Against the odds she had come to trust him. For a few moments her mind had even started to accept that it might be safe to love him. Her feelings for Owen had been just for her, something new and unspoiled. She had only just started to find her way. Now, as she felt the happiness ooze from her, Tess wondered if it had all been based on shifting sand.

"It wasn't really like that," Joanna said after a moment.

"Tell me how it was, then," Tess said. Her words came out flatly when in her head they sounded like a scream.

"Owen helped me when David treated me very badly," Joanna said in a rush. "You know that my first marriage was not happy." She paused and then as Tess nodded she hurried on. "David assaulted me and Owen paid someone to protect me, that is all. It was one of the boxers from Tom Cribb's tavern. You may remember that I was a Lady of the Fancy before I married Alex, and went to all the boxing matches." Joanna was chattering now, the words spilling over Tess's head and rushing past her unnoticed like a river in full flood. Owen had helped Joanna when she had been in trouble. Well, that was not so bad. Any decent man would surely have done the same. Except… Tess felt doubt nibble at the corners of her mind. Owen had protected *her* when she had been in trouble. Perhaps he had some sort of compulsion to rescue women in distress.

"But by then, of course, I was married to Alex," Joanna was saying, and Tess realised that her sister was still talking, quickly, almost feverishly, avoiding her gaze, shredding the heads of the roses until they looked as though they had had a very bad haircut. "Owen knew I was not happy," Joanna said, "and it is true that he did ask me to elope with him, but I refused and I am sure that he thought no more of it."

Tess found her voice. "Wait," she said. Another roll of sickness beat through her. "Owen asked you to elope with him *after* you had married Alex?"

Again she waited for the denial, because she knew that Owen and Alex had been friends and comrades for years and years, and surely no man would put a woman before that unless he truly loved her and believed her worth smashing to smithereens years of trust. Unless he loved her body, heart and soul, the way she now realised she wanted Owen to love her.…

The deep blush in Joanna's cheeks deepened further. Her expression was furtive but Tess thought there was also a hint of triumph there. She was sure of it. From the nursery Joanna had always wanted everything first, the prettiest clothes, the new dolls—not the books; Merryn was allowed those, since they bored Joanna—the attention, first from their parents and brother, later from men.... Joanna had always been first. Tess simply had not expected her to extend this to being first with her husband, any of her husbands. But particularly not this husband since he was the only one she loved with all her heart and soul.

"I see," she said. Her voice shook, echoing the tremor inside her. She stood up. Even her legs felt a little shaky. "And you were never going to tell me this?"

"I didn't tell you because it was all over a long time ago," Joanna argued. She had got to her feet as well. She put a hand out, took Tess's hand in hers. Hers was warm, as warm as the gentleness in her blue eyes. Tess wished she could believe Joanna was sincere, but she was racked by cold doubt and fear now. It was horrible to imagine that Owen had married her only because he could not have Joanna. It was equally impossible not to think it. And even if he had not, he must have loved Joanna so much, so *very* much—and here the jealously scored her again with its deep claws—to have wanted her to run away with him.

"It meant nothing," Joanna repeated.

Tess snatched her hand away. "It does not mean nothing for a man to ask you to elope with him," she said.

She felt a spurt of anger. "Don't belittle both of you by pretending!"

"Well, no." Joanna was frowning, confused. Tess could see that she was groping for words, words to put matters right or at the least not to make the situation worse. Unfortunately there were no words that could do that.

"As I said, it was a long time ago and I daresay Owen has forgotten," Joanna said.

"*You* have not forgotten!" Tess burst out. She smoothed her skirts in jerky little gestures, creasing and recreasing the lavender silk. Her throat burned with hot tears. She hated herself for her jealousy. She hated that she felt it, that she could not control it. It was like a canker eating away at her.

"Lady Martindale wanted you to decorate the house," she said. It was another vicious little pinprick, the thought of her sister renovating the Clarges Street house that might under different circumstances have been her own. She gave a shudder. "I feel as though you're present in every aspect of my marriage."

"Don't be ridiculous!" Joanna said, sharply now.

"How would you feel if you thought Alex was in love with someone else and that he only married you as second best?" Tess burst out.

A rueful expression touched Joanna's eyes. "Perhaps I understand that better than you think," she said. "When I married Alex I was haunted by the ghost of his first wife." She spread her hands. "But my jealousy was needless and that is how it is for you and Owen, Tess. Ask him. He'll tell you the truth."

Tess rubbed the back of her hand across her eyes. That was what she was afraid of. Owen would tell her the truth because he always did. And she was not entirely sure she wanted to hear it.

She started to walk towards the door. It seemed a very long way.

"I didn't want to hurt you," Joanna said suddenly, from behind her. "Tess, all I want is for you to be happy."

Tess stopped. Her chest felt constricted, as though it was bound very tight.

"Tess…" Joanna said again, and Tess could hear the tears in her sister's voice now.

Her shoulders slumped. She turned. "I know," she said, through the huge lump in her throat. She wanted to be angry with Joanna, wanted to blame her, but it was not possible. She remembered her sister giving her a home after she had been widowed for a third time, remembered Joanna's dogged attempts to reach out to her even though she rebuffed her time and again. It was impossible to hate the sister who loved her and it was unworthy to want to.

"You didn't sleep with him, did you?" she asked. "I don't think I could bear that."

"No!" Joanna looked horrified. "I never even kissed him! I promise you."

Tess nodded. They looked at one another and then they grabbed each other and hugged very tightly.

"I'm sorry," Joanna said, muffled. "Tess, I'm so sorry...."

They hugged again.

"Go to him," Joanna said, loosing Tess, giving her a little shake. "Ask him." She looked dubious. "Or don't, if you prefer not."

"I only wish he had told me of his own accord," Tess said.

She felt miserable as she walked back to Clarges Street through the melting snow. The November wind was bitter even though the sun was out. Tess felt the raw chill on her feverishly hot cheeks. Her eyes felt gritty and sore with suppressed tears and the cold made them sting. Her nose was red. There was little to recommend marriage, she thought, when it totally ruined one's appearance.

Her gloom deepened when she stepped inside the house. It was so dark and murky, overlooked by those ghastly marble busts and stone statues. In a flash of despair she imagined how Joanna would have stamped her mark on the house and made it bright and welcoming and somehow her own.

"Is it true that you wanted to elope with Joanna?" She burst in, flinging open the door of the library. She had not intended to accost Owen like this, but now the jealousy was driving her hard again and she could not hold her tongue. There was a pain about her heart. She had never realised that love could hurt so profoundly.

Garrick Farne was with Owen. Tess registered his presence then ignored him. She planted herself in front of Owen's desk.

"Well?" she demanded.

Garrick got to his feet. "I don't think you need me anymore, do you, Rothbury?"

"No," Owen said. He eyed Tess thoughtfully. "I am sure I can make a hash of this on my own, thank you, Farne."

Garrick grinned. He bowed to Tess and went out.

Tess slapped her gloves down on the table. "Is it true that you—"

"I heard you the first time," Owen said curtly, cutting her off.

Tess stared at him. He had always been so patient with her, so courteous, that she was utterly unprepared for a different reaction. There was a hard, angry light in his eyes. With a shock to the heart Tess realised that this mattered to him. It mattered a great deal. She felt sick despair twist in her stomach.

"Yes," Owen said. "Yes, it's true. I asked Joanna to run away with me. I was in love with her."

She had not even asked that and he was offering the information. Anger at the obtuseness of men in general and her husband in particular lit Tess with a vivid fury.

"So you married me because you could not have her?" she asked sharply.

The darkness in Owen's eyes deepened. The hot, angry atmosphere of the library simmered up several notches.

"That is unworthy of both of you," he said, biting off the words.

All Tess wanted to hear were the words Joanna had spoken—that it had been over a long time ago, that it had meant nothing to him, that she was the one who mattered now. But being a man, he was not going to say the right thing.

"Every time," she said slowly, "when we have been together, I thought you were thinking of me. I can't bear to think that you were thinking of her whilst making love to me."

"I wasn't," Owen said.

"Perhaps you have some sort of obsession with rescuing damsels in distress," Tess continued, as though he had not spoken. The pain sliced through her and she could not prevent herself from inflicting it on him too. "You should consult a physician for a cure before it happens again," she said.

"I don't need a cure," Owen said. He got up and came around the desk. Tess could feel the controlled fury in him as he walked slowly towards her.

"Teresa," he said. "Don't do this. Don't break something so fragile."

"I am not the one spoiling things!" Tess said furiously. "Were you ever going to tell me, Owen? Or did you think I would never find out?" She turned away.

The ache inside her was excruciating. "I trusted you," she said. "I told you every last one of my secrets. I never realised that you told me nothing in return. Now I know why."

There was a long, heavy pause in which even the tick of the clock on the mantel seemed to slow and then Owen grabbed her and kissed her. There was no warning and no time to prepare. It was so utterly out of character that her mind reeled with the shock. And this time he was not being careful. His kiss was fierce, harsh and glorious.

"Does it feel as though I am thinking of anyone but you?" he demanded, as his lips left hers. "Does it feel as though I want anyone but you?"

The turbulent expression in his eyes demanded an answer. It demanded honesty from her.

"No," Tess squeaked. Her heart was beating hard against the silk of her bodice. She thought she should have been frightened by the anger and violence she sensed in him but she was not. Throughout the past ten days he had shown her nothing but tenderness. He had come to her bed every night and made love to her and it had been blissful. But always he had held something back. She had not realised it at the time but she recognised it now. Owen had been careful and considerate with her always, putting her needs and desires first. Not once had he betrayed her trust. He had treated her with absolute tenderness. Now Tess found she did not want that gentleness anymore. Now there was an edge of darkness in him and she responded to it instantly. There was fire here that he had not shown her before and a wild passion. She had sensed that depth of emotion in him but she had never experienced it. Now she felt her own passion rise to meet his.

She stared into his eyes. Her lips parted. Owen made an inarticulate sound and dragged her back into his arms. His mouth came down on hers again, blotting out all thought.

OWEN HAD NEVER INTENDED TO lose control. He had been angry with Tess for her demeaning of his feelings and for the way she had confronted him, but he had intended to talk the matter out calmly and with restraint. Then he had made the mistake of kissing her instead.

All week he had been holding himself back when he touched her, making love to her with exquisite care, trying to make certain that he did not frighten her by asking too much of her too soon. It had been bliss but it had been torment too. To hold her delicious, lush body and treat it like china when he wanted to claim her with everything he possessed, to exercise iron constraint over his own needs and desires when he wanted to plunder her and drive them both to the far shores of pleasure... The strength of his feelings had consistently shocked him. He had never wanted a woman as much as he wanted Tess. Yet it was not simply lust. It never had been.

Owen kissed her again and felt her response, eager and totally unrestrained, and the shock and sheer visceral power of it pushed him right over the edge. He dragged her down onto the wide chaise longue and yanked her close beneath him, moulding every last one of her curves to his, feeling her softness and the heat in her. Her mouth opened beneath his and he kissed her deeply, hungrily, his mind reeling when he heard her voice, a broken whisper, begging for more.

He raised himself above her and searched her face with an urgent gaze. Her eyelashes fanned thick and black against her flushed cheeks. Her lips were parted, stung rosy with his kisses. She was panting.

"These have to go," he said. She was wearing far too many clothes. So was he. He dealt summarily with the buttons and bows on her bodice. Her hands bumped his, impatient as he. Something ripped. Was it his clothes or hers? He did not care. He stopped to kiss her again, and lost himself in the maelstrom of feeling. He felt her hands against his bare chest and groaned.

Her bodice hung open but her skirts, obdurate as they were, were never going to oblige him. He dropped his head to her breast and took her in his mouth so that she cried out. The need that drove him was sharper than anything he had known, blotting out reason, blotting out thought. He lifted her skirts, slid a hand up her thigh and met the hot, damp centre of her. She cried out again and he stroked her, loving the way in which she lifted her hips to beg his touch. She was all heat and fire as he drove her on, his mouth at her breast, his fingers at her core until she trembled for him so much he could wait no longer.

His body was hard and aching. He tossed her skirts and petticoats up to her waist, spread her wide, lifted her hips and pushed deep into her heat. He had not intended it to be so quick but he was beyond control now. She came immediately, with a keening cry, and her body closed around his in pulses so tight and smooth that he almost lost his mind. He thrust into her over and over, deeper and deeper, his hands braced against the rough velvet of the chaise, plunging into her sleek, warm body hard and fast as he possessed her with relentless intensity. He could not seem to quench his need; it left him shaking. He wanted to conquer her completely and claim her forever.

He felt Tess's body gather again and clasp his and he shattered too in a climax so powerful it left him dazed. He had never fallen so swiftly and so completely in all his life and he had certainly never lost all restraint with any woman.

They were both breathing hard. Owen rested his forehead against hers, utterly shocked at his total lack of control and the fierce way he had taken her.

Tess opened dazed eyes, so deep and vivid a blue that his heart clenched. She smiled at him and raised her head a little to kiss him. Her lips, deliciously soft, brushed his. He could feel her smiling against his mouth. Owen thought of Joanna then but only to dismiss her ghost, so pale now in comparison to the deep feelings he had for Tess. Loving Joanna, he thought ruefully, had been something of a habit for him. It was only now he realised how hollow those emotions had become over the years, how empty of real feeling.

"We were supposed to be talking," he said slowly.

"I'm sorry." Tess looked impossibly pleased with herself. "I misunderstood."

She looked so tousled and so slumberous that Owen was ambushed by a sharp desire to kiss her again, to make love to her over and over until he had possessed her with the ravenous need he felt within. He forced himself to draw back, sitting up on the sofa, pulling her close into the curve of his arm.

Regret, bitter and sharp, pierced him for the way he had used her.

"No," he said. "I'm the one who should be sorry."

She shifted beside him; he felt her touch his cheek, her fingertips soft against the roughness of his stubble.

"I'll never understand sex," she said drily. "I thought it was delicious. Unimaginably exciting. And then you apologise."

Owen grimaced. "I was rough. I treated you with less consideration than I should."

"Consideration." Tess's voice had warmed into humour. "I can bear a great deal less consideration if it means that you make love to me like that, Owen."

Owen glanced quickly at her. She was snuggling into his embrace, her cheek rubbing his shoulder, all dishevelled clothing and lush, warm woman. His senses tightened even as he rejected the renewed arousal of his body.

"You don't understand," he said roughly. He felt weighted down with regret. "I don't lose control. I cannot. It's too dangerous."

The sleepiness fled her eyes at his tone. She sat up, a little away from him, tucking her feet beneath her rumpled skirts.

"What do I not understand?" she said simply. "Tell me."

In the end Owen found it easy to tell Tess the one thing that caused him so much shame he had never spoken of it, not even to those of his friends who knew what had happened. He talked and Tess sat with her chin resting on her hand, listening.

"You asked me if I had a compulsion to help women in trouble," Owen said. "I had never thought of it that way before but I suppose that I do."

Tess's eyes narrowed but she said nothing. He had thought she might ask him about his feelings for Joanna again but there was a new awareness in her face as though she had moved beyond the jealousy that had driven her before. She waited.

"There was a woman, a long time ago," Owen said. "A girl." He glanced at Tess quickly as she moved a little. "Oh, not like that," he said. "I did not love her. I did not even know her name. I was a young midshipman in those days and full of ambition. We were in Southampton, and a rougher port you'd be hard-pressed to find." He shrugged. "We had been drinking that night and I was more than three-parts cut. As we came out of the tavern I saw that the ship's first officer—a brute called Bates—had picked up a girl. They were arguing and then he started to hit her." He stopped. The image of that dark alley and the woman's pale flesh and ripped clothes, and the sound of her screams were seared on his mind, something he had never forgotten.

"She was a prostitute," he said. "Little more than a child. It was hideous. Intolerable." He moved uncomfortably as the unbearable memories flooded his mind. "I had always been brought up to respect women," he said. "I was young and it gave me a shock to see things differently. Oh, I knew—" He stopped and shifted his shoulders again. He could not feel comfortable. The memories were too bleak and their legacy too painful. "I was not naive. I knew such things went on. But this was my commanding officer. So perhaps I *was* naive after all if I thought that such men would always behave with honour."

Tess was sitting very hunched and still. "What happened?" she whispered.

"I wanted to intervene," Owen said, "but the others held me back. I shook them off—I was full of idealism and pride and nobility." He gave a short laugh. "I went to plant Bates a facer. I was spoiling for a fight. And he was so angry to have his authority challenged. He was full of violence and fury. But instead of hitting me he took the girl and..." His throat convulsed and he swallowed hard. "He hit her so fast and so hard that she fell and cracked her head against the wall and was killed. He did it deliberately, like a display of power, to show me his absolute dominance over her, to prove that nothing I could do would make a difference. I hated him for it." His voice shook. Tess was silent, watching him. "And after that, subordinate or not, I laid into him as though I was possessed by the devil himself. I lost control and let my anger drive me. The others pulled me off in the end, but by then..." He paused. "I had half killed him."

He heard Tess give a horrified gasp. The colour left her face, leaving it white and stark. "That was why you left the Navy," she said.

Owen raised his eyes to hers. "I had no choice," he said. "There was a frightful scandal. I lost my commission and was thrown out. My family had scrimped and saved and gone without and I threw away all that they had given me in one careless night because I lacked the self-control to restrain my violence."

"Oh, Owen." Tess put her arms about him and burrowed closer into his side. She felt warm and soft and very giving and Owen felt the cold tension start to drain from his bones. He pulled her to him and buried his face in her hair. "It was not your fault," she said, her words muffled against his skin. "That was not justice."

"It may not have been justice but it was my fault that I could not control my anger," Owen said. The bitter taste of failure was still in his mouth. "Over and over, time and again, I have reproached myself. I could have stopped Bates, reasoned with him—"

"You could not have known what the outcome would be," Tess argued. "His was the crime, not yours."

"My crime was a lack of judgement and control," Owen said tonelessly. "And I failed the girl. I couldn't save her. She was young and defenceless but I could not help her." He loosed Tess a little. "And as if that were not bad enough, I threw away all that my family had given me. I owed them so much and I let them down."

Tess touched his cheek. "You were young," she said softly, "and idealistic. We have all made mistakes."

"I was not making any more," Owen said fiercely. He realised that he was holding Tess hard, tension in his grip, and deliberately freed her, running his hands down her arms to link his fingers with hers. She held him tightly. Her eyes were steady on his.

"After I was thrown out of the Navy I went my own way," he said. "I had my own code. I worked for all I had because I had to prove myself." He slanted a look at her. "You once asked me if I was a pirate. Well, I was never that because I respected the rule of law too much to break it again."

"That was why you worked for Sidmouth, wasn't it?" Tess said slowly. "Because you wanted to uphold the law and do what you thought was right. You have spent your life trying to make amends." She leaned forwards and kissed him. Owen felt the brush of her lashes against his cheek. "You are a good man, Owen, but even good men can make mistakes." She drew back; smiled at him. "I understand about Joanna now," she said simply. "When you saw the way that her first husband treated her you must have hated him so much."

"David Ware was a bastard," Owen said. "Everyone thought him a hero but all I saw in him was abuse of power and disrespect. I had nothing but contempt for him. I wanted to kill him—that damned violence in me again—and to take Joanna away from him and show her that it need not be like that." He shook his head. "Then Joanna married Alex and she seemed unhappy again. It made me angry."

"I'm sorry," Tess said. She was looking down at their interlinked hands. "Sorry that she hurt you."

Owen smiled ruefully. "It was lucky that she did," he said. "Joanna was wiser than I. She knew that to run away with me was no answer. She loved Alex and he loved her and they were able to resolve their differences. I am glad for them." He rubbed Tess's bare shoulder very gently beneath the loosened bodice of her gown, relishing the silken smoothness of her skin, her warmth. She felt so bountiful, so giving. He had not known such generosity in a woman and had not thought to find it in Tess.

"You should not think that I love Joanna still," he said, wanting to meet Tess's openness with the honesty it deserved. "It is not true. I stopped loving her a while ago but I did not realise it."

He saw Tess's face light with soft pleasure. "I am

glad," she admitted. "I was very jealous. It hurt so much and I was so unprepared for it." Her lips curved into a smile. "You had been patient with me and generous and endlessly considerate." She laughed. "I thought you a saint and then when I heard you had wanted to run off with your best friend's wife I felt disillusioned as well as horribly jealous."

"A saint!" Owen said. He started to laugh. "I am very far from sainthood, I assure you."

Tess looked down at their dishevelled clothing. "So it seems," she murmured. "And actually I find I much prefer you as a mere man." She leaned forwards and took his face in her palms, kissing him. Her bodice gaped open, and Owen saw her breasts, lush and round, pink-tipped, so tempting. His whole body leapt to arousal.

"I understand that you feel a need to keep control," Tess whispered, against his mouth, "but you need not be so careful with me anymore." She nipped his lower lip, sliding her tongue into his mouth where it entwined with his in an erotic dance.

"I like what I have learned about myself," she whispered, "and I like what you do to me."

She slid her hand into his pantaloons and took his cock, already hard, in her hand. Owen groaned and grabbed her, tumbling her back into his arms where she lay smiling up at him, all wanton provocation.

"I suppose we should not do it again," she said quickly, regretfully. "The door is not locked and anyone might walk in. Poor Houghton might announce a guest. Your aunt Martindale, for example. That would sink my reputation with her beyond repair."

"God forbid. You are quite right." Owen freed himself and strolled over to the door, registering the look of keen disappointment on Tess's face as she started to button her bodice.

"Don't do that," he said, turning the key. "I shall only be obliged to undo them all over again." He tugged his cravat off and threw it aside as he walked back towards her.

"Owen!" Tess's face flushed rosy-pink. "Can we? Again? Here? Now?"

"Certainly we can," Owen said. And did.

CHAPTER FIFTEEN

IT WAS MUCH LATER, WHEN OWEN had left belatedly for his meeting with the maritime broker, that Tess wandered upstairs to her bedroom where Margery was stolidly placing clean linen into the armada chest, folding it in with sprigs of lavender and rosemary. The room was fresh with the scent of herbs and bright with the cold winter light of early afternoon.

"Is all well, milady?" Margery asked, viewing Tess's crumpled gown and inexpertly pinned hair with some amusement.

"All is very well, thank you, Margery," Tess agreed, and the maid smiled and turned back to the linens.

"Perhaps you should change gowns if you are thinking of going out, ma'am," she said.

"Perhaps I should," Tess agreed dreamily.

It had been a long journey, she thought, but now, against all odds, she felt whole again. In the beginning she had been a frightened girl who had lost so much, and endured so much. She had taken up Robert's political cause to fill the empty spaces in her life and she had developed a true passion and loyalty to it. But now her loyalties had changed.

She sat down on the edge of the bed and took Robert Barstow's miniature out of the drawer and looked at it for a moment. His painted picture smiled at her, young, boyish, idealistic. He had had so many hopes for the future. Death had robbed him of his plans, but she had picked up his cause and she had done her best, and now it was time for others to take on her role. There were many, many people now who supported the radical movement. In time they would achieve the reforms that they sought, fair wages and food on the table for all and the right for their voices to be heard. And she might no longer draw satirical cartoons or run the Jupiter Club but she could still fund her charities and be a philanthropist.

Margery was looking over her shoulder at the portrait. "Handsome boy," she said.

"My first husband," Tess said. "He was…" She paused. Robert had not been her love, she thought, but she had loved him dearly. "Very special to me," she finished.

"But now you are in love with Lord Rothbury," Margery said.

Tess's lips twitched at her maid's matter-of-fact manner. "Yes," she said. "It is quite different, Margery."

"So it seems," Margery said, her gaze flickering over Tess's ruined gown once again. She went to the wardrobe and started to sort through Tess's petticoats.

"Will you be going to the radical meeting this afternoon, ma'am?" she said. She glanced at Tess over her shoulder. Her face was troubled.

Tess jumped. "I didn't know anyone knew about that," she said. She felt a stirring of guilt. Today was the date of the largest political rally of the year, but she had not mentioned it to Owen because she had not wanted to stir up trouble between them. She had wanted nothing else to spoil her happiness. Not now, when it was so new and precious and felt so true.

"All of London knows that Orator Hunt is to address the crowds, ma'am," Margery said. "Spa Fields, isn't it? You should stay away, ma'am. There's bound to be trouble."

"I know," Tess said. She thought of Owen warning her that Justin Brooke was not to be trusted. But Justin did not need to know that she would be there. No one would know. She could go one last time and make her farewell to the radical cause. She needed to do it for Robert's sake. This was the last thing that she had to do before she could close the door on the past.

"I swear I'll be careful," she said. She looked at the maid's stubborn face. "It's the last time," she said. "I have to say goodbye."

She pushed Robert's miniature into her pocket, dressed swiftly and went out.

OWEN WAS LATE COMING BACK from the city. The appointment with the maritime broker at Lloyds had taken longer than he had expected. He did not like the atmosphere on the streets. It felt loaded and dangerous with the promise of trouble. Those people who were out were scurrying furtively, heads down, wanting to reach their destinations as quickly as possible.

Owen had thought about mentioning the meeting at Spa Fields to Tess but had decided against it because he did not want it to appear that he did not trust her. She had given him her word that she would not involve herself in politics again and he had accepted it. But as the carriage rolled through the quiet streets, the wheels echoing ominously on the cobbles, he felt a clutch of fear about his heart, a question impossible to avoid, difficult to answer. He was not sure if he really did trust Tess to have abandoned her political affiliations. Her devotion to the radical cause had been a part of her life for so long. It had been fundamentally important to her and to the person she was.

"Where is Lady Rothbury?" he demanded, as he strode into the hall at Clarges Street, throwing his gloves down onto the table and loosening his greatcoat. He wanted to hear that Tess was in the drawing room, or perhaps shopping with Joanna Grant. Then the shadow of doubt that dogged his heels could be put to rest.

"Her ladyship is from home, my lord," Houghton said. "She left several hours ago."

Cold fear grabbed Owen's heart. "Did she tell you where she was going?" he asked.

The butler shook his head, his long face growing even longer.

"Did she call a hackney?" Owen could feel both his anger and his fear rising sharply now.

"She went to the political meeting." It was Margery who spoke up from the shadows of the hall. She came forwards, bobbing Owen a curtsy. "Your pardon, my lord. Lady Rothbury has gone to Spa Fields to hear Orator Hunt speak. She said..." Margery hesitated. "She said that she had to make an end. She took the miniature with her, sir."

"The miniature?" Owen questioned.

"Of her late husband, sir. Mr. Barstow," Margery said. "She said she had to say farewell."

Owen felt simultaneously vastly relieved and almost blinded by anger. So Tess was saying goodbye to the cause she had held fast to for so long. He felt a huge tenderness for her swell inside him, but it was almost eclipsed by anxiety and dread. If Brooke should see her, if Sidmouth's men should identify her, then this time Tess would be undone. They would have the evidence they needed to link her to the radical cause. And Sidmouth would without a doubt be using this opportunity to incite the crowds to riot so that he could arrest the most prominent radicals and crush the movement once and for all. It was foolhardy in the extreme of Tess to go, even if she had felt driven to it.

He grabbed his coat again.

"Do you require the carriage, my lord?" Houghton asked.

"No," Owen said. "I'll take a horse. It's quicker." He

would never be able to drive through a rioting mob, he thought grimly. They would smash the coach and then he would be obliged to shoot someone and the whole thing would become even more of a disaster than it already promised to be.

It was a shade darker out on the streets, the short winter afternoon turning to evening. The wind cut like a blade. As he rode back into the city Owen saw the first signs of trouble. There were bands of drunken men roaming the streets armed with clubs; there were carriages broken in the road and set on fire, windows smashed, shops looted. Rolls of black smoke mingled with sudden bursts of flame. And everywhere there was the feeling of violence hanging in the air.

Scraps of paper were fluttering in the wind, pamphlets and cartoons. Owen leaned down and grabbed one. His heart contracted. It was a caricature of Lord Sidmouth bestriding the country, trampling the people beneath the heel of his boot. It was signed in that unmistakable black scrawl, Jupiter. Owen jumped down from the horse and grabbed another. There was another, and another, dozens of Jupiter's cartoons, vicious incitements to violence. There was an element of cruelty in them that Owen had never seen before, their humour gone and in its place a raw anger that made his heart jolt. This had to be Tess's work. It could be no other. Owen felt as though he had never really known her at all.

A chill disillusionment swept through him. Tess had

given him her word that she had abandoned the caricatures and he had believed her sincere. Now he found
she had been sketching these ever since they had wed.
He had thought that they had built up something very
honest and real between them, but Tess evidently had
older, deeper loyalties and all the time she had been
true to them and not to him. She had deceived him from
the first and she had never really stopped. Owen tasted
the bitterness of betrayal and savage disappointment.
He was angry with Tess but he was even angrier with
himself for believing in her.

It was then that he caught sight of her, cloaked,
scurrying down a side alley. For a second the wind
blew back her hood and the faint light gleamed on her
hair before she raised her hand to pull the hood back
into place. Owen turned his horse. He caught her from
behind, reaching down to capture her about the waist
and swing her up onto the horse in front of him. She
screamed and spun around, her knife at his throat, and
he closed his hand so hard about her wrist that she
dropped it with a clatter on the cobbles.

"Owen," she said on a breath of profound relief. "Oh,
thank God."

He did not reply, could not. He was so angry with
her and yet he was shaking with relief that she was safe.
She was trembling too.

"It's terrifying out here," she said.

"What did you expect?" Owen said savagely, and
she heard the note in his voice and fell silent.

It took only fifteen minutes to reach Clarges Street and they did not speak once on the journey. Owen rode into the mews, handed the horse over to the groom and gave it a grateful stroke on the nose. Tess was watching him, her eyes wide, her face troubled. There was a long rent in her cloak and her gloves were dirty and torn. Seeing the evidence of the physical danger she had placed herself in, Owen felt his temper soar.

"Owen..." she said, as he practically dragged her through the entrance hall and into the library, slamming the double doors behind them. "I'm sorry." Her blue eyes, so wide, so honest, touched his face. "Please let me explain."

She had tried that last time, Owen thought bitterly, and it had worked. He had believed her. No more, though.

"You told me you would never attend another meeting," he ground out.

Her gaze fell. "I wanted to go to say goodbye," she said softly. She opened her hand. Something sparkled as she cast it down on the table. He saw it was a locket.

"The radical cause was Robert's cause," she said. She looked up suddenly and Owen's heart shifted in his chest at the sincerity in her eyes. "I was saying farewell."

Almost he believed her. He wanted to believe her, but he could not because there were the cartoons with their vicious incitement to violence. He put his hand into the pocket of his coat and drew out the drawings, letting them scatter on the table.

"What of these?" he demanded.

Tess nodded. Her expression was odd, he thought, distressed, but a little furtive. "These are not my work," she said.

"Please." Owen felt a rush of contempt. He had not expected her to lie. "They are signed Jupiter, are they not? What is this, Tess?" His voice grated. "Just another betrayal?"

"No!" Her voice rang clear. There was a slight frown between her eyes now. "I tell you, I did not draw these!" Her gaze searched his face. Her voice dropped. There was flat calm in it now. "You don't believe me," she said.

"No," Owen said. "Of course I don't believe you! You gave me your word you would not attend a political rally and yet I find you there despite your promise, despite the danger. You gave me your word you would never draw these again—" he ripped one of the cartoons in two "—and yet here they are with your signature on them."

"You don't trust me." Her eyes had not left his face. "You can. Owen, please—"

The library door burst open.

"Yes?" Owen snapped, not taking his eyes off Tess.

"My lord." The quiver in Houghton's voice was more fear than outrage. "There are soldiers here—" They were already pushing past Houghton into the room, filling it with a blur of red coats.

"We are here on Lord Sidmouth's orders to arrest Lady Rothbury on a charge of treason and sedition." The young captain of the dragoons looked nervously from Owen to Tess and back again.

Owen saw Tess turn chalk-white. She swayed, clutching the edge of the table to steady herself. The remaining cartoons scattered to the floor like confetti.

Owen tore his gaze from Tess's face and stared down the captain. The only thing he could do now was to bluff and hope that the man would be sufficiently intimidated to back off. It was the biggest gamble of his life and he could feel the tension tight across his shoulders.

"Don't be ridiculous, man," he said, very coldly. "Lady Rothbury a criminal? Your wits have gone begging."

"Lord Sidmouth's orders, sir." The man was dogged. "There are political cartoons circulating that are her work—" he gestured to the ragged papers on the floor "—and she was witnessed attending the meeting at Spa Fields earlier this afternoon. We are here to take her to the Tower of London, my lord, so that Lord Sidmouth may question her further."

Owen looked at Tess. For a moment he saw abject horror in her eyes. He remembered in that moment what Tess had confided to him about her fear of the dark, the door closing on her, locking her into Brokeby's nightmare. He thought of the gaol and the terror and the darkness and the locked doors. He felt the despair roll over him. He knew what life was like in a British gaol. He had been there before. Sidmouth's methods would not be gentle. He could deal with that. Tess could not. Whatever she had done, he would never let that happen to her.

"The cartoons are mine," Owen said. "I am the man Lord Sidmouth seeks."

Tess made an involuntary movement. He heard her gasp. Her eyes were wide and terrified. Owen gestured to her to be silent. He kept his gaze on the Captain of the Dragoons. "I am an American, a known sympathiser with the reformers' cause," he said. "I was a prisoner of war a mere two years ago for fighting against the British."

Tess started forwards. "Owen—" she said.

Owen shook his head very sharply. "Don't say anything, Teresa."

He turned back to the captain. "I am afraid I have been working against the government from within," he said. "As Sidmouth's man I had access to a great deal of useful information."

A ripple went through the soldiers like wind through the grass. At least half of them looked as though they wanted to shoot him on the spot. The captain was dithering now, uncertain what to do. Owen held his gaze. Tess had obeyed him; she was standing quite still, but there was tension in every line of her slender body and her eyes were riveted on his face.

Owen picked up the cartoons and let them slide through his fingers. "What are you waiting for?" he said to the captain. "I've confessed. I am the man you seek. Lady Rothbury is and always has been innocent."

"My lord." The captain looked confused. "Lord Sidmouth—"

"I assure you," Owen said, "that Lord Sidmouth will be very happy to have me in place of my wife."

The captain drew himself up. "Very well," he said. "We shall see what his lordship says." He turned to his men. "Take him away."

Tess moved then, running forwards into his arms even as the soldiers moved to surround him.

"No!" Owen felt her tears hot against his cheek, heard her agonised whisper. "No! I won't let you do this!"

"It's better this way." For a moment Owen held her tight and close, so close, against his heart, then he put her from him with iron control. Any more and he knew he would be lost. As he stepped back they were pulling him roughly away from her and the distance between them was lengthening even as Tess held her hands out to him in a vain gesture.

"I love you," she said. "I love you so much. You made me whole again."

Owen heard the words long after they had taken him away.

THE WATCH WAS CALLING TWO in the morning but Tess could not sleep. She had not slept for seven nights now, not since the soldiers had taken Owen away. She had not eaten either. Joanna and Merryn fussed over her. Lady Martindale, suddenly her staunchest support, called upon her each day. None of them could get her to eat or even speak. Because there was nothing that she could say.

She had gone to Lord Sidmouth the morning after Owen had been arrested and she had told the Home Secretary that he had got the wrong man, that he knew she was the guilty party and that he should let Owen go and take her instead. She told him she knew that Justin Brooke had betrayed her. She even offered to draw some cartoons for Sidmouth to prove that she was Jupiter. She had snatched his quill up from the desk and drawn a few quick lines, and Sidmouth had sat back in his chair and had smiled indulgently at her as though she were no more than a featherbrained female and told her that it must have been a frightful shock to her to discover that her husband was a traitor but what did she expect when he had been a prisoner of war. Leopards, Sidmouth had said, puffing on a pungent cigar, never changed their spots.

Tess had been furious and had pointed out that Owen had fought for the British at Trafalgar and that he had sworn his allegiance when he had taken his oath to the king, but Sidmouth had only shrugged. He would not let her see Owen, even though she had humbled her pride and begged.

"Why is he doing this?" Tess had wailed later, abandoning her reserve and crying all over Joanna and Alex.

"He knows full well it was me! Why is he going to punish Owen instead?"

And Alex, who was looking grimmer than Tess had ever seen him, had said, "Because he could not hang you, Tess. He couldn't hang the daughter of the Earl of Fenner. Yes, he knows you were Jupiter, but he needs a scapegoat. And he has the perfect one in a man whom he can remind everyone was born a foreigner."

Tess had understood then, and her world had caved in on itself, extinguishing the light and hope forever. Because she knew that Alex was right. Owen had given himself up for her and he was indeed the most perfect person for Lord Sidmouth to blame.

Even Lady Martindale had gone to Sidmouth to petition him on behalf of her great-nephew, but Sidmouth had been as unaffected by her pleas as he had been by Tess's. And then Tess had heard that Rupert Montmorency had been boasting in his cups that he had conspired against Owen in the hope that Lady Martindale would change her will to leave everything to him, and that after Owen's death he would petition the courts for the Rothbury title as well. Tess had been so enraged that she had stormed into White's, past all the gentlemen who said she could not enter because she was a female, and had poured a glass of port all over Rupert, ruining his cravat and his silver lace waistcoat. So everyone was talking about her all over again. But she did not care because nothing mattered except saving Owen.

Now Tess sat by the window watching the cold

winter moonlight flicker across the darkened garden and she felt lonelier than ever in her life, empty and alone down to her soul. She tried to reach out to Owen through the dark, to imagine where he might be and what he might be doing but she could not sense his presence. She felt smothered by the house and by all the old musty drapes and those damned statues with their blank eyes. She hated it. She had to get away. She had to think.

She went over to her dresser and took out her drawing book with the sketch of Owen she had done when first she had gone to him to ask him to marry her. She traced the lines of his face, the slash of his cheekbones, the fall of hair across his forehead. Impossible to imagine that she might never see him again. Unacceptable to think that Sidmouth might hang him for a crime he had not committed. She could not bear to think of it; she could not bear to lose him when she had only just found him.

She turned the page and started to draw. Within a few strokes of the pencil *Sea Witch* had started to come to life, sails billowing as they caught the wind, prow raised to the waves.

Sea Witch...

Tess closed the book very softly. She knew now what she had to do.

"YOU BLOODY FOOL," GARRICK Farne said, marching into Owen's prison cell in the Tower of London and planting himself foursquare in front of him. "What the hell

did you have to confess to something like this for?"
Then, as Owen did not answer: "I don't think I can get
you out. Grant and I have both tried. Sidmouth doesn't
want to know."

"Of course not," Owen said. "I was the one who
questioned his judgement and told him he was corrupt."
His mouth twisted. "Sidmouth doesn't really appreciate
opposition."

Sidmouth, Owen thought, had been notably unsym-
pathetic to him so far. He had had him thrown into a
damp cell in a forgotten corner of the White Tower and
had left him to rot. The room had a pallet for a bed, a
broken chair and one narrow window, barred. It smelled
of damp and decay and hopelessness. He was inordinately glad that Tess had never had to endure this place
where light and dark merged and nameless horrors rose
to taunt him in the depths of the night.

"Plus you are a foreigner, a known Republican sympathiser, a former prisoner of war and a reputed pirate."
Garrick rubbed his forehead. "Hell, Rothbury, you'll be
hanged before you know it." He scowled. "Why did you
have to confess to this when you did not even do it?"

"Why do you think?" Owen demanded.

Garrick stared at him. "Tess," he said heavily, after
a moment. "So it's true. She really was Jupiter." He ran
a distracted hand through his hair. "She said that she
was, but I thought she was run half-mad, wanting to
save you. So that night at the brothel—"

"She was running away from the radical meeting,"

Owen said. "Yes. Your wife is not the only bluestocking firebrand in that family, Farne."

"Bloody hell," Garrick said. He frowned, dragging the most recent of Jupiter's cartoons from his pocket. "But Tess didn't draw these cartoons," he said.

Owen did not even look at it. "Yes, she did," he said tiredly. He felt sick with misery and disappointment. Tess had promised him she would not go to the radical meeting but he had found her at Spa Fields. She had told him she had not drawn the cartoons but he could not believe her. He wished she had kept her promise to him. But more than that he wished they had not quarrelled, not now when very likely he would not be permitted ever to speak to her in private again. He would never have the chance to tell her how much he loved her.

"Tess didn't draw those cartoons," Garrick insisted. "Lady Emma Bradshaw drew them."

"What?" Owen shot to his feet. "Lady Emma? She cannot have done."

Garrick passed the cartoons over. "Look at them," he growled. "They aren't as good as the other ones."

"They were drawn in a hurry," Owen argued.

Garrick shook his head. "Emma came to me and confessed," he said, with grim satisfaction. "She was all set to confess to Sidmouth too, but I told her it would do no good. He won't release you. He wants to make an example of Jupiter, but he couldn't hang either the daughter of the Earl of Brooke or the daughter of the

Earl of Fenner. That would look frightfully bad. So you—" Garrick shot Owen a glance in which fury and exasperation were mingled equally "—are his sacrifice."

"It's worth it," Owen said bleakly. Then, as Garrick just looked at him, he burst out, "Devil take it, Farne, what would *you* have done? Let Merryn go to gaol? Let her die?"

Garrick's expression hardened. "No, of course not." He raised both hands in a gesture of appeasement. "But there had to have been another way."

"There wasn't," Owen snapped. "You said it yourself. Sidmouth has to be seen to make an example of someone." He sat down heavily on the flimsy pallet bed. "So Tess was innocent of these." His hand scattered the cartoons. "Damnation. I wish I had believed her." In his mind's eye he could see Tess's pale, strained face as she had sworn to him that this time the caricatures had not been her work. He had not trusted her. He felt a great sweep of desolation.

"The two of you are as bad as each other," Garrick said. "Did you know Tess went to Sidmouth to try to persuade him of her guilt? If anyone else claims to be Jupiter, this whole thing will start to look like a farce." He ran a hand through his hair, suddenly looking very tired. "You know what is going to happen, Rothbury? You do understand? They only let me see you because they are going to hang you."

They stared at one another.

"I had thought to try to help you escape to *Sea Witch*," Garrick said suddenly, "but if I started to hire a crew Sidmouth really would sit up and take notice and I'd end up in here with you."

"A pity I can't crew her alone," Owen said, with a faint smile, "but that is beyond even my powers." He shook his head. "It doesn't matter," he said. "As you say, Sidmouth has to hang someone. People are terrified of the radicals running out of control and starting a revolution like the one in France."

"Sidmouth encouraged those rumours deliberately so that he could crack down on his political enemies," Garrick said grimly.

Owen shrugged. "That's beside the point." He looked away. "Tell Tess that I am sorry I doubted her," he said, with difficulty. He stood up, offered Garrick his hand. "And look after her for me, Farne. I want her to be happy. I hope she finds husband number five," he added wryly.

"She won't," Garrick said. "Don't you know she loves you, Rothbury? A pity that when she finally finds a man worthy of her he has to do the quixotic thing of dying for her." He hesitated, shook Owen's hand. "We'll keep trying for you," he said. "We'll do our best."

It sounded like an epitaph.

The door closed behind him, leaving Owen in the dark.

Tom had been waiting for Emma all day. He knew she had gone to Garrick Farne and that his half-brother had told her not to go to Sidmouth to confess, but Tom knew his Emma and he knew that she would come anyway. Emma loved Tess Rothbury and she would never let Tess lose Owen if there was a single thing that she could do to prevent it. Emma was honest like that, honourable, true and good, all the things that Tom was not and now wished he had been in order to deserve her. He passed the long, cold day of waiting in thinking of all the bad things he had done. Soon, he knew he would have ample time to sit and reflect on his sins, on all the people he had robbed and cheated and black-mailed, on the time he had left Merryn to die and had tried to shoot Garrick. He thought of all the women he had betrayed. He closed his eyes and saw Tess stumbling down dark corridors towards an open door, a door that he had closed in her face.

It was the sound of footsteps that roused him. The clock on St. Margaret's Church had just struck the hour of six. The cold darkness was settling over the quiet street and the snow was starting to fall, and there was Emma, hooded and cloaked, a slender shadow amongst the dark. Tom felt his heart surge and then the dull weight of denial settled on him as he remembered she would never be his again. Soon, very soon, she would be a widow. He knew what he had to do.

He ran up the steps to Lord Sidmouth's house and rang the bell. Emma had checked as she had seen him by the door ahead of her. He knew she had not recognised him. For a moment she hesitated then her steps resumed. She walked past the house, turned the corner of the street and was lost from his sight. The door opened. Tom stepped inside.

IT WAS LATE WHEN THE CELL DOOR clanged open, rousing Owen from half-sleep.

"You're free to go, my lord," the turnkey said with a great deal more respect than he had shown Owen over the previous week. "Lord Sidmouth's orders. All an unfortunate misunderstanding, his lordship says. We've got the real culprit. Nothing but trouble, this one, right from the start." He pushed Tom Bradshaw into the cell. Bradshaw stumbled and almost fell, righted himself and shook himself like a dog. Chains clanked. Owen noticed there were iron manacles on his wrists and his ankles.

"Bradshaw?" he said incredulously.

"Wants a word with you," the jailer said. "You don't need to talk to him though, sir, if you don't want."

"Such respect," Bradshaw sneered, "now my Lord Rothbury is no longer a criminal."

The jailer kicked him. "Enough from you."

"I'll talk to him," Owen said. He saw the jailer's look of surprise before the man went out, leaving the two of them alone with one small candle to light the cell.

"I hope it doesn't hurt your pride, Rothbury," Bradshaw said, "that Sidmouth wanted to hang me more than he wanted to hang you."

So that was it. Owen looked at Bradshaw's dark cynical face and felt shock and profound relief mingled with an odd sort of regret.

"I am surprised Sidmouth didn't just hang both of us," he said drily.

"You've got powerful friends," Bradshaw said. "They didn't like it. Kicked up a big fuss. Lady Martindale…" He shook his head. "Never get on the wrong side of that woman. Sidmouth was in a bind. So when I came along—" He grinned. "Manna from heaven. No questions asked."

"You gave yourself up?" There was stark incredulity in Owen's tone. Self-sacrifice was so far from Tom Bradshaw's way of life that he was sure the man must be lying.

Bradshaw grinned. "Difficult to believe, isn't it?"

"Impossible," Owen said.

Bradshaw's smile faded. "Some things are worth more than others," he said softly. "That's why you are here, isn't it, Rothbury? Because you love your wife so much that you would die rather than see her hurt?"

"Sidmouth would never have arrested Lady Emma," Owen said.

"Emma would have made him do it," Tom said quietly. "She was going to confess. And if Sidmouth ignored her confession she would have announced it on the streets, published it in the papers, declared her guilt and her identity as Jupiter to everyone so that Sidmouth could not ignore her and was forced to act." For a brief second he dropped his face into his hands then raised his head, haggard. "Emma has too much integrity to let an innocent man die," he said. "She and Lady Rothbury. They were both Jupiter, from the very first. They took it in turns to draw the cartoons. When you were hunting Jupiter, Lady Rothbury protected Emma. Now Emma wants to do the same for her."

For a second time Owen felt the shock hit him with the power of a blow. Emma and Tess, both Jupiter, both the radicals' cartoonist. He would never have guessed. Tess had not lied to him; she *had* been Jupiter and she was prepared to own up to that fact. But she had wanted to protect Emma too because she was strong and generous, and helping those who needed her was what she had always done.

"You gave yourself up to keep Lady Emma safe," Owen said.

"I made Sidmouth a deal," Tom said. "He knows I'm not Jupiter. He knows those latest cartoons were Emma's work. But he won't touch her because it's a greater triumph to arrest me and hang me and make a huge spectacle of it." His mouth twisted. "The Duke of Farne's bastard son, criminal and murderer, caught at last."

"And what if Lady Emma won't let you die for her?" Owen said. "She wouldn't hand you over before."

"She won't know until it's too late," Tom said. "That's part of the deal. Sidmouth keeps this quiet until the last minute when it is too late for Emma to do anything about it." He looked up. "It's not just for Emma," he said slowly. "It's for Lady Rothbury too."

Owen's attention sharpened. "Because Teresa saved Emma when she was thrown out onto the street?"

"That too," Tom said. He shifted. "And because I did her a terrible wrong."

The atmosphere in the cell moved and thickened. Owen could feel the tension in his blood.

"I heard you were looking for Brokeby's cronies," Bradshaw said.

Owen went very still. "How did you know that?" he said softly.

Bradshaw shrugged. "I hear things." He shifted his shoulders against the wall. "I heard you were looking for revenge." He shrugged. "I can't blame you. But you've been robbed by time." He met Owen's eyes. "They're all dead, Rothbury. All dead, except me."

Owen made an involuntary movement towards him. Bradshaw was watching him with those dark, unreadable eyes, waiting for his reaction. Owen knew all about Tom Bradshaw and the games he played. He knew how Bradshaw had manipulated Merryn and tried to blackmail James Devlin and all the other things he had done. He knew Bradshaw was a man who exulted in his power to hurt people. He felt the anger and the violence spread beneath his skin and infiltrate every part of his body, but still he did not move.

"Why are you telling me this?" he said.

Bradshaw smiled. It was a bitter smile this time.

"Think of it as my confession, Rothbury. It's been on my conscience, and me thinking I did not even have a conscience."

"What did you do?" Owen's blood felt ice-cold with rage now, sick with dread.

"I didn't touch her." Bradshaw had heard the note in Owen's voice too. He put out a hand as though to ward off a blow, the blow Owen wanted so deeply to administer and yet held back. "I swear it." He laughed, a short, mirthless laugh. "Well, I would say that, wouldn't I? But it's true."

"Then what did you do?" Owen said. He scarcely recognised his own voice, thick with anger and violence.

"I was the one who closed the door," Bradshaw said. His look scoured Owen's face. "I see she told you about that," he said. "Well, I was the one who locked her in there, Rothbury, with Melton and Brokeby and Brokeby's friends. I thought it was just a bit of fun—I didn't even know who she was! Some of the others had brought women with them and they were playing all manner of games…. I thought she might even have been paid, you know. Paid to try and run away, and be caught and brought back…."

"You thought that Teresa was just another whore to treat as you wanted," Owen said. "You loathsome—" The murderous hatred closed his throat. He was so close to the edge with his abhorrence for what Bradshaw had done and his disgust for those men and their vile games. His heart was breaking for Tess all over again.

"It's not too late, though, is it, Rothbury?" Bradshaw said, and Owen could hear the hope in his voice. "She has you now. You opened the door. You can show her the light."

Owen clenched his fists so tight that he felt the bones ache. He wanted to kill Bradshaw, to take him apart, not only for what he had done to Tess but also because the man was the last remnant of Brokeby's repulsive legacy, the only man left whom he could vent his anger and revenge upon. The fury raked him again, but beneath it he could sense Tess's presence, feel her touch on his cheek.

"I love you. You made me whole again..."

He had no need to kill Bradshaw. Sidmouth would do that for him, coldly, clinically, with the full weight of the law behind him. The only thing that mattered was Tess. What mattered now was their future, not the past.

He walked to the door. His body felt cold and tired, aching in his bones as though he had been in combat.

Bradshaw had not moved, nor even looked up.

Owen stopped. "We will take care of Lady Emma," he said. "I promise you."

Bradshaw's head came up slowly. He gave a crooked smile. "I know," he said. "I tried to be good enough for her, but it was always too late."

"In the end I think you were," Owen said. He rapped sharply on the door and the jailer let him out.

"Vermin," the man said, jerking his head towards the darkened cell. "Scum of the earth." He kicked the door shut and turned the key with a grating creak of satisfaction. "You'll be wanting to be away now, my lord," he added. "Now that this unfortunate misunderstanding is resolved."

"Unfortunate misunderstanding," Owen said. He could just imagine Sidmouth uttering those words, full of sanctimony and self-righteousness. "Yes, indeed, most unfortunate."

He went out into the street. The air was cold. Snow was gathering. He had never been so grateful to be free. He turned for home.

CHAPTER SIXTEEN

NIGHT HAD FALLEN OVER THE Greenwich dock but on the deck of *Sea Witch* lanterns burned as they had done late into the night for the past two nights. The air was rich with the fumes of fresh paint and tar, thick with snow. Men moved in the rigging of the ship, shadowy figures swarming from bow to stern. Owen stood at the corner of Wharf Street in the shelter of the warehouses and looked on in astonishment.

He had come directly from Clarges Street.

"Lady Rothbury is currently living on board a *ship*, my lord," Houghton had told him, lips very tightly pursed, sounding as disapproving as if Tess had taken up residence in a brothel. "Her maid is with her," he added, as though that gave Tess a spurious respectability.

Owen had grinned and slapped him on the shoulder and had called for a horse and was gone before the butler could even protest that he smelled like a week in gaol. He knew exactly where Tess was and he loved her all the more for it.

As he watched, Tess came up onto *Sea Witch*'s deck. For a moment Owen saw the lantern light gleam on her auburn hair before she pulled her shawl over her head to protect against the swirling snow. She stood there for a moment, a lonely figure looking out across the dark river, and then she paused and turned towards where he was standing.

Owen was not aware that he had moved but he found himself running down the narrow street towards the quay. He reached *Sea Witch* and vaulted aboard in one jump. Tess had not moved. She was looking at him, lips parted, eyes bright in the lantern light, as though she could not quite believe what she was seeing. She pressed one hand to her throat. Then she took a step towards him.

"I thought it was you," she said slowly. Her voice was hoarse. "I felt it—"

Owen reached out and grabbed her, pulling her into his arms. She gave a little sound, half sob, half laugh, and then he held her against him and felt her arms go around him. Her heart was beating wildly against his and he kissed her, clumsily, desperately, with all the passion that was in his soul, and she was warm and vibrant in his arms and he felt at peace at last, sloughing off the darkness and dread of the prison cell and stepping into the light. He tangled his hands in her hair and kissed her again and tasted her tears and heard her muffled protest.

"You're so dirty!" She drew back. "You didn't even trouble to change before you came to find me!" But she could not let him go, touching his cheek as though she could not quite believe he was there.

"I love you," Owen said. "I never told you. And I am so sorry I did not believe you when you said you had not drawn the cartoons." He stopped as Tess pressed her fingers to his lips.

"Hush," she said, drawing his head back down to kiss him again. The lanterns guttered and hissed in the snow and the crew gave a ragged round of applause.

"You've been busy," Owen said. He blinked to see the number of men on deck now.

"I had plans," Tess said demurely. Her eyes sparkled. "I still do. You can sail with me if you like."

Owen kissed her again and tasted the hot salt of her tears once more mingled with the cold snow.

"Let's go below," he said as he released her. "I don't want an audience for this." And Tess nodded and pulled him down the companionway as the crew cheered her on.

"Where on earth did you find the crew?" Owen asked. It was some considerable time later and Owen had told Tess all about Tom and his release from the Tower, and she was lying in his arms in the captain's cabin. There was a bottle of bumbo on the table, more than half-finished, and Tess was feeling happy and a little dizzy and yet very safe because Owen was holding her, his arms strong and hard about her, and she knew nothing would ever part them again.

"I asked your broker to recommend a boatswain,"

she said, "and then he and I went into the Eagle Tavern and asked if any man wanted to crew for you." She pressed a kiss against Owen's jaw. "And then we stood back in order to avoid being trampled in the rush," she added drily.

"Really?" Owen looked so surprised Tess felt the need to kiss him again for his modesty, a kiss he returned with interest.

"Really," she said. "They all admire you tremendously."

"Except that they would have been crewing for you, not me," Owen said.

"Only until we got you out," Tess said. She looked at him under her lashes. "That was the plan," she said. "To sail upriver to the Tower and rescue you." She saw Owen's shoulders shaking with suppressed laughter and poked him sharply in the ribs.

"You ungrateful wretch!" she said. "It might have worked."

Owen slid his hand into her hair, cupped her head and kissed her again. "With you in charge," he said, "it would surely have worked. I defy even Sidmouth to withstand you."

He released her and studied her face, his eyes so warm with love and happiness that Tess felt she might drown in the unguarded emotion she saw there.

"So you love *Sea Witch*," he said softly.

"Almost as much as I love you," Tess said. "This was the only place I felt close to you," she added, looking around the sparkling little cabin that she and Margery had scrubbed so lovingly. "I hated the house. It felt unbearably empty and cold. So I came here because I knew there was so much of you in *Sea Witch* and so much of her in you that surely I would find you again. And I did." She snuggled closer into his arms. "I can scarce believe that we have another chance." She raised her head and looked at him. "Where shall we go? We could visit all the Rothbury estates by sea rather than land."

"That," Owen said, "sounds like an excellent idea."

"And Joanna wishes us to visit them at Fenners for Christmas so we had best put into Bristol in a couple of weeks," Tess said.

"Capital," Owen said. His voice was sleepy now, content. He smiled at her, twining his fingers in her curls. "We'll sail together," he said. "I love you so much and I thought I had lost you forever."

Tess sighed. "Alas that I will have no chance to find husband number five now," she said.

She squeaked as Owen ruthlessly tumbled her beneath him on the bunk. He smoothed her hair back from her brow with gentle, loving fingers. "Do you remember asking me how it was possible to make love in so enclosed a space as this?" he questioned softly.

Tess blushed. "I did not ask that!"

"But you were thinking it," Owen said. "Would you like to find out?"

He kissed her and the happiness burst through her

like starlight, dazzlingly bright. Her heart expanded with all the love she had thought never to find. Tess gave herself up to it and stepped into the light.

* * * * *

When the *ton*'s most notorious heartbreaker meets London's most disreputable rake

Susanna Burney is society's most sought-after matchbreaker, paid by wealthy parents to part unsuitable couples. Until her latest assignment brings her face to face with the man who'd once taught her an intimate lesson in heartache...

James Devlin has everything he's always wanted, but the woman who's just met his eyes across a crowded ballroom could cost him everything.

To put the past to rest once and for all, Dev just might have to play Susanna at her own wicked game.

www.mirabooks.co.uk

M252_N

"Perfect for fans of Downton Abbey"
—*Now* magazine

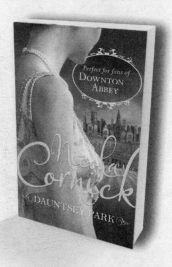

Jack Kestrel is the dissolute and dangerous son of the family of the Dukes of Kestrel, who finds himself in London, not to enjoy the many temptations on offer, but to uphold his family's honour. But it's Sally Bowes, owner of the fashionable Blue Parrot nightclub, where the upper echelons of London society come to sparkle under dazzling chandeliers, who has all of his attention…

Set in the bustle and boom of Edwardian London, *Dauntsey Park* captures the roar and glamour of the early twentieth century.

www.mirabooks.co.uk

M241_DP

For a reputation compromised,
there are but two options:
marriage—or infamy...

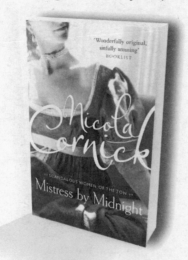

'Wonderfully original,
sinfully amusing'
BOOKLIST

Nicola Cornick

SCANDALOUS WOMEN OF THE TON

Mistress by Midnight

London, May 1811

After her family name was tarnished at his hands,
Merryn has waited ten years to satisfy her revenge
against sensual, mysterious Garrick Northesk,
Duke of Farne.

Yet when a disaster traps Merryn and Garrick
together, white-hot desire stirs between the two
sworn enemies. Her reputation utterly compromised,
Merryn is forced to do the one thing she cannot
bear: accept the scandalous marriage proposal
of the man she has vowed to ruin.

HARLEQUIN®MIRA®
www.mirabooks.co.uk

*"I hired you as a novelty, an
attraction, the most notorious
woman in London..."*

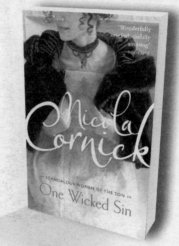

London, July 1813

Once the toast of the *ton*, Lottie Cummings is now
divorced—and penniless. Shunned by society, the destitute
beauty is forced to become a courtesan. Refusing to
oblige her customers, Lottie's about to be turned out on to
the streets. Until a dangerous rake saves her with
a scandalous offer.

The illegitimate son of a duke, Ethan Ryder rose to the
ranks of Napoleon's most trusted officer—until his capture
landed him in England as prisoner of war. Now Ethan
is planning his most audacious coup yet. But he needs to
create a spectacular diversion. And having the
infamous Lottie as his mistress will certainly
do that...

www.mirabooks.co.uk

*One whisper of scandal and
a reputation dies...*

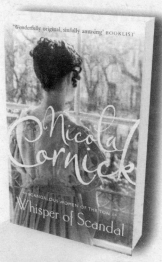

London, May 1811

Widow Lady Joanna Ware has no desire to wed again
but that doesn't stop the flurry of suitors knocking on
her door. Desperate to thwart another proposal, Joanna
brazenly kisses Arctic explorer Alex, Lord Grant.   But
matters are complicated when she learns her deceased
husband has bequeathed his illegitimate child to her and
his friend Alex; and they must travel to the Arctic to
claim the orphan. Battling blizzards, dangerous wild life,
and a treacherous plot, Alex must protect Joanna but
not before he wickedly seduces her...

Scandalous Women of the Ton continues in
One Wicked Sin and *Mistress by Midnight*

www.mirabooks.co.uk

M216_WOS

One marriage. Three people.
Proud king. Loving wife.
Infamous mistress.

1362, Philippa of Hainault selects a young orphan
from a convent. Alice Perrers, a girl born with
nothing but ambition.

The young virgin is secretly delivered to
King Edward III—to perform the wifely duties of
which ailing Philippa is no longer capable.

Mistress to the King. Confidante of the Queen.
Whore to the court. Power has a price, and
Alice Perrers will pay it.

**'Anne O'Brien has joined the exclusive club
of excellent historical novelists.'**
—*Sunday Express*

www.mirabooks.co.uk